LAST MAN STANDING

THE EARTHBURST SAGA: BOOK 1

© 2022

CRAIG A. FALCONER

Last Man Standing
© 2022 Craig A. Falconer

The characters and events herein are entirely fictional.
Any resemblance to real persons, living or dead, is purely coincidental.

ISBN: 9798358715394

For Sarah.

1

Nine minutes.

After everything that's brought me here, it all comes down to this.

I can't take my eyes off the steel ball in the test chamber. What it does when the timer runs out could change the world forever.

It feels like time has been passing in slow motion in the hour since I started this final make-or-break fuel enrichment experiment.

And believe me... with how slowly the hours seem to pass up here at the best of times, that's saying a lot.

Life on a space station — even The Beacon — isn't nearly as glamorous as I imagined as a kid. Back when I was telling my high school career advisor that I'd do whatever it took to make it here one day, I wasn't factoring in any of the downsides.

Don't get me wrong, I know how lucky I am to be here. The last two months have just taught me that I'm really not built for solitude.

I guess the biggest difference between 15-year-old Ray and 35-year-old Ray is that *he* had a family he couldn't wait to get away from and *I* have one I can't wait to get back to.

The one thing that keeps me sane is knowing that I'll be

back home with Eva and Joe once my placement ends in a few days, no matter what happens with this experiment. But from the moment the placement started, I've been working my ass off to make every second up here count.

Opportunities like this don't come around twice. Not even my unbridled high-school optimism let me believe I'd *ever* have a chance to do something as important as the work I'm doing right now.

Because if the reaction in my test chamber plays out like I know it should, we're going to be looking at the biggest scientific breakthrough of the decade — at *least*.

Very few people know what I'm doing, even among my colleagues on the station. Calling them colleagues is kind of a stretch in itself since I'm an outsider in their eyes, technically designated as a "Visiting Researcher" on placement from my university.

Pretty much everyone else on The Beacon works directly for ZolaCore, the company that built it.

My understanding is that legal credit and future proceeds from my work here will be spilt three ways, like it would often be split between a researcher and their employer on the ground.

ZolaCore stepped up with an offer of unimpeded lab access when my research proposal was officially deemed "too dangerous for Earth," so I don't begrudge them for taking a cut.

But about the danger…

Okay, I'll admit it. A slight oversight on my part could, *in theory*, create the most powerful explosion in human history.

Granted: I'm working with a recently discovered mineral at temperatures no one else has ever tested it and I'm introducing it to BioZol, a next-gen biofuel whose value lies in its sheer combustibility.

No argument on that one.

But the whole point of my research is to harness the unique natural properties of theocite to bring out the best in our easily synthesized new fuel, which means greatly increasing the potency while stabilizing it at the same time.

That's right: introducing the right concentration of theocite at the right temperature can make BioZol *more* stable, not less.

The bottom line is that I wouldn't be here if I wasn't completely sure my work is safe. I have way too much to live for to do anything reckless in the name of progress. That's even true for something that can deliver the mind-boggling level of progress *this* work can bring.

Is my experiment inherently dangerous? Sure. But is it reckless? Not for a second.

I'll prove that in a few minutes, along with my broader thesis, just as soon as the ultra-heated theocite feeds into the BioZol and the controlled explosion takes place.

Because I'm working in one of the station's four off-shoot labs, completely sealed off from the main body, no one else will see my breakthrough in real-time.

My supervisor is a senior ZolaCore guy named Justin, who has really taken me under his wing.

He chuckled when he laid out the reality of why I'm so isolated in here: "The bosses on Earth think this stuff is too dangerous for the surface, and the bosses at ZolaCore think it's too dangerous for the main station!"

That's why I'm basically on an island right now.

Each of our four offshoot labs is separated from the rest of the station by a long buffer walkway, kind of like the ones that connect a plane to an airport terminal.

So yeah… if you picture The Beacon as an island in the hostile and lifeless ocean of space, I'm the guy talking to crabs and coconuts on the even smaller island that lies beyond it.

When it comes to the nitty gritty, Justin is as confident as I am in the process I've come up with. He even wanted to join me in here to see the final reaction. He wasn't allowed, though, so he's not going to know it works until I run out to the main station and tell him.

I guess he'll know before then that it hasn't *not* worked.

3

After all, our two outcomes are basically success and disaster. Justin knows exactly when I'll be feeding in the theocite and he'll see that my lab hasn't exploded.

A lot of cutting-edge research takes place on The Beacon. That's why ZolaCore built it and that's why it attracts the best of the best. But these offshoot labs are specifically designed for *extra* dangerous research — to the extent that they'll instantly and automatically sever from the main station if any sensor picks up the first sign of something going wrong.

If that happens, which it won't, the incredibly thick walkway would split from my lab's reinforced entrance.

The walkway would then rapidly transform into an extra line of defense, physically shielding the station body against any kind of damage.

I guess it's understandable for the station's full-time researchers to resent guys like me who waltz in for a few months to do risky research on their doorstep.

Maybe I'd feel the same way in their shoes. But at the end of the day they all work for Ignacio Zola — the guy who personally signs off on every single research project just like he signs their paychecks.

I've never met Zola. The university's management said he was extremely accommodating and interested in my work, though, so I'm sure he's going to be delighted to see my final results when Justin sends the news down to Earth.

Justin is the one guy up here I really can't wait to tell, and he'll be first to know. But most of all I'm looking forward to calling Joe.

I used to think I was all about space as a kid, but man… Joe takes it to another level. He's seven and I still remember how he was *so* proud that I was going to be an astronaut.

Leaving him and Eva was the hardest thing I've ever had to do, even for a once-in-a-lifetime opportunity like this.

If my placement had been an opportunity for personal glory or recognition, I would still be sitting at home in Salt Lake City with them right now. But that's *not* what this is. This is an opportunity to make a positive difference to the kind of world Joe will grow up in.

The synergistic properties of theocite-enriched BioZol could truly revolutionize space travel. Even more immediately, it could work alongside ZolaCore's fledgling asteroid-mining program to open up solutions for some of Earth's crippling resource problems.

When I have proof of viability in a few more minutes, our family will be set for life. But this is bigger than that. This really could help humanity as a whole.

I'm not here to claim credit for anything and I definitely can't claim credit for *everything*.

I didn't single-handedly develop my university team's fuel synthesization process, let alone take it far enough to develop BioZol. That was ZolaCore.

I also didn't play *any* part in ZolaCore's discovery of the undersea theocite deposits that have made my final break-through possible.

I just saw a way to bring two discoveries together — ours and theirs.

Maybe you could say opportunity met preparation. However you want to frame it, I'm grateful to everyone who played a part in getting me here and I'll make sure they get their due credit.

As for Joe, I guess we're soon going to find out if one kid can get any prouder.

Eva and I didn't tell him that I'm technically not an astronaut, even though ZolaCore's extensive insurance documentation makes it very clear that I'm a C-word... *civilian*.

I used to dream of being a real astronaut. The accident put an end to that, thanks to the physical limitations it left me with, but I'm just glad my research work has finally gotten me into space.

Oh, and speaking of insurance. Here's a little pro-tip in case you ever find yourself trying to calm your partner's totally understandable concerns about the highly dangerous thing you're about to do: *don't* repeatedly mention the generous payout she'll get if you die while you're doing it.

Trust me, that one doesn't work as well as you might think.

I learned the hard way so you don't have to. You're welcome!

When I got the invitation to come here, we were three weeks away from a long-planned trip to Hawaii to mark five years since Eva and I first met.

The engagement ring I was going to give her on the beach is in my pocket right now. As soon as I see her again, it's going to be on her finger.

No more waiting for the perfect moment.

Two months of near-total isolation has taught me that the present moment is the only one that counts, and I'm not going to let any more slip by.

The present moment I'm in right now, meanwhile, is without a doubt the most tense of my life.

Everything rests on what happens next.

I glance at the countdown and gulp.

Here we go…

2

I've always dreamed of the day when humanity can reach a new world. Hell, even just exploring beyond this one will be a great start.

When I was a kid, my grandfather told me that I *might* live to see humans colonize another planet but that my hair would probably be as gray as his before it ever happened.

I think about those words a lot. I've spent my whole career working on a fuel source that could make it possible and I've never once touched up my hair with any of the gray-prevention products that commercials always push on guys my age.

Call me superstitious, but if Pops was right about the timeline then I definitely don't want to let vanity get in the way.

But for real... the idea that my work really could play an important part in humanity's future is mind-blowing in all of the best ways.

I've done a pretty good job of distracting myself with all these thoughts during the final nine-minute countdown, but there's no more time to kill.

There's no more time to wonder.

No more time to beg.

No more time to pray.

There's no going back now.

I close my eyes for a few seconds and try to get a hold of my runaway breath. I thought I knew what tension was, but damn. *This* is something else.

If this works, everything is going to change for the better. The world needs some good news and all I care about is creating some. I don't care one bit about being the guy who delivers it.

I'm not here to be a hero. A hero to Joe, sure. A step-dad he can be proud of, to give him a better start than I had. But I'll be happy to get home and live on the sidelines while the breakthrough speaks for itself.

It's going to be an *explosive* breakthrough, one way or another.

Until now I haven't given much thought to the *wrong* way this could go. Everything has been checked and double-checked and triple-checked, by me and by Justin and by the guys at the university. We've all but ruled out the wrong kind of explosion and we're all but certain I'll get the right kind.

"All but" ruled out and "all but" certain suddenly feel like pretty big qualifiers, though. There's no "we" anymore, either.

I'm the only one in this offshoot lab, standing inches from the reaction chamber.

However unlikely a disastrous miscalculation feels in my mind, the stakes are making my heart beat faster than ever.

I want to see the chamber's steel ball propelled upwards from its volcano-like support cylinder to a height of precisely two meters. That will prove that my theocite reaction has enhanced the BioZol underneath in a controlled, predicted and replicable manner.

But with seconds to go, I'm suddenly so nervous that I almost feel like I'd settle for a damp squib of a failure — no explosion at all.

If the reaction fails and the ball doesn't move, at least there's no risk. At least—

No.

No.

I didn't come here to fail, safely or not. It's easy to forget from up here, but the world *really* needs some good news.

My eyes flick to the clock. Nine minutes has become nine *seconds*.

I return my gaze to the all-important steel ball.

Come on, I urge as the ultra-heated theocite is about to feed in. *Don't let me down.*

I'm wearing goggles, ear protectors, the whole shebang.

It's all for show. I know these things won't make any tangible difference.

If things go well, the explosion will be controlled and the chamber's insulation will comfortably handle it.

If things go badly, I'll be dead before I know it.

I'm going along with the pointless safety checklist because wearing protective equipment is a condition of my insurance coverage. If anything does go wrong, the only thing that matters to me is that Eva and Joe are looked after.

With the ear protectors in place, all I can hear is my heart. Given how fast it's beating, I think I'd hear it anyway.

One second left.

My eyes want to close, but I don't let them.

I have to see.

And what a sight it is!

The steel ball shoots upwards, right to the two-meter line, before The Beacon's artificial gravity takes over and returns it safely to its starting point.

Oh. My. God.

It worked!

We did it!

I lift my ear protectors off and hear myself holler in delight. Anyone seeing this who didn't understand the context would think I was insane, celebrating such an unspectacular-looking outcome. But *I* know why that ball just moved and *I* know what it means.

Justin knows, too, so I set off to tell him right away.

What will I say? I don't know what words will come out first.

Not that it matters — he'll see my face.

He'll probably grab me in a bearhug and give me more credit than I deserve.

But what really counts is all the things this will enable. We've not only harnessed theocite, a remarkable material that we knew could change space travel even before we knew how. We've synergistically paired it with an already well-optimized fuel.

Sure, we'll have to wait for peer review, but this is going to be ready to roll out in no time.

At last, the tantalizing asteroid-based resources we've been unable to reach for so long are finally going to be accessible. And the efficiency gains here are *so* great, we could finally be ushering in an era of ultra long-distance space travel.

"Justin!" I yell as I unlock my lab's thick door.

I figure there's a good chance he'll be waiting on the other side of this door. It's as close as he could get and I know he'll be keen to toast the moment as soon as possible.

All he'll know for sure by now is that I haven't blown myself up, but he's always had even more faith than me that we'd get an unambiguously successful result.

I seriously can't wait to see the smile on his face.

For half a second I think about trying to put on a glum expression, pretending it didn't work so he'll be even more excited when my smile cracks and he realizes I was kidding.

But I can't even kid *myself* — there's no way I could hide this smile even if I wanted to.

I push the door open.

"Huh," I mutter in surprise.

Justin's not there.

Maybe he's gathered some of the other researchers to greet me in the central area of the main station? That would make sense.

Maybe he just wanted to give me some space in case the news wasn't good? That would, too.

Or maybe he had some natural doubts after all, and wanted to be safely clear of the walkway in case I blew my offshoot lab to pieces? I couldn't begrudge him that.

In the few moments when my eager mind is whirring through these possibilities, my eyes flick along the rest of the corridor and then to the ground in front of me.

Instantly, I feel my stomach heave.

"N-no," I stammer. "No!"

Because Justin *is* there.

Sprawled on the floor, inches from my door, Justin is there.

Dead.

3

"Justin!" I yell.

Instinct sends my body recoiling back against the thick door.

Justin's lifeless body instantly brings back an image I've spent my whole adult life trying to forget, but for once that horrible memory isn't the worst thing I have to contend with.

No breathing exercises or mindfulness tactics can shake away present reality like they can sometimes stop the flashbacks.

There's nothing I can do to calm myself down in the here and now. Even worse, there's nothing I can do to help Justin, either.

Unless I'm not too late...

I drop to my knees and desperately feel for a pulse. But as soon as I touch his skin, the pulse question disappears.

He's gone.

His skin is *so* cold... if I didn't already know for sure, I do now.

My best friend on the station is dead.

Time isn't moving in slow motion anymore. Now, it feels like time doesn't even exist.

I get back to my feet and stand dumbly over my fallen

supervisor. Justin is so close to my lab's outer security door, it seems like he must have been on his way inside. But his skin is too cold for this to have just happened... whatever the hell "*this*" even is.

A heart attack?

Anything is possible and I know appearances can lie, but Justin was probably the healthiest-looking person here. I can't see it being something like that.

And the timing...

Sure, coincidence is a thing, but *come on*.

For a healthy researcher to die literally *while* I was proving our thesis on the other side of the door, purely by chance?

I'm not buying it.

But what else could it be?

My mind is running a mile a minute.

All I know for sure is that something isn't right. The fact that Justin is laying here on his own makes me think no one else knows he's dead, which raises even more questions.

The main body of the station is only a one-minute walk from here, along the length of the walkway that keeps my offshoot at a supposedly safe distance.

I guess anyone who saw Justin enter the walkway would have figured he was going the whole way to see me, so the fact he didn't return wouldn't necessarily worry them.

The Beacon is a big enough station for a lot to happen without anyone else seeing it, anyway. No one lingers in the central areas for long and for all I know Justin might have come to see me in the middle of the night, when no one lingers anywhere.

I'm trying not to jump to any conclusions. But no matter what I do, all kinds of intrusive thoughts and regrets swirl in my brain.

I've been in the lab for two and a half days.

What if something happened to Justin yesterday and I could have gotten him medical attention, in time to help, if only I'd been less obsessed with the experiment?

I even slept in there for a few hours last night instead of going to my dorm, all because I didn't want to talk to anyone else — including Justin — until I had the good news I've been promising for so long.

Nothing was ever too much for Justin when it came to equipping my lab. It breaks my heart that he'll never know we did it. He'll never know I made the replicable breakthrough we've both craved for so long.

Now that I have a whole other kind of unwelcome news to share with everyone else, that breakthrough is suddenly taking a backseat. Because whatever has happened here, I sure as hell can't handle this on my own.

I take a deep breath and set off along the walkway.

"Someone help!" I bellow as I run.

I instinctively call for Yannick, a computer technician who has just taken over the mantle as my closest friend on the station.

The nature of my periphery working arrangements means I can't think of anyone else's name off the top of my head. I know a lot of faces and in normal circumstances I would know some names, too, but the stress of the moment is making low-level neural connections feel unreachable.

Almost everyone here is a full-time ZolaCore worker. They're a pretty tight knit group and haven't exactly gone out of their way to bring me in. I don't care about any of that right now, though, and by the time I reach the main area of the station I'm screaming loudly for help from anyone who might hear.

"Justin is down!" I yell. "Help!"

Nothing but silence comes back.

It *is* the central area, I tell myself. No one spends much time here and the sound probably won't carry to the rest of the station.

I decide to head for the entrance to the dorms.

But I don't even make it ten more steps before the most harrowing sight of my life stops me in my tracks.

Straight ahead of me, right by the airlock that leads to the emergency evacuation dock, no less than twelve other researchers are slumped lifelessly on the floor.

Holy shit.

It's not just Justin, it's everyone.

All of them…

They're all dead.

4

I've seen some things in my life.

But without *any* doubt, the sight before my eyes is by far the most horrific I've ever encountered.

Even though I feel like I can't bear to look, the whole scene is just *so* disturbing and *so* incongruent that I can't tear my gaze away.

These people…

These poor, poor people…

They were trying to open the airlock.

It only opens from the outside to enable evacuations from the emergency dock, but I can see from some of their positions that they were trying to get out.

Whatever happened in here, these men and women of science were driven to try to escape into the void of space.

I eventually look away after counting at least fourteen bodies. I don't want to get ahead of myself and start assuming things are even worse than they might be. But whether this is a disaster or — I'll just say it: an *attack* — what's clear now is that it happened on a scale I couldn't have imagined just a few minutes ago.

Is there *anyone* else alive on the station?

And why am *I* alive?

Sure, my lab is completely self-contained. Ironically that was supposed to protect the rest of the station from my dangerous experiments, and in the end it looks like the setup has protected *me* from whatever happened here.

I understand that part.

But so far it seems like something probably happened with the air supply, whether the problem was too little oxygen or too much of something less breathable.

The big issue with that line of thinking, pretty obviously, is that I'm breathing the air right now without any problems.

But *should* I be?

I glance again at my fallen colleagues.

I'm no detective but it looks to me like they died pretty quickly and that their last moments were frantic.

That doesn't strike me as something that would come from prolonged exposure to suboptimal air. It looks like they knew something wasn't right and they did all they could to get the hell away from it.

My eyes scan the walls and the rest of the floor, looking for any kind of hints about what I've walked into.

There's no one near any of the other doors within view, which all lock for basic security purposes rather than to act as safety seals.

Only the station's four offshoot labs have high-level air seals, and as soon as this thought is at the forefront of my mind it gives me a little bit of hope.

Maybe some people made it into one of the other offshoots?

Maybe Justin had the right idea in trying to reach my lab, knowing it's completely self-contained?

The poor guy… he got so close.

And as much as I want to go deeper into the station to find some other survivors, or at the very least call Earth for help, thinking about the safety of the offshoot labs puts one more "maybe" in my mind:

Maybe sheltering in my lab is *still* the right idea?

I have no idea what happened out here, but what if it happens again?

I'm alive because I was in my lab. Do I really want to end up dead because I'm out of it?

My heart is thumping like I've never known. The eerie totality of the silence around me doesn't help.

The station's complex life support systems don't even give off a gentle hum like you might imagine, so when I say silent I really do mean *silent*.

My body wants to run back to the lab and hide.

My mind is conflicted.

It's not like I can rationalize waiting this out, since I don't know what this is or even if it's something I possibly *could* wait out.

There's a chance that my sub-amateur detective skills of observation are failing me and there *has* been a mundane system failure — one that's made the air unbreathable in a way that my short-term exposure hasn't picked up on yet. If that is the case, waiting things out won't be an option.

And although my lab is completely self-contained, it's not truly self-sufficient. It keeps a few days' supply of emergency everything. Air, water, power, you name it. But after that, it has to tap back into the main station.

Another huge issue is that there's no way of contacting Earth from in there, or even of contacting the rest of the station. That's because although my dangerous work had to be kept completely *separate* from everything else's, rumor has it that some of the other offshoots were used for research that Zola-Core wanted to keep completely *secret* from everyone else.

Long story short: if I go back into the lab to curl up and hide, no one else will know I'm alive.

The shock I'm feeling is making it hard to wrestle with what I know, let alone think about what anyone else might know, but I have to make the decision that gives me the best chance of getting home to Joe and Eva.

If there's a group of survivors at the other end of the station working on an escape plan, or safely waiting for a rescue craft from Earth, can I count on them to come knocking on every door?

I don't think so.

And on the other side of the coin, what if there are no other survivors up here?

If no one is calling Earth for help, no one from Earth is coming *to* help. They'll come eventually to figure out what happened, clear up the carnage and salvage as much research as they can... but when?

Why would ZolaCore or any public agencies risk sending people up to a station where it looks like everyone has been killed by some invisible force?

"They wouldn't," I say out loud.

The sound of my voice sharpens my mind. They really wouldn't, I figure... at least not until it's too late.

This will already be huge news on Earth, whether anyone from the station has been in contact or not.

Contact being lost is news in itself, obviously, and it breaks my heart to think of the worry Eva must be feeling. I know she'll be doing her best to protect Joe from it all, but how much can she really do?

I turn towards the main body of the station. I know what I have to do.

"For them," I tell myself.

The sound of my voice really does sharpen my mind all over again.

I don't know if it's just because humans aren't wired for this kind of unnatural silence, but I'm starting to see why some people talk to themselves.

Whenever I wasn't in full-focus mode in the lab, I always had music playing to keep me sane. Right now there's nothing I wouldn't give to hear a chord, or a voice, or even the clap of a footstep that isn't my own.

Pretty much any sound would be better than nothing.

Or so I think.

The timing of a blaring alarm, suddenly piercing the silence right as I ponder this, is so uncanny that I momentarily wonder if I'm imagining it.

As a red light starts flashing overhead, I know I'm not.

My voice didn't sharpen my mind half as much as this does.

When the words of the automated message start repeating, a rueful feeling of "be careful what you wish for" slaps me on both ears.

WARNING: CRITICAL LEAK.
WARNING: CRITICAL LEAK.
WARNING…

5

Is this it?

Did some kind of "critical leak" kill all these people?

Is it happening again?

Did another survivor temporarily patch it up? Did the system itself temporarily patch it up?

Questions without answers are like cars without wheels, and these ones really are taking me nowhere fast.

I don't know if this is the first time the alarm has sounded. Right now I guess that's immaterial.

What's clearer than ever is the futility of trying to shelter in the lab. Because if there's a leak on the station with no one else around to fix it, every minute I spend delaying my effort is a minute I spend reducing my chances of survival.

I know there's an emergency control hub on the other side of the station's center, near the Canteen. That's the only place I can think of where I *might* be able to do anything. There's the Control Center, too, but I don't have the right biometric security credentials to get inside.

I've never used the hub's touchscreen system so I don't know what all is on there. Now that I'm thinking about it, though, I don't think it's wildly optimistic to think there might be some kind of way to contact Earth.

I can always grab my own phone from the dorm and try to make contact if — *big* if — the station's internet uplink is still live. That doesn't seem *too* wildly optimistic, either, since the lights and everything else here still seem to be working.

A *lot* of things are still working.

And yeah, the fact that I'm facing a critical leak is worse than bad news. It's an urgent problem that I don't know how effectively I can tackle on my own. But if I'm searching for a silver lining, at least the station's systems are still functional enough to warn me about it.

I set off in a sprint towards the hub. I feel the weight of every step *way* more than usual thanks to the elevated heart-rate I've been running ever since I stepped out of my lab and almost literally stumbled on Justin.

The Beacon usually feels airy and open, with soft overhead lighting and wide corridors that aren't claustrophobic or industrial like the space stations in the sci-fi movies I grew up watching. It never felt like somewhere that, sooner or later, something bad was going to happen.

Needless to say, there's a different vibe today.

When I reach the hub I'm instantly surprised that I don't see many bodies littered on the floor.

There are maybe five or six in the whole area. Once the initial surprise wears off that five or six isn't fifty or sixty, I recognize how morbid it is that the sight of these poor souls doesn't register the kind of visceral shock and sorrow it would have just a few minutes ago.

The human survival instinct is a powerful thing.

Our brains are adaptive and can selectively focus to an extent I'm just starting to appreciate now. Mine is working overtime, trying its best to filter out everything that isn't helpful in dealing with the immediate and urgent problem at hand.

As I approach the pillar that contains the emergency control hub as well as a public noticeboard, I pass the open entrance to the Canteen.

Okay, my brain's focus-filtering system is strong... but it wasn't built for *this*.

All of the bodies I didn't find out here?

Yeah. They're in there.

My feet stop of their own accord to let me glance into the Canteen.

The strewn bodies make for a sight that's beyond grim.

My eye line also reveals a second grim scene against the other airlock on the far wall, in another spot where an evacuation craft could dock in an emergency.

Just like at the airlock nearer the dorms, these people were trying to get out.

I can't even imagine what must have been going through their terrified minds and breathless bodies. The only visuals I can liken this to are the harrowing images of people jumping to the ground from burning buildings, or into icy water from sinking ships.

I guess when death is absolutely certain, quick beats slow.

I wonder for a second if there might have been something else going on at the airlocks. An attempted evacuation, maybe, or some kind of airlock malfunction these people were trying to fix.

That second thought doesn't make any sense when I reflect on it, though. The airlocks are clearly working — my lungs are sure of that one — and they're only operable from the outside.

Once a rescue craft is docked, it would form a seal around the airlock. The crew would then open the airlock from the outside to access the station. In a real emergency where there *was* an airlock malfunction that stopped the rescuers outside from opening it, I'm sure they would just blow it off.

So whatever happened, it wasn't that.

With the alarm still blaring, I turn away from the Canteen and its harrowingly crowded airlock. I focus back on the control hub.

I can hardly believe how quickly the high I felt from the greatest success of my life — and one of the biggest scientific breakthroughs in decades — has given way to these morbid sights and realities.

But I am where I am. And at least now that I'm in front of the control hub, there *might* be something I can do.

The system and its screen are new to me, like I said, but it's not alien. The Status Overview screen that's displayed when I arrive is flashing with the same three ominous words that keep repeating in my ears.

Safe to say, by now I feel sufficiently warned about this damn critical leak.

What I need is a helping hand in doing something about it.

My eyes scan the rest of the screen.

I don't like the look of the red WiFi symbol in the corner. Instinctively I reach out and tap it.

I know from life at home that two things can be wrong with WiFi: a local fault with the router, or a fault with the incoming signal. I also know that one is a lot easier to solve than the other.

Unfortunately, the words "NO INCOMING SIGNAL" tell me there's almost definitely a bigger fault than anything I could hope to solve with a reboot. That's if a reboot is even going to be within my power from here, which is far from guaranteed.

It's a huge blow to know that my phone isn't going to work either, since its WiFi comes from the same relayed signal that's not reaching the main system like it should.

With my phone ruled out, the best hope for making contact is going to rest on accessing the station's radio comms.

I'm hoping beyond hope there's a radio control built into this hub. Otherwise I'll need to find a way into the Observation Deck or the high-security Control Center, which is probably also the only place where I could try to reboot the incoming data signal.

I close the WiFi information pop-up and look for another icon. I'd settle for a radio, a satellite dish, a phone handset... any icon that indicates a communications system.

It seems like that's too much to hope for right now and this blaring alarm is a constant reminder that I don't have any time to spare.

I tap the huge warning message on the home screen, hoping something happens.

Something *does* happen: a rudimentary 2-D diagram of the station appears. Helpfully, one small section of external pipework is colored red and flashing steadily.

I tap this section of the map, homing in.

Okay... *here* we are. A much clearer and more detailed diagram of the pipework appears. There's even a real photographic image of it, too.

There's a robotic arm in the picture, which looks like it knocked the pipe out of place. That thing has to be remotely controlled from inside the station... but as hard as I'm looking, I'm struggling to make sense of it.

Or do I have it all backwards?

After a closer look, I think the arm was holding the pipe. Maybe an interruption hit when someone was controlling the arm to replace this small pipe for routine maintenance?

It's a maybe.

But if someone *was* in the process of replacing a section of pipework when everything went down, that seems like another case of suspiciously bad timing.

All of that is for later, I tell myself. I can't afford to get lost in the questions of why this happened or who might know more.

Right now, I need to focus on the only thing in my sphere of control: what I can do next.

Can I fix this?

Can I get to wherever the robotic repair system is controlled, hope it's still working, and take over from the poor worker who might have died halfway through the job?

Well... I can *try*.

In a strictly technical sense, this strikes me as a very easy fix. Controlling the robotic arm might not be as easy as it sounds, but it's a very small pipe that looks like it should clip right back into place.

I'm no mechanical engineer, but if this was an *internal* pipe I would have no problem clipping it into place. That's what I mean about it looking easy in the technical sense — it's not like I'd be using a robot arm to thread the eye of a needle.

If there's anyone else alive here who has EVA training, I reckon they could go out there and fix the pipe almost as easily as I could do it in here. It's primarily an access problem.

Side bar: as far as euphemisms go, I've always thought that referring to spacewalks as "Extra Vehicular Activity" is one of the biggest. It makes it sound *way* too easy.

And although *I'm* definitely not the guy with suitable EVA training, I'm also not the guy who's giving up hope that there might be more survivors.

The corpse-littered floor of the Canteen is the worst thing I've ever seen and it strongly suggests that at least *almost* everyone is dead, but it's not like I've been doing a headcount. Besides… if there's even *one* other survivor, I bet right now they have no idea I'm alive.

That's a thought I want to hang on to: I'm proof that there's a chance.

Where there's life there's hope — and maybe someone else got lucky, too.

I close the station diagram for now to see what else I can find on this system. It's publicly accessible so I'm not expecting access to *everything*, just hoping for something I can work with.

The next thing I tap is a bell-shaped icon, like the one for notifications on my phone. This brings me the welcome option to override the warning system, hitting mute on the near-deafening alarm.

I do it.

Believe me: if anyone else is alive outside of the offshoot labs, they've heard it by now.

As soon as the sound stops, my brain feels freer.

Just like I'd never understood the oppressiveness of real

silence until I stepped out of my lab a few minutes ago, I realize now that I never really appreciated how overwhelming the *opposite* of silence can be until that damn alarm kicked in.

The only icon I haven't hit yet is shaped like a question mark.

Might as well tap, I figure.

It opens up a menu screen with dull-sounding options like *Operating System License, System Status* and *Touchscreen Calibration.*

I feel growing disappointment until I notice two new icons at the bottom of this screen, replacing the ones that were there on the home screen. I tap a gear-shaped one first. It brings up options for changing the brightness and contrast of the screen itself. Not what I need.

The other new icon, which feels like my last hope here, is shaped like the silhouette of a person's upper body. This kind of icon usually leads to a user selection or login screen, but I hit it, anyway. This probably won't tell me anything new but it doesn't hurt to check.

Immediately, I see that my curiosity was well-founded.

Not that I'm glad...

Because what I'm looking at now is *not* a user selection screen, and it *does* tell me something new about my situation.

The screen now displays a top-down diagram of the station's interior.

There's one green dot visible in the center, in the exact spot where I'm standing. To the right of the diagram, there's a single heading: *PERSONNEL.*

The bad news lies underneath that heading.

I gulp.

I can't take my eyes off the name — *my* name — because that's the big question settled.

A solitary name for the sole survivor.

The screen doesn't lie and there really is no one else left alive up here.

Ray Barclay...

Last man standing.

6

As a scientist, I know there's value in clarity and I know that making distinctions — even unwelcome ones — can ultimately aid in problem solving.

But this?

This isn't the clarity I wanted. This isn't a distinction I can use.

Everyone else is dead. There's no one here to do an EVA to fix the pipe and there's no one here to help me access the secured areas I have to reach to contact Earth.

I'm all alone on this island in space, facing a kind of solitude no one should ever have to know.

I take a deep breath.

At least I can still do that, I tell myself. I'm still breathing and the air tastes and smells relatively okay, which I'm taking as a small mercy. I might owe that to the small amounts of chemical additives in our air supply.

Because without trying to sound insensitive, the condition of my colleagues would definitely be causing more problems if I was surrounded by this many of their corpses on Earth.

If I go back to playing detective for a second, I don't think the issue with the pipework is what killed them. I think that's become an issue *because* everyone is dead.

I navigate back out of the Personnel screen and head into System Status. I tap more in hope than expectation that I'll find anything useful.

The word Status sounds pretty passive, so I don't expect to be able to control any locks from here, or anything else as useful as that.

In fact, with this being a publicly accessible system, I'm absolutely sure I *won't* be able to control the locks. That would kind of defeat the point.

A menu option like System *Control* would have been nice, for sure, but this isn't exactly my lucky day.

Figuring out how to get into the high-security Control Center is probably the only way I can gain the kind of control I need.

The System Status screen resembles a long checklist, with everything except Data Uplink having a happy green checkmark beside it.

A solitary red X in that spot reaffirms what I already know about the internet uplink not working. Aside from that, the remaining sea of green is a welcome sight.

I already knew the power was okay, but it's good news that the emergency Escape Pod is still here and online.

Let me rephrase that: it's not *bad* news.

There's a huge caveat, though, because the Escape Pod is not an emergency return capsule.

It can't return to Earth, it can only launch from the station to be intercepted by a rescue craft. Although it does technically offer a way out of this place, it doesn't offer a way home.

Still, it's better than nothing and it means I have a theoretical way out — *if* I can contact someone on Earth. A working Escape Pod removes the need for them to send a dockable craft, which could be crucial for my bid to leave before this critical leak gets the better of me.

We'll just gloss over the fact that making contact is the biggest *if* of my life. That's one ounce of hope I'm not giving up without a fight.

For the same reason, I'm also not going to dwell on knowing almost nothing about the Pod's operation. It's got to be designed to be easy to launch, I figure, and I like to think I can be a pretty smart guy.

Pressure isn't usually my friend and being alone at the helm of an unfamiliar vehicle brings back crippling memories I can do without, but I don't want to think about any of that right now.

Needless to say, evacuating to be intercepted by another craft rests upon making contact with one in the first place.... and *that* rests upon accessing some areas that are specifically designed to be inaccessible to low-ranking outsiders like me.

It's not going to be easy.

I belatedly notice a little asterisk beside the green checkmark that tells me Life Support systems are functional.

Given that I know there's a leak, I'm surprised there isn't a giant red X like there is for the Data Uplink.

I tap the asterisk, by now expecting that more details will pop up. Sure enough, they do.

My eyes close almost instantly in reaction to the pop-up. It's not what I want to see.

By now I should also have expected that more news would be bad news, and my God… this time it *really* is.

The green checkmark suddenly feels totally out of place, accurate only in the very narrow sense that the Life Support systems are currently online. The size of the asterisk had no connection to the size of the problem, though, because things are definitely not okay.

The words *"Leak Detected; Isolated"* might have seemed quite promising on their own. After all, if you already know there's a leak, detection and isolation are pretty good words to see.

But *"Emergency Backup Operational"* is less promising, particularly when my eyes reach the third line of text — *"Evacuation Window Estimate"* — and the numbers that follow.

The lifespan of the emergency backup that's providing my oxygen is displayed in the form of a six-digit timer.

Counting down.

From eleven hours.

7

Think, Ray.

Think.

Everything I've learned in the last few minutes has made things even worse, but there's no sense in trying to massage the truth.

Here are the facts: I'm all alone. The station is running on emergency backup reserves. I have eleven hours left to evacuate. I can't get into any of the rooms that will let me contact Earth.

This isn't necessarily just about the air supply, either, which would naturally last longer with only me breathing it than it would if everyone else was still alive.

No… it's the whole system.

Right now I might technically owe my life to a backup power supply rather than a backup oxygen supply. I don't know. From here, it's impossible to say. All I know is that the station is a holistic self-sustaining system. When a pipe is totally out of place and the leakage is as bad as this, everything breaks down.

I need to fix it.

What seemed like enormous problems when I left the lab — stuff like figuring out what the hell happened here and worrying about whether it *might* happen again — aren't even featuring on the list anymore.

There's no space in my problem box right now to think about what caused this. There's no space to worry that it *might* happen again. Not when the knock-on effects are *definitely* going to kill me unless I can do something to fix this.

One unhelpful thought that keeps swirling is that I was supposed to be going home in a few days. If only my placement had been a single week shorter, I'd already be down there with Eva and Joe.

Sure, if I'd gone home early I wouldn't have made the all-important breakthrough we've been working on for so long. But right now I don't even know if the world will ever find out about it.

All the good things this breakthrough could eventually usher in might never come to fruition. Long-distance travel, clean energy generation, asteroid mining... all of it. Or should I say, *none* of it.

The more these intrusive thoughts circle, and the more I think about just how much my results will change things if I'm ever able to share them, the more sure I'm getting that none of this is a coincidence.

Granted, we were sitting ducks in a metal can in the hostile void of space. And granted, accidents happen.

But *everyone* on a ZolaCore space station dying, just as our biggest breakthrough was about to come?

I'm *really* not buying it.

The fact this was all supposed to be secret doesn't mean much. Not at this level.

There are some very powerful interests who wouldn't want the benefits of my work to come to pass. And maybe just as importantly, there are a lot of powerful people who wouldn't want ZolaCore to profit from any of it.

Ignacio Zola has made of lot of enemies — not just in business, but in politics, too. Zola is wealthy enough to be able to destabilize national economies when he wants to pressure

leaders into passing favorable legislation, and
before.

Maybe he pushed his luck too far.

I've always appreciated the mountains of
thrown at space research. Unlike some others who have
and gone, he even invests in the unglamorous stuff that doesn't
have any real prospect of financial returns. Still, that doesn't
mean I've been fooling myself into thinking he's a nice guy.

Call me cynical, but you don't get to *that* level of power in
today's world by being a nice guy.

With Zola on my brain, I can't even imagine what's
happening on Earth.

If this *isn't* an accident, he's not going to take it lying down.
Zola is known for being rash. He's a *shoot first, ask later* kind of
guy. There will be hell to pay for what's happened here, and
for all I know things could already be kicking off.

I just hope and pray Eva and Joe are okay. I wish more than
anything that I could talk to them right now.

Whatever it takes to see them again, I'll do it.

All of this brings me back to the one thing I need above all
else: contact with Earth.

Since everyone else is dead, there's obviously been no
ongoing contact with Earth while I've been in the lab.

No one on the ground has any reason to think there's a
survivor up here. That means there's going to be no rescue
mission unless I can find a way to call for one.

Sure, they'll come eventually to find out what happened. I
already thought about that… before I found out I have literally
hours left to live up here.

In an unprecedentedly stressful situation like this, it's especially hard to line up what's most important and what's most
urgent.

Calling Earth is the most important thing, hands down. But
fixing the dislodged exterior pipe is clearly the most urgent. I
have eleven hours of emergency life support. Without fixing
the pipe, that could be all the time I'll ever have — period.

But there's nothing I can do about the pipe until I can get to the Maintenance Bay. And even then, I would be fumbling around with zero robotics experience to call on.

Time, help, a way out... all the things I need are the things I don't have.

A way out would be awesome but right now I'm struggling for a way forward. What's the next step? Where's the path?

The biggest obstacle in my way is the core security setup of The Beacon, which is based on biometric credentials unlocking various doors. That's what's stopping me from getting into the Maintenance Bay. It's stopping me from getting into the Control Center, too, and I feel like that's where I should be aiming first.

The sooner I call for help, the sooner a rescue mission could get off the ground. But on top of that, someone on Earth would at the very least be able to talk me through the pipe-repair process.

Hell, they might even be able to remotely repair the pipe from Earth once we establish an open link to the robotic arm. Surgeons on one continent can control robots on another, to perform operations that need *way* more precision than we'll need here. Is something like that too much to hope for? I don't think so.

It does feel pretty unrealistic to think anyone could reach me within an eleven-hour window with no prior notice, but help with fixing the pipe will change my situation in a heartbeat.

Once I have the regular life support systems back online, there *is* no window. I would just have to wait a little bit longer for them to arrive.

I have food, I have water... hell, I even have a lot of data to document and collate. A little wait wouldn't be the end of the world.

I'm swiping and tapping my way through every last mundane-looking option on the control hub's screen as I try to wrestle with my thoughts — being as thorough as I can with my hands, as well as with my brain — but so far there's been nothing else worth seeing.

A couple of moderately reassuring thoughts come to mind as I look again at the digital diagram of the station and tap on everything in the hope some new data might appear. It doesn't.

When The Beacon's design was first revealed, some reporters took to calling it "The Beetle" due to its rudimentary shape. The 2-D diagram I'm looking at now is a reminder of why.

The general shape is a horizontal oval, with the Docking Bay protruding to the "north" and the Observation Deck to the "south," as ZolaCore-produced maps encouraged people to think of the positions.

Zola didn't want people to consider The Beacon as a vessel so much as a place, and he was vocal about his preference for cardinal points over the usual port and starboard terminology. Because he gave wall maps to every school in the country, any kid who's interested in science could probably point to our Greenhouse or Maintenance Bay on one map as easily as they could point to Georgia or Alabama on another.

The Beetle nickname comes from the way the long walkways to the four offshoot labs, like mine, each protrude diagonally.

It *does* kind of look like a six-legged bug if you squint hard enough, albeit with the two central legs being much shorter and thicker than the others.

The Leisure Zone is close to this control hub, slightly to the east in the very center of the station. That circular area is divided into four main sections along with a smaller entrance to the Maintenance Bay. Permanently stationed researchers work in labs to the east and west, with their dorms to the far east and the Control Center to the far west.

Staring at the diagram might not have brought any new data, but seeing my lab and the Docking Bay does lead to a realization.

If I can contact Earth but for some reason they *can't* help with the pipe, I still might be able to survive for a few more days.

My lab has its own 24-hour emergency backup system that would kick in when the main station supply stops feeding it. And without wanting to assume too much, the fact that I didn't get any warnings while I was in there makes me think the main station's emergency countdown probably just started.

In theory, I could shelter in the lab until someone can get here from Earth.

There are EVA suits and oxygen tanks in various accessible parts of the station, too. Utilizing those could give me a few more hours.

Thinking about that feels kind of like putting on some water wings to jump into shark infested waters, though. What I really need is a lifeboat.

The Escape Pod is more like an inflatable dinghy, closer to those water wings than a lifeboat. It can't really take me anywhere except out of this place. If I get desperate enough to launch in that thing, I'd be like a shipwreck survivor counting on a bigger ship to come along and pick me up.

But come to think of it, the Escape Pod should have a radio of its own. I don't know if it would be long-range, but it *might* be.

That's another possible place I can contact Earth from. Too bad it takes me back to square one: not having any way past the security locks. The Docking Bay is locked, too.

If only I knew any of the technicians who worked there or in the Maintenance Bay, I could look for them and hope that dead people's fingerprints still work on the scanners by the doors.

That's a morbid thought, I know. But what are my other options?

The problem is that I don't know who's who around here. I've been an outsider since the day I arrived. The only people whose work I really know much about are Justin and—

That's it... Yannick!

My buddy Yannick is… well, *was*… a computer technician. He was *the* computer technician. When something went wrong, he fixed it.

The Maintenance Bay's door is just on the other side of the Canteen, and I've definitely seen Yannick unlock it with his finger.

If I can find him, I should have a good chance of getting in there!

Okay, it's only the Maintenance Bay. And okay, even successfully fixing the pipe would be like putting a bandaid on a gunshot wound when what I really need to do is call for an ambulance.

But Yannick's important job and longstanding position at ZolaCore might also give him security clearance to access *other* locked rooms… like one that contains a radio I can use to reach Earth.

I take a deep breath.

The path in front of me is still littered with enormous obstacles, but at least I have a first step.

In the shape of my poor buddy Yannick's fingerprint, I think I finally have a real lead.

8

I don't think there's a single icon or option left on this touchscreen system that I haven't tapped by now.

But before I go looking for Yannick, there's one thing I want to check that might help me out. If this hunch is right, it could *really* help me.

I navigate back to the map that depressingly confirmed my status as The Beacon's last man standing, by way of the solitary green dot it displayed right where I am.

My name is the only one on the screen.

Going on nothing more than a hunch, I have a sudden urge to check if the map might have a toggle I missed first time around. Maybe there's a way to make it also show me the location of the others who weren't so lucky?

Since I have no idea how this tracking system works, I don't know if this is a reasonable hope. Is it based on facial recognition? And either way, how would it know who's dead? Advanced thermal imaging, maybe?

Who knows.

More like who cares, Ray, I scold myself.

Curiosity about stuff like this isn't my friend right now. I need to control my thinking. I need to focus on what counts. I need to focus on what can *help*.

It's worth looking for this "dead people i
because knowing where Yannick met his end
saving me a lot of searching time. But as hard
not seeing any more options. Every passing
hopes.

I sigh.

Nope… there's no way of locating him so easily.

Trying to stay positive, I reflect that I at least have something to go on. I really think Yannick can get me into the Maintenance Bay, for starters. Quite possibly some other locked
areas, too.

I return the screen to its default menu and glance to the left
of the main control hub.

There's a non-digital noticeboard containing a few pieces of
paper. Most are scribbled notes about lost and found items,
scattered around a printed flyer for an upcoming poker night.

There's one other large sheet of paper that I've noticed
before, mainly because it's been here longer than I have. It's a
running scorecard for an epic Speed Chess challenge between
the station's North American and European researchers.
They've always recorded the results of three one-on-one games
per day, one at the end of each eight-hour shift block.

I know from Yannick's anecdotes that he and the other
players take their cumulative records pretty damn seriously.

I lean in for a closer look, suddenly realizing that this score-
board could actually tell me something very important.

I glance at my watch to make sure I'm totally clear on the
time and date, then look back at the last recorded score.

Immediately, I can see that five games are missing.

The last recorded score is for a game that took place 42
hours ago — a game Yannick played in and won, ironically
enough. After that, there's nothing. This single scorecard goes
back several weeks and there isn't a single gap until these five
missing games.

"Okay…" I say, thinking out loud. "So they played the
scheduled game 42 hours ago, but something happened

...n that game and the next one. So everything went down .een 34 and 42 hours ago."

Hey, it's *something*.

My hand reaches for my chin as I try to put a timeline together to build a clearer picture.

I was in my sealed lab for two and half a days and didn't come out even for a second.

When I went in, Justin knew how close I was to confirming the breakthrough with a replicable experiment. That means whoever he reported to will have known, too, but I hadn't actually sealed the deal yet.

Was someone trying to stop me from doing it?

And let's see... *eleven* hours of backup life support.

So if I consider the 11 hours the main station has left and factor in that things went to hell somewhere between 34 and 42 hours ago...

I'd guess it happened 37 hours ago, which could be when a 48-hour backup kicked in.

48 hours seems like a reasonable assumption for a main backup, considering my lab has 24, and it makes the 11 and 37 work.

This isn't an exact science but at least it gives me a picture to work with.

One thing I can't figure out is why the critical leak alarm only started when it did.

The best idea I can come up with is that until I left my lab, the system knew there was no one alive in the main body of the station. Maybe it didn't want to waste any of the remaining power on a message no one would hear?

But wait...

Does that mean it didn't know I was alive in my lab? Is that why it didn't warn me in there?

And does *that* mean there might still be people alive in the other fully sealed offshoot labs after all, and this screen isn't showing them as green dots because it doesn't know they're there?

I would knock on the doors if it would do any good, but it won't. Through two thick doors and along an extensive walkway, no one would hear anything even if they are sheltering alive in one of the other labs.

All I can do is live in the faint hope that someone really is hiding away and that they'll show themselves before it's too late.

I'm not kidding myself, though: the hope *is* faint. I don't know why the map would show the offshoot labs shaded white like the rest of the station if it couldn't detect living people inside them.

I also don't know why anyone would still be hiding in a lab after 37 hours, anyway, because surely they'd be out here trying to get to a radio, too. I know I would.

I don't have good answers for any of that and I don't have any time to wait around, either way. It was a positive thought while it lasted but I've already pretty much talked myself out of hoping to find anyone else alive around here.

More importantly, I know that Yannick isn't going to find himself.

If my deductive reasoning is right, I think he ended a shift around five hours before this all happened. That means there's a good chance he was asleep in the dorms. Since it looks like everyone died quickly, *that* means there's a good chance he'll be in that area of the station.

It would make sense that the internet died at the same time as my colleagues, around 37 hours ago. Thinking about the dorms is giving me the idea to grab my phone from its charger to see if I got any emergency notifications before that happened.

It could also be helpful to see the last notifications or messages I got from Earth, in case this *was* caused by some kind of natural celestial disaster that they saw coming from the ground.

I don't know.

I'll say that again: I don't know, and I won't pretend to.

I'm trying to think of all possibilities and I'm trying to do it while taking action to move forward.

I've utterly exhausted what this emergency control hub and noticeboard can tell me. Thanks to what I've found, I know I'm the only living soul left on The Beacon and I'm pretty sure the others all died around 37 hours ago.

The most important thing I know is still the most urgent — that I have less than 11 hours of breathable air left in here.

The biggest hope I've gained is that finding Yannick could be a big first step towards getting home to Eva and Joe.

"Come on, Yannick," I plead as I set off for the dorms. "Help me out one last time…"

.

9

My feet carry me to the dorms as quickly as they can, which isn't as quickly as I'd like.

I feel lightheaded and hot. Worry kicks in as soon as I notice how hot my forehead is. Does this have something to do with the air?

Is the backup supply not working properly? Is it going to get me, too? Did everyone else die slowly after all?

Maybe the ones who look like they died in panic near the airlocks were the ones who saw others fall first, then they started rushing around and doing whatever it took to try to avoid the same fate?

"Stop," I implore myself.

Catastrophizing isn't going to help.

I'm hot and panicked because I have a hell of a lot to be hot and panicked about. And come to think of it, I don't know when I last took in any nutrients or even had a drink of water. I'll grab a bottle when I see one.

The finale of my fuel enrichment experiment was supposed to be a big moment of exhalation. I was supposed to finally be able to relax. Those two months of intense focus were supposed to usher in a few days of celebration, until my placement officially ended and I could get home to Eva and Joe.

But instead of relaxing, the moment when I'm most tired from my single-minded focus on work has turned out to be the very moment when I need to be more clear-minded than ever. All I'm thinking as I near the dorms is that survival depends on rising to a challenge like nothing I've ever faced.

Okay... I'm here.

Unusually, the entrance to the dorms is pitch black. Flicking the light switch has no effect. I don't know what's going on here but it seems like some kind of localized power outage.

I'd know the way to my own dorm with my eyes closed, though, and that comes in pretty handy as I navigate the darkness.

Reaching my phone and its flashlight will illuminate the way to Yannick. I do know where his door is relative to my own, I just don't have as much muscle memory and I wouldn't trust myself to find it quickly in the dark.

In my dorm, I grab my phone from its charging dock.

"*Shit*," I curse under my breath.

A critical battery warning pops up as soon as I touch the screen.

1%.

I guess the power in here died around 37 hours ago and my phone has been bleeding battery life since then.

Joe's phone is newer than mine and he's seven years old. I guess I'm paying for my over-attachment to this old thing now. I just hate the planned obsolescence and the yearly upgrade cycle everyone else seems happy to go along with, so I've squeezed as much life out of this phone as I could. But again, damn if I'm not paying for that now.

"First-aid kit," I say, snapping my fingers in a Eureka moment.

That's right: there's a small flashlight in the standard issue first-aid kit under my bed. That means I don't need the phone to find Yannick. Since it's in my hand right now I figure I might as well take a second to check for notifications and messages before the battery dies, because who knows what I might see.

My lab still has full power so I know I'll be able to charge it there once I've found Yannick. I never take my phone into the lab since the shielding doesn't let any signal in, anyway, and right now I'm very glad I *did* leave it in here.

I don't know what help they might bring, but whatever notifications or messages my phone has received in the past two-and-a-half days wouldn't have arrived if it had been with me in the lab.

Let's see what we have, then…

I unlock my phone and immediately see that there are no warnings or any other push notifications from The Beacon's centralized app, which keeps us informed about all kinds of things.

I'm not overly surprised about that. After all, my thinking since seeing the chaos in the central areas has always been that the shit hit the fan *very* quickly, leaving no time for warnings.

Like you'd expect after a few days, I have a bunch of texts and missed calls, along with a downloaded voicemail. With so little battery power I decide to look at the texts first, since this seems like the most efficient way to take in some info.

I have four messages, all containing images and all from Eva. Only one actually has any text: "*Someone is excited… XOXO.*"

The first picture shows little Joe busily making a "Welcome Home" banner, complete with spaceman stickers and an impressive attempt to draw The Beacon. He's such a good kid.

I have to blink a few times to regain my focus and keep the pent-up tears at bay. A few seconds later I move onto the other three images Eva has sent. At first glance they all look like blank squares… solid blackness and nothing else.

And on second glance…

Nope, still blank.

Hmm. There must have been some kind of glitch, I figure.

I look at the timestamps of when they came through. The photo of Joe came in right after I last left my dorm for the lab, but the glitched images are more recent. 41 hours ago, 39 hours ago, 38 hours ago.

Just before it all happened.

So why are they blank?

Could it have something to do with the battery life? Maybe these photos reached my phone but are too high-resolution for it to display them in low-battery mode? Maybe they're animated GIFs that won't play for the same reason?

I could be grasping at straws, but it's possible.

For all I know, the pictures that aren't loading could be more everyday shots of Eva and Joe. But they could also be something else.

For her to send three within such a short time, and so close to the Now-Minus-37-hours mark I've pinpointed as the likely start of the station's deadly chaos... it just seems like it *has* to be something else.

Next I head straight to my voicemail inbox. There's only one, automatically downloaded to the phone's local storage, and once again it's from Eva. The message isn't transcribed into text — I really *am* paying for still having this old phone — but I can see when it came in.

42 hours ago... just before she sent the first of the weirdly blank images.

It's *really* not like her to have left a voicemail. In all the time we've been together, the only times she ever has were when she's run into another friend who wanted to say hi when I wasn't able to take a call. Like pretty much everyone else, she's normally a texter.

Come to think of it, it's more than a little bit weird that she sent three images without any comments, or even her usual "XOXO" sign-off.

I click play on the voicemail.

"Piece of shit!" I roar as the phone's one percent battery life drops to zero and the screen turns black.

It's all I can do not to throw the damn thing at the wall in frustration.

I take a calming breath — or at least try to — and put the phone in my pocket. I grab a charging cable for good measure then reach under my bed for the first-aid kit.

Flashlight in hand, I head for Yannick's dorm.

I pass a few other doorways on the way and, well... I can't not look.

I don't know what I hope to find but I'm keeping an open mind that some clues, answers or even survivors might show up where I least expect them.

For the sake of a few extra seconds, I feel like it would be irresponsible *not* to look everywhere I can.

Using my shoulder to force open the first door, which isn't seriously locked like the offshoot labs and other high-security rooms, I easily enter the dorm.

A woman is lying in the bed, so serenely peaceful-looking that I have to check for a pulse to make sure she's dead and not just asleep.

I get the confirmation I didn't want but fully expected, then cover her face with the top of the bedsheet. My colleagues deserve that respect, at least.

The same process plays out in two more rooms. Each time, I shine my flashlight around the room for anything that jumps out. Nothing does. Each time, I cover the face of an innocent victim of whatever happened here.

I pause before Yannick's door.

None of the three people I've found so far showed any signs of discomfort, but they're all dead just the same. I don't understand... it just doesn't vibe with the chaotic scenes in the more central and western areas of the station.

It's impossible not to be moved by finding them like this, and I'm not going to lie: I don't think that in itself is a bad thing.

I don't *want* to lose my sense of humanity here. Each of these people is an individual victim of whatever happened, with loved ones on Earth who'll be worried sick just like Eva and Joe must be about me.

I'm not numb to any of this and I don't *want* to be, I just have to work through it it. Not past it — through it.

I'll turn the temperature as low as I can once I reach the Control Center. I'll see to it that everyone here gets a dignified send-off, too, just as soon as I can reach Earth to secure my own immediate future.

Aside from everything else, the only way to make sure these victims have dignity in death is for me to stay alive.

If I was one of these guys who didn't make it off the station, I know I'd want the survivor to make sure someone does.

More and more, this doesn't feel like an accident. And more and more, I know it's on me to make sure word gets out.

I've only vaguely recognized the three peaceful faces I've found so far, but I know that won't be the case with Yannick. That one will be even tougher to deal with. I also know that finding him is just the start of the discomfort coming my way.

Trying not to get ahead of myself and think too much about the challenging minutes to follow, I burst in.

A slow sigh escapes my lips. Yannick's not there.

His bed is unmade, so I'm pretty sure he *did* come in here after his shift ended and after he won that game of chess.

That might seem like an assumption to anyone who doesn't know Yannick, but I know him too well to think anything else. He's an organized guy. He *was* an organized guy — that's a tough tense to get used to — and there's just no way he would set out for the day without making his bed.

When I glance to the side I spot his uniform is folded on his chair, with his name badge showing. Okay… so he *definitely* came here after his shift.

I also see a pile of empty soda pouches on the bedside table. I rarely saw Yannick without one of those things. As I try to piece everything together, it makes as much sense as anything else to guess that he might have gotten up in the night to fetch another one from the Canteen's vending machine.

From the start, the two places I figured he might be were

here or in the Canteen. I try to push aside my disappointment and consider that I've ruled out one of the two likely options.

That means I should have *more* confidence I'll find him in the Canteen, not less. Even still, it's tough to stay positive.

I'm going to run to my lab first to start recharging my phone and get some overdue hydration, then it's onto the grim business of finding Yannick in the Canteen.

I could hardly bear to peer inside when I saw how many people were in there but I'm not going in because I want to. I'm going in because I *need* to.

This is bigger than me.

More than anything else I'm fighting to get home for Eva and Joe, but I also want to make sure all of these innocent people aren't forgotten.

I didn't ask for any of this, but it's here and I'm the only one who can do anything about it.

Whatever happened on this station 37 hours ago, only I can bring it to light.

Every passing second makes me more sure that someone did this, and every passing second makes me more determined that they're going to pay for it.

10

It's a short walk to my lab from the darkened dorms. But with each step I take, I almost find myself wishing the lights were out in the main body of the station, too.

At least that way I wouldn't be getting this visual reminder of the high body count.

I have nothing on-hand to cover these victims' faces. As I pass, I silently vow to them that they'll be taken care of with dignity. Just like for the people in the dorms and the many more I'll soon have to confront in the Canteen, I'll see to that.

I quickly reach my quiet and deathless lab. It's a welcome sanctuary.

But this isn't like earlier when I was contemplating holing up in here until things blow over and work themselves out — which I now know they won't. This time, I know my respite is temporary.

I plug in my phone's charger. It's going to take at least a few minutes to power up again, like always, and those are minutes I can't afford to waste right now.

I grab a bottle of water from the wheeled trolley next to my desk and finish it in no time.

It's only when the water hits my mouth that I realize just how parched I've let myself become.

I also grab a little resealable bag of sunflower seeds from beside the water. I don't eat them right away but I know I'll need to take in some calories at some point soon.

Everything is *go-go-go* now that I know what needs to be done. I feel like I've pieced together as much as I can, and I've done all I can do without getting through the locked doors that Yannick is hopefully going to open.

The second phase starts now.

Before heading out again, I look around for anything else that might be useful.

I have a tool box and some fire extinguishers and all the other things you might expect. It's not like I'll be leaving the lab forever, though, so I don't see any sense in taking anything I don't need right away. That would only slow me down.

The one thing that gives me pause for thought is the wheeled trolley itself. It's pretty big, and my current circumstances are macabre enough to reflect that it's probably sturdy enough to support a man's weight.

Yannick was always something of a big fellow, to put it more than a little euphemistically. Even though I keep myself fit and wouldn't have too much trouble lifting him, carrying him from one fingerprint scanner to another would be a serious challenge.

Again though, I decide against taking the trolley with me. I know there are a bunch just like it in the Canteen, which is where I'm going, anyway.

Needless to say, everything that will come next rests on Yannick's biometric credentials working as well as I hope.

I glance at my phone before leaving, just in case. There's no progress yet, still just the red battery symbol. I force myself away from it, because "one more minute" could easily turn to five before it powers up.

Once I contact Earth and we can do something about the imminent expiration of the backup life support system, I'll have as many *one more minutes* as I want.

But not now. For now, I just don't have the luxury of time.

I hurry back along the walkway and into the main station. As I briefly glance straight ahead at the next closest offshoot lab — one of only three others — something makes me stop dead in my tracks.

I can't kick myself for not noticing it earlier.

What I'm seeing now is only easily apparent from this angle — which I wasn't looking from last time I left the lab, when poor Justin was the only thing I could focus on.

A slight distance from three fallen colleagues, I notice one man lying on the ground between the airlock they were trying to open and the walkway to the other offshoot lab.

Even more tellingly, I can see that the guy has a blue name badge — like mine — that designates him as a visiting researcher.

"That's his lab," I realize out loud.

Which means he can get me inside…

11

Okay, checking out this lab next wasn't part of the plan. But the plan is in flux. It *has* to be.

It's only going to take a few minutes to see what's inside this guy's fully sealed lab.

For all I know, the rumors could be true and he and the other visitors could be conducting research that's too *secret* to be conducted in the main body of the station, instead of too *dangerous* like mine.

Even if it ends up being pretty mundane in there, the guy could have tools that let me blow my way through the doors to the Control Center or Observation Deck, which I have no strong reason to think Yannick's fingerprint will open.

My mind is settled: I have to look.

"Sorry about this, man," I say to the guy as I crouch down and move his arm. I do this so I can read the name badge.

L. Barnet.

It doesn't ring any bells, but then I don't know why it would.

All kinds of research happens on The Beacon, so it's not like I should expect anyone I find to be familiar to me from my own field.

Unlike Yannick, Barnet is a small guy. He's wiry and quite a bit older than me. I figure that running back to get the trolley would take more effort than lifting him, especially when we're already so close to the door.

It would probably be the most obvious thing in the world to say "I don't like dead bodies," but I *really* don't like dead bodies. I can't watch crime shows or anything like that — it brings back too many memories of the day I've spent twenty years trying to forget.

The reason I'm thinking about that kind of thing is that I have no idea how long Barnet has been dead. Someone who watches those shows might know more about rigor mortis and the other stages that follow, giving them a detective-like ability to say when the victim died. Not me.

I vaguely recall hearing that rigor mortis usually happens in the first day and often *only* on the first day after death, but I wouldn't want to be quoted on that. All I know is that Barnet's arm didn't feel overly stiff.

I could *maybe* read something into that… something like he's probably been dead for more than twenty-four hours, I guess.

Another factor to consider here is that we're not on Earth. We're a *long* way from home. And as much as the air tastes and feels like the natural stuff we're used to, it's a long way from being exactly the same.

There are small amounts of chemical agents in the station's air supply to ensure people can thrive here for months and years at a time. Those additives might be why the air doesn't *feel* as death-filled as an enclosed space on Earth would if there were so many sadly departed people lying around inside it.

The "fortified" air supply up here could definitely have an impact on this kind of natural organic decay. I know our food doesn't rot as quickly here, for one thing, so it's not much of a stretch.

This all adds up to me still not knowing for sure when Barnet and the others died.

The little I think I know about rigor mortis still fits in with the 37-hour timeline, though, and the difference in our air could explain why people aren't in as bad of a condition as they would be on Earth after so long.

Looking at poor Barnet, and especially having felt that he's not overly rigid, I know I can lift him. That's what counts right now.

I apologize again, hold my breath, and pick him up.

Let me rephrase that: I *try* to pick him up.

It's not the weight. Like I said, Barnet is no giant.

Twenty years of steady training has made me a strong enough guy, too, even with the nerve damage in my right hand making it difficult to hold a regular grip.

No — my problem here isn't a physical one.

When I try to pick Barnet up, I feel my arms recoil before I've even gotten started. My breathing speeds up, which my heart-rate seems to take as a challenge to race ahead even faster.

My eyes feel like they're pulsing in a way I haven't felt for years as my surroundings give way to a haunting vision of the worst day of my life.

As clear as when it all happened, I feel paralyzed by a painfully immersive flashback to the teenage accident that caused my nerve damage in the first place, along with a whole lot of bigger issues.

I back up to the nearest wall and close my eyes.

You have time to breathe, I tell myself. *Take it.*

I cup my hands around my mouth and breathe as slowly as I can.

When this first started happening, a few weeks after the accident, the therapist I had to see told me that even if every-thing else in the world felt like it was outside of my control, I could always be in control of my breathing.

That didn't always seem true, especially at first, but the exercises we worked on *have* helped when things come flooding back.

Unfortunately the situation I'm in now isn't one that steady breathing can get me out of. The need to lift a dead body is just *such* a direct reminder of the accident itself, as on-the-nose as anything could be.

When I slowly reopen my eyes, another comment from the therapist comes back to me. It was the last thing she ever said to me and I've leaned on it more than once. Right now, it feels more applicable than ever:

"Always remember one thing, Ray: You didn't survive that day to let anything else beat you."

I force out a hard breath and look over at Barnet.

I can do this. This won't beat me. I can lift him to the door and he can get me into the locked lab.

He's not big, he's not far from where I need to take him, and his life isn't in my hands. Those are three ways it's easier than the incident I'm fighting to push from my mind.

With some control over my thinking again, I know I can get Barnet to the first door. If he gets me through, I figure it probably will be worth fetching a trolley to wheel him the rest of the way to the inner door. Knowing how long the safety walkways are, it just doesn't make sense to think about carrying him that far.

There's also no way in hell I'm dragging him, possible or not, so trolley it is.

If his fingerprint unlocks the door.

It will, I tell myself.

This has to be his offshoot lab — his blue badge, his direction of movement and his proximity to the door all combine to convince me of that.

I move in to lift Barnet again, and this time I succeed. I carry him to the door.

Awkwardly and still apologetically, I lift his right hand towards the fingerprint scanner and pray it's going to work.

It does!

A welcome clicking sound as the door unseals brings a rush of relief flooding through me. I don't have anything to smile about yet, but for the first time since the end of my experiment I finally feel like I've achieved something tangible.

I gently lower Barnet to a sitting position against the wall.

"Thanks," I tell him.

I might look and sound crazy if anyone else was around to witness this, but it's important to me. Barnet is not just a corpse, he's my brother. Living in space is no walk in the park and there aren't many people who share that bond.

Although I don't know who Barnet has left on Earth, I know the kinds of lifelong sacrifices that it takes to have gotten up here. It's not glamorous and it doesn't usually pay anywhere near what most people would expect, but that's not why we do it.

If Barnet is anything like me, he left Earth for a little while to try to make it a better place for a whole lot longer.

It breaks my heart that he and the others will never see Earth again.

Rueful about that but boosted by the breakthrough Barnet has delivered, I run back to my lab to get the trolley. I stop only for a second to check my phone.

It *still* hasn't powered up.

Good thing I didn't wait, I muse, reflecting on the fact that I've made a potentially major breakthrough in what would otherwise have been dead time.

I hurry to Barnet again and place him on the trolley. It's more than big enough for him, which means it should work for Yannick, too. Another good sign.

I wheel the trolley to the far end of the walkway and lift Barnet off. I pause for a moment, *almost* doubting myself, but push through the doubt.

There's no choice here. I have to go in.

My hesitation came from a momentary concern about what might be in his lab, but it looked for all the world like Barnet was trying to get back in before he died — with no protective equipment or anything else I don't have.

I have no reason to think it'll be unsafe in there.

At the point of no return, I hold Barnet's finger against the inner door's fingerprint scanner and wait for the click.

It comes.

I breathe another sigh of relief. Even though there was no reason to think this inner door *wouldn't* unlock, I've already learned not to get too confident with any expectations around here.

But when the click gives way to another sound, I instantly freeze.

I wish Barnet was alive for all kinds of reasons.

Top of the list right now? So I could ask him if I'm going crazy, or if I really *did* just hear what I thought I heard.

An unmistakable sound of movement comes next.

I feel the hairs on my neck stand up just before the first sound repeats.

I'm *not* crazy. There *is* a voice!

It only speaks one word, in a fairly high pitch, but I definitely hear it.

The sound of movement grows progressively louder, clearly getting closer and closer to the door.

And then the voice comes louder then ever:

"Hello?"

12

———

"What the—"

I literally fall over in shock when it reaches the door and shoots past me.

That's right: not *he*, not *she*… *it*.

The voice, the movement — it was a parrot.

A big one, too.

Blue and yellow and clearly well looked after, it flies down the walkway like a genie escaping a lamp.

Barnet fell with me and I apologize to him for that. I'm sure he would have warned me about the huge bird if he'd had the chance.

I place Barnet on the trolley again and stand quietly in the doorway for a few seconds. I cough, trying to draw out anything else that might be in there.

No more sound comes for several seconds. When I'm sure no more is coming at all, I step in.

As soon as I see inside, my jaw drops at the sheer scale of the room.

The lab is the same size as mine, but it *feels* so much bigger. I guess that's because a huge section of mine is taken up by the reaction chamber, which I was told is the largest ever developed in space.

But it's not *just* the scale of this place that's caught me off-guard. It's also the content.

Glass-fronted enclosures fill both long walls, most of them filled by animals. Unlike the parrot, none of them are moving.

The parrot's cage is lying on its side in the middle of the floor, with the door seemingly having opened in the fall. It looks to me like the poor thing knocked it over in a frenzy, maybe after being left alone for so long.

At least it had a chance to get out, I sigh, looking at the grid-like arrangement of test subjects who weren't so lucky.

When I get to Barnet's desk, though, I see that his computer screen is displaying a series of vital signs for "Dormouse 002."

I'm no doctor and definitely no veterinarian, but one of the lines is moving like a very slow heartbeat. Not just slow for a dormouse, either… we're talking *seriously* slow.

A little ironically, there's an old-school computer mouse next to the keyboard. I move it and left-click — haven't done that in a while — to select a backwards-facing arrow. The screen changes.

Hmm… Dormouse 001 seems to be alive, too.

As I keep clicking, it really does seem like everything is still alive. I only look at five or six more examples, including a cobra and a coati.

I glance around and start to wonder if Barnet's middle name is Noah.

I walk along the length of one wall to see if my eyes can discern any signs of life. I don't know *why* I don't trust what the computer is telling me, but it can't hurt to look.

My eyesight is pretty good as long as I'm wearing the only contact lenses in space, which is a story for another day, but I'm finding it hard to see much breathing going on.

Granted, most of these animals are pretty small. There are no apes or big cats or any of the other headliners I'd be looking for if this was a zoo.

Some of the animals are *really* small, as I notice when I reach some poison dart frogs and tiny spiders. There are cockroaches, too.

All of these little guys have moveable glass screens in front of their tanks. The screens are like panels and seem to have different levels of magnification. They remind me of the butterfly collection Joe loves at our local museum. That display has one clear panel you can move into your eye line, pretty much working as a magnifying glass.

I continue past the bugs and don't stop again until I reach the coati. He's the biggest dude I've seen so far and looks very peaceful. *Too* peaceful, I start to worry, until I see a slow breath after a few seconds of staring.

When I say slow, I guess I really mean infrequent. I don't know how fast or how deep an individual coati breath should be, I just figure they're usually a lot more frequent than this.

I look around again, taking in the vastness of the room.

"Suspension pods…" I muse out loud.

That *has* to be it. Barnet was testing some kind of suspended animation technology!

Run of the mill animal testing isn't the kind of thing I would expect Ignacio Zola to sanction on his station, especially in one of the four offshoot labs. These are universally seen as the most prime scientific real estate *anywhere*.

I venture back to Barnet's desk and glance at the papers he's strewn around. Some are on the floor, too, but I figure the frantically escaping parrot is probably more responsible for this mess than Barnet himself.

If Barnet had found my handwritten notes on my own work, they'd probably make about as much sense to him as his do to me: *zero*.

Through a combination of rushed handwriting and some kind of shorthand system intended solely for himself, it's all totally unintelligible. I unironically think I could get more answers from the parrot than from these notes — that's how little I can make out.

As *for* the parrot…

I'll hold my hands up and say I'm totally ignorant to the nature of parrots' speech. Do they even know what they're saying, or is it all mimicry? Do they self-learn, or do they have to be patiently taught? I just don't know.

Jeez, Ray, I catch myself thinking. *It's a desperate time when you're hoping a bird is going to fill in the blanks.*

Yeah. I won't count on that.

I don't want to touch anything else on Barnet's computer, in case I disrupt any variables that might be keeping his animals alive.

I'm already as driven as a man can be to get home to Joe and Eva, and making sure my fallen colleagues can have some dignity in death is pushing me forward, too.

But when a situation is as bleak as this one, I'm always going to be happy to grab extra motivation wherever I can find it. In this lab, I just found some.

Doing whatever I can to make sure these innocent animals wake up again is one more thing I'm determined to achieve.

I walk back to the little coati, who's lying there peacefully with no IV drip or anything else I can see. Is there something special in the tank's air supply?

A sudden thought hits my mind, making me consider that Ignacio Zola might have been working on a *much* bigger picture than I thought. The technology being tested here... this development in suspended animation... it could very conceivably combine with my fuel breakthrough to make long-distance space travel viable.

This makes sense given that Zola's wealth grants him the pick of research projects and personnel from anywhere on Earth, but I've never really thought about his grander plans. He keeps things so close to his chest, speculation has always felt futile.

I'm now more curious than ever about what's in the *other* two labs, but with the clock relentlessly ticking down I know I've spent enough time in this one.

I came in here because I thought I might find something

tangibly useful, and in that regard the unplanned excursion has been a failure.

But I did find a parrot… if that helps?

"I'll be back," I tell the unconscious coati. "Hopefully with someone who knows what they're doing."

Before leaving, I turn the parrot's cage upright and decide that I'll leave the lab's doors open, too. That way it can come back inside for its spilled food and bottle of water.

I also decide to wheel Barnet all the way into the lab, to leave him where he spent most of his time.

"I'll be back for you too, man," I vow. "And that's a promise."

I mean what I say. But for this promise to mean anything, I have to get back on track and find Yannick as soon as I can.

We need to unlock the doors to the radios.

And from there?

All eyes on Earth.

13

On my way to the Canteen, I start thinking more about Barnet and the blue badge that told me he was another visiting researcher.

My badge is blue, like his, to distinguish us from the resident researchers whose name badges are all white. My supervisor Justin wears standard white. Well, he *wore* standard white.

I'll get used to the fact that everyone else is past-tense dead at some point, I swear.

Anyway, I don't think Justin or the other white-badgers ever had any access privileges I don't. Each of us can enter our own locked labs as well as all public areas, but no more. What I do know is that Yannick definitely *did* have greater security access.

And here's the hopeful point I'm realizing now: he wasn't the only one.

Yannick is the only person with higher-level security who I knew personally, but there are others. His badge is yellow and so are theirs. That definitely gives me something new to go on when I get to the Canteen.

If I can't find Yannick, I can check other people's badges and look for another yellow one.

Granted, I'll be counting on them wearing their uniforms... which Yannick wasn't when he died. I saw it folded on his armchair, badge and all. That means if I stumbled upon Yannick in the Canteen without knowing him already, I'd have no way of knowing he had high-level access.

Fortunately he took some time to warmly introduce himself when I first arrived here, unlike most of the others. No one ever said anything outright hostile, but they didn't have to.

I sensed resentment from more than a few of the resident researchers and Yannick told me that was pretty normal. Unlike me and the other visitors, they were all here for the long haul.

They also worked in labs much smaller than mine and had to clear their equipment requests with a financial oversight team, instead of benefiting from Ignacio Zola's blank checks like I did.

I get it. I also have to take my share of responsibility for not reaching out more than I did, to either the resident researchers or my fellow visitors.

I arrived from Earth on my own with nothing but cargo and a supply crew for company. I'll be first to admit that my focus on the work I came here to do has been pretty obsessive from the get-go.

I've barely raised my eyes from my own paper in the past two months. I guess I didn't see a whole lot of point getting too close to the residents when the date of my return journey has always been set in stone.

The only reason my self-imposed isolation is a source of regret now is that it's the reason I can't put faces to names or roles. It's left me dependent on variously colored name badges for clues.

But I'll know Yannick as soon as I see him, I remind myself, and he's a hard man to miss.

I speed up. The Canteen's entrance is in sight now.

As I draw near, a squawk startles me from further ahead.

No words can do justice to the level of silence I'm operating in, so the parrot's call really does make me jolt.

This squawk would have been a lot *more* startling if I hadn't already seen and heard the bird, though, and I figure the poor thing has to be at least as panicked as I am.

It lived in a pretty big cage and was clearly more like a pet to Barnet than the rest of the animals on the other side of those weird glass screens, but it's still pretty obvious that captivity is all it's ever known.

Being loose in a weird place like this must be disorienting. Maybe he's the lucky one, though, free from a full under-standing of how perilous our situation really is.

Our situation.

Yup… it's me and the bird.

For a fleeting moment I wonder if I can use it for something.

If this was a movie I'd work out some kind of plan to tempt it into an air vent, so it could fly through the inner workings of the station and unlock all the important doors from the inside.

If this was a movie I'd also fast-forward through the part when I'm about to step into the Canteen of death, but sadly there's no magical remote control in my hand. I'm working in the real world, warts and all.

Standing at the threshold of the open doorway, I force myself inside and take a deep breath.

I look around.

At first glance I'd say there are thirty or forty people in here. Needless to say, I'm the only one alive. I *am* the last man standing, but I'm more than a little bit surprised to see that some of these men and women seemingly died sitting down.

They didn't die scrambling around in a desperate bid to open any airlocks. Not most of them, anyway. Some show no signs of panic at all. There's a group in the far corner, gath-ered around a table, who look like they didn't even move an inch.

The ones lying on the ground look like they were standing

when it happened. Some of the ones who were sitting down have tipped in their chairs, but they're all tightly crowded.

A pattern is unmistakable.

From my vantage point near the door, I can actually *see* the difference as my eyes move across the Canteen.

Whatever happened, it looks like it killed the people in the far corner instantly and spread across the room like a wave to take out the others.

No one got far, which tells me we're looking at a timescale of seconds rather than minutes.

For the guys in the corner, though? I really think it was practically instant.

The difference between these groups isn't as stark as the difference between the people who died sleeping in their dorms and the ones who were clawing at the airlocks just a short walk away. But seeing the variation in here all at once brings it into a sharper focus.

Although I don't want to jump to any conclusions just yet, it's looking increasingly like the air supply was compromised in some way, possibly with a fast-acting toxin. I figure the guys in the corner must have been closest to a vent.

My initial glances haven't spotted Yannick.

I do see some food on the tables, though.

There's a peeled banana, half-eaten, and it's only slightly brown. At home it would be *full-on* brown by now, which is a clear sign of the difference in our air.

I really do think that's played a part in keeping the air relatively fresh, because I don't think I could stand for one minute in a room on Earth with this many 37-hour-old corpses for company.

I head over to the far corner to begin my closer inspection. After just a few steps, I notice there's a chess board on the table that the group was crowded around. Knowing Yannick's interest in the endless intercontinental tournament, I dare to hope — with fair reason — that he might have walked over to check it out.

The news gets better as I get closer: everyone I can see around the table is wearing a uniform. That's a big contrast from the rest of the room, where a solid two-thirds are wearing their off-duty clothes.

This difference between the chess guys and everyone else makes sense, since they do usually play right after their eight-hour shifts end. That routine means I have a chance of spotting some yellow badges among them.

A yellow badge isn't quite a golden ticket, but it could definitely open some doors.

The bad news is that Yannick isn't with the group. After several checks of their area, I'm sure of that.

I sigh. I shouldn't have *expected* it to be that easy, but hanging on to hope is all I can do.

The three people still sitting at the table all have white name badges, and so does the woman whose chair has tipped over.

The others are all face-down.

"Sorry about this," I whisper with discomfort as I turn the first person over.

I see another white badge. I'm sorry about *that*, too.

Five more bodies and five more apologies later, I'm no further forward. All of the chess players and spectators were everyday resident researchers, with no greater security access than I have.

Even though there are still a lot more people to check, with no Yannick and no yellow badges to show for my efforts it's getting harder to stay upbeat.

"He has to be somewhere," I tell myself.

He does. Even if he's not in here and even if no one else can help, Yannick really does have to be *somewhere*

This is no wild goose chase. I'm looking for a guy who is definitely here. I'm not looking for something that can't be found.

Then a terrible thought hits me: what if I *am*?

What if I am looking for something that can't be found…because what if Yannick was already in one of the locked rooms when he died? What if he's somewhere I can't reach?

What do I do then? Work through the dozens of people who aren't wearing a badge, taking each one to the doors I need to pass and hoping someone's fingerprint will unlock them?

I don't have time for that. I wouldn't have time even if there was a reason to be sure one of them had high-level access, and that in itself is a blind assumption.

My chest tightens.

Shit.

A task that felt grim but eminently achievable just a moment ago now feels a whole lot less certain to end in a breakthrough.

"Keep moving forward," I say out loud, trying to gather myself. "It's the only way to go."

This three-word imperative, my closest thing to a mantra, has made a positive difference in my life since a therapist introduced it to me twenty-some years ago.

Moving past the accident wasn't easy and I needed all the help I could get. Since then I've gotten through other tough times by reminding myself that I made it through the aftermath of all that, but *nothing* has been as trying as this. Not even close.

Even on that terrible day, it all happened so fast. I wasn't desperately clinging on to life in a dying space station, and I wasn't running into one brick wall after another like I am now.

I turn away from the chess board and the fallen researchers who surround it.

One by one, I have to check every other uniform I can see and hope one is sporting a yellow badge.

I wish that was a bigger task than it's going to be. I wish every person in here was wearing a uniform instead of only a third of them. But if wishes meant anything I'd already be on my way back to Earth, so there's no sense in lingering on all the luck I'm missing.

The next group of victims, five in plain clothes and two in uniforms, bring me no closer to a breakthrough.

I wouldn't say hope is fading, but I'm definitely having to cling on tighter to keep hold of it.

I look around to choose my next area of focus.

Two more groups and a few more individuals later, I'm *still* no further forward.

Every badge I've found so far has been white white white. I'm running out of places to look. I'm also struggling to keep my thoughts away from the bigger picture of how grim all of this is.

I'm literally surrounded by death at every turn, on a space station that's supposed to be the home of progressive research driving humanity towards a brighter future.

That was Zola's whole idea and that's why he called it The Beacon.

But what is it now? *The Mortuary?*

My discomfort keeps my eyes moving — most of the time, at least. Every now and then they pause on something.

Wait a second…

This time, my eyes full-on stop as they come across something totally new: bizarre debris on the wall, in the near-left corner that I couldn't see from the doorway.

The white wall is partially covered in a black dust that almost looks like soot. The mark is narrow at the bottom and widens, with less density, until it stops around five feet from the ground.

My eyes continue along that wall, towards the trash cans and vending machines.

Only now do I see that the soda machine has tipped over.

There's another area of black debris behind where it stood — blowback from some kind of controlled explosion, if I had to guess — but what makes my heart sink is what's *underneath* the machine.

The one man I wanted to find, in the last place I wanted to find him.

Trapped beneath a 1,000-pound machine I'd need multiple helpers to lift...

Yannick.

14

I think it was Archimedes who said, *"Give me a lever long enough and a fulcrum on which to place it, and I shall move the world."*

I wonder what he could do with a four-foot crowbar? Because that's all I have access to.

Seconds feel like minutes as I stare at my poor friend and the heavy machine on top of him.

One consolation is that it hasn't *crushed* him in the grossest sense that it might have.

The other people closest to the charred marks on the wall look like they died instantly, too. This not only strengthens my theory of something rapidly poisoning the air, it also gives me hope that Yannick was already gone when the machine toppled onto it.

Okay, that doesn't make any material difference to his situation or to mine. But the guy was my friend. I just pray he didn't suffer for long.

My initial goal coming in here was to find Yannick. To that extent, I guess you could say I'm on track.

I'm at least back in the position of knowing what I have to do next, instead of worrying that I might not find him at all. That's where I was a few minutes ago.

But when what I have to do next is as difficult as moving this monstrous machine all by myself, it feels like another case where the details don't matter.

I look again at the vending machine. I don't think *two* of me could lift that thing.

There's nothing in my lab or dorm that could help with a manual task as big as this and I didn't see anything useful in amongst Barnet's weird animal collection, either.

There might be a jack or some other lifting equipment in the Maintenance Bay, but that takes us back to square one. Because guess who I need to unlock its door?

Yup, the very guy I need to free from underneath the machine. As circular problems go, this one is a doozy.

It's too bad Barnet didn't have a few trained elephants in his lab instead of a pet parrot, I think to myself. There's nothing to laugh about, believe me, but sometimes it doesn't hurt to try.

I crouch down beside Yannick and size up the machine.

It *looks* heavy, but how can I be sure? I know it contains a lot of water and some flavoring agents that mix together before delivering passable soda to the reusable pouches, but the actual machine could be lighter than a standard one on Earth.

Even when money is no object for a guy like Zola, I doubt he would waste it by launching anything heavier than necessary from Earth.

A lot of water has already leaked out, too, I realize as my knees quickly dampen. Maybe this is good. Maybe now it's not going to be anywhere near as heavy as I first thought?

Without making any claims of being especially strong, I'm a well-trained lifter. I started seriously lifting weights out of stubborn defiance as much as anything else, as soon as my post-accident physical therapy was done.

I worked around my right hand's major grip issues with some special wrist straps in the beginning. As I got older and had some money to spend, I graduated to more specialized equipment adapted to my needs.

I brought my old straps to use in the Gym here, since bringing bigger equipment wasn't an option. Even though they won't come in handy for this task, which isn't the kind of lifting motion that needs any concentrated grip, I'm hoping they've helped me hold on to enough strength to make this possible.

You couldn't tell from looking at me that my right hand is incapable of holding anything heavy, and in a lineup with nine other average guys you'd probably think I'd have a better chance than most of them of lifting this machine.

And with this water leakage, it's not necessarily impossible.

I wouldn't say I'm confident but I'm also not ruling myself out.

I take a deep breath and put everything I have into one big heave.

Nope… there's no way.

I don't know how heavy it actually is, only that it's *too* heavy. It feels like trying to lift a car. As hard as I heave, it doesn't budge at all.

I know from the accident that too heavy is too heavy, even when it feels *just* too heavy. But this thing is way beyond *just* too much for me to deal with.

It's humbling.

There's literally no way I can move this machine with the limited hand-tools I have access to, just like there's no way I can use those tools to skip all of this bullshit and smash my way through the locked metal doors that stand between me and any hope of survival.

I'm not just on my own in dealing all of this — I'm basically empty-handed, too.

Weighing everything up, no pun intended, I think my only hope is that I can somehow pull Yannick out from under this thing.

Like I said, he hasn't been crushed or squashed or anything quite as brutal as that. He's just trapped.

There's that word again: *just*.

Yannick is *just* trapped. I *just* have to get through a locked door and call Earth.

Just just just.

Right now that word feels more like a four-letter taunt than anything else, so I'm *just* going to eliminate it from my mental vocabulary altogether.

"Okay," I exhale, preparing to reach my hand further under the machine and feel for a good gripping point.

My left hand is the one doing the scouting. After the accident damaged my right hand, I had to learn to use the left for everyday tasks like writing and even brushing my teeth. That was harder than it sounds.

My right hand has regained strength and its fingers have regained a lot of dexterity since then, but I'm still limited by my right thumb's inability to hold a precision grip of even light objects.

Everything above Yannick's chest is already free from the machine, along with his right arm and the top of his right leg. The angle of his standing position at the time of the fall has trapped everything else, but it feels like I might be able to start shimmying him out if I can get a grip under his left shoulder.

I should probably get some objects to prop the machine up at its current height before I try pulling him, I figure. That would stop it from crushing his lower body even more as soon as gravity gives it the chance.

For now, I'm feeling around for a place to grip. I want to get a sense of the viability of this idea.

But as soon as I reach my left hand further under, feeling the cold water on my hands as I try to free my friend's lifeless body, I slump backwards and find myself in a losing fight with the harrowing memories.

Breathe, Ray, I implore myself. But it doesn't work so well this time. I'm not even able to say it out loud.

It's too much. Too similar. The memories are too close.

Trying to carry Barnet brought them flooding back and even thinking about trying to free Yannick sharpened the focus, but feeling the water like this has taken me over the edge.

I can still see the moment it happened.

I can still see his face etched in my mind, his expression just as blank as Yannick's. I couldn't save him. I couldn't save my own brother.

However much I tell myself the mindfulness techniques work and however much I distract myself with work, that image haunts me every day.

After feeling the chill of water on my desperate fingers just like I did back then, it's never been in sharper focus.

I couldn't save my older brother that day and I don't know how the hell I'm going to pull it together and do what it takes to save myself today.

I know what he would say: he'd punch me in the shoulder and tell me to man up.

That used to work when I got scared, and if he was still around it probably still would. But he's *not* around, because I couldn't save him. He's dead because I failed — just like *I'll* be dead if I fail again here.

If I fail here I'll never see Joe and Eva again, just like I'll never see my brother. And just like then it'll be my fault.

I hold my breath for as long as I can, then sharply fire it out.

No.

Not again. Not today.

"Keep moving forward, Ray," I mutter weakly. "It's the only way."

I move back towards the machine and try again.

The coldness of the water isn't a shock this time and I go in with my brother's face already playing on repeat in my mental cinema, so there's no instant recoil.

What there is, though, is an instant recognition that I can't do it. Physics is against me and I have as much chance of pulling Yannick out from the machine as I do of lifting it off him — the square root of absolute zero.

My left hand rubs against the side of Yannick's face as I

move out to sit up. His skin is cold, but that's no surprise and it's not the realization that suddenly changes my thinking.

The idea I've just had *does* change my thinking and give me a new way forward, but it's an idea so hard to stomach that I almost wish I hadn't thought of it.

I close my eyes and gulp, trying not to judge my desperate mind too much for even thinking of this.

Yannick's body is completely stuck under the vending machine, giving me no way of getting him to the locked doors I absolutely *have* to open.

I force my eyes open and stare intently at the key I've been looking for.

Because I don't need Yannick's whole body…

I only need his finger.

15
_____

I don't have to talk myself into it.

This idea is so unpalatable, the fact I've even *had* it says everything. Desperate times call for desperate measures and that's never been truer than it is right now.

I haven't found anyone else with a yellow badge indicating that they could unlock the locked doors and getting this far has already taken much longer than I wanted it to.

There's no time to haul everyone else to the doors on the off-chance they have the biometric credentials I'm looking for. Not while my seconds of breathable air are literally ticking down, even as I kneel here beside Yannick and the only chance I have to keep moving forward.

I push myself to my feet. My legs feel weak, partly as the reality of what I'm about to do sinks in and partly in the continued aftermath of the most intense flashback I've felt for years.

I steady myself and look down at poor Yannick. He was one of the funniest guys I've ever known. If anyone could lighten the mood right now, it would have been him.

"At least it's a fingerprint reader," he might have said, "and not a retina scanner."

I shiver at the thought.

Thank the Lord for small mercies, as they say.

I know *what* I have to do.

I know the *when* is ASAP.

And when this story is eventually told — whether it's by me or the security cameras or whatever else — I hope everyone will understand the strength of my *why*.

The one unanswered question is *how*.

I mentally run through the contents of the toolbox under my bed. There are pliers, a little hacksaw, and a few other things that could theoretically do what has to be done, but not cleanly and not in any way that would let either of us retain much dignity.

I look around the room until my eyes rest on the door to the kitchen.

The idea is obvious. It's the opposite of glamorous, but it's obvious.

I don't want to dwell on this and I'm not going to. It just stands to reason that the sharpest things I'm going to find will be in the kitchen, so I head right there.

The doorway to the kitchen opens easily, which is something I hadn't even considered.

I guess there's no need to secure it. The doors to most other rooms here are locked on reasonable security-related grounds, with my lab and a few others also being fully sealed on broader safety grounds.

Not the kitchen, it turns out.

I've never been in the kitchen. The best view I've had was a glimpse of some staff clearing away dishes and cutlery, when I was sitting at a table near the door.

Ignacio Zola is a big believer in everyone chipping in to do their part, so there have never been any full-time menial workers on the station. There were two chefs, but all of the resident researchers had to take a shift or two every month to do the cleaning up and other similar jobs.

As a visiting researcher who was headhunted to come here for a limited time, I didn't have any obligations like that. Now that I think about it, that probably played a part in the luke-warm welcome I got from everyone else.

When I get into the kitchen, it feels pretty big. There were a lot of mouths to feed, I guess, and it's still a lot more compact than the staff kitchen on my university campus.

I don't know where to look first or even the best thing to look for, but straight away my eyes fall upon a knife block.

Like I said, I'm not dwelling on this.

Say my apologies to Yannick, get it done, apologize some more, and move on.

That's the plan.

I take a look at the knives and take an exceptionally sharp looking one. I don't know my culinary terminology very well but it looks like a butcher's knife rather than a basic kitchen knife.

I didn't want anything overly serrated, just something that can do the deed as quickly as possible. The last thing I want to do is to drag this out. One downward movement is the aim, like a guillotine, as quick and as dignified as I can possibly make this horrible process.

There are some rutabagas on the counter, raw and fresh from the Greenhouse, but I really don't need to test the knife's sharpness.

I spot a blue rubber glove by the sink and pick it up. I wouldn't say I'm any more squeamish than the average guy, but let's just say that feeling the texture of a severed finger wasn't on my to-do list this morning.

The only other thing I want to grab before I go back is some clingfilm, to keep the rest of his fingers back so I don't do any more damage than I have to. I've been served fruit wrapped in this stuff so I know it's in here somewhere.

Thankfully the search is short. I find it in the second drawer.

Without wasting another second, I rush back to the vending machine and crouch down beside my departed friend.

No dwelling, I implore myself.

I try to dissociate from the process as I pull three fingers and a thumb out of the way and use the clingfilm to keep them clear of his all-important pointer finger. That's the one the biometric reader needs.

Thinking makes it worse.

If I do get out of here alive, I'm going to need forgiveness from Yannick's family more than anyone else. I hope they can find it in themselves to understand.

The level of desperation and necessity pushing me forward is the only reason I think I might ever forgive *myself*. And if I was only trying to save my *own* life — not doing this for my family, and to make sure someone is held accountable for all of this carnage — I don't think I could do it.

Self preservation is a strong drive but I feel sick thinking about what I'm about to do. Truly, having a reason bigger than my own survival is all that's making it seem possible.

I feel all kinds of things right now. Sitting near the very top is a burning rage at whoever played a part in what happened here.

Since seeing the suspicious marks on the walls and the incongruent way people have died in different areas of the station, my mind has pretty much abandoned any thoughts about this being an accident.

Someone did this, and because of them I'm about to do this.

Someone has forced me into this corner, leaning over my friend's corpse with a butcher's knife in my hand and tears in my eyes.

I position the knife above the bottom knuckle and take a deep breath.

I can't even look.

I swing the knife downwards once, in a very firm but controlled motion. I toss it away just as quickly.

Still without looking, I fumble with my hand. It's morbid, but the feeling of a severed finger brings a conflicted sigh of relief.

I clasp my gloved hand around it and finally look back towards Yannick.

"I'm more sorry than you'll ever know," I say out loud. "It was the only way."

With the gruesome key in my hand, I leave the Canteen with one thought in my mind:

This better work.

16

I know for a fact Yannick had access to the Maintenance Bay, so at the very least I should safely get in there.

Even though I'm not expecting to find a radio behind its door, getting in would open up the possibility of trying to fix the pipe with the robotic arm. It *might* also enable me to reboot the power in other areas.

Hell, there might even be something in there I could use to break through the other high-security doors by force.

My priority has always been contacting Earth ASAP. The best chance of doing that is by getting into one of the rooms where there are *definitely* radios: the Observation Deck and the Control Center.

I'm going for the jugular first: the Control Center.

As the name suggests, that's the real heart of the station.

The station Commanders work in there, making sure everything runs smoothly.

I figure that *has* to be where they monitor everything the ubiquitous security cameras pick up, too. So once I've contacted Earth and someone helps me stabilize the life support systems, I can utilize my hours waiting for the rescue craft by poring through the footage to see exactly what happened.

Okay, okay, I know. I'm getting ten steps ahead. I'm thinking of success as something that's waiting to happen, rather than something I have to chase down like a battle-weary lion stalking the only gazelle in sight.

The Control Center is also the place where I'm more likely to be able to reboot the power system in the areas where it's gone down. I think major systems like that will all be controlled in there, not in the Maintenance Bay or Observation Deck.

I think the same about the temperature control system, which is going to be important for preserving the others until they can be returned to Earth for the proper send-offs they deserve.

I make a mental note to move everyone else into the Canteen and close the door once they're in, just as soon as I get through to someone on Earth and secure my own survival beyond the next... what is it now... nine and a half hours?

Wow, getting this far has taken *that* long?

Time flies when you're fighting for your life.

I try not to beat myself up.

I *have* gotten this far, despite everything piling up to stop me. I've moved forward one step at a time even when those steps were harrowingly difficult. If I can keep doing that, I might have half a chance.

I reach the Control Center quickly.

Unfortunately, I even more quickly realize that I'm not getting any further.

There *is* a fingerprint scanner on the reinforced door... but it sits alongside a numeric touchpad. I need a code.

As the most important room on the station, I guess it makes sense that there would be an extra layer of security here.

I hope the same isn't true of the Observation Deck. I know there's no keypad at the Maintenance Bay, but there won't be a radio in there.

Getting hold of Yannick's biometric credentials was tough in a way I couldn't have imagined. If after all of that I fail to reach a radio within the next five minutes, this mountain of challenges I'm climbing could start to feel like a never-ending stairway to nowhere.

I don't know the layout of this western side of the station well enough to know the most efficient pathways between each room. Aside from the densely packed residential research labs and dorms, the hallways are very open. This at least means I don't have to keep turning corners and reorienting myself, which is a damn good thing given how overworked my brain already feels.

I don't pass many bodies at all as I walk between the Control Center and Observation Deck, which I put down to this section of hallway being a low-traffic area.

Most researchers would usually only move between their dorms, their labs and the Canteen. Justin and Yannick both told me that hardly anyone used the facilities in the Leisure Zone, like the Library and the Gym and the Greenhouse seating areas, so I'm not reading much into this.

As soon as I reach the Observation Deck, my eyes are all over the door like a hawk scanning a meadow.

Fingerprint scanner… check.

Keypad for code entry… nope.

Finally, some good news!

I'm still wearing a bright blue rubber glove and grasping poor Yannick's index finger like my life depends on it, because quite frankly I think it does.

This absolutely *has* to work.

I open my hand and shuffle the gruesome key from my palm towards my own fingers, then hold it against the scanner.

I've hoped and I've begged and I've prayed for a lot of things in my life, but never as desperately as this.

I've never wanted anything as much as this. I've never *needed* anything as much as this.

The silence around me is utterly suffocating, right until it's broken by the most welcome sound I've ever heard.

The click is faint, but it might as well be a celebratory symphony.

It worked!

I look at Yannick's finger, less squeamish than I've felt until now.

"Thank you, brother," I whisper.

We've cleared the first hurdle.

But as I push open the door, I immediately feel my body sag with an instinctive sigh of disappointment.

"Shit," I curse under my breath.

It's dark. No power.

I take a deep breath and try to psych myself up. Like I've been thinking all along, there's a small but non-zero chance that I might be able to reboot everything from the Maintenance Bay, and there might still be a working radio in the Escape Pod.

Hell, the radio in here might even be on backup power. It certainly *should* be, shouldn't it?

This line of thinking eases my mind a little bit, making it so my first steps into the Observation Deck are filled with something more like tentatively hopeful anticipation than all-out trepidation.

It only takes a few steps for me to catch my first sight of the room's staff. There are four of them. All four are wearing yellow name badges, and all four are as dead as everyone else I've found.

What strikes me here, even more so than anyone in the Canteen, is just how suddenly these people seem to have died.

Two of them still have their hands on their screens. The other two are facing each other like they were in conversation.

Their bodies have slouched in the chairs, naturally, but aside from that they look eerily like waxworks frozen in time.

With my flashlight in one hand and Yannick's finger in the other, I step forward some more to get a good view of the control console. I see a bunch of screens, all dark. I can only hope that the radio system is going to be easily identifiable and still running.

I'm sure I could figure it out if I can find it, and I feel like I have enough wits about me to rig it up to a working power circuit even if everything in here is offline.

Time is a luxury I don't have, but there's power in the lighting rig all along the hallway on the other side of the doorway I just entered.

That gives me a fall-back, at least. It means that if I *don't* find a working radio here or in the Escape Pod, and if I *can't* reboot everything from the Maintenance Bay, I still won't be totally out of hope.

Beyond the control console, the Observation Deck's huge glass front provides a window to Earth.

I take a belated look through that window, thinking it will spur me on.

Never have I ever been so wrong.

As soon as I look up, I drop everything.

It all hits the ground. Flashlight, finger... even me.

I literally stumble forward, catching myself on a chair only after my knees crash to the hard floor. At least I don't smash my head, too, but what difference does it even make now?

Because on the other side of the window, I don't see a blue planet.

I see Earth in flames, thick with volcano-like smoke.

Just as bad, I see none of the electrical lighting that usually signposts human civilization from above.

There's nothing.

Nothing.

Like a scene from an apocalyptic nightmare, Earth looks as dead as this damn station.

It hits me like a brick to the skull:

I'm not just alone *here*...

I think I'm alone, period.

17

I can't believe what I'm seeing.

Truthfully, utterly, *literally*… my brain simply won't accept the images my eyes are sending its way.

It can't be real.

It can't be true.

Earth can't be in flames. There *can* be smoke without fire.

All of the death and destruction that's occurred up here can't be a tiny footnote compared to whatever has ravaged our beautiful planet.

No… my eyes are kidding me. They have to be.

This is when I wake up.

It *has* to be.

"Wake up," I tell myself, the voice so weak and hollow that I barely even recognize it as my own.

I close my eyes and massage my temples. I psych myself up to look again.

The trauma is playing tricks with my mind. The corpses, the finger, all of it… it has to be messing with my perception.

But it's not.

When I reopen my eyes, the sight somehow seems even worse.

Who am I kidding? There are no tricks.

I *have* been through a lot and my brain *does* feel frazzled by everything it's had to deal with in the past few hours, but that doesn't change the reality of what's in front of me.

Earth is in ruins.

Where there should be evening lights concentrated in our cities and touching almost every area of our landmasses, I see nothing.

Nothing good, anyway.

I do see what looks like thick smoke billowing from multiple areas.

Are those volcanoes?

Is it fallout from some kind of attack? Maybe the nuclear war we always worried about, with an electromagnetic pulse thrown in to totally kill the electrical grid?

My heart is pounding, but who cares whether I'm looking at nuclear fallout or volcanic fallout? Whatever it is, there's *nothing* else!

Something has clearly happened down there that totally dwarfs the horrible things I've seen up here.

I've already seen things no one should ever see and done something I don't know if I'll ever forgive myself for, however necessary it felt. But nothing could have prepared me for this.

The sight itself is horrible in a way that would make anyone recoil, like the visual equivalent of nails on a chalkboard.

Except this is worse, with all kinds of horrible implications connected to the innately unsettling sensory stimulus. So if I'm comparing this to a sound it shouldn't be nails on a chalkboard… more like a cacophony of bloodcurdling screams.

Whatever has happened on Earth to cause it, there's no mistaking what I'm staring at: death on a previously unimaginable scale.

"Extinction-level event" is a term I've only heard in movies and sensationalist news reports. Right now, though, my gut is telling me it's the best phrase for what I'm looking at.

Eva.

Joe.

Their helplessness down there was the first thought I had when I saw this awful sight. It's the thought that sent me stumbling off my feet.

Of all the two-month periods in our lives, why did it have to be now? Why did it have to be when I was here, when I'd left them alone?

And in all the millions of years since the last planetary disaster on any scale close to this, why did it have to happen in their lifespans at all?

Neither of them have ever hurt a soul. They shouldn't have had to live through this.

Live through this.

These words echo inside my brain, feeling like they've been sent to haunt me. The huge unknowable point right now is whether *anyone* has lived through this.

Picturing Joe and Eva being confronted by the chaotic moments when everything went to hell brings a chill to my veins.

Unlike me, they definitely weren't holed up in an isolated lab. They weren't blissfully unaware of the hell unfolding outside. They were *there*.

Depending on what actually happened they might have heard the warning sirens, seen the breaking news broadcasts, watched helplessly as the waves or the smoke rolled in.

I can't see North America right now and the power outage in here means I can't access any satellite imagery. I also don't know enough about volcanoes to know if some kind of eruption cascade is the source of the distinct towers of smoke rising from our broken marble of a planet.

All I know is that our home in Salt Lake City is only around 250 miles from Yellowstone. I figure anything that could set off a global volcanic cascade would place the two people I care about most right in the firing line. It's way too close for comfort.

I hate the idea that they had to experience whatever happened, but the idea of them somehow scrambling for survival is better than the alternative. I flat-out refuse to let myself think that a sudden end might have been a more merciful fate.

I can't start thinking like that.

For what could be five more seconds or could just as easily be a full minute, I stare at Earth.

Enough light is coming through the open door behind me to create a slight reflection in the window. I notice only now that my hand is instinctively covering my mouth. With the silhouette I'm casting, I can't help but think that I look like a heartbroken farmer staring out at a tornado-flattened barn.

If only, I lament.

If only it was something like that... something we could rebuild.

From here, I don't have any good reason to think there's even anyone left to rebuild *anything*. It's hard to put this into words. I can't see rivers of lava — not without any telescopes or satellite assistance — but I can see the smoke.

As well as the immediately noticeable huge towers of smoke, my longer look reveals several areas of burning land on a much greater scale than any wildfire I've seen.

It's unmistakable. Earth is burning.

But worst of all, in terms of the implications, is what I *can't* see. I've figured out that everything up here went to hell around 38 hours ago, and the lights on Earth are still off.

I'm assuming a few things here, with the pretty obvious one being that things went to hell down there first.

Whatever happened here is either a direct side-effect of whatever caused the disaster, or some kind of knock-on effect from our Earth-based control systems going haywire in a way no one could have seen coming.

What I'm saying is that everything up here must have happened after it started on Earth.

The weird marks I saw on the walls could be some kind of incidental leakage through the walls or blowback from the vents, I guess, because I just can't see an angle where it still makes sense to think the station was hit by a sabotage attack.

If it was, how does any of that fit in with whatever happened on Earth?

Until a few minutes ago, I thought we'd been sabotaged because we were about to prove what theocite can do and someone wanted to stop us while they could.

The timing seemed too much of a coincidence… but that was before I knew anything had happened on Earth, let alone something on this horrible, awful, *sickening* scale.

The best word I have for Earth is destroyed.

If not *Earth* then at least our human *world*, given the natural darkness as far as my eyes can see.

Yup… destroyed.

My head is a mess. If all my dead colleagues on this station *were* victims of an attack, everyone on Earth must have been too. But who the hell would launch attacks that destroy their own planet?

Unless…

I hear my heart beating, faster than ever.

"It's not aliens, Ray," I say out loud, trying to get that idea straight out of my head.

Maybe I've seen too many movies, or maybe I'm just seeing something that makes so little sense that a nonsensical answer seems no worse than any other.

So… volcanoes? I wonder again.

Caused by…. a comet impact?

I almost find myself hoping I'm right. Something like that — something natural — might be survivable for people far enough away from the impact site. That would be better than some kind of attack from an extraterrestrial civiliz—

"There's no way," I say to myself, cutting off a crazy thought that just won't quit.

That effort lasts all of two seconds. The thought comes back almost as soon as I shake it away, because given what my eyes are looking at, is it really so crazy to think Earth really might have been attacked by—

"No!" I repeat, louder this time. "It's *not* aliens."

Right now, my mind feels like a hand trying to control a nuclear-powered yoyo.

All I can do is try to reason myself out of the craziness.

If there's been an alien attack on Earth, what the hell happened here?

But wait... even if there has "only" been some kind of unprecedented *natural* disaster on Earth, what the hell happened here?

Something like a colossal asteroid impact could do this to Earth, but how exactly would that lead to the death and chaos all around me on the station?

"The same way an alien attack on Earth could do this," I say.

The part of my mind that's still working knows it's beyond weird to silently consider most of an internal debate and speak the rest out loud, but I am where I am.

Although The Beacon is supposed to be a self-sustaining station, it's in constant contact with Earth and all kinds of operations can be controlled from the ground. That's why I was hoping they could remotely help me with the broken pipe.

I figure it *might* be theoretically possible that some kind of massive surge, or some other major unexpected malfunction in the Earth-based control systems, *could* have somehow kicked off problems with the station's life support.

What seems *more* likely, and increasingly so as I focus on how *un*likely the last idea sounds, is that whatever happened on Earth had a more direct effect here.

Solar flares, cometary debris, hell, even my craziest idea of alien weaponry... any of those things could have easily done collateral damage to the station.

After all, we're so close to home. Barely any further than the old International Space Station was.

I focus down on one of the smoke towers again. It's so wide, I can't help but wonder what the sky must look like from the ground.

A tingle runs down my spine. The hairs on the back of my neck stand up.

The sky from the ground.

Suddenly it hits me that even if there are survivors on Earth, maybe in government bunkers far enough away from the fallout, they're going to be looking up at this station and writing it off.

If they still have power to contact us, they'll know we've gone dark. They'll see that we have an air leak no one is fixing. They won't for one second be considering that I'm standing here looking down at them.

Why would they? Why would anyone think a lone survivor had been lucky enough to be isolated in a sealed chamber when this happened?

I take a deep breath.

But I *was* in the lab.

I *am* standing here.

So maybe, just maybe, some people *did* make it to safety before the mysterious chaos down there caught up with them.

Maybe some people *were* able to outrun death, just like I was able to escape it.

I have a long way to go. The air leak is getting closer to being a deadly issue with every passing second and I now have no prospect of reaching anyone else to help me fix it in time.

But here's the headline: I'm not dead yet.

I'm down but not out... and maybe *they* are, too.

I have to cling on to hope. My own life means nothing if there's no one else left, so there has to be.

There have to be people left and Joe and Eva have to be two of them.

No other thoughts will do me any good, so I'm going to do all I can to make sure no other thoughts get in.

I wish more than anything I could talk to them, but with no signal and no—

Like a whippet released from its trap, I'm gone before my legs even know it.

My phone!

It has to be charged by now. At the very least I can listen to Eva's voicemail and get some idea of what was happening. Her messages and the blank images came in a few hours apart, so maybe she had some kind of warning of what was going to hit.

I wouldn't call my current feeling optimism, because it's not. But it's not the abject hopelessness of the past few minutes, either.

As I rush towards my lab, all I can do is beg for some news that doesn't make things worse.

Give me something to cling on to, I plead to whoever is listening.

If there's any hope worth living for, I can still get into the Maintenance Bay to try to fix the air leak. After that, there's still a chance I can restore power to the Observation Deck in the hope of contacting someone.

I reach the lab and pick up my phone. At last, it's powered up.

As I navigate to Eva's voicemail, I'm only looking for one thing.

Right now I have nothing, but I know what I need.

"Just an ounce of hope they're okay," I say out loud. "Please…"

18

I'm scared to listen.

I'm desperate to know what Eva's voicemail can reveal. I'm just as desperate to hear her voice at all, but I can't shake the feeling that this is going to be a defining before-and-after moment.

I could get the modicum of hope I'm looking for, or I could get a final goodbye that leaves me with nothing to live for.

Everything I've already done since finding Justin dead outside my lab has been painful. Everything I've done has been grim.

But most importantly, everything I've done has only been possible because I've had a reason to do it: the hope that I'll see Joe and Eva again, and the drive to make sure that if someone *was* responsible for this they'll pay for all they've done.

Fixing the air leak and surviving any longer is going to be physically and operationally difficult, even if these messages give me a reason to keep going.

Without that reason, why keep fighting to keep suffering alone?

I know I can't win in the next few minutes, but I can definitely lose.

I'm holding my phone tightly. It's charged and ready to

reveal what it can, but my thumb is hesitant to tap the play button next to Eva's message.

I know that whichever way this sends me, there's no going back.

I exhale sharply and force myself to tap the button, because there's sure as hell no staying where I am.

When I first looked at my phone, I saw the photo of Joe, three blank images, and one voicemail.

The voicemail came in *before* the blank photos, which could be important. If nothing else, it tells me that Eva was still trying to contact me after leaving the message I'm about to hear.

It also tells me that the station was still getting a signal from Earth a few hours after she recorded this. That doesn't mean much right now, without knowing what she's going to say, but it's worth reminding myself.

My phone shows Eva's voicemail as the only one I have, delivered before the station lost all contact, and the recording is just one more thumb tap away.

I gulp and tap the button to play the message.

"Ray…" Eva begins.

Straight away, it feels like everything is in slow motion.

I don't just hear my name, I hear the breathy way she says it and I hear every sound in the background.

There are no wailing sirens or screaming victims or honking horns.

So far, at least, it doesn't sound like she's in a post-apocalyptic movie scene.

There's a long pause after her first word, so long that I know it's not just my hyper-focusing brain making it *feel* long. It's also long enough for me to identify the main background sound, which I can ninety-nine percent confidently identify as shoes in the dryer.

It's not the first time I've heard that lately. Eva always calls from our sun room, just off the utility closet. Joe has started playing a lot of soccer and she says his boots collect mud like nothing else.

The everyday mundanity of the dryer's hum and the rhythmic thudding of the boots only amplifies my sorrow over what's been lost.

Because whatever Eva says and however widespread this disaster is, I know there are no dryers spinning in the homes under the smoke I saw from the window.

I know there are no families sitting at those dinner tables talking about how soccer practice went, or what everyone is most excited about for tomorrow.

"Call me as soon as you can," Eva goes on. This time her words come out unusually fast, more thrown than spoken. "*Please.*"

I hear her sniffle, either fighting back tears or gathering her thoughts amid an evident storm of worry. She exhales very loudly a few times, gathering herself for what she's about to say next.

"Ray, they're saying on TV that all contact has been lost with The Beacon. The control team on Earth has lost access to the monitoring systems and no one is answering any calls. Calls are getting through but none of the other researchers are picking up. The news reporters started talking about an air leak but now they're saying it could be something worse."

I hit pause.

Nothing is moving in slow motion anymore, and I need to think this out.

Earth lost contact with station personnel *before* the station lost its data signal?

Damn, that changes everything. That means whatever killed everyone up here *didn't* kill the comms straight away.

In turn that has to mean that something happened *inside* the station, not *to* the station, just like I was thinking at first.

If the deaths here were a side-effect of a bigger incident, like the station being physically hit by something, everything would have gone down at once. The Beacon is a marvel of human engineering, but it's still as exposed as a kayak in the ocean. If something hit us, we'd be *done*.

My eyes suddenly widen as I realize I've missed the forest for the trees.

Sure, it's a confusing surprise that the station's data link was still live after all of my colleagues died. I would have put money on the opposite being true, but that's not the biggest point.

The biggest point, with implications I can hardly even start to get my head around, is that *everything* happened up here before *anything* happened down there.

And not seconds or minutes before, either. *Hours* before.

One of the blank text messages from Eva came in three hours after this voicemail. Earth still had power and the station still had a data link three full hours after everyone here died.

But how?

How can any of that make sense?

The timing of everyone dying here, coming while I was in the process of proving that our world-changing fuel enrichment process works, was already too much to handle. I just can't buy that as a coincidence.

But for Earth to then be ravaged by... *something*... just a few hours later?

No. I'm not buying that as a coincidence, either.

Right now I don't know what I think or what I believe has happened, but I sure as hell know what I *don't* believe.

All of this is connected, and it's *all* starting to look less and less like an accident.

I hit unpause, resuming the playback.

"They're saying it could be an attack," Eva continues. "They think the station might have been sabotaged. We don't know what to believe but an eco-terrorist cell has claimed credit and they say it's just the start. President Williams has told everyone to stay calm but alert... not to give up hope for the brave researchers on The Beacon, but not to go to any large gatherings or travel unless we need to. It feels like he's taking the threats seriously and knows a lot more than he's telling us. I just hope you're in that lab right now, Ray... that's all I can hope. If you are, and if you hear this message, don't give up. I know you'll find a way to let us know you're still there, and I know we'll find a way to get you down."

Another voice comes in, getting louder as it gets closer.

"What did the president mean about Dad's station?" Joe asks.

My throat tightens. The poor kid. He's always called me Dad — I'm all he's ever known — but he's never sounded as scared as he does now.

"I love you," Eva whispers into the phone. "Please: hold on to faith."

The message ends abruptly, no doubt as she turned to reassure Joe that things weren't as bad as they seemed.

As soon as it ends, I navigate to the blank images I saw earlier in the hope that my phone is able to display them now that the battery is charged.

I wait for several seconds but they stay blank. I can't be sure if the glitch was at Eva's end or if my phone failed to properly download them. Either way, with no internet signal anywhere on the station there's no chance of them showing up now.

Although this is a major disappointment to end on, I've already learned a lot from the voicemail.

My mind is reeling, but I've learned a hell of a lot.

Really, my mind is reeling *because* I've learned so much.

Right up until I saw Earth, I was thinking that my colleagues up here didn't just die — they were killed.

Now that I know President Williams has warned people to be vigilant about more attacks on Earth, things are starting to fit together again in my mind.

I'm as environmentally conscious as the next guy, but the phrase *eco-terrorist cell* is one that sends shivers down my spine.

A few minutes ago I was wondering why anyone would do something like this to their own planet. I was wondering that so hard, I started to think about some kind of alien involvement.

But now? Well, I might have just gotten my unwanted answer.

Some of the extreme groups that have been growing in the past few years go beyond nihilism and right into full-on anti-humanism. We're talking mass public immolation, suicide promotion on college campuses, anti-natalism as a core principle... all of it rolled into one position that sees humanity as a scourge.

At the fringe, these guys think they have a duty to Earth and the rest of the universe to bring our civilization to an end.

Is that what we're looking at? Ideologically motivated murder-suicide on a planetary-scale?

I still don't know. I still can't make it make sense.

I mean, why would a group like that attack the station first? And why would they happen to do it in the tiny slice of time when I was all set to change the world with my discovery?

I don't know why this all happened and I still don't know exactly *what* happened, but there is one thing I know for sure.

"It happened here first," I reflect out loud, "and then it happened on Earth."

I take a deep breath.

Okay...

I know what I need to do.

19

Eva's words have changed how I'm looking at *everything*.

She said a lot of things. One of the most important was that despite how things looked, she kept holding on to hope that I might have been safely sheltering in my lab.

It doesn't even matter whether she really believed that or just couldn't handle considering the alternative. The point is: she was right.

When she left that message, it seems like everyone on Earth understandably assumed that everyone on this station was already dead. Just like anyone looking at Earth from up here could now understandably assume that everyone on *Earth* is already dead.

The devastation I saw from the window really was *that* bad. But at the very least, I now know that the government was aware of an imminent threat.

I'm not jumping to a definite conclusion that Earth was hit by the largest terrorist attack ever seen. Because although that seems likely given what President Williams said, I still can't let myself become too sure of anything.

Either way, what counts most is that reflecting on *my* survival against the odds offers hope that Joe and Eva have survived, too.

I was sheltered in my lab by chance. If someone sabotaged the station, I guess they either didn't know I was there or didn't know how much protection it would give me.

And obviously *I* was in there to do my work, with no idea I'd be shielded from anything. I didn't have any warning that something was going to happen. I got lucky.

On Earth, though? Survival wouldn't be by chance. They wouldn't have needed dumb luck.

If President Williams knew the station had been sabotaged and had intelligence of more attacks to come, surely he would have taken action.

We have large nuclear bunkers as a matter of public record. Who knows what even bigger underground facilities could exist, built to survive incoming comet impacts and other existential threats?

It goes without saying that not everyone could be saved. No underground facilities could have *that* much space.

But Eva is an internationally published expert in early years childhood development. If this is like the movies where the government has lists of people with jobs we would need to rebuild society after a huge disaster, it's not impossible that she might have gotten in.

Come to think of it, I've heard talk that Ignacio Zola has his own emergency bunkers, too.

If he does, is it a stretch to think that the families of his researchers might get a spot?

That seems more likely than the first thought about a government list.

In a matter of seconds, I've gone from no hope to two hopes. However relatively small they might be, they're big enough to pierce the fatalistic cloud that's been engulfing me like the smoke engulfing Earth.

Gripping my phone tightly, I start to feel for the first time like this *isn't* necessarily a lost cause.

I'm the longest shot of all, and here I am. Still alive. Still kicking.

Sure, the Observation Deck's radio has no power and there's no visible sign of life on Earth.

Eva was right, though: if I can do my part and find a way to signal that I'm alive, someone might — just might — be able to come and get me. Now that I'm considering the bunkers and contingency plans both the government and ZolaCore must have in place, I think there *could* still be a usable spacecraft down there.

I might be able to help investigators on Earth put all of this together, bring justice to whoever did it, and make sure things don't get even worse.

And like I said, I know what I have to do next.

There's power I could possibly restore to the radio, and there are doors to open to find other ways of alerting Earth that I'm here. Both are important goals but I can't risk delaying the most urgent step for another minute.

I have food for way longer than I want to think about needing it.

I have power in most areas and water reclamation is all tied in to the core life support system.

Air is the choke point — no pun intended — and I need to fix that damn pipe. If I don't shore up the air supply, nothing else matters.

I don't know exactly what it will take but I know what I am. I know *who* I am. I know *where* I am. Most of all, I know why I'm here.

I'm a scientist, *in space*, and I was sent here for a reason.

Discovering solutions and solving problems is what I do.

I'm not giving up hope that my family is alive and I'm not giving up hope that I'll see them again.

Hell, I'm not even giving up hope that one of my old physics teachers is still alive somewhere, too. He's always been the one person I want to prove wrong, like Eva and Joe have always been the two I want to make proud.

Maybe I was a smart-ass, reading too far ahead in the textbooks and raising my hand too much. Maybe Mr. Lindell just had it out for me.

Either way, he didn't think I had it in me to be a real astronaut like I always dreamed of. Even before the accident ruled that out, he told me to take my head out of the clouds.

My other teachers were the opposite. Their helpfulness played a big part in my studies and my career, but Mr. Lindell is the guy whose words really stuck.

"Ray tends to falter under pressure," he wrote on my report card.

We'll see about that, Lindell.

Because all by myself, I have an air leak to take care of.

20

Like I reflected earlier, I've personally seen Yannick enter the Maintenance Bay via the finger-scanner. Even with confidence in short supply, I feel like it's safe to think his finger will get me inside today.

I can't count on much else, but my path forward is going to be illuminated pretty quickly.

Illumination is a big consideration in itself, really, because everything is going to be a lot easier if there's still power in the Bay.

So far the dark areas have been the Observation Deck to the station's "south" and the dorms to the east, which are both pretty far from the center. If there's been a fault somewhere in the system, it seems to have occurred towards the edges.

That doesn't sit well for the Control Center to the far west. That's where I'll definitely find another radio and hopefully gain access to the security camera recordings — *if* I can find a way in… and *if* there's power.

The Maintenance Bay, my next port of call, is where I'm hoping to restore power to everywhere else once I've fixed the leak. A lack of power in *there* would be a huge hurdle I don't want to consider. I'd have no choice but to rig it up to one of the circuits that are still live, and I have no idea what kind of draw the machinery and computers down there will need.

Yeah — down there.

The entrance to the Bay is in the center of the station, right next to the Canteen, but it leads down to the lower levels where all the wiring and plumbing and everything else lives. I've never been down there and I've never previously wanted to, but right now I'm just glad it's an option.

I think it's the only place where I can possibly fix the air leak. I'm crossing every finger and toe that the remote-controlled robot arm I saw in the pictures is going to be fixable in itself, because the alternative hardly bears thinking about.

But when even the hellish prospect of a last-resort and impromptu spacewalk is equally dependent on access to the Maintenance Bay, I can only worry about one hurdle at a time.

Still, I feel tense when I reach the door. I hope to hell poor Yannick's finger will still work.

And please, God, let there be light, I silently pray as I stand in front of the locked door.

I place Yannick's fingertip on the scanner, still hating what I've had to do to make this possible, and wait for a click.

Nothing happens within the usual half-second it takes to register an approved fingerprint. My heart rate reaches an all-new spike.

A full second passes, then another.

I reposition the fingertip, feeling antsy and already beginning to brainstorm ways of smashing through the door. It doesn't look as seriously reinforced as the one outside my lab, or even the one outside the Control Center.

Off the top of my head, I can't think of anything I have access to that could help me break my way in. Ironically — and *cruelly* so — all the potentially useful tools are locked behind this very door.

I reposition Yannick's finger again, trying to touch it against the scanner at a natural angle as if it was my own. This is so much easier said than done.

I move it slowly and press with different intensities. But with each passing moment I'm starting to worry there might be some kind of heat component to the security, on top of the fingerprint verification, to defend against the kind of thing I'm doing now.

But he was cold when I found him and his finger unlocked the Observation Deck, I think to myself. It doesn't make sense for—

Click.

My eyes close as a flood of relief rushes over me.

I'm almost certain the unlocking delay must have been down to user error, with me holding Yannick's finger at the wrong angle or using the wrong amount of pressure.

I feel like I did the same thing that worked instantly at the Observation Deck, though, so it's hard to shake the lingering thought that the effectiveness of Yannick's biological key might somehow be fading with time.

I paused for a second. I can't control that, but I can react to it.

I make a mental note to leave every door jammed open once I unlock it. This seems obvious in hindsight but I didn't do it a few minutes ago. I guess I can't beat myself up about that given everything else that was going on.

I'm also not going to rush back and jam the Observation Deck open right now, because I'm very confident there *will* be tools in the Maintenance Bay that could smash me back in there if that ends up being necessary.

I should really be jamming doors open from the inside, too, in case I run into any unexpected security systems. I've been in countless secure lab buildings on Earth where you need a code to get *out*, and anything like that would leave me up the creek without a paddle.

All of that is for later, though, and the relief of *this* little victory is still swirling as I get ready to push open the unlocked door.

I've cleared one hurdle. Now it's time to see what's inside.

And hopefully I *will* be able to see it, I muse, returning to my prayer for light.

I inhale deeply and push the door open without wasting another second.

The lights are on!

The silence unsurprisingly tells me that no one is home, but the lights are on.

Hurdle two — cleared.

Okay, let's see what we're dealing with.

At first glance it looks kind of like an air traffic control room, with a bunch of seats facing screens all along the walls. In the back right corner I can see the staircase leading down to the lower level. I haven't even thought about whether that might have its own access restrictions, but you'd better believe the concern is here now.

I take off a shoe and jam it in the doorway. Knowing for sure I can safely get out, I head further in towards the staircase.

It's totally open.

Phew, I sigh. I guess they decided one lock is enough, and I'm sure not complaining.

It's good to know I can go down there if I need to, but that's not why I'm here. Focusing on the reason I *am*, I study the rows of computer screens.

Some but not all of the chairs are occupied by six sadly deceased station workers. I'll never get used to seeing death up close like this and I never want to.

Being able to detach my emotions might make leaning over these people to read their screens a little bit easier, but at what cost? My humanity?

The workers here look like they died very quickly, just like in the Observation Deck.

Just like being indifferent to death, there's another potentially useful thing I don't want to be able to do *too* easily: get into the mindset of the kind of maniac who would ever do something like this.

But if I *had* to?

It definitely makes some demented sense that I would prioritize taking out people who were in a position to raise the alarm. The workers in here and in the Observation Deck are the ones with a direct radio line to Earth. If there's been a toxin attack or something along those lines, I can see why it would be focused on those areas. Maybe that's why they died so quickly?

In the Canteen and the main walkways, the way people were sprawled out and trying to open the airlocks is a surefire sign that they clearly didn't meet the same instant fate.

What I don't understand about that is why no one contacted their loved ones on Earth in the last moments they had, like people do during big hijackings or fires.

I now know the data signal was still working at that point. I have a voicemail from Eva that arrived *after* station-to-Earth contact was lost, which is proof of that.

All I can think of is that some signal-jamming technology could have been applied at the time of an attack.

Yeah... that could be it. Maybe the signal was actively blocked during the attack, my messages came in when the signal-jamming stopped, and then the internet signal went down later when the station shifted to emergency life support?

Maybe.

It seems to me that communications should be left online as a higher priority than overhead lighting, so I'm definitely skeptical. It's a theory, though, and my life might get easier if it's true.

After all, the idea that I could restore a data connection as a side effect of fixing the air supply and returning the station to regular functionality is an intoxicating one. And now, at last, I'm in the right room to make a go of it.

I'm not giving up my hope that I can reboot some other systems from in here, either. The general look and feel of the room tells me it's more focused on routine maintenance, though, and I think the Control Center is the place I'll be more likely to have that kind of success.

If I can get in, that is.

But right now I'm in *here*, and the power on these computer screens is a sight for sore eyes.

Granted, the first one I'm looking at is filled with a massive warning about the air leak. Fortunately there's an X-shaped icon I can tap to close the warning, not unlike on the big touchscreen outside where I muted the loud alarm.

*Un*fortunately, tapping X closes the warning but brings something just as unhelpful in its place.

I see a login box, with blank spaces in both the username and password fields.

"Shit…" I mutter.

None of the machines have been used for a day and a half. There'd be something majorly wrong with basic IT protocol if they *weren't* logged out. I know that, but it doesn't mean my stress-frazzled brain saw it coming.

Telling myself to stay calm, I move to the next machine. The same thing happens again. A fingerprint scanner on each keyboard would come in pretty damn handy, what with the users sitting right here. Today it just seems that luck like that isn't for guys like me.

I keep going.

All of the computers along the first wall lead me to the same dead end, but I quickly notice that the first one on the left isn't showing the leak warning.

Instead, *its* screen has a diagram of the pipework and shows the issue in red. Again, it's like what I saw outside.

This computer's operator is the only person so far whose hand is still on his mouse, and I think that might be why his system hasn't logged out. I could be wrong, but it's possible that a pressure sensor in the mouse is keeping the computer awake.

I crouch down.

"Sorry, man," I say, moving his hand away.

That cold lifelessness… it doesn't get any easier to handle.

The mouse is an unfamiliar and very odd shape, clearly for

highly specialized work. It's only a mouse in the sense that moving it on the desk will control something that happens on the screen, but I immediately sense that it's going to do a lot more than move a cursor.

The weird shape is designed for a right hand. The thumb and finger grooves rule out using my left. That would be *hugely* preferable, what with the trouble I have doing precise tasks with my right thanks to the nerve damage.

You would have taken this a few minutes ago, I tell myself, trying not to let a minor disappointment cloud what could be a major breakthrough.

It's not like I can't do anything with my right hand, this is just going to be tougher than it could have been.

On the screen, I see a few icons. One looks like a camera.

Moving automatically, my finger taps it before I can even wonder what's coming next.

My eyes widen instantly.

I'm now looking at a camera feed from outside the station, focused on the broken pipe. I can even see the robotic arm gripping it.

A pop-up notice catches me by surprise and gets in the way of the live feed, but I'm the opposite of frustrated.

"RESUME REMOTE CONTROL?" the dialogue window offers.

I feel a smile cross my face for the first time since my BioZol enrichment experiment reached its climax.

"Resume control?" I muse out loud. "Don't mind if I do…"

21

A few impossibly long hours ago, when the experiment ended, I was happy to see a steel ball propelled with the precise level of force I'd hoped for.

Right now, I'm almost giddy at the thought of remotely controlling this robotic arm and using it to place the metal pipe where it belongs.

I tap the big green *YES* button and place my right hand back on the multi-sided mouse. I'm sure this thing has all kinds of sensors, but I'll start slowly and be very careful not to make any sudden movements.

Even spreading my fingers to fit in the grooves creates an uncomfortable feeling of tension at the base of my wrist. It's not unbearable — not even close — but I know it's going to get worse with time and that applying much pressure with my thumb is going to be especially difficult.

Let's hope that won't cost me.

I start by turning the entire mouse very slightly to the right. As I do, the arm moves slightly on the screen.

"No way," I beam.

This is a live feed — from a real camera. This is actually happening. I'm actually controlling it!

I pause to take stock of the situation, looking much more

closely at the nature of the problem. With my right hand staying on the mouse, I use my left to tap the screen's controls and move the focus of the camera.

This lets me see exactly where I have to move the pipe. I have to tilt it more to the right, bring it slightly down, and then push it inwards.

I take a few deep breaths and turn the mouse further to the right.

So far so good.

Next comes downwards.

Okay…

And then *inwards*.

Inwards.

"In!" I groan aloud, imploring the robotic arm. "In the way!"

It's really myself I'm frustrated with. How do I tell this mouse I want the arm to move the pipe inwards?

Up and down, left and right, those I can do. But a three dimensional mouse just isn't something I'm used to.

And the pipe is *so* close.

I left the other screens around me on the air supply countdown, and they tell me I haven't fixed anything yet.

The live feed shows me just how close I am. *So* close. So tantalizingly close.

It's perfectly lined up… all it needs is a slight push.

I look on the screen for a help icon, maybe a question mark, but there's nothing like that. Why would there be? This guy is obviously an expert in his field and you wouldn't find instructions on the steering wheel of a racing car.

I push my palm down on the mouse, hoping *that* will do something.

It doesn't.

Next I try squeezing the sides with my thumb and pinky.

I wish I could tell if this idea works, but I can't squeeze hard enough with my thumb to perform the task. It can't feel the same feedback I feel in my pinky.

In everyday life I've found all kinds of ways to work around the nerve damage that limits my right hand, from improving the dexterity of my left to utilizing straps and other assistive devices.

For this mouse, though? I'm stumped.

If only this guy had been left-handed, the grooves would be the right shape for me to do it easily.

An idea suddenly hits. What if I can use my left hand here... not instead of my right, but *as well*?

Without wasting another second, I use my left thumb to push my right thumb firmly enough to apply the pressure it can't provide on its own.

I instantly feel a mild vibration telling me I've pushed hard enough. Unfortunately the good news ends there, because nothing happens on the screen.

I slowly release the grip, feeling a physical relief as the tension in my wrist eases but experiencing the total opposite internal feeling as the tension in the air rises.

There *must* be instructions somewhere, I think to myself. Maybe on an earlier stage of the computer's menu system, or there could even be a printed guide lying around somewhere.

I let go of the mouse altogether. My eyes are already scanning the room for drawers or a filing cabinet while I lift my hands away. I lift them slowly, taking no risk of any accidental movements.

There's nothing within sight.

When I turn back to the screen, though, I immediately notice something.

Something I wish I didn't.

I was careful. I lifted my hands away slowly. I didn't move the mouse anywhere.

But none of that matters. It doesn't matter what function I accidentally engaged, because the robotic arm is gone.

All I can guess is that my thumb-and-pinky squeeze made it hold the pipe more tightly, and that releasing my grip of the mouse made the arm release its grip of the pipe.

I rush to control the camera via the touchscreen. It takes a few seconds, but I locate the arm.

It hasn't moved very far, just enough to click securely into a storage slot next to a second identical arm.

It must be possible to control both of these arms at once, I figure. Either two people controlling one each or one impressively dexterous person controlling two.

I don't know. And with no left-handed mouse or instructional guide to be found, none of this helps me, anyway.

The camera feed cuts off automatically once the arm is back in place.

I try not to panic over my failure.

I'm in control here, I tell myself. I might not know how to work every aspect of the controls just yet, but I was definitely getting somewhere. That pipe was *so* close to being back in place.

From the menu that appears in the feed's place, I tap the obvious option:

"INITIATE NEW REMOTE PROCEDURE?"

That seems like what I need. I'm happy to see it.

When the next screen appears, I'm suddenly less happy.

A *lot* less happy.

"ENTER REMOTE PROCEDURE AUTHORIZATION CODE," it demands.

I feel my knees buckle.

Because life isn't a Hollywood movie, I couldn't guess this guy's unknowable authorization code if I had nine years to do it, let alone nine hours.

The pipe is lined up perfectly. All it needs is a firm push inwards to get it fully back in place. The air supply would be back online and the time pressure that's stopping me from focusing on anything else right now would be gone.

If I don't fix this, I'm done for. And as close as I just came, I know I can't get any closer with the mouse.

I can't fix this from here.

I turn towards the stairway, which leads not only to the utility access level but also to the emergency EVA hatch.

AKA, the exit door for spacewalks.

Well, Ray, you know what they say: if you want something done right, you have to do it yourself.

I gulp harder than ever, because there's only one thing I can do and there's only one place I can do it.

Yup.

I have to push the pipe back into place.

I have to go outside.

22

The possibility has been there since I first saw the nature of the unsecured pipe. I just didn't want to focus on it.

But now that my dead-end with the remote repair system has made an EVA the only other way forward? There's nothing else I *can* focus on.

One thing I don't want to get hung up on is that I've never worn a full space suit outside of a single three-hour emergency training scenario on Earth. That was little more than a box-ticking exercise for insurance purposes and I understood why ZolaCore didn't spend any more time on it than they had to.

I took up my invitation to work here at pretty short notice and it's not like anyone ever expected me to have to do something like this.

After all, it's not like any random member of an aircraft's cabin crew can fly the plane or patch up the engines in an emergency. If things go so wrong that all the capable people die at the same time, it's game over.

Which also makes a fair amount of sense, since most incidents capable of taking out *almost* an entire crew are likely to take out everyone, anyway.

As a visiting researcher I guess I'm also kind of like a performer on a cruise ship. I'm here for a few months, and definitely not expected to steer the damn thing if the captain goes down.

To labor that metaphor, it's safe to say all expectations went out the window when the station was hit by an iceberg no one could have seen coming.

I had one afternoon of training to familiarize myself with the suit. That was to prepare for an emergency evacuation where a fully sealed docking procedure couldn't be guaranteed.

At the airlocks people were desperately trying to open in their dying moments, a craft could have attached itself outside. If there was any hitch to prevent a full seal, like if a publicly-built rescue craft didn't have full operational compatibility with this ZolaCore-built station, knowing how to wear the suit could have saved my life.

That's as far as it goes.

Basically, I know how to put the suit on and walk in it so that I don't die right away. I know how to survive a few seconds of exposure to the nothingness that might have lay between the atmosphere in here and the safety of a rescue craft.

I've had zero EVA training. Extravehicular activity wasn't on my docket. Just like the cabin crew who aren't supposed to step in to fly the plane, I'm not the guy who's supposed to step out and fix a pipe.

But that's the thing: here, now, in *this* situation... I am that guy, because I'm the *only* guy.

In my regular disaster-free life, I work with fuel.

It used to be jet fuel for aviation, but most of the work moved towards rocketry a while ago.

My work has major implications for space travel — especially now that the experiment has proven the stable viability of my theocite enrichment method — but I wouldn't introduce myself to anyone as a space scientist.

I'm not a space scientist, I'm a scientist in space.

And trust me, the trepidation flooding through my veins is a surefire sign that this is more than a lexical distinction.

I try to psych myself up with the thought that it's going to be much easier to manipulate the pipe with my own hands than it was to control the robotic hand with that weird mouse.

I mean, controlling something with my own hands *is* the root of the word manipulate. How's that for some lexicology!

The trouble is, right now I'm not an easy man to convince. Sure, circumstances were against me with the mouse and my hand issues. But at the end of the day, I failed with the remote repair.

If I fail with the space walk, for any reason, the result is going to be a lot worse.

Let's just say it: the result could be sudden death.

Those are the stakes I'm playing with when I step outside.

Unlike everything else I've done so far, one wrong move means disaster — not just disappointment.

I know there are a bunch of emergency suits out in the hallways.

I'm not totally sure why the people out there didn't go for them before trying to open the airlocks. I would have guessed they would, in the same futile way people who have to jump from burning buildings might try to make a parachute out of a jacket. I guess the speed of the unfolding chaos had a part to play in everything.

Every time I think about my dead colleagues, I grow more determined to find out exactly what happened here.

I *will* find out. As soon as the life support system is back online, accessing the camera recordings in the Control Center will become my second priority after somehow alerting Earth's survivors that I'm here.

Come on... work with me, Ray, I tell myself.

I have to believe there are survivors, just like I have to think about my next step after dealing with this huge EVA challenge. It's not about getting ahead of myself, it's about having a vision of a future that can pull me through the present.

And take it from me: when the present is as rough as it is right now, you need all the pull-through you can get.

Back in the present, I know there are suits in the hallway but I figure there have to be some downstairs, too, nearer the EVA point. I decide I'll try there since I have to go down, anyway.

I look around the Maintenance Bay's main room one last time, this time physically searching for an instruction manual as well as visually scanning. Still nothing.

Guessing the authorization code for another attempt at a remote fix is totally off the cards, too, so there's nowhere left to turn.

I head to the stairs but stop halfway.

Wait…

What if I need a code to get outside, too?

My shoulders sink. Every time I think I'm getting somewhere, something new gets in the way.

"Breathe," I tell myself.

I haven't hit that stumbling block yet.

There might be no need for an exit code. After all, I'm already in the Maintenance Bay and it's not like I'm trying to access a certain person's computer system. I'm trying to exit via an *emergency* hatch for exterior repairs here, and what kind of emergency exit has a password?

Yeah… I think I'm worrying over nothing with that one. I mean, it's not like a saboteur could do more damage from the outside than if they were already in here.

Maybe I only needed a code for the remote repair because that system was meant for one guy, with a very specific and very valuable skillset?

Maybe his role let him remotely control way more than just the robotic arm he was using when everyone died?

And, I don't know, maybe a lot more could go wrong with all that than with an EVA?

Putting on a suit to fix something outside is definitely risky as hell for the person doing it, but it's a whole different kind of thing. My hands wouldn't be strong enough to rip out pipework like the robots might be.

Come to think of it, I just hope I'm strong enough to push the pipe back *in* where it needs to be. It should be light enough but the level of pressure it'll need is totally unknowable until I'm out there.

I think I only have to click it into place — hardly move it at all — and I'm hopeful it won't offer much resistance. Time will tell.

Yeah... time.

Time *will* tell, and I don't have much of it.

I continue down the stairway and set foot on the station's lower level for the first time.

My first thought is that it's very industrial looking. This is definitely more like you might expect a space station's corridors to look, versus the surprisingly airy spaces upstairs.

Janitorial is another word I'd go for. That works, too.

Fortunately the corridor is well enough lit for me to walk without any problems.

I know which emergency EVA hatch I'm heading for since I know where the pipe is dislodged. Thanks to the two-level map I saw on the screens, I also know that the hatch is *fairly* near the problem. It's all relative.

I'd like the door to be even closer to where I'm going, giving me a shorter EVA, but I'm thankful it's not a *lot* further. Seeing its position felt kind of like rolling a five. Six would've been awesome, but I'll take it.

I have hours of air left, not minutes, so it makes sense to open some doors as I pass them. There's no telling what could be inside and I'm glad to find that none are locked.

I find mountains of innocuous supplies of just about everything.

Meal packs, cleaning equipment, you name it. Nothing in the first few rooms and storage areas jumps out as useful for smashing through the doors that are designed *not* to be smashed through, but we'll cross that bridge when we get there.

One door leads to a large workshop with all manner of large power tools inside.

I see large desk-mounted saws, vices, and plenty more equipment that I couldn't even name.

What I don't see are any portable tools I could use to *drill* through any of the locked doors upstairs — another possible method — but I'll be sure to have a real look in here later. You know, once I've dealt with this whole *time-sensitive air leak* thing.

Right after the workshop, I find a supply closet full of medicine and first-aid stuff. The stock goes way beyond what I have in my small kit upstairs. Like the workshop, this could be important later… but only after I've shored up the air supply to make sure I even *have* a later.

Nothing else really stands out as I progress towards my exit door. I can still hardly believe I have plans to use an *exit* door, but we are where we are.

Right next to that final, frightening door, I see three EVA suits.

I don't see any keypad for a code. Finally, a welcome relief.

I'm also glad that I *do* see a printed safety notice on the wall. It details the core safety information for emergency procedures, which is the kind of thing I need to know.

I read every word.

The writing gets small, making me extra thankful for my contact lenses. Really, though, I wouldn't even be able to read the headings without them.

The headings introduce topics like *AUTONOMOUS EMERGENCY RETURN MODULE*. Judging by the descriptions and diagrams, this could just as accurately be titled *JETPACK CONTROLS*.

I've never worn a suit equipped with one of these jetpacks, but I know they haven't changed very much since the boxy NASA ones came along in the mid 1990s.

It's basically a powered life jacket. And trust me: you *really* don't want to need it.

The hand-based controls for the thrusters and steering look simpler than the mouse upstairs. I spend a minute or two taking it all in, just in case.

Only a few minutes, though, because I'm very fortunate that the incident site is close enough for me to reach without having to untether. I'll always be attached to the station. With that in mind, I spend the vast majority of my time reading the other sections.

The end of the notice refers to a second page, which I gratefully find behind the first. At first I thought the notice was just laminated on the wall, but it was actually inside a pouch and there are nine pages of information where I thought I only had one.

This is good.

When I'm doing something so new and so inherently dangerous — one hell of a combination — a full rundown like this is exactly what I need.

Even if I only had *one* hour of air left, I'd pay attention to this stuff before going outside to take one big swing at the problem.

An old Lincoln quote comes to mind: *"Give me six hours to chop down a tree and I will spend the first four sharpening the axe."*

Okay, I'm not going to use up *two-thirds* of my remaining time getting ready to do the EVA. But still, I am being fairly thorough.

I sit down and read every section at least twice, challenging myself to remember the most important parts verbatim.

I'll be wearing a pretty new ZolaCore suit design. It seems very intuitive, and before long I learn how I'll be able to use the touch-sensitive control pad on my left wrist to control options on my visor's HUD.

This heads-up display isn't too far away from the technology that shows directional arrows on your car's windshield, synced up with the navigation system so you don't have to look away from the road.

I pay most attention to how to get back inside, naturally.

Second place goes to what I should do if I run into any kind of difficulty during my maneuvers.

Before getting back inside I obviously have to get *outside*, and fortunately the notice confirms that I can open both the safety door and the final emergency hatch without a code.

One of the options I'll see on the HUD is titled *EMERGENCY RECALL*. Apparently, that one would reel me back in as quickly as it's safe to do so. I don't plan to fall back on any procedure with the word emergency in its name, but it's always better to be prepared.

Once I've digested everything, I gulp away my final doubts and reach for a suit.

A *space*suit.

For my spacewalk.

In space.

23

_____

I'm not surprised that the suit feels pretty weighty in the station's gravity, what with the pre-fueled jetpack and all, but it's totally manageable.

As a kid I would have absolutely loved the idea of doing a space walk like this, and I can't help but think that maybe I wasn't careful enough with what I wished for.

I step into the suit, breathing as steadily as I can and trying hard to visualize success.

I'll be back here in no time, I tell myself, *taking this thing off as soon as the job is done.*

An information screen near the door shows the air supply countdown. It's down to just under seven hours. I guess I've been sharpening the axe for a little while longer than I meant to, but it doesn't really matter at this stage.

This really does feel like my last big swing.

I can't leave anything on the table, and if there had been any advantage to using *more* time I would have gladly done it. I stopped when I started to feel like I've internalized as much as I'm ever going to from these written instructions, and that running over things any more could do more harm than good.

Paralysis through analysis... that whole thing. It's not a wall I want to hit.

I walk to the informational touchscreen by the hatch and tap an icon to undo something I did earlier.

It feels like a lifetime ago when I silenced the alarm to give myself a chance to think. Now that I'm heading outside, it's time to hear that blaring siren all over again.

When I get back inside, I'll want to know right away that I've succeeded. The absence of this ear-piercing alarm will tell me just that.

Wow.

I literally flinch when the alarm resumes.

Almost unbelievably, it's even louder down here that it was in the upstairs hallway.

I pull my suit's gloves on, with my left hand doing most of the work, and smile at the clicking sound as they snap into a full seal.

It sounds almost like a hydraulic hiss — undeniably cool. I know childhood Ray would have loved that, because even I can appreciate it for a few seconds amid all of this tension.

I'm able to hear the hiss over the alarm only because my ears have done their best to adjust to the din. Seriously, though, it is *loud*.

Even when I first put on my helmet, I can still faintly hear the siren.

The sound stops completely when my helmet's seal engages.

Silence.

Standing in front of this door is the most frightening moment of my life. I try to focus on the series of ordered steps that I have to complete in a very disciplined way, because I know structure brings safety.

I close my eyes and run through the steps.

Go outside. Tether. Go *all* the way outside. Maneuver to the pipe. Click the pipe into place. Maneuver back. Come inside. Untether. Come *all* the way inside.

I feel like I've got this, but when I reopen my eyes I really feel the closeness of the visor.

I breathe slowly and think back to my few hours of suit training. I remember the instructor talking me through calming techniques to avoid feelings of claustrophobia, which I'm apparently more prone to than most.

Those hours were worth it just for that, I think to myself as the woman's words echo in my mind. They help me push the negative thoughts to one side.

In a few moments when I'm confronted with the vastness of space, I figure I'll probably be feeling agoraphobic about that rather than claustrophobic about the suit.

I'll have no well-rehearsed way of handling that, but I'm working to a "don't look down" style plan to never look away from the station — and especially not towards the soul-crushing specter of Earth.

Last-minute hesitation is making the suit feel a whole lot heavier.

I close my eyes and think about when I was standing at the edge of my lab, debating whether to shelter inside or come out to stare death in the face. I did the right thing then, as hard as it felt.

Now that sheltering anywhere is no longer an option, I have to go one step further.

It feels more like a giant leap than a small step, but I'm the only man who can take it.

"You can do this," I say.

And I'm right.

With my breathing as controlled as it's going to get, I open the first door.

It's a full seal, naturally, and the outer hatch won't open until I close this one again.

I step into a small compartment where I find my all-important tether. I reseal the inner door and tether myself to the station.

After that, there's only one thing left to do.

Shit out of options and praying I'm not equally out of luck, I open the outer hatch and step into space.

24

Go outside, check.

Tether, check.

Go *all* the way outside, check.

I'd love to kid myself that I'm a third of the way to success. In reality these three steps, and the opposite three at the end, are the easiest by far.

The actual pipe-fixing and the maneuvering on either side of it are my stumbling blocks. They're where things could go wrong.

Getting out was an important challenge to overcome, but potential missteps in that phase didn't come with the stakes that they do now.

One wrong move out here and I could be toast. *Space* toast.

The station-mounted grip rail is exactly where I expected it to be, courtesy of the thorough instructions I found. Those notes were a godsend and in a sense they're making me feel like I'm not totally alone.

I'm the only one who can do this, sure. But I'm doing it with the help of the ZolaCore team who left everything I need to do it.

When you're the only person left breathing on an otherwise dead space station, a connection to the past is important. It helps to center me; it helps me to remember that this moment will eventually be in the past, too, just like every other one I've ever made it through.

Better still, considering that this moment is fleeting brings the future more sharply into my mind. I'm doing this with the help of the people who came before me, and once I've done it I can get help from others who'll come to save me.

I'll help *them*, too, with all the evidence and intelligence I can gather about what happened here.

Together we can get to the bottom of things. From that bottom, we can set our foundation to rebuild.

But first…

Okay, Ray, no more waiting. No more delays.

I grab on to the grip rail and carefully place my feet on the lower track. As though walking on the world's thinnest ice, I do my best ballerina impression to sidestep in the direction of the pipe. It's really not far, but I really don't want to rush.

I count each and every step, for no real reason other than to give my mind something to focus on. Making controlled movements is easier than I expected, to the extent that the mental battle not to look down really is the toughest one I'm fighting right now.

By the time I count my forty-seventh step — as slight and as careful as all forty-six before it — I'm exactly where I need to be.

I see the loose section of pipework, achingly close to its correct position. I'm at once proud of myself for so nearly doing the job with the robotic arm and frustrated with myself for not being able to inch across the finishing line.

It's so close, *inch* really is an appropriate word.

I slowly take my left hand from the grip rail. Making sure not to move quickly enough to throw off my balance, I take hold of the pipe.

"Easy does it," I murmur to myself.

I gulp and put a little bit of force into my arm. Even erring on the side of extreme caution, aware that pushing too hard is the only way I can mess this up, I push hard enough for it to clip into place on the first move.

I don't hear anything, obviously, but I definitely feel the feedback of a sealing click. Better yet, the pipe doesn't move when I gently jimmy it to be sure.

After all the note-reading and axe-sharpening, I think I've done it! As easy as that, I really think I've done it.

I turn back towards the access hatch on the main body of the station, where my tether is coming from. It doesn't look nearly as far away as the pipe did when I set out.

Looking at the door makes me wish I had initiated up a radio relay to one of the other suits, so I would have been able to hear whether or not the alarm has stopped.

It definitely looks and feels like I've clipped the pipe back into place. But still, a decisive sensory confirmation while I'm out here would have been nice.

If something still isn't right when I go in, I can always come back out now that I'm more comfortable with the movements. I pray it doesn't come to that, though, because I don't know what else I could do with the pipe.

Basically, it's either working or it's not.

I take my hand off the pipe for good and re-grasp the rail.

The last thing I want to do is entangle myself in the tether when I start stepping back the way I came, so I glance down at my foot to make sure everything is clear.

Don't look down, I scold myself.

I quickly raise my head again and turn the other way.

Too far the other way.

I don't even know if it's direct sunlight or if it's reflecting off something closer, but a beam of light reflects off the far end of the handrail and momentarily blinds me.

For eyes like mine that are sensitive at the best of times, the worst of times are *bad*.

I'm totally flash-blinded.

I can't see a damn thing!

I try to tell myself it will pass, but everything happens so fast… everything is so disorienting…

I lose my footing.

My right hand — my stupid, useless right hand — has already instinctively and unthinkingly reached for the eyes it can't get to through the helmet that's keeping me alive. Without a steady footing and with the sudden imbalance of a single-handed grip, my left hand can't hold on.

In an instant, I've gone from feeling totally in control of the situation to being totally blind and totally free.

Free in the very worst way.

Emergency Recall, I implore myself. *Do it!*

This is what the tether is for. This is why I read those notes.

I tap my left wrist and desperately squint to look for the right menu option on my HUD.

Too bad I can hardly see anything.

A giant white shape fills my vision, like an artifact of the biggest camera flash ever. It surely won't last forever but that doesn't help me now.

Squinting again, I move my head slightly. I want the digitally projected writing on the inside of my helmet to sit in the less-affected extreme peripheral of my vision.

There it is, I think, seeing the right words. I use the control pad to move down to the right option and then tap.

"Confirmation required," a digital voice booms in my helmet.

I squint and tilt my head some more to make sure I'm selecting the green checkmark rather than the red X.

I tap it.

The emergency procedure begins.

But the first millisecond is all it takes for me to know that the *wrong* emergency procedure has begun.

The tether doesn't start pulling me back towards the station like I want it to.

No.

I *didn't* see the rights words.

In my flash-blinded panic, I didn't request and confirm an Emergency *Recall*.

The tether detaches from my suit and leaves me slowly floating away from the station...

Because I asked for an Emergency *Release*.

25

We've all heard that when you're facing death, your whole life is supposed to flash before your eyes.

I guess old Ray just *has* to be different.

For me, the flash in my eyes is the *reason* I'm facing death. It's the reason I can barely even see the tether — and the station — getting further and further away.

I can't beat myself up for choosing Emergency Release over Emergency Recall, because I literally couldn't read the full second word. Now because of that, I'm floating away from the station with nothing in reach that I can grab on to.

Except the controls... I realize.

Except the controls for my one last hope: the Autonomous Emergency Return Module.

Yup. It's all riding on the jetpack.

I couldn't test it out inside, obviously, and my limited training never covered this. All I trained for was putting on the suit and not taking it off until I was back in a controlled atmosphere. I guess ZolaCore's trainers must run a jetpack class for emergency repair workers, but that class understandably wasn't extended to the likes of me.

The cabin crew doesn't fly the plane, after all.

But right now there's no one else to help. No trainers to talk me through it, let alone a pilot to do the flying. My life is in my own hands.

Everyday jetpack-style flight is something that my BioZol-enrichment breakthrough could finally make into a reality. It's not one of the breakthroughs I've given much thought, though, and for that reason I've never operated anything like this — in any kind of environment.

I really am in at the deep end.

Sink or swim, I think to myself.

The biggest irony is that I successfully reattached the pipe to the station, only to *un*-attach *myself* from the station a few moments later.

My only hope now lies in boosting myself close enough to grab on to something, then carefully sidestepping the rest of the way back to the hatch.

It's not far in absolute terms but the distance is growing by the second. This level of pressure is like nothing I've ever felt, even though the controls aren't inherently complicated.

I feel trepidation rather than hesitation, and only necessity pushes me forward. I gulp away any further notion of over-thinking. It's now or never.

I engage the AERM.

There's a kind of inbuilt handle on the waist region of my suit, to the left, which functions as a joystick. It's not like any control method I've seen before and the best adjective I could throw at it is *futuristic*.

Like most other ZolaCore developments, it's impressively intuitive. I read the notes inside and had a quick dummy run, familiarizing myself with the handle's controls without engaging anything.

It's a hell of a lot more intuitive than the mouse that almost let me avoid all of this with a remote fix, I'll tell you that. The joystick is also reachable with my left hand, albeit awkwardly. That's a major boost since the grip and dexterity I need to operate it are beyond the powers of my right.

I take a deep breath. Unlike when I very conservatively

pushed the pipe inwards as gently as I could, this time I'm erring on the side of using too much thrust.

I don't know the real-world range of these things or when they were last tested, so I don't want to get an inch further away from the station than I have to. I don't want to leave it too late.

As soon as I squeeze the handle to engage the AERM — okay, let's just say jetpack — I feel a surprising level of power.

Wow.

With a tank of theocite-enriched BioZol, these things would be insane.

I use the joystick to align myself, like the notes instructed, then squeeze again for another forward boost.

Yes…

Yes...

It's working!

I'm getting closer!

I ease off the thrust, but momentum doesn't carry me as far or as quickly as I expected.

If I knew the mass of my suit, the power of the device, the distance to the railing... all of that... sure, I'd be able to precisely work out exactly how much juice I need to give this thing.

That is my job, after all.

But I've got to give myself a break — I don't have good data for any of those variables, least of all the distance. My vision is still shot to shit by the flash, even now that I can sense the effect is very gradually abating.

I tilt a little to straighten up and squeeze again to bring myself in.

This time the thrust pushes me forward much faster than I expected. Maybe this is because there was no inertia to overcome or maybe it's because everything was warm.

Either way, I positively *shoot* towards the railing — so quickly that my hands can't fully brace my arrival.

The impact is rough.

It's more of a collision than a full-on crash, but you better believe I feel it.

I'm winded, and worst of all my right shin feels like someone just dropped a hammer on it.

I scream in reaction to the pain, but my hands grasp the railing like the life-saving object it is. My left does most of the work, as always, but my right squeezes with all its might and I can't fault it for fighting bravely to hold on.

A two-handed grip gives me enough stability to work with.

I see absolutely nothing now, with my eyes closed tight in a wincing reaction to the impact. But even through the pain in my leg I feel the wonderful firmness of the railing against my hands, and I put every ounce of my resolve into holding on.

I hold and I hold until the rest of my body feels strong enough to do what I tell it to. Breathing quickly, I heave myself along the track one pained side-step at a time.

Even with my eyes open again, I still can't see much of anything. I see just enough of the external hatch to know when it's close, and my relatively unscathed peripheral vision lets me see where I have to open it.

I manage to open the hatch and stumble inside.

As soon as the hatch is open, my detached tether starts automatically winding around its drum like a giant fire hose. I wait until it's done then reseal the hatch and open the inner door.

Relief floods over me as I step back into the Maintenance Bay's lower level.

The readings in my HUD quickly turn green, confirming that I'm once again surrounded by the station's hospitable atmosphere.

It's only when I remove my helmet that I realize there's no alarm.

There's no alarm.

There's no alarm!

I grit my teeth and take a few labored steps towards the

screen by the hatch. I remove my gloves and tap a few options until I'm looking at a diagram of the station.

It's the same diagram I saw earlier. The same one that showed me a red-for-dead pipe.

Through my slowly recovering vision, I can see that the pipework is now all green. It's working!

There's no countdown.

Life support is back online.

I did it!

I'm struggling to walk or even breathe normally due to the heavy impact I've just taken, but at least I know there's going to be air for me to breathe beyond the next few hours.

With a long exhalation, I fall to my knees and ultimately lay down.

Pain, exhaustion, relief... who knows which is strongest, but I need to lie down for a minute.

I actually did it, I think to myself.

I went outside — into *space* — and I fixed the pipe.

I'm hurt, maybe more than I want to accept right now.

But by God...

I *did* it.

26

My breathing returns to something close to normal after a few minutes on the floor.

Call it respite.

This is the first time I've been off the clock since that alarm started. The relief of restoring full life support is genuinely immense, even if it's tempered by the pain in my right leg and the discomfort in my eyes.

My vision has improved more than the leg, which positively *aches*. I'm mainly pleased that my sternum feels better after the brief but intense winded feeling I got from colliding with the station harder than I planned.

I get to my feet and fully step out of my suit.

There's no visible bruise on my shin. It feels like there should be, but with the protection of the suit I suppose it was a different kind of impact than would normally be the case.

And it was better for my shin to bear the brunt of it than my head, I figure, searching for a silver lining.

My eyes are bothering me a lot, though, despite how much the flash has faded from its apex. I feel like I need to get these contacts out and splash some water around.

As far as I know, mine are the only pair of contact lenses in space. They're only here because I got special dispensation when I was headhunted by Ignacio Zola himself.

I'm medically unable to get corrective laser surgery, as *another* result of the injuries I suffered on the day my brother died.

Until they made an exception for me, ZolaCore had strict requirements for unaided vision and hearing.

The rest of the physical tests are nowhere near as strenuous as they were in the old days, when rocket launches were way more demanding than the runway takeoffs our craft use now. Back then, the list of tests people had to pass to be considered space-worthy was as long as your arm.

I never quite understood why Zola had such a hang up about any "sensory deficiencies," as his rules called it, but at the end of the day they were *his* rules and that was that.

No one here ever had glasses or hearing aids. Researchers were allowed to arrive with *implanted* hearing aids or laser-corrected eyesight, but they couldn't rely on anything wearable — even contacts.

Like I said… until me. Zola *really* wanted me here for the enrichment work and I couldn't do it without my contacts, so he rewrote the old rules.

My lenses aren't adaptive or augmented like some that are hitting the market. They're just plain old corrective lenses. The most important thing is that I never have to take them out, which isn't yet true for the adaptive lenses.

I'm not switching until the tech catches up.

They were expensive as hell, too. But if I ever get down from here and there's a civilization left to return to, I'll finally be able to buy myself a few backup pairs. Even though I'm not going to see a huge percentage of the fortune my breakthrough is going to make Zola and the university, I'll get a small slice of a massive pie.

I limp along the industrial-looking lower level corridor, towards a door where I saw a toilet and sink on my way past in the other direction.

I open another door first, grabbing some painkillers from the medical supply closet. I can make out the brand name and I'm pretty sure I should only take one of these at a time. They're strong, which is definitely not a bad thing.

I pop one of the pills and hurry into the small bathroom.

Very carefully, I take my lenses out and place them on some toilet paper by the sink. My eyes don't feel any different when I take them out, but holy hell is this a reminder of how much I need those things!

I can hardly even recognize myself in the mirror above the sink — everything is so blurry.

I don't know if my eyes have become dependent on the lenses in a way that makes my vision worse than it would have been if I didn't have them, or if I've just had them in for so long that I've forgotten how much work they do.

I'm trying to think how long it *has* been since I got these life-changing, always-in lenses. The surest I can be is that it was somewhere between 17 and 19 months ago. I know it was last year, in the time between Joe and Eva's birthdays.

The feeling of cool water brings a pleasant relief to my strained eyes. I really haven't been drinking enough, either, so my parched lips are grateful for the drops that fall towards them.

Looking at myself for the first time since this nightmare started, I get a new sense of how alone I am.

I exhale sharply, trying not to dwell on this.

The blurriness of my vision will be here for as long as I leave the lenses out, but I'm getting a sense that the flash is fading more quickly than it was. Whether that's because I took the lenses out or because a certain amount of time has passed, I don't know.

I also don't care. What counts is that it's happening.

A sudden flapping sound startles me, literally making me jump.

My mind eases when I realize it's just the parrot's wings.

It's outside, in the corridor.

The parrot... I'd forgotten all about it.

"Hey," I say.

Does it talk? I know it said *"hello"* when I first opened the door to that guy Barnet's weird animal-filled lab, but can it actually understand anything?

Are macaws talkers, or just mimics? I still have no idea. I'll readily admit that parrot communication isn't exactly my speciality subject.

It's a big bird, for sure. But now that I can see the shape up close, albeit lacking visual detail without my lenses in, it's clearly not as big as some I've seen in zoos. I guess it's a young one.

"Hello," it squawks, flying through the door.

It lands on the ground and looks up at me. Only a second later, it lifts off again... but not back towards the door.

"Woah!" I call, holding out a futile hand to try to keep it back.

"Water, water," the parrot says, evidently attracted to the still-flowing tap.

The blue and yellow bird perches its huge claws — *talons*? — on the edge of the sink.

It tilts its head and shuffles its feet to get its beak under the tap.

My unaided vision is blurry, but not too blurry to see what the damn bird does as it moves in to quench its thirst:

It knocks my contact lenses down the drain.

27

"Stupid bird!" I bellow, grasping fruitlessly towards the drain in the hope that I can catch my contacts before they're gone for good.

I can't.

I slouch over the sink, crushed by another defeated feeling right after the high of a long-awaited success.

Why?

Why does it have to go like that?

First the experiment works, I'm ecstatic, I go to tell Justin… and I find out Justin is dead, along with everyone else.

Now I fix an air pipe *on the outside of a space station*, and the rare positive feelings have barely settled by the time another disaster strikes.

I look up at the blurry man in the mirror.

"No feeling sorry for yourself," I say. I don't like that trait in others and I don't want it growing in myself.

But no one else has ever been in a situation *this* bad, the commiserating half of my brain counters.

I do all I can to shake that voice away.

I really can't see any details on my face. I look down at the faucet and only see blue and red. I can't make out the C for Cold or H for Hot.

I'm nowhere near as flash-blinded as I was a few minutes ago, but this is even worse. When the flash was causing problems, I misread a small digital projection of the word *Release* as *Recall*. Right now I can't even make out a single letter at arm's length.

Maybe this is why people with bad vision shouldn't be in space after all, I think with a long sigh.

There are a lot of downsides to being on your own like this. Leaving aside the main ones, like the reasons *why* I'm alone and the fact that I feel genuinely alone rather than just physically isolated, one thing I wouldn't have predicted is the way your brain talks to itself.

I never experience this in normal times, but here I am with two sides of the same psyche arguing and picking holes in their prior thoughts.

Maybe that's the natural scientist in me. Maybe that's my brain going for the closest thing to peer review it can muster.

Yeah… I'll tell myself that. It's probably better than admitting I'm going cuckoo.

I can't see the parrot at all now that it's flown away, scared by my angry reaction. I wasn't going to hurt the stupid thing, but *come on*. Was I supposed to be quiet and shrug stoically?

I keep blinking as I look around the small bathroom, hoping this level of blurriness is temporary. Maybe it's only this bad because of the water I've splashed around, or as an after-effect of the flash, or just a result of wearing the contacts for so long and then finally taking them out.

I can't deny reality, though: unlike the flash-blindness, the blurriness is not getting better.

It actually feels like it's getting *worse*, but I know there's no logic in that. It surely only seems that way due to the increased attention I'm paying to just how little I can make out.

My phone is back in my pocket, returned to its usual spot after I stepped out of the spacesuit. I pull it out to take a look, trying to gauge just how bad this is.

Aaaaand I'm screwed.

I can't even see the numbers on my Lock Screen.

I look and I look and I look, squinting and widening and blinking my eyes. Even knowing which number is in which place, I don't recognize any of them. They might as well be blank circles.

Muscle memory helps me tap in the six-digit code to access my home screen. When it appears, the photo of Eva and Joe is my final straw.

Sure, it's not the closest-up shot you'll ever see. But they could be *anyone*.

The two faces I long to see in the flesh might as well belong to two random strangers in this photo. That's how bad my vision is.

I feel a familiar and painful flashback coming on, because this hits way too close to home. On the day my brother died, I lost my glasses trying to save him in the water. My vision wasn't this bad back then, but I remember trying to wake him up and not even being sure if his eyes were slightly open or not.

The injury that ruled me out as a candidate for corrective laser eye surgery came right after that... at the part I *really* don't want to think about.

"Keep moving forward," I speak as firmly as I can, returning to the therapist's mantra that got me through so many dark teenage nights after it all went down. "It's the only way to go."

I take a deep breath.

Forward *is* the only way to go, and right now I think there's only one route.

I have to do something about my eyes.

Seriously: I could barely function like this over a quiet weekend at home, let alone manage to carry out difficult operations with unfamiliar technologies in places I've never been.

The shooting pain in my shin is still there but suddenly feels very secondary. It's nothing compared to this massive mountain-sized bump in the road that's just appeared in front of me, in the middle of a path that was finally starting to look traversable.

There's no getting around this and there's just no way I can work through it.

With this level of unaided vision I can't read instructions, I can't recognize faces, and I can't control computer systems.

It's already crossed my mind that I could try to isolate this drain's output and look for the lenses. It's also already left my mind as a workable idea. Even if I knew where to start with something like that in such a non-standard plumbing system, there's literally no chance I could do it without being able to see properly.

Just once, a happy stroke of irony would be nice. It's like each instance keeps getting crueler than the last, like they're competing to kick me hardest when I'm already down.

One more unwelcome irony is that the exception Zola made for me has put me in an especially terrible spot, since the *old* rule means there are no other contact lenses or corrective glasses anywhere on the station.

I need to fix this.

A sore leg is something I can limp through, because I can go without a perfect gait.

But functioning eyesight? That's not a luxury. Not here and not now.

Clear vision might not be as crucial for my immediate-term survival as ensuring a supply of oxygen was, but it's really on that level when it comes to having any chance of getting out of here.

However hard I rack my brain for an alternative, I know there's only one thing to do.

I look at myself again in the mirror.

"No getting around it," I say. "We're going to need to engineer ourselves some glasses."

28

The glasses don't have to be perfect, I tell my doubting thoughts as I set off for the stairway.

Hell, they're not *going* to be perfect. Let's just clear that up now.

All I need to do is improve my vision enough to function. I don't have to get it back to how it was with the contacts.

Good enough is good enough.

Walking takes longer than usual due to my injured leg, but after a while I find my gait returning to something closer to normal. Impact injuries are no joke. This one reminds me of when I smashed *both* shins into a metal railing while sliding down an icy hill with a bunch of my equally moronic school friends.

Still, though, it's not debilitating. Once the painkiller I took fully kicks in, this shouldn't hold me back at all. That's a lot more than I can say for this whole vision problem.

If my brain is good at one thing, it's running through a lot of options quickly and narrowing the field down to a few viable ones.

From the flashes of ideas that come to me before I reach the stairway to the main level of the Maintenance Bay, a handful make the initial cut.

There are going to be telescopes and microscopes everywhere, for one thing, so I'm not short on actual lenses.

Lenses with a level of magnification even remotely close to what I need to remedy my poor short-range vision, though? Yeah... probably not so much.

There are magnifying glasses of different sizes, too, including one on a little credit-card sized multi-tool in my own lab.

Even holding something like that in front of one eye might help me read text when I need to. If I can find two of them, I'm sure I could come up with something simple to hold them in place at a working distance. I guess that'd be somewhere between contacts and glasses.

Again, I'm not kidding myself that I'll have some nice frames sitting snugly on the bridge of my nose. But I'll be damned if I can't hook something basic around my ears and attach some makeshift lenses to it.

That's not asking too much, is it?

As soon as I'm upstairs, I hightail it to my lab.

It's a longer walk than I'd like, especially when my leg is still thumping despite the painkiller I took downstairs. It's necessary, though, because my lab is the one place where I know what I'll find. And while time might not be as pressing as it was when my remaining air supply was literally ticking away by the second, I still have to be as optimal with my movements as I can.

I still don't know what the current situation is on Earth. Things could be getting worse, for all I know. Something I've learned up here, or maybe something I haven't learned *yet*, might even be the only way to *stop* things from getting worse down there.

Maybe Eva and Joe are *okay for now*, just like me.

What I'm getting at is that time is no more of a luxury than working vision.

I reach the lab after a few increasingly painful minutes and open the top drawer of my desk right away.

My eyes scan around for the multi-tool but actually land on something else first: safety goggles.

Hmmm, I ponder.

These could work as the basis, saving me from having to make frames.

I figure I could cut out the protective fronts and make a nice place for whatever lenses I settle on. There won't be any distance control, like I could get if I was making frames to spec, but making *anything* with my current level of vision is tough — and that's without even thinking about whether I'll find the materials in the first place.

That's the whole point. It's not that I don't want to do anything elaborate, it's that I *can't*.

Once I regain workable eyesight and do whatever I can to send an SOS signal to Earth, I can always use the benefits of my first solution to come up with a better second iteration.

Safety goggles like these aren't a rare commodity around here, so I grab a pair of scissors and set my mind to cutting out their fronts.

I squint like my life depends on it, because who's to say it doesn't? I *have to* be able to see if I'm going to have a chance of contacting anyone on Earth, and I have to have something to hold in place the lenses I'm hoping to find in the next few minutes.

And speaking of having something to hold things, I take great care not to cut any of my blurry-looking fingers.

These scissors are nothing compared to the knife that gave me poor Yannick's finger, though, so I'm not in danger of cutting one *off*.

This also doesn't have to be the world's most precise procedure, so I err on the side of speed over caution. I'm planning to secure working lenses to the inside of these goggles and getting rid of their plastic fronts is really just a way to give me the clearest view I can get.

Glass on top of the plastic would be way better than the

blurriness I'm facing now, but it wouldn't allow the same level of clarity as just glass.

Piercing the goggles and cutting two rudimentary circles doesn't take long. And even if it doesn't achieve anything tangible quite yet, it's a start.

I put them on and look around. They're comfortable enough and the sides aren't obstructive, so this could definitely work.

Now for the lenses.

My eyes pass right over my two go-to microscopes, because those aren't the kind of lenses I need. They'll be way too powerful, even for my worse-than-I-ever-realized vision. Besides, they're also too small to work at the distance the goggles allow.

So what do I actually need?, I muse. *What am I actually looking for?*

I need something with a relatively minor level of magnification, in terms of scientific instruments or tools. Ideally something that's already used as a screen of some kind, or maybe—

Barnet!

Barnet and his weird animal lab, where I found the parrot!

My feet are moving before the *a-ha* moment even finishes playing out.

In that room with all the animals in suspended animation, he had tanks of insects and poison dart frogs that had slidable magnifying panels at the front.

Going by what I can remember of his setup, some of those panels must be roughly the right kind of magnification. They were at the right kind of distance and were used for looking at the right size of things to be in the right ballpark, at least.

It's not far to Barnet's lab from here, even with my leg still complaining about every step.

As I walk I'm now trying to think of how I could make some kind of visor, to attach a large piece of glass at a suitable distance from my face.

I can't, I decide.

The idea of glasses-shaped glasses, for lack of a better term, is the best one I have. Admittedly that's going to require the use of some fairly heavy duty glass-cutting machinery, but I know where I can find that.

What I don't know is how I'll safely *use* that machinery with the very imprecise vision at my disposal.

So yeah... that thing I said about not being in danger of cutting any of my fingers off?

We'll see.

My usual work, as skilled and volatile as it is, doesn't require the dexterity and steadiness of cutting through glass. I can also usually see what the hell I'm doing.

These thoughts fade when I get to Barnet's lab and see that the parrot is back by its cage.

Even with *these* eyes I'd be able to see its blue and yellow feathers from the other end of the hallway. Up close, it's impressively vivid.

The bird is right next to the cage, which I left open so it could come back if it wanted to.

"Water, water," it squawks, like it doesn't remember what happened last time.

I look around and see a bottle on Barnet's desk. It's close enough for me to discern the shape, but I don't know if there's anything inside until I lift it up and feel the weight.

I open the bottle and place it on the floor. The bird doesn't do anything.

"Water," I say, gesturing to the open bottle. "For you."

Still, it just looks.

"Did he lobotomize you or something?" I ask.

"Hello," it replies. "Squawk!"

I can't help but shake my head and stifle a chuckle at the absurdity of all this.

But I guess none of it is this little guy's fault. He shouldn't be here, but he is — and that makes him my responsibility. I move closer to his cage and reach for the special water bottle that's clipped on.

When I lift it, I feel that it's empty.

I squint as I hold the bottle out at arm's length, giving myself the best level of focus I can achieve. I tip it upside down and unscrew the dripper part. There's probably another word for it, but let's go with that.

Either way, I fill this bottle with the water from Barnet's, then reattach it to the cage.

I do this by feel more than by sight, but it gets the job done.

The bird hops into the unlocked cage and drinks like it's never tasted a drop of water in its life.

"Cheers," I say, because why not?

"Cheers," the bird says back, pausing for a second before getting back to its drinking. "Squawk!"

A grin crosses my face. I still don't know if it's just mimicking me or if this bird knows what it's saying. But aside from the whole *destroy-my-vision* incident, it doesn't seem too bad.

With the parrot happily moving between its water bottle and some seeds on the floor, I turn back to the insect tank I came to see. I lean in close.

There are five layers of magnification panels. None are in place to begin with. When I slide the first to the center, not much changes in terms of the visual clarity.

I try the second and feel some optimism when it makes the ugly cockroach slightly less blurred.

And when I try the third panel? That ugly cockroach becomes the most beautiful thing I've ever seen — because I really can *see* the damn thing.

I'd be kidding myself to say it's perfect, but it's better than anything I've been realistically expecting.

The fourth panel proves to be *too* magnified and the fifth even more so, but number three can do the job.

Three out of five, right in the middle.

I remove all five panels — the only way I can do it — then gratefully pick out my lovely little slab of Goldilocks glass.

I'm still wearing the lens-less safety goggles, where I plan to attach the glass circles I'll cut out of the panel.

That means I have the two components I need, right here on my person. All that's left is putting them together.

And the small feat of cutting out the circles in the first place, I reflect with an increasing weight of reality sinking in.

I look at the parrot and decide that during the cutting procedure I'll absolutely *have to* break my rule about leaving doors open. The workshop door has to be closed. I just can't risk that thing flying around in there while I'm doing something so dangerous.

Before leaving I also check-in on the little coati I saw last time, whose slow breathing confirmed that all of these creatures are alive despite how it looked at first glance.

Naturally I can't see much detail this time, but I remember which tank-like enclosure it's in.

"I'll be back, buddy," I promise one more time, not that I can be sure it's still breathing.

I might as well be ten beers deep at this point, because this really is the blurriest vision I've ever had.

For now, though, I have some glass to cut.

Yay.

29

Down in the Maintenance Bay's corridor, one of the doors I opened en route to the EVA hatch looked like a multi-purpose workshop.

Its ceiling light worked when I hit the switch, so I'm pretty hopeful the machinery will work too.

As quickly as I can walk, that's where I'm heading.

It's been a long time since I cut glass. Even then I was standing back most of the time, watching in awe as my grandfather trimmed a large pane to replace one that had smashed in his Greenhouse.

Pops was the kind of guy who always had a pencil behind his ear and three screwdrivers in the cutlery drawer. The kind of guy who'd buy a standard-sized replacement pane instead of a pre-cut one, then call five friends to track down the tool he needed to trim it.

I don't think it was the ten-dollar saving that motivated him so much as a driving desire to just *do* stuff.

He taught me the old mantra that *"he who chops the wood warms himself twice."* To this day, that's something I can get behind.

I wish I had paid more attention to everything Pops told me when I watched him cut that glass. In my defense, I couldn't have been more than ten or eleven years old.

I don't know which month it was when we repaired the Greenhouse. I just know it was the winter before he died. I always remember that, because he never got to see how tall the tomatoes grew the year after we patched it all up.

Any resourcefulness I have comes from him, no doubt. My dad wasn't around and Steve was a step-*asshole* more than a stepfather, even before the accident. A lot of kids don't see any positive male influences at all so I'm grateful I had Pops, even though he went too soon.

Guys who grew up like me often do all they can to be the opposite of the father figures we had to live with. I'm lucky that I have those memories of Pops to give me a positive role model, too. But still... I have to admit that most of the time when I'm thinking about how to handle something with Joe, I *am* trying to be the opposite of Steve.

Pops was a good influence in all kinds of ways. Unlike some of his buddies who used to come around to help on projects from time to time, he was all about safety.

"Spend ten seconds double-checking everything is right, or spend a lifetime wishing you had," he'd always say.

I'll bear it all in mind, today more than ever.

I walk into the workshop and flick on the light. As I look around, it seems pretty clear that this is The Beacon's main workshop — if not the only one. It's *huge*.

A far cry from Pops' garage, that's for sure.

Everything is shiny and new-looking. I always expect tidiness and cleanliness around here since Zola is famously insistent on a tightly run ship. But this stuff is *so* pristine, a lot of it looks like it's never been used.

The air seems fresher, too. As soon as I notice that, I realize why: there are no bodies in here.

In fact, I haven't found a single person *anywhere* on this lower level.

The systems on a station like this are designed to run as

self-sustainingly as possible, I guess. These rooms don't seem like places where people would carry out routine work.

I walk the perimeter of the workshop, taking in the different machines.

Needless to say, this is a lot easier when I hold the magnifying panel in front of them. The panel also lets me read the various notices on the walls next to some of the power tools.

They must have gotten through a lot of yellow and red ink, is all I'll say. Seriously: the number of exclamation-point warning signs is off the charts.

I guess Zola and the people he put in charge of safety around here had a lot in common with Pops. I can respect that, especially in a controlled environment like this.

You can't be too careful when the stakes are so high.

This workshop would have been heaven to Pops, in the same way my custom-layout lab felt like heaven to me when I first walked in. With all these tools, he would have been like a kid in a candy store.

And I'm not going to lie: I'm pretty excited myself.

I didn't look in here properly when I first passed by, because I didn't think I'd need any of this. But now that I'm here I see that I have choices on choices on choices, with at least four machines I could *probably* use to get this glass into two more workably sized pieces.

I stop at one tool in particular when I spot the word "glass" on its warning notice.

The context is good — "*If cutting glass, be sure to…*" and then a list of bullet points.

"You'll do," I say, tapping on the bandsaw's label. It reads: PlatinumCut 1080-B.

Just like at the EVA hatch, I find several sheets of paper behind the main warning notice, in the clear pouch it sits inside.

I'm a little bit disappointed that there's no printed version of the full instruction manual. In its place is a QR code that would apparently take me to one if I was lucky enough to have an internet signal.

The quick-start guide's diagrams look helpful enough, though, and enough is all I'm going for.

The magnification on this glass panel is good enough to help me read and the information I have for using the bandsaw is good enough to follow.

If perfect is the enemy of the good, I'm more than happy to make best friends with the good *enough*.

I take five minutes to hunt down everything else I think I'll need. First I find some heavy duty gloves, which are an absolute must.

Next I pick up an unmodified pair of safety goggles, with their protective plastic fronts still in place. Lastly I pick up an adjustable chair. That'll allow me to sit comfortably at the right height.

I struggle through most of this gathering stage with my right hand, since I need the left to grip the glass panel that's letting me see what I'm picking up.

Not for much longer, I tell myself.

With everything set in place and double-checked, just like Pops would want, I power up the bandsaw. By now, I know *way* better than to take anything for granted around here. That's why seeing a red power light appear when I flick the switch feels like a small win in itself.

Sure, in a lot of contexts a red light means STOP.

Sure, in a lot of contexts a red light means WARNING.

If I was watching from afar, I would tell someone with blurry vision to bear those facts in mind and reconsider this course of action.

But believe me: I wouldn't be doing this if I didn't have to…

30

The surface of the tool doesn't give me any way to position my magnifying panel at a useful angle.

I can't hold it in front of my eyes, either. Cutting glass is a two-handed job.

I have to start with the vision I've got, which means I need to add an extra step to my original plan.

The first thing I have to do is cut the panel in half. The second thing is to cut one of the halves in half again.

One quarter of the panel should be small enough for me to safely attach it over the outside of my goggles. I'm sure that would be way too cumbersome for a permanent solution, though. Picture lenses twice the size of the frames they're meant for, attached crudely to the outside.

Besides, every little bit closer I can get the glass to my eyes is going to make my vision better. I want to attach some makeshift lenses to the inner part of the goggles, not the front.

Basically, I'll do a *very* crude job to start with and then use the benefits it brings to help me do a slightly more precise job.

I'll cut out two rough squares and use them to let me cut out two neater circles.

Make sense?

I'd like to think Pops would be saying yes.

Following all the warnings I've seen, I use two hands to guide the center of my panel towards the fast-moving serrated blade.

I move slowly but smoothly. I try to do exactly what the notices tell to me to, making sure to never stop moving or applying pressure.

My panel is big enough to allow a relatively comfortable amount of space to hold it at either side. My hands aren't too close to the saw. Still, I'm glad of the heavy-duty gloves I picked out of a well-stocked drawer full of safety equipment.

I'm not using any of the ear protectors I found in there. There's no sound warning on this thing, which isn't overly loud, and I want to be able to listen for any signs of a problem. It doesn't make up for the details I can't *see*, but right now I want all of the sensory input I can get.

As I squint at the blade in a vain hope of drawing it into focus, the irony of this situation cuts deep. I can't help but feel that having to engineer a pair of makeshift glasses without functioning eyesight is kind of like an energy-sapped and starving lion having to catch a spritely antelope.

When you need to do it most, you're least able to do it.

Such is life, I guess.

The power tool I'm using might be made by PlatinumCut, but after just a few seconds I'm all for giving those guys a gold medal. This thing works like a dream.

The blade cuts through my pane so well, I don't think "knife through butter" would even cover it.

Wire through cheese, scissors through paper, they're all way too mundane.

How about: lion's tooth through antelope's jugular.

I grin. That metaphor will do. Because just like a hungry old lion catching his prey when he's up against the odds, I'm actually winning.

I repeat the process with extra care. The half-sized panel is still big enough to be handled safely, even with my blurry vision.

This second cut gives me the quarter-pane sized pieces I wanted.

I'm majorly impressed by how smooth the cut is. Not impressed by myself, I mean, but more so by the bandsaw.

I guess I did okay to hold steady and move smoothly, but the saw did the rest. It's the real MVP.

I grab a tube of maximum strength glue and stick the square pieces of glass to the front of my pre-cut goggles.

I take just as much care with the glue as I did with the saw. This is probably because while I've never been cut by a powerful saw, I *have* messed up with powerful glue. Painful memories of a school dare gone wrong are etched in my mind, and for this more precise task I have to lose the gloves.

The glue sets quickly.

I put my gloves back on for the final stage of the process, which is going to involve some circular cutting.

The awkwardly square goggles I put on a few seconds later look goofy as all hell. There's no getting around that. But as soon as I put them on, I'm floored by how much better I can see already.

I can make out the logo and product name on the bandsaw, for one thing. Sure, I can't easily read the text on the wall-based notices, but I can make some words out when I squint.

As a test, I remove the goggles and try them backwards. When I hold them in front of my eyes like this, with the outer glass as close as it'll be after I complete the job, my vision hits the magic level:

Good enough.

The smallest page numbers, which I could have read effortlessly with my contacts, still take some squinting to make out. But in the grand scheme of things, I'd say getting back to eighty percent of my previous vision is a huge win.

All I have to do now is cut some smaller pieces I can glue *inside* the goggles, to bring the makeshift lenses half an inch closer to my eyes.

That might not sound like much, but it makes a huge difference. I'm sure anyone who wears glasses would have a hard time if they woke up and the temples had grown half an inch, taking the lenses further from their eyes.

The goggles as they are probably give me forty percent clarity. With all the reading and other close-up tasks I have to do around here, a move from forty to eighty percent will be a major game-changer.

If the saw didn't feel so safe, I *might* think about sticking at forty percent. But let me tell you, the guys at PlatinumCut knew what they were doing when they put this thing together.

Note to self: when I make it back to Earth, they're going on my Christmas card list. Either that or I'm buying some stock.

Before making any more cuts, I use a marker pen to draw circular guidelines on my remaining half-pane of glass.

Aided by my square-framed goggles, I cut the remaining half-pane into quarters like I did with the first half. Next I make four straight cuts at the corners of each quarter.

I look at the result and decide that there's no need to go any further. I don't need perfectly round lenses. After all, the goggles themselves aren't perfect circles.

All I'm going to do is cut two holes in an untouched pair and stick my lenses inside. Those holes can be any shape I want now that the lenses are small enough.

Making round cuts would take a lot more dexterity than what I've done so far, I figure. That's even truer now that the glass is so much smaller than the panel I started with. And since there's no tangible benefit to rounding off the corners of these lenses, I'm leaving them like this.

Good enough.

I power down the bandsaw as soon as I'm done. Only the sudden silence makes me realize how loud it was.

Looking down at my smoothly cut glass and my intact fingers, I smile wider than I have all day.

I keep my clunky square goggles on for now, majorly glad of the help they provided. I'm also glad that their safety-giving properties weren't called into action.

The gloves didn't end up being necessary, either, but I'd always prefer to have that last line of defense than not have it. Pops ingrained that much in me, for sure.

The forty percent vision gain given by this first crude attempt makes it easy for me to cut perfectly smooth holes in another pair of goggles. The finish is much cleaner than on my earlier half-blind attempt. They also make it much easier for me to apply the quick-setting glue in the right places.

The end result is a new pair of safety goggles with most of their plastic fronts cut out and some magnified glass lenses secured neatly in their place.

I switch into the pair and smile from ear to ear, even wider than a few minutes ago.

I'm not going to be winning any awards for style, but I'm pretty damn proud of what I've thrown together here.

They work. Not perfectly, but pretty damn well.

They just *work*.

I look in a mirror on the wall, which sits under a sign that says: "SAFETY IS STYLISH: BE PREPARED."

The first thing I notice is that I can read those words effortlessly, which was decisively *not* the case earlier. The second thing to note is how awkward the goggles still look. But hey, that's a small price to pay.

Most ironic is the third thing I notice. Standing close to the mirror, I see a few gray hairs creeping through on my hairline.

Stress will do that to a guy, I suppose, but I can't help but think about the day Pops told me that my hair would be gray before humanity left Earth in the quest for new worlds.

For me to spot my first grays right after perfecting the fuel enrichment process that could have taken us to those worlds, but also right after a cataclysm did so much damage to our own...

Well, once again, it's not the kind of irony I like.

I step away from the mirror and shake these thoughts away for now. The past few minutes have been a rare triumph.

Lamenting what's already happened shouldn't get in the way of recognizing that.

Sure: in objective terms, I'm worse off now than I was before the parrot knocked my contacts down the drain.

Emotionally, though? In terms of my morale? There's a lot to be said for the value of a win. And Pops was right about something else, too: there's a lot to be said for chopping your own wood.

I've just done a spacewalk to shore up the station's life support while an alarm counted down my remaining air supply and I've just made myself working glasses while I could hardly see past the end of my nose.

That's without even getting into what I had to do to poor Yannick, which was another thing I'd *never* have imagined myself being capable of doing.

Since I first found Justin I've felt crushing pressure on my shoulders in more ways than I could ever have imagined. But despite what grumpy old Mr. Lindell said in my report card, I haven't faltered just yet.

I'm still here.

That's a problem, obviously, because I don't *want* to be here for another second. But it's also a success.

Because despite everything this place and whoever sabotaged it has thrown at me, I'm still standing.

Where there's life there's hope, and I feel like I've finally broken through a few walls and finally have some momentum on my side.

I know what comes next, too: one way or another, I have to get into the Control Center.

Eva's voicemail gave me a lot of new contexts to consider, along with a lot of new questions. But most importantly, it gave me a new idea for my immediate next move.

The adrenaline that came with cutting the glass is fading now, and as soon as I stand up my leg encourages me to take a look at the box of painkillers I grabbed earlier. I took one before

I could read the instructions, and now that I can see clearly I understand why it didn't do much.

I see the brand name I thought I recognized from the box's color scheme, but now I see that these pills are an "easy swallow" variant. One pill contains only a *third* of a full dose.

That explains it, I figure.

I pop two more and gulp them down.

I step back into the corridor and set off towards the stairway.

I still don't know what happened here, or on Earth. But when I get upstairs and gather the items Eva's message has inspired me to analyze, I have a feeling I'm going to start filling in a *lot* of the blanks.

Knowledge is power... and I know just where I can find some.

31

As I leave the workshop, I take the marker pen that I used to draw my guidelines on the glass.

I also take a large bag. I'm going to need both for the first part of my next step.

This isn't going to be a pleasant step so I'm not going to dwell on it. But given how much I learned from a single voice-mail on my phone, it would be reckless not to check as many of my dead colleagues' phones as possible.

Hopefully a lot of them will still have battery power. That's a pretty realistic hope if they're newer than mine. A few days without any use shouldn't have drained too much.

I can always charge them, too, but there's a logistical reason I really want to be able to use them as soon as I gather them.

We'll get to that.

My first port of call is the Maintenance Bay's main level, where there are six workers dead in their chairs.

I hate the sight of these unfortunate souls. I hate even more that I have to get close enough to check their pockets. There's no other way, though, so I hold my breath and do what has to be done.

I'm not lingering on the reasons for holding my breath, either. All I'll say is that as soon as I get into the Control Center,

I really *do* have to designate one area as a cold storage zone and move everyone in there.

I'll probably use the Canteen for that since it's where most people already are. Moving a person is a hell of a task at the best of times, let alone with my leg acting up. Minimizing the number of trips required to bring everyone together is the smart move.

I hope to have bigger solutions to bigger problems by then, too. The main one is contacting Earth so someone can come to take me home, ideally with the others in tow. But realistically, that might take a few trips.

I'm not trying to ignore the reality that these are dead bodies I'm brushing up against, because I really don't want to become someone who can dissociate like that.

Instead I'm trying to move as respectfully as I can, working *despite* the emotional difficulty rather than trying to block it all out.

The first guy I reach, whose badge names him as Bryce Nolan, has a phone in his front left pocket. Better yet, it has power.

Two steps out of three, clear.

The third step is unlocking it.

I don't know Bryce's passcode but I do have his face. I try the facial recognition feature.

It doesn't work. I try again but there's still no progress. I have a hunch it's because his eyes are closed.

"I'm going to get whoever did this to you," I tell Bryce. "Sorry I have to do this first."

I place his phone on the desk in front of him, with the screen and its camera angled upwards.

A shiver runs down my spine as I move in to open Bryce's eyes. Touching a dead man's face is so much worse than touching his hand. I don't know why and I wish I hadn't just found out, but believe me: it is.

As soon as I hold the poor guy's eyelids open from behind, the phone unlocks.

I know facial recognition on consumer tech is more for convenience than real security, but I don't think it even saw his irises. It seems like it just wanted to see a sign that he wasn't asleep. Or, you know… dead.

I immediately navigate through the phone's menus to remove all of Bryce's Lock Screen security settings. I use my marker to write his name on the back of the phone, along with the number 1.

I get three more phones from the other five workers. Two have battery power. One of those unlocks with a closed-eyed facial ID shot and the other needs the same action as Bryce. I'll charge the third later.

Before I leave the room, I take a wide-angled photo on my own phone. I quickly annotate it with the numbers I've attributed to each person.

When I'm looking through these phones later, I want to know who each of them belonged to and where that person died. I'm being as thorough as I can be here, trying to anticipate things I soon might regret not doing if I don't do them now.

I decide to mark powerless and still-locked phones with an X as well as a number. That'll make it easy to pull them aside and charge them all as quickly as possible.

I keep up this grim person-to-person process outside in the hallway. Next comes the dorms, and then the heavily populated Canteen.

I can't get to poor Yannick's pockets because of the damned vending machine that necessitated an even grimmer process earlier. But when all is said and done, I have dozens of potential new leads in my bag.

I also have an adequate dose of painkilling medication working its way through my veins, so this shin should stop complaining anytime now.

I've picked up a bunch of chargers as I've come across them, too, as well as a few battery banks.

I'll start recharging the dead phones while I look through

the others. As I've been doing my rounds I've been brainstorming what kinds of things I should look for, so I think it'll be pretty efficient.

Messages and call records are the obvious places to start. From there I'm also going to check out people's news apps in case anything has been downloaded automatically.

Updates could have come in even after everyone up here died. I know the data signal was live for hours after people on Earth realized something was wrong, so there's a pretty good chance of that.

As part of my bid to stay focused on things I care about in a world whose media companies seem like they're *trying* to drive everyone to madness, I usually don't follow the news.

Most other people do, though, and I know that the main apps spam "breaking news" notifications all the time. I think some of them even push short-form video content that downloads automatically. That means there's a chance that some reports could still be accessible, despite everything on the station now being offline.

It's pretty weird when I think about it.

I'm on a space station jam-packed with some of the most high-tech equipment you could imagine. Yet here I am, all set to play detective by poring through the same devices that kids use to send each other memes and selfies.

Really, my biggest obstacle at the moment is the fact that the most high-tech areas of all, like the Control Center and the other two offshoot labs, are locked up and out of reach.

A piece of new information stored on one of these phones could be the vital key I need. If nothing else, I feel confident that I'll get more context on what happened on Earth.

Other workers must have received worried messages from their families, just like I did. I'm willing to bet that at least someone up here was able to fire off a text message in the few moments between when the chaos kicked off and when they breathed their last breath. That's where I could *really* fill in some blanks.

This information-gathering idea doesn't feel a million miles away from investigative tasks in some of the escape room experiences I've done with Eva. She *loves* those like nothing else. I have a feeling her well-honed eye would already be spotting things I'm missing.

All I can do is keep moving forward in my bid to get back home to her and Joe. They're the future I'm not giving up on.

With my bag full of phones, I step out of the Canteen and peek through the doors of the Greenhouse. It's a vast area where a lot of our food is grown, but the layout makes it easy to see right away that there's no one on any of the paths. I hardly ever saw anyone else in the times I've been in there, so I'm not surprised.

After that I take a few steps towards the only accessible place I haven't been yet.

Whatever anyone says about Ignacio Zola, no one can deny the guy has an eye for design. His business towers on Earth are modern wonders of the world, and all four parts of the station's Leisure Zone are incredible in their own way.

I go to the Gym most days and I've spent a little bit of time in the Library. Both are great. I've only seen the Music Hall for a few minutes during my introductory tour, so I can't say too much about that. But like everyone else here, I quickly took to the charms of the miniature Greek-style Theater.

I check the other three areas before the Theater. Again, there are no bodies in any of them. I figure the people I've already found in the hallway probably spilled out from these places.

I take a few minutes to look around the Gym for anything that could be useful, but nothing catches my eye. It's mainly basic equipment and plate-based machines — nothing I can use as a powerful battering ram, or anything like that.

Last of all, I walk to the Theater.

Zola is Spanish by descent and the Theater's design is inspired by those of Ancient Greece. Considering those points, I don't know why he gave it an Italian name.

That's just Zola all over, though; inspired by everything,

always looking to take what he likes from various sources and bring it together however he sees fit.

Almost everyone has always called the Theater "the cinema." As I pass under the arched entrance and the name *Teatro Lorenzini* looms large over my head, the screen comes into view.

I turn to the seats — empty — then back to the impressive screen.

I can send content from the phones onto that screen. Whatever I find can be blown up to a pretty massive size, making it much clearer. That will help a lot, given the better-but-still-imperfect vision I'm working with.

Good or bad, whatever I find is going to hit harder when I see it on such a big screen.

The screen is easy to power up. With that task quickly achieved, I take a seat in the furthest back of the compact Theater's twelve rows.

I root through my bag for the first phone: Bryce Nolan's.

Once I find it, I use the wireless sharing feature to mirror its display onto the screen. I look at the phone as I'm controlling it, but the big screen is definitely going to come in handy once I find some pictures or video content.

Straight away, I see a string of messages that arrived on Bryce's phone right around the time Eva tried to call me.

None have been read. That makes sense since Nolan would have been dead by then, but the very first line of the very first message is enough to get me sitting up straight.

Well well well, I think to myself.

What *do* we have here?

32

Bunker.

The word jumps out at me like a penguin in the desert.

There's a long way to go before I start counting any chickens, but that word popping up several times in the unread messages on Bryce Nolan's phone is a sight for sore eyes.

Literally, my sore eyes are ecstatic to see it.

Molly, who I'm guessing is Bryce's wife, has sent him nine texts after the time I've identified as the moment of sabotage. The first few are frantic requests for him to call and reassure her, using similar language to Eva's voicemail.

The *next* text is where things start to get interesting.

"Kevin Hull just asked the group chat if anyone else has been called to an emergency bunker in Culpeper, Virginia," she writes. "He doesn't know if it's real or if the terrorists are trying to round up ZolaCore staff and their families for more leverage. Do you know anything?"

My eyes widen.

Bryce doesn't reply, obviously, because the poor guy was dead when this message came in.

From there, Molly gets increasingly frantic.

"It's on the news. There IS a bunker. What do you know? Hurry — please!"

Eight minutes pass before the next message.

"It was supposed to stay secret and they're saying no one will get in without a valid invitation and ID. Did they send the invitation to you?"

The final message comes in twenty-five minutes after that.

"It's too late," Molly says. "I love you, Bryce. Always. XXX"

Wow... talk about an emotional roller coaster.

I take a few deep breaths and look up from Bryce's phone. Everything in this Theater has been made to look like sun-whitened concrete, but the seating is as comfortable as any I've known.

What feels *less* comfortable is taking solace from the heart-breaking messages I've just read. Molly didn't make it to the bunker, and her final send off makes it sound like she *knew* that meant she wasn't going to make it past whatever was coming.

That hurts to read. For Molly's sake I can only hope she has found peace now, back with Bryce on the other side of all this suffering.

But for my sake?

And much more importantly... for Eva's sake? For Joe's sake?

Suddenly I feel more justified in hoping they found a lot more than a peaceful end.

There really *is* a bunker, and it sounds like some of the researchers' spouses are being invited. I don't know if it's a government bunker or one of Zola's, which we've all heard rumors about. Either way, I have reasons to be optimistic.

Like I was reflecting earlier, Eva's own professional reputation as a childhood development expert makes her the kind of person who could definitely earn a slot in a public evacuation program on her own merits.

And with my unique position as a visiting researcher hand-picked by Zola himself, I think my family has an especially good chance of being on the list for any private bunker that might exist.

I don't like the sound of the part about terrorists, or Molly

Nolan's initial speculation that it might all be some kind of honeypot trap. Something eased *her* mind on that between the first and lasts texts, though, so I'm not going to get stuck on it.

The name Kevin Hull, who Molly mentioned, sends my mind to a woman I found with the same surname on her badge. I'll look in my bag for her phone next.

There's a fair chance her husband could be the Kevin Hull who got an invite to the bunker. If that's the case, there's a *great* chance he'll have contacted her about it and that I might learn a lot more from whatever messages he sent.

Before I put Bryce's phone down, I run through the mental checklist I put together a few minutes ago. I check all of the messaging apps I can see, along with his email and everything else. There's nothing revelatory, just a bunch of texts from worried friends as they began hearing news that all contact had been lost with the station.

I guess the lack of friend-derived messages on my phone is a reflection of how much I've focused on work for the past decade. Work and family, since Eva came along. There really hasn't been a lot of time for friends.

I feel a little uneasy scanning all of Bryce's messages, even with the best and least-invasive intentions, but it has to be done.

Next I look for notifications from other apps. He has the YNN app on his home screen — Your News Now — and there's a little red notification circle next to it.

Interesting.

Since I can't quite read the tiny number on the phone, I look at the large cinema screen.

It's *so* much clearer at that size, and the text in the circle is pretty promising, too: 9+.

At least ten news stories have downloaded to Bryce's phone since he last opened the app.

That doesn't guarantee they arrived after this all went down, but the fact he has the app on his home screen tells me he's probably something of a news junkie. I'm guessing he wouldn't let the number get so high without taking a look if he was able to.

I open the app, staring at the big screen as I touch the phone. I immediately feel my head nodding in success.

Kind of like with the messages from Molly, though, the nature of what I see stops me from feeling too happy about it.

Sure, I wanted to see some news from Earth to get a better indication of what happened here and what happened there. I also wasn't foolish enough to expect any of the news to be good, but I still wasn't expecting this.

The very top thumbnail is blank, with a notice about a lack of internet connectivity. But below that, in the "Ready To View" section of automatically downloaded clips, I see some extremely unsettling images.

There are timestamps telling me how many hours ago each clip was downloaded. They all fit perfectly with the timeline I've put together. I swipe along to the oldest, which shows a newsreader sitting at a desk.

Looking at the giant screen, I take a deep breath and hit play.

"We have some unsettling news coming in from ZolaCore headquarters in Auckland, New Zealand," the anchorman begins. "ZolaCore has experienced a sudden and total loss of contact with its flagship space station, The Beacon. I'm told we have no reports of any solar flares, magnetic anomalies or any other identifiable interference. Our understanding is that public space agencies are working urgently with ZolaCore to identify the issue and ensure the safety of the station's large research crew. We'll bring you more on this developing story just as soon as we can."

This checks out with everything I already know, so I skip forward to the next clip. It's short, too. They all are — around thirty seconds each.

The next three feature the same reporter, giving similar non-updates about the station's situation. He really just restates that they don't know what's going on, albeit in an increasingly glum tone with each passing clip.

It's the fifth video that really gets things rolling.

A few hours after the station went dark, a report comes in from the moment when two huge earthquakes hit on two continents at almost exactly the same time. More follow within minutes and the next few videos show harrowing images of falling buildings and collapsing bridges.

Watching this on a giant cinema screen has the natural effect of making it seem like a high-budget disaster movie. And *oh* how I wish that was the case. How I wish the screaming and panicked crowds were made up of actors... oh how I wish those buildings and bridges were made of CGI pixels instead of concrete and steel.

After the earthquakes come the eruptions.

This is when I start finding it even more difficult to look.

The cascade of disasters is utterly unprecedented. It's so unprecedented, I don't think the term "natural disasters" even fits. Sure, isolated things like this can happen on their own. But things like this don't happen *together*.

Not by chance.

I've had more than enough fire and brimstone for one day, so the thumbnail of a TV reporter in an airport terminal looks like something of a respite from the helicopter footage of flowing lava and raging waves.

A sea of people rushes around in the background, frantically gazing at departure boards and trying to get away from whichever airport this is. I guess they're probably aiming as far inland and as far from any major fault lines as they can get.

But things go from chaos to all-out bedlam when someone near the reporter overhears her comments to the camera:

"Hold on a second, Kurt," she says, pressing into her earpiece. "I'm hearing from airport management that *all* commercial flights have now been grounded per an immediate federal ruling. We don't know when we can expect—"

The poor reporter is rushed by the panicked crowd before

she can get another word out. As the news spreads further back, people start pushing their way past airline staff at the departure gates in the vain hope that the planes they're boarding will ever take off.

I close the video and move on to the next.

This one is shot from a helicopter over the streets of New York. There's no immediate sign of disaster here, but the streets and bridges are utterly gridlocked.

"We now know beyond any doubt that an emergency government evacuation procedure is under way," the reporter yells over the noise of his chopper. "Reports have reached us that selected citizens are being moved to at least three secure locations across the country, with similar stories coming in from Europe and the Middle East. Resentment among those who haven't been chosen is manifesting in all the ways you might expect, Bob. It's ugly down there, and it's only going to get worse."

I have two videos left.

The next one features President Noah Williams, standing on an airfield flanked by several unusually animated Secret Service agents.

"Confirmation will come when we have it," Williams tells a news crew. "For now, I can tell you that we are *not* treating these events as a natural occurrence. We are engaging emergency measures to ensure the survival of our democracy. There are no easy choices and nothing I can say will reassure you like I wish I could. The United States and our allies will not be defeated by the enemies of freedom. Freedom will strike back, and it will not miss."

As the reporters shout over each other with their questions about bunkers and terrorists and contingency plans, one of the president's guardians rushes to his ear.

The whispered message Williams receives visibly makes his spine stiffen like a yardstick.

Before President Williams can say anything else to the news crews, two agents rush him away towards Marine One. The one who delivered the message moves to the reporters and pushes their cameras to the ground.

As politicians go, I don't think Williams is too bad. And until the last few seconds of this video he was probably doing as a good a job of delivering a calming message as anyone could in those circumstances.

The abruptness of the ending has undone it all, though. That could only raise the panic levels even higher, with people speculating over what he was told and why he was so unceremoniously led away.

I exhale deeply, starting to feel overwhelmed.

But while I'm going, I know I have to *keep* going.

One video left…

This one has an especially ominous heading: *"ECO CELL ISSUES ZOLA ULTIMATUM."*

When the video begins, a young and strikingly telegenic woman stands in front of a metallic surface, illuminated by a cool white lighting rig.

I'm no expert and there's not much to go on, but I think she's in a bunker.

"This doesn't have to happen," the woman begins, a very slight southern twang in her voice. "We can stop escalating at any point and we can still call off the *coup de grace*. Your Beacon is down, Zola, but Earth doesn't have to go with it. You know what we want: give yourself up and commit to an immediate halting of all space-related activity. No more exploration, no more mining, no more compromises. Humanity has done more than enough damage here and we will not let you spread the disease of conquest any further."

The woman makes a show of looking at her watch. "Earth will survive this reset if you force our hand," she continues with a demented grin, "but humanity will not. You wanted to be the man to take us to the stars, Zola. But if you don't step forward and do what we say, you're going to be the man responsible for turning this broken world to dust. The choice is yours."

The video ends.

There are no more clips on Bryce's phone and the time-stamp shows that this one was downloaded just before my last blank message from Eva.

I can hardly believe what I've seen here, and I'm trying not to feel selfish for focusing on the one positive I can take from it. But maybe I *shouldn't* feel too bad about the details I've just learned?

After all, the destruction on Earth is no surprise — I've already seen the fallout with my own eyes, no news reports required.

Sure, I *have* just seen way too much close-up chaos and suffering for one man to process. But I've also just learned that there really are working bunkers and that Eva and Joe really might have a chance of being in one.

That evil woman's talk of a *coup de grace* has me worrying that even bunkers might not have been enough to survive whatever their group's final move was, but I can't think like that.

I have to follow the leads I have, and right now that means finding out what Kevin Hull told his wife about the bunkers.

Because the more I know about where people might still be alive, the better chance I have of reaching them…

33

The time I took to record everyone's positions and number their phones is paying off already. I find Lisa Hull's phone within less than a minute.

I immediately click into her messages and just as quickly see the ones I'm looking for.

They're from her husband Kevin and they make it clear that he and their son really *were* invited to a bunker in Virginia.

Kevin says that if they could reach Newark airport they would be allowed to board the evacuation flight to Charlottesville and then be driven to the final location: Culpeper.

Things take an awful turn in the next few messages, though. Kevin reveals that his invitation has been revoked because he broke the cardinal rule of not telling anyone about it.

"I only asked the others in the spouse group in case we could work together to get to Newark," he laments. "I thought it might be a ZolaCore bunker, but now the government information line is saying they won't let us in even if we can get there. I'm so sorry."

Wow. I feel for the guy.

I mean, it's a rule that exists for a reason… but I can see

why he asked in his group chat with other researchers' spouses.

I don't know whether it's good or bad news that the bunker that definitely exists is a government one. Eva still has a chance of getting in, for sure, but it feels lower than if the bunker was for chosen ZolaCore workers and their families.

On the other hand, at least I know a genuine government bunker is *definitely* not a honeypot trap for Zola-hating terrorists.

I closely check the time of Kevin Hull's texts and work them into the overall timeline. They all came after the earth-quakes and volcanoes, but just before commercial flights were grounded.

I quickly grab my own phone and look at the blank messages from Eva one more time. The first of them comes in right around the same time as Kevin's last, with *her* last coming two hours later.

Eva has never sent me a blank message before. She's more tech savvy than I am with that kind of thing. I also still don't know what kind of glitch could make an image load all black rather than not at all.

Was she trying to tell me something?

Was she trying to *show* me something?

Maybe Eva knew she couldn't say anything about an invita-tion but wanted to give me some kind of sign that she was okay?

I open my phone's image editor and try to increase the brightness of the first image. At every level, there's nothing there.

The information bar at the top tells me it was a screenshot. It also tells me the time and location.

I sit up straight.

The location.

This blank screenshot was taken at our house, just outside of Salt Lake City.

I swipe to the next and check its metadata.

Yes!

This one, forty minutes later, is from SLC airport. They were leaving!

I move on to the final image's metadata, not sure what to expect.

"Please be somewhere else," I beg. "Please, Eva... tell me they got you on a plane."

Colorado Springs.

I never thought those two words could make me feel so much, but they just did.

Eva made it onto a plane, and there's no way in this world she would have boarded without Joe.

They both got on a plane to Colorado Springs.

That seems like somewhere the government would have a bunker nearby. Surrounded by mountains, inland, abundant Air Force personnel and tech already in the area...

It makes sense to me!

For the first time since this all started, I really feel like my faith is no longer blind.

Eva and Joe were evacuated.

Even if Zola didn't give himself up and even if those evil terrorists did go through with their promise to turn the whole world to dust, maybe Eva and Joe survived it in their bunker just like I survived the attack up here in my lab?

All along, whether it was baseless or not, I always had hope. And now, *at last*, I know it really does have a valid foundation.

I grab my phone and navigate back to the photos of where I found each of the others. I look for who was nearby Lisa Hull when she died.

My thinking is that she might have had a job up here that made her family a high priority for the evacuation, and that she might have been surrounded by immediate colleagues whose phones can tell me even more.

I quickly see that she was in the Canteen, near the chess

players but not with them. No one in her vicinity seems closer or more connected to her than anyone else.

Oh well, it was worth a shot.

There's no instruction manual for all of this and I'm just going by my own instincts to look for—

Wait wait wait wait wait.

Hold the hell up.

With the Canteen photo blown up on the giant screen, something sticks out like a sore thumb.

I didn't notice it when I gathered the phones, when so much was running through my mind and I had the untamed leg pain to deal with alongside everything else. But now? I can't miss that there's something weird about one of the bodies.

He's laying in the middle of the floor, at least ten feet from anyone else, and he's facing away from almost all of them.

Most unsettlingly of all — and this is the part I'm surprised I missed at close range — he's wearing gloves.

I marked this guy down as number 32, so I rifle through my bag and grab the phone I scribbled that number on. It's one of the ones that had power, and one I was able to permanently unlock using facial recognition.

He's not wearing a name badge. That wasn't a red flag at the time, but it adds to my suspicions now.

I immediately look for his messages, but there's no icon to take me there.

Very conspicuously, this guy's home screen has only one icon: a notebook.

I tap into that and see four note previews in the left-hand sidebar. One full note is open to their right.

"Holy shit," I groan, seeing painful confirmation of what I had already started to suspect.

It was *him*.

34

No more assumptions.

No more supposition.

No more *thinking* I know what happened here without knowing it for sure.

The Beacon was sabotaged from the inside, and this piece of shit was the one responsible.

A checklist on his phone, coldly callous in its simplicity, lays out what he did.

The note mentions canisters in the Canteen, which fits perfectly with the marks on its walls and the relatively slow deaths of its inhabitants.

Another step confirms that a faster-acting toxin was used to target the HSC workers. HSC means "high security clearance" around here.

That fits with the staff dying faster in the smaller locked rooms, like the Observation Deck and presumably the Control Center.

How this asshole pulled everything isn't clear. Neither is who else was in on it. Not yet, anyway. But a few of my biggest questions *have* just been answered. This is a major breakthrough.

Another checklist point jumps out: *"Confirm VRs in main body (phone locations)."*

On this station, a VR is a visiting researcher. I can only assume this means he wanted to be sure that me and the three others were out of our protective labs when he did his dirty work. I guess some Wi-Fi based way of tracking our phone locations is how he planned to tell.

"Confirm" feels like a strong word if that's all he was relying on. My survival is testament to that, all because I left my phone charging in my dorm.

Then again, what else could he do? He couldn't exactly walk into each of our dorms to check if we were there with our phones — not without looking suspicious.

This small point makes me think he probably *wasn't* working with anyone else in a higher position.

After all, access to the security cameras would have shown him that I entered the lab and didn't come back out. The offshoot labs themselves don't have any cameras inside, but footage of our comings and goings is all he'd have needed.

I keep hold of the scumbag's phone and return to the Canteen for a closer look at him.

He looks to be around my age, mid thirties or a little older, and there's nothing remarkable about him.

No scars under his eyes, no handlebar mustache, no golden teeth. He doesn't scream "bad guy," is all I'm getting at. I can't blame myself for missing it.

His arms are up at an odd angle, too, away from his pockets, so I can almost forgive myself for not noticing the gloves when I was taking his phone.

It's not an odd enough angle to be suspicious on its own, just odd enough to mean the gloves weren't immediately noticeable when my focus was so firmly on his pockets.

I really was going between everyone at a mile a minute back then. I was basically working with my blinkers on and just doing the same regimented and uncomfortable tasks over and over again for each person.

He has a small bag. This didn't raise any suspicions at the time, either, because a lot of people come to the Canteen to grab some snacks and drinks to take away.

I pick it up and look inside. All I find is a small bottle of pills.

One of the early items on his checklist mentioned so-called toxicity blockers, and a big part of me hopes this idiot thought they would protect him.

The kind of people who could mastermind something like this wouldn't want to leave any loose ends, and they wouldn't be above misleading a henchman.

That could mean this wasn't a suicide mission, if he thought he would survive it. He might have been motivated by cold hard cash, rather than really caring about the eco-terrorist cell's apparent goal of stopping all space exploration in its tracks.

I wish I knew his name.

I wish there were other notes on his phone.

I wish I knew what I could do with what I've just learned.

I'll track his movements on the security camera once I can get into the Control Center and access those systems, which is the second thing I'll do after sending out my SOS calls to Earth. For now, though, this discovery isn't giving me a lot to work with.

Thinking about the security footage makes me think of the only time I've ever had my photo taken on the station.

It was in the Library, right next to the Theater and the other sections of the Leisure Zone. It's a long shot, but if this guy ever borrowed one of the holographic text-readers like I did, I might be able to put a name to this face.

That would give me something to search for everywhere else, and it could reveal any accomplices if they've ever spoken to him — or about him — on their phones.

I'm close to the Library and I planned to head back to the Theater next door, anyway, so I turn away from the scoundrel on the ground and make my way there.

In keeping with the Theater and Music Hall, Zola wanted the station's Library to be grand.

It contains no physical books but has ten distinct and immersive reading nooks. Everything is compact, with wall decorations and seating arrangements making inventive use of the available space.

One nook is styled on a Parisian coffeeshop of the early twentieth century. Another feels like the inside of a North African bazaar. It all feels a little on the kitschy side to me, but the nooks were always pretty popular and I can see what Zola was going for.

The holographic text-readers are the real stars of the show, with ten kept on-site and ten available for overnight borrowing.

Every book registered with the Library of Congress is available on The Beacon's local storage system, which Zola saw as an important way to ensure his researchers' souls and minds were nourished along with their bodies.

When I walk behind the desk to access the computer system, I find Margo, the friendly librarian, dead on the floor.

I guess I wasn't thorough enough when I glanced in here earlier. Her proximity to the computer makes it physically easy to login via her keyboard's fingerprint scanner, but I still find it emotionally difficult.

"Sorry about this," I whisper to Margo. "And thanks."

Once I'm in, I head straight to the borrower records and start scrolling through faces. As soon as I start, I'm doubting myself.

Why would *he* borrow a text-reader and have his photo taken unnecessarily?

He wouldn't, and he didn't. It wouldn't make sense.

It only takes me a few minutes to confirm this. At least I didn't waste too long, I figure, and I'm never going to scold myself for looking under too many rocks.

I take a text-reader before heading out, in case I need to look for something later. I don't need an internet signal since all the digital book files are stored locally, so this could actually be a major help.

Everything from encyclopedias to user guides will be at my fingertips. There's no telling when that might come in handy.

I also grab a handful of sunflower seeds from the gumball-style dispenser on Margo's desk.

A few seconds later, I hear a loud squawk.

The parrot.

Anticipating another unsettling flurry of wings, I turn around and look for the bird. I guess it heard or smelled the seeds coming out of the dispenser. There's no sign of it, though.

I walk into the hallway and hear another squawk.

Only then do I see it, standing at the threshold of another wondrous place I've glanced inside but not looked around: the Greenhouse.

"Hello," the bird calls. "Food? Food?"

The words are so clear.

"Uh, yeah," I say, holding out my hand. "Food."

But instead of coming towards me for the free seeds, it turns and flies into the Greenhouse.

"Yes, yes. Hello!" the bird calls as it goes.

I scratch my chin and breathe slowly.

If I didn't know any better, I'd think it wants me to go in there…

35

The station's Greenhouse is a working kitchen garden, but it's also an area where people can sit and relax. When you're so far from Earth, the greenery really does go a long way.

I understand why the parrot likes it, too, given that the poor thing's natural instinct is to sit in trees and not in a cage.

And as soon as I enter and see the bird sitting on one of the tallest trees just a short distance in, I know I've majorly over-analyzed the interaction we just had.

Of course it wasn't calling me in here to see something helpful it just found. Talk about wishful thinking.

"Squawk, food," it calls. "Food."

I throw some of my sunflower seeds to the ground. It flies down quite gracefully, in a way that makes me wonder why it couldn't have been so controlled when it flew into the downstairs bathroom like a tornado and knocked my contacts down the drain.

It didn't mean to, I remind myself. And I guess I can understand its excitement over the running water.

There are sprinklers in here, along with the heat lamps, but they might only come on at certain hours.

I sit on the bench next to the parrot and lift the killer's phone from my pocket once more. The air feels fresher in here, which is understandable for two reasons. The first is the presence of trees. The second… well, to be blunt, the second reason is the absence of corpses.

Among my options, this really isn't a bad place to be.

The Beacon is an incredible place and that's even more apparent in the Greenhouse than anywhere else. Benches, soil, even trees… it's all here — in space.

From the moment I arrived on the station I've been too busy with work to fully appreciate the surroundings. From the moment I found Justin's corpse, I've been too frantic to notice much of anything.

There's a relative serenity in here, though.

You can't beat nature.

When science and nature combine like this, bringing plant life into space, it's a reminder that the two don't have to be in conflict. That's what I was hoping for with my enrichment work: that we could use science to harness the natural properties of theocite and use the results to do good.

Now that I've identified the killer and recovered his phone, I figure there has to be more I can find out about him. He only has one icon on his home screen, but that doesn't mean he doesn't have other apps.

I swipe down until the search bar appears, then type in the word *Messages*.

There's a little download symbol next to the app icon, telling me he doesn't have it on his phone. The same happens when I search for all the other messaging and email apps I can think of.

"Hello," the bird calls, suddenly perching on the back of my bench.

I've given it water and now I've given it food, too, so I guess that makes us friends.

"Hey," I say. "I'm Ray. *Ray.*"

I point at myself a few times.

Just when I start reminding myself that I'm trying to make friends with a parrot, a member of the animal family that gives us the term *bird-brained*, it tips its head to the side and replies:

"Hello, Ray Ray!"

"Not Ray Ray," I correct it, gesturing horizontally with my hands to emphasize the point. "Just Ray."

It looks at me for a few seconds. "Ray Ray," it says.

I blow air from my lips. It's a losing battle. I'm stuck on a space station with one potential friend and it's insistent on calling me Ray Ray.

It seems to like me, at least.

It's hard to tell. I never had any pets growing up. My stepfather Steve didn't like them. He didn't like a lot of things. Some of my friends had the usual cats and dogs and rabbits, but I can't remember anyone even having a cockatoo or a parakeet, let alone something like a macaw.

"What's your name?" I ask. "Polly? Polly wants a cracker?"

It doesn't look amused.

No… I'm not calling it Polly.

We're in space, I tell myself. Let's go with *Laika*.

"You can be Laika," I say. "Like the dog. Except I'll make sure you stay alive. Deal?"

With this thought in my mind, I pull out the text-reader and search for books about parrots. The device is incredible. If you select the holographic setting, it projects text on what truly seems like thin air.

I figure I might need to feed my new friend something more than sunflower seeds at some point, and I have no idea what that should be or when "some point" might come.

The highest-rated book about parrot care opens instantly when I select it from the search results. I flip to the contents and see that the first section is on physiology. The first thing I see is that there are no reliable physical differences between male and female macaws.

"Let's just go with you being a *he*," I tell Laika.

Sure, the dog I'm borrowing the name from was a *she*, but I figure Eva would prefer to think of me stranded alone up here with another guy.

Before I get to the feeding section, Laika flies down and lands next to me. He's dangerously close to the killer's phone so I grab for it before he can accidentally knock it off.

"Easy, there," I say. "We need this thing."

"Ray Ray?" he replies, tilting his head like it's a question as he keeps looking at the phone.

I pick up the phone, with the search bar still on the screen.

An idea enters my mind. It's worth a shot.

I type in my own name, just the one *Ray*, taking a harmless swing that there might be a note hidden somewhere about what the killer knew of me and my work.

He swings and he connects!

There *is* a note containing my name.

I look at Laika, hardly believing that his annoying call of Ray Ray gave me that idea.

I guess you make your own luck, though, and I *did* feed him and *did* introduce myself despite what he did in the bathroom. I also *did* search for my name once he put the idea in my head. Still, I'm not discounting his part.

For a bird, he's not so bad.

He's just made up for the contact lenses, that's for sure.

Because this note containing my name also contains a few *others*, too, and one of them is about to take me into the third offshoot lab.

36

The document I've just found contains more detail than the first checklist.

It doesn't have any new action steps, but some are expanded. The one about checking the visiting researchers' locations via our phones names me, Barnet, and a guy called Michael Vinner.

Only three.

I guess the fourth offshoot lab mustn't have been occupied by anyone recently. Maybe someone was due to arrive on the craft that was supposed to take me home in a few days.

In any case, identifying Vinner's phone is a piece of cake thanks to the marking system I devised.

He's one of the many people who was asleep in his dorm when the attack happened. That was surely the best way to go. His phone was next to his bed, half-charged, and easily unlockable in the usual way.

I look at its contents for the first time. Nothing immediately jumps out. All I see are a bunch of sad but by-now standard messages from worried friends and family.

There are no clues about what kind of work he was doing, and I figure I'd be wasting time looking for too long when I can go into his offshoot lab and see for myself.

I head over to his dorm, grabbing the first trolley I pass. When I get there I apologetically lift him onto it and wheel him all the way back to his lab.

I don't know exactly what I'm hoping for, but I'd like to think the sky is the limit.

The dream find would be something I can use to drill or even safely *blow* my way into the Control Center, but there could also be some information or research that helps indirectly.

Hell, there might even be something that helps me raise the alarm to Earth without needing to access the radio.

What would that be? I don't know... something I can explode *outside* the station? Something I can fire, like an SOS flare?

ZolaCore is into *all* kinds of stuff, so I don't think any kind of research is off the table. Vinner could have been working on quite literally anything.

The walk to Vinner's lab from the dorms is something of a trek. As trips within the station goes this is almost as far as it gets. Fortunately my leg isn't complaining too much now that the painkillers are working.

At the outer door, Vinner's finger works on the first try.

I wheel him along the safety walkway.

At the inner seal, we hit a snag.

It won't unlock.

I try not to panic, recalling the trouble I had with Yannick's finger at the Maintenance Bay. It's harder to repeatedly reposition a finger that's still attached to a whole body, but I try my best.

On our fourth attempt, I hear the welcome click of success.

I step back and listen carefully for any signs of movement, wary of another unexpected Laika-esque moment. None comes.

Silence.

"Thanks, buddy," I say to Vinner.

With the door unlocked, I wheel him into his lab to see what he's been up to.

.

37

Wow.

Vinner's lab is a *much* classier place than mine or Barnet's. It has an academic feel to it, with a huge whiteboard on each side of a large wooden desk.

It also has a much sparser feel. Mainly because there's no sealed test chamber like in my lab and no wall-filling animal tanks like in Barnet's, I figure. The lack of any dominant feature like those leaves a lot of space that Vinner seems to have been content to leave empty.

The whiteboards are frustratingly clear of any scribblings. That leaves me reliant on the papers on his desk for any early clues as to what kind of thing he's been doing in here.

Thankfully, Vinner hasn't been so thorough in keeping his entire lab free of information as he has free of clutter.

"*Oh,*" I say out loud as I get close enough to read the first of many pages.

I'm something of a space nerd — who knew? — and I keep my ear to the ground when it comes to new exoplanet discoveries. I read the monthly digests, I listen to the podcasts, I follow the main researchers online. You name it, I'm on board.

But I've never heard of Michael Vinner and I've never heard of the planet *Bayzen 108b*.

I also don't know why seemingly uncontroversial astronomical research needs a lab like this, but that's not the most important thing for now.

Bayzen 108b is what has my eye.

I read the notes and grow more intrigued with every line. The planet is apparently 5.9 light years away. That's almost fifty percent further than Proxima Centauri b, but if the data on this page is correct then it's safely within the top five closest habitable exoplanets.

Habitable is a very important word here. But as I take note of the numbers on Vinner's paper, it might not be strong enough.

Hell, if these numbers are right, Bayzen 108b is straight-up *Earth-like*.

My theocite-enriched BioZol fuel breakthrough could plausibly take us there, I figure, and the suspended animation tests Barnet was working on in the other lab could be something Zola was exploring to make a *manned* journey tolerable.

Holy smokes.

Zola handpicks his visiting researchers, personally signing off on every one. We've always worked with our heads down, eyes on our own paper, but it makes sense to realize that we've all been working on one part of a much bigger whole.

I don't know if Vinner discovered this planet or if he's just been studying it.

More to the point, how does no one *else* know about this? And why have I never heard of someone who seems to have been working at the top of a field I'm so interested in?

Needless to say, I have a lot more questions than answers right now.

Maybe Vinner is pioneering a whole new approach to the search for exoplanets? It's possible he's discovered Bayzen using some all-new scanning technique I don't know anything about.

On the other hand, he might simply have access to equipment that offers an incremental improvement on existing methods. Incremental improvements aren't as sexy as novel approaches, but they're responsible for most discoveries in most fields.

A bunch of the highest-profile candidate planets were all identified within a few years of each other, from around 2015 to 2018. We owe that burst of discoveries to advances in Doppler spectroscopy.

Come to think of it, there *has* been talk for a few years that Zola was throwing serious money at a next-generation spectrograph.

My eyes scan everything on Vinner's papers as quickly as they can. The adapted goggles are still working like a charm, even if my eyes are starting to feel a little strained. That's probably down to a lack of sleep as much as anything else, I figure.

I take some photos of the paperwork, too, so I can look at it all later without having to carry it around. Ideally I'll read every word in the Control Center when I'm waiting for my rescue craft to arrive.

A guy can hope.

But without access to Vinner's computer, which frustratingly needs a password instead of just a fingerprint, I can't dig much deeper right now.

I open the top desk drawer. Another pile of papers lies inside.

It's a little bit disappointing not to find something more visceral or useful than written information, I'll admit, but I take the pages out for a quick scan.

Right away, I see that these notes are about asteroid mining.

That's been a *huge* part of ZolaCore's focus for a long time. It's one of the main ways Zola plans to fund distant exploration.

I've never met the guy but in my pre-placement meetings with senior management, I heard that he saw my fuel enrichment process as a way to ensure quick access to some asteroids they've already identified as being colossally profitable. We're talking *trillions* of dollars in rare minerals and other materials, just from their top few targets.

One of the rare minerals in question is theocite itself.

That means that reaching these asteroids with a relatively small amount of theocite, mined from Earth's seabed, could grant access to much more of it, which is what we need to propel us even further afield.

Vinner's notes contain intensely detailed calculations regarding the drilling power needed to get to the largest undersea deposits, along with what seems to be the greatest drilling power he thinks we can achieve right now.

It looks like we're close, for at least some of the targets, but we're not there yet. All five sheets in this stapled bundle are filled with the same kind of notes.

Besides from drilling, some of Vinner's calculations relate to the force needed to safely extract theocite via controlled detonations. My eyes widen on the third page when I see calculations showing how hard it will be to access some deposits at depths where I didn't even know any deposits existed.

Adding up the numbers on all the sheets, I think I've just learned that ZolaCore is aware of more than *fifty times* as much Earth-based theocite as anyone has ever publicly declared.

Fifty times.

I'm flat-out stunned.

Vinner's notes on theocite end with a red-pen reminder to himself to: "Stress the dangers of overzealous excavation. CANNOT OVERSTATE the need to slow down."

He seems like a smart guy. Theocite is volatile as hell and he knows it.

If anyone tried to get to these incredibly rich and incredibly deep undersea deposits by impatiently blowing through the smaller accessible quantities I already knew about, they'd be playing with fire.

As this thought settles in my mind, a new one rises. It's one of the most uncomfortable I've ever had.

"Oh shit…" I mutter.

I know the station was compromised and sabotaged by that glove-wearing rat in the Canteen, and I still don't think the timing could be coincidental.

And if he knew what *I've* been working on, chances are good he knew what Vinner has been working on, too. Chances are good he knew how much damage blowing through even the most accessible theocite deposits could do.

Chances are good that the consequences could be brutal.

Hell, the consequences could be what I saw when I looked down at Earth. The Zola-hating terrorists who threatened a world-destroying *coup de grace* if he didn't surrender might have just turned our research against us.

I wish I wasn't thinking this, but I am. They might have used theocite as a weapon.

The idea is crushing. I know I was trying to do good and I've no reason to think Vinner wasn't, too, but our research might have loaded the gun for those maniacs to pull the trigger.

I take photos of these last few pages and rifle through Vinner's drawers in search of more.

There's nothing. I think about going back to his dorm to see if there's anything else in his bags or if he has a briefcase, because this doesn't seem like enough work for a lab of this size.

But when I turn to leave, I freeze.

Right beside the doorway, I see the last thing I expect.

I walked straight past it on my way in, wholly focused on what might lie ahead, but I can't miss it now.

First I see the torso, standing perfectly straight.

And then I look up.

That's when I see the wide open eyes, staring straight into mine…

38

Okay.

I knew there had to be more to Vinner and his lab than a bunch of documents about exoplanets and mining deposits, but I didn't expect this.

Nope. I didn't expect a robot.

I've never seen anything like it. It's so... robust.

They haven't wasted time trying to make it look like a human, beyond the bionic-looking eyes and ears. Even those are probably just for necessary sensory input, I figure, because there really has been no attention paid to making it look like a person.

The body looks like, well, the inside of a robot.

It's like they haven't gotten around to putting the 'shell' on yet. Most striking of all are the thick arms. When I say thick, I mean thick. We're talking more silverback than man.

There are no hands, just stumps. When I look to the wall behind the robot I see why.

Resting on wall-mounted holders like rifles proudly displayed behind a bar, there are three pairs of attachments. One pair are hands, one pair are drills, and one pair are, for lack of a better term, bona fide wrecking balls.

"Woah," is all I can say.

I walk over to the hand-shaped attachments and notice a button on the wall beside them. I press it automatically. Within seconds, I'm watching in awe as the shelf-like supports the attachments are resting upon come out from the wall on telescopic rails and rotate towards me.

Oh, I get it.

These are way too heavy for a person to move, so they slot onto the robot's arms from their resting place.

Below the wall-mounted attachments, right behind the robot's huge block-shaped feet, I spot a cable. It's plugged into the wall outlet at one end and into the robot at the other.

If this thing can be useful to me in any way, the fact that it's recently been charged is definitely a good thing.

More good news comes when I find a box in the same area. It's not locked and the lid isn't heavy, so I get inside with no difficulty.

A bizarre-looking pair of gloves is all I see at first, until I move them out of the way and find a fairly standard-looking remote control.

There are two joystick-like levers, one with two arrows indicating forwards and backwards and one with full circular motion. The only writing on the face of the remote says *ROBEX-2*.

"Robex," I muse out loud, looking back at the robot's face. "Let's go with Bex."

I'm already thinking of Laika as a *he*, so it makes sense to even things up.

Under the remote, I find one last item in the box: an instruction manual for the remote.

Jackpot.

It's limited, like the quick-start instructions I had for my EVA suit, but it's a hell of a lot better than nothing.

One thing to note is that this manual is strictly for the remote control, not for Bex herself, so it doesn't tell me much about what she can do.

I carefully disconnect the charger then flick the transmitter switch on the remote and move its left arrow forward. As soon as I do, Bex takes a step towards me.

"Sweet," I instinctively grin.

Okay, my situation is grim. But I'm controlling a robot!

I would have loved this as a kid and I'm not ashamed to say I love it now. The fact that Bex might be able to help me is what really counts, but now more than ever I have to try to appreciate cool moments whenever I can find one.

I look again at the attachments. With the wrecking balls and the drills, especially in the context of the room I've found her in, I have a feeling our girl Bex might be in development for some remote mining applications.

I can't take my eyes off the gloves, though, because I have a hunch what they might be for.

I use the remote to turn Bex around and position her so she's standing directly in front of the hand-shaped attachments. I'm not bragging when I say this is pretty easy for me, as a dude who grew up with more remote-controlled friends than real ones.

I move Bex towards her perfectly aligned hand attachments until a clear double clicking sound confirms they're in place.

As soon as they are, I move her backwards to be clear of the wall.

I reach down and put the gloves on my hands.

A huge smile instantly crosses my face, because my hunch was right.

When I open and close my left hand, Bex opens and closes hers.

When I slash through the air with my right, she mimics the move.

These are precision control gloves! As long as I keep them on, Bex is going to mimic every hand movement I make — in real-time!

The first thing I think of is how useful this kind of thing would be for repairing pipes on the outside of space stations, negating the need for complex mouse controls.

Can't imagine where I'd get an idea like that...

But really, this is incredible.

I'm not going to mess around with the drill, but I do want to try something with the wrecking balls. I maneuver Bex to put the hand attachments back on their holding rack. They unclick as soon as they're in place, evidently thanks to some kind of pressure sensor.

I press a button on the wall beside the wrecking balls, bringing them forth to be attached. I control Bex to get them on her arms within no more than a minute. Once they're securely on, I ball my fists and swing to see if she still follows the physical orders.

To my moderate but delighted surprise, she does.

There's no dexterity with these, obviously, but the more I move each hand, the more she moves the ball.

The faster I move each hand, the faster she moves the ball.

It's not just her hands, either. Even though the gloves stop at my wrists, her metallic forearm follows a similar motion to mine.

The accelerometers and whatever else is in the gloves must know my arm has to be moving to generate a certain level of speed and power, I figure.

I don't spend more than a few seconds pondering the robot's inner workings because the result is right in front of me. And believe me: I like what I see.

When I arc back and lurch forward in my best impression of a boxer, she follows.

She follows *hard*.

Instantly, I have two ideas. The first is primarily a test and the second could finally be the big solution I've been looking for.

I position Bex so that *one* of the ball attachments comes off, then replace it with a hand.

Her asymmetry is a weird look, I can't deny that, but this setup could deliver a huge breakthrough.

I lower my hands to my sides then remove the gloves. This

is my way of making sure that Bex's wrecking ball and giant hand stay at *her* sides, too.

I really don't want them thrashing around when I walk her to the Canteen.

I let Bex walk in front, less out of chivalry than practicality. I mainly want to make sure she doesn't walk into anything and damage either it or herself.

There's another reason, too. Call me crazy… but while there's no such thing as too many sci-fi movies, I've seen enough of them to feel uncomfortable turning my back to a large humanoid robot.

I'm joking on that, I think, but this thing can definitely do some damage. I'm glad the power is in my hands — literally — and I'm very eager to see how far I can take it.

Laika is a cool enough guy to have around, and talking to a parrot is better than talking to no one at all.

But Bex?

I don't think I've found a friend here, but I do think I've just discovered a new secret weapon.

39

Controlling Bex's legs with the remote might not be as intuitive as controlling her hands with the gloves that recognize my hand movements for her to replicate, but it's still pretty damn easy.

I just keep holding the left stick forward to make her walk and tilting the right stick slightly whenever I need her to turn. That aspect really is similar to some of the toys I had as a kid.

Make no mistake, though, Bex is anything but a toy.

We get to the Canteen fairly quickly. Inside, I march her straight over to the vending machine.

I move a chair from a nearby table then put the left glove back on my hand. I move my hand so that hers hovers over the chair, then I lower it and grasp at thin air.

Like I hoped, she grasps the chair.

There really must be a lot of cutting edge tech going on inside this glove, from accelerometers to pressure sensors to I don't even *know* what else. All I know is, it works.

That knowledge is reinforced when I thrust my hand forward and release my grip as if throwing a dart. Bex throws the chair at the wall like it weighs nothing. To her, I guess it basically *does*.

I use the remote to turn her back towards the vending

machine, and it's funny to watch as her left hand mimics mine. There's no remote in her hand, obviously, but her dexterous fingers move as if there is. This time she's the one gripping thin air.

As soon as she's in the right position, I try to make Bex grab on to the vending machine's opening.

My plan is to push my arm upwards and see if she's strong enough to lift the machine. That could free Yannick's body — a win in itself — and it would confirm that she's capable of what I want her to do next.

The problem is, I don't know how to make Bex crouch and I can't get her hand low enough when she's standing.

I decide to switch strategies. I take the left glove off and put the right one on, to control the wrecking ball attached to Bex's right arm.

I figured it made sense to put the wrecking ball on her right side, since that's the hand I can't control with as much precision or grip strength.

I swing my hand slowly at first, then faster.

When I crash the ball into the side of the machine, my arm is moving with a punching motion that hasn't had much practice in the last two decades. Incredibly, this is still more than enough for her to smash a huge hole in the side of the machine.

Just... wow.

This suddenly feels like *so* much power.

I punch even harder, leading Bex to all but *destroy* the side of the vending machine.

When that's done I switch gloves again, encouraged and not a little frightened by how much damage I've been able to do so quickly. I take advantage of that damage by using the hand attachment to make Bex grab hold of a newly exposed piece of the machine's inner structure.

"Let's see what you can really do," I say. I position her hand in place by moving my own, then grasp tightly and yank my arm up as fast as I can without unclenching my fist.

Even through the glove, I feel my fingernails digging into my palm as I squeeze as hard as I can.

Bingo.

They say seeing is believing, but damn if I'm not still struggling to believe this.

Bex pulls the vending machine up like it's made of cardboard.

Before it has a chance to fall again, I move my whole other arm in front of me so Bex does the same. This blocks the machine until I pull Yannick away with my other gloved hand.

Without making any sudden moves that might make the wrecking ball swing violently again, I pull my poor friend clear into the open.

I then remove both gloves and let the machine fall back to Earth with a thud.

Yannick was a sci-fi nerd like me. He would have *loved* Bex.

I take his phone from his pocket just in case I might need it, then apologize one last time for what I had to do to his finger.

Bex, meanwhile, has just proven herself beyond any doubt.

There's a drill in Vinner's lab if we need it. But after what I've just seen, I don't feel like we will.

For more hours than I'd care to count, I've known where I need to go.

And now, at last, *at last, at last…* I think I finally have my way in.

40

I know I shouldn't celebrate until the job is done, but try telling that to the smile on my face.

With Bex leading the way, I make the short walk to the Control Center with excitement in every step.

The ironies have been adding up since everything started going down, and I've spent long enough lamenting the fact that they've only gotten crueler.

For once, though, I kind of like this irony.

I kind of like the fact that inside this greatest of all technological marvels — a state of the art space station housing some of the most cutting-edge technology ever developed — my solution to getting through a locked door is a big-ass robot with a big-ass wrecking ball for a fist.

When I arrive, I stand before the Control Center's entrance with a thousand thoughts running through my mind.

This door isn't an airlock or a seal to guard against toxicity, like in my lab or down at the EVA hatch. It's built for security, not safety, and it was designed to keep out *people* — not robots.

With Bex in position, I put on the all-important glove and instruct her to take a swing at the passcode keypad. The frazzling sound of dying electronics is pretty cool, but not half as cool as the click that follows.

I stand in disbelief.

Did she just do it? Did she just get me in?

I try to push the door, but it doesn't move.

Hmm, I muse.

I guess that would have been *too* easy.

That was just a prelude to my main attempt, though, which comes when I line Bex up for a thunderous swing at the door itself.

My left arm is slightly stronger than my right, so I contemplate returning to Vinner's lab to switch out Bex's left hand attachment for another wrecking ball on *that* side.

You're overthinking, I tell myself.

Less think, more swing.

Taking this advice, I wind up my right arm and power it forward, striking at a slight downwards angle in the hope that will increase Bex's chances of breaking the door.

Again, I was overthinking. Because forget cardboard... that thing falls from its hinges like a domino when her massive wrecking ball makes its concentrated impact.

"You beautiful metal bastard," I beam, taking off the glove before I accidentally do any more damage.

It takes me a few seconds to fully accept how much everything has just changed.

I'm in.

I'm really in.

Standing at the threshold, I almost feel like one of those circus elephants who's been forced to stay in a circle for long enough that they'll then stay there forever even when they don't have to.

It's as though I've internalized the idea that the Control Center is somewhere I can't go.

But with one decisive swing, Bex just changed all of that.

And better yet, I can see from here that the overhead lights are on.

That in itself is huge. There's power!

I should have already realized this since the keypad was

working until I smashed it, but my mind was too focused on getting in.

The Control Center has power.

I repeat: the Control Center has power.

There are bunkers on Earth, Eva and Joe were chosen for the evacuation, and the Control Center has power.

It's been a good hour for yours truly after way too many bad ones in a row.

And as the flattened door invites me inside, I have a feeling it's about to get a whole lot better.

41

Earth looms large through the window up ahead, both calling me forward in hope and wrenching my heart all over again.

Still, nothing will ever compare to the crippling shock of seeing our burning world for the first time. My eventual success in entering the Observation Deck took me from joy to desolation in the blink of an eye. The first cut really is the deepest.

At least, that's what I think as I step into the Control Center.

But now that I've seen some of what happened in footage from the ground, the sight hits differently.

I've seen the physically destructive earthquakes. I've seen the volcanic eruptions. I've seen the global societal chaos those disasters provoked.

Terrified expressions are etched in my mind, along with the disaster-movie visuals I saw on the big screen.

It's no longer an abstract cataclysm. I know what happened. *Some* of it, anyway.

Now that I know an eco-terrorist cell threatened to turn the world to dust if Zola didn't surrender himself by their deadline, I can put two and two together and assume he didn't give them what they wanted.

The scale of the devastation visible from here is too great for anything else to make sense.

I feel sick thinking that my research might have had something to do with the impossibly coincidental timing. Hard as I try, it's hard to escape that idea.

The saboteur knew who was in the offshoot labs, which means his civilization-hating cronies on Earth knew what Vinner and I were working on.

They knew how theocite can be mined.

They knew how volatile it is. They knew Zola saw harnessing its power as the key to finally achieving ultra-long-distance space exploration.

Seeing Earth again like this, a question thumps at my soul with all the power of Bex's wrecking ball:

Is this my fault?

Fault is too big of a word, I decide.

Surely, no one could throw *that* at me. But a slightly looser version of the question feels all too valid: would this have happened without my research?

Would this have happened if *I* hadn't assisted the team who developed the BioZol synthesization technique in the first place, and if *I* hadn't theorized I could make it an order of magnitude more potent by enriching it with ultra-heated theocite?

I wish I could say no and believe myself, but I just can't.

After a few seconds, I catch myself staring glumly at Earth. I slap myself on the cheek — *hard*.

Snap out of it, Ray, I implore myself.

The road to hell is paved with good intentions, but what's done is done.

Seeing Earth like this could send anyone into a doom spiral of depression, so I'm not going to beat myself up for wasting the last sixty seconds. But I have to shake it off. I came in here with a job to do.

The surface of Earth might look like a burning hellscape, but thanks to what I've learned from my phone-based investigations I know that an underground evacuation was under-way. I also know Eva and Joe were part of it.

I now know that if I can put out an SOS call, it won't be a pointless scream into the void of space. People *are* down there.

Okay, I'm counting on someone looking or listening in the right place. But for all I know, thousands of satellites could still be online. People could still be monitoring them from the government bunkers with their backup supplies.

Hell, Zola himself could be holed up in New Zealand. And if he is, his base is definitely going to have radio contact with the station. Our station Commander routinely reported to ZolaCore HQ in Auckland, so there's a chance that a two-way channel is already going to be open.

Which is all great… if I can get a radio working.

As I finally look away from Earth, the first thing to say about my surroundings is that this Control Center is a *lot* smaller than I expected.

It's the hub of the station, located at the extreme western tip on the standard maps I'm used to seeing. I knew it couldn't be very big given its location, but the borderline claustrophobic feeling is still a surprise.

I guess I'm used to my abnormally spacious lab. It's all rela-tive, I guess, since even that now seems like a tight squeeze compared to Vinner's almost empty lab where I just found my priceless ally Bex.

There are only two chairs in here, both taken.

I know who is in them before I look. Commander Harrison sits alongside his more personable Deputy, Lily Paulson.

Lily gave me my introductory tour when I arrived here. She went out of her way to make sure I felt comfortable in the first few days, and for someone of such high rank and experience she was unusually insistent on using first-name terms.

No one around here ever had a bad word to say about Commander Harrison, either, but he was a more old-school kind of guy. He was the type who would have gone down with his ship and would have been the last one to board an evacuation craft if any had come.

From the way they're both sitting, I can instantly tell that they died as quickly as the people in the Observation Deck.

I now know that wasn't by accident, thanks to the demented checklist I found on the sick killer's phone. I now find myself wondering what kind of toxin was used. What could kill them so quickly but leave the air totally breathable now, just two days after poisoning such an enclosed space?

There isn't a lot of screen space in here and there aren't a lot of machines. When I crouch to look under the main surface, I see countless dials and knobs on what has to be the main control board.

Everything *seems* to still have power in here — the switches are all flicked the same way, with no fuses visibly tripped — but the screens are disconcertingly blank.

On the control board, I see a green button marked MASTER REBOOT.

It's all but begging to be pressed.

"This is what you wanted, Ray," I say out loud, psyching myself up.

I close my eyes and press the button.

42

Through my eyelids, I see the overhead lights cut off.

That on its own is no surprise and no cause for concern.

What *does* concern me is the sudden and total silence, which instantly makes me miss the gentle hum of electricity that I barely noticed before the reboot.

I reopen my eyes in a panic. Only now do I realize that I'm still depressing the button with my finger.

As soon as I release it, the lights and the hum kick back into gear.

And better yet, *so* much better yet, the two screens come to life, too.

Success!

I can't help but wonder if I just returned power to the Observation Deck, too. But my main goal in there was to access a radio, and I know I can do that in here.

Even though my heart has been racing for most of the past day, the current elevated pace feels different somehow.

For once, there's more anticipation than trepidation.

I finally feel like I could be on the brink of my big break-through, no longer just walking an endless tightrope of survival from one disaster to another.

Commander Harrison's large touchscreen display goes

through a brief reboot process before quickly settling on a desktop-style layout.

His background image is of The Beacon itself, shot from a craft on its way to dock. This job must have been a dream come true for him.

Lily's background image is more emotionally impactful when it loads, showing her with three kids who I know from our conversations to be her niece and nephews. They're on a beach somewhere, smiling like only the truly happy ever can.

Sorrow and rage are roommates in my mind.

As the rage swirls, I don't even know if I can keep telling myself that the bastards who did this are going to pay. I mean, are they even still around?

Those lunatics think humanity itself is a scourge to be eradicated. Would they have *wanted* to shelter from the so-called coup de grace they planned to unleash?

It's weird that these thoughts are arising now. All I can do is try to push them aside and take Lily's background image as a reminder of what counts most of all: not vengeance, but family.

Touching Harrison's screen brings up a security verification pop-up. Apparently a login is required after any reboot or extended period of inactivity. I cross my fingers that one of *his* will be enough to unlock things.

Tapping the option for Biometric Verification quickly reveals that a fingerprint alone won't be enough. It needs a combination of that plus facial identification.

The touchscreen's in-built camera proves fussier than those on everyone else's phones. It takes a few awkward and apologetic attempts, but I eventually manage to hold Harrison's eyelids open without my own fingers getting in the way too much for his face to be recognized.

Without stopping to let the discomfort build any further, I do the same for Lily.

I truly don't think words could express how glad I am that I'll never have to do anything like this again.

Vengeance might not be what counts most, but believe me:

it's hard *not* to feel rage at the culprits.

It's hard for my blood *not* to boil when I've seen so much death at such close quarters, let alone when I've physically felt it through the unfortunate need to move my fallen colleagues around and use their biological credentials like this.

Once I'm in, I go back to Harrison's touchscreen and immediately tap the Call icon. This pulls up a screen I'm unfamiliar with, but it looks happily self-explanatory.

Scrap that. *Delightfully* self-explanatory.

There's a recent calls list, showing that his last call was with ZolaCore HQ.

"*2 days*" is as specific as the timing gets. Unspecific, but consistent with my timeline.

I tap the text in hope that it will start a new call, only to be confronted with an unwelcome message about a lack of data signal.

Duh, I scold myself.

The internet signal is down because it's dependent on a relay from Earth — which doesn't exactly look like it's very online right now.

I'm counting on radio contact, not VOIP.

I close the Call menu to look for another useful icon. My eyes scan them all until I spot one the looks like a satellite dish. It's a radio telescope… just the kind of icon I wanted to see.

I tap it and wait.

And wait.

And sigh.

When the screen changes, there are so many fields and options that I barely even know what I'm looking at. The options are impenetrable.

The overcrowded layout makes me feel like I'm looking at a physical switchboard in an old radio transmission center. It's the opposite of the intuitive Call menu, but I consciously try not to let myself get too concerned.

"You're here," I say out loud. "You're in."

It's a good reminder.

I've done things I would never have believed I could do and I've gotten up from gut-punches I would never have believed I could take.

This isn't an air leak. This isn't my best friend trapped underneath a vending machine. Hell, this isn't even a locked door with no way through. This is a radio control screen designed to be used.

Sure, it's overwhelming… but it's definitely not insurmountable.

I can't see anything about choosing a target, selecting a channel, or anything else that's obviously helpful. I step back and quickly look for an instruction manual.

Unfortunately I can't even see any spots where one might be hiding, with no sign of drawers or anything else in this small room.

There has to be something, though, I assure myself. Even just a digital guide somewhere else inside this all-access system I now have at my fingertips.

When I look back at the screen after glancing around, the benefit of fresh eyes pays off with unexpected speed. I notice something new.

In the lower right corner, I see a small red circle with a white exclamation mark inside and red lines emanating from the circle like rays.

Rays of hope?

Ray can hope.

I tap the icon.

And… yes!

Yes!

A new pop-up covers everything else on the screen, with three huge words above three options. The word *emergency* is one I've seen and relied on way too often lately, especially during my spacewalk, but I've never been so glad to see it.

The three words are simple:

EMERGENCY ASSISTANCE SIGNAL.

The three options are simple, too:

TARGETED // ALL CHANNELS // CANCEL.

As soon as I see the options, I tap ALL CHANNELS with all the speed of a frog's tongue shooting for a passing fly.

The screen changes right away. It now shows a larger version of the satellite dish icon, with a constantly looping progress bar underneath. The bar is orange. I don't know what that means. It's not green but it's also not red.

A sound begins to emanate from the screen's speakers, not unlike an old telephone's calling tone.

The words "STATUS: TRANSMITTING" appear under the bar a few seconds later.

I nod in relief and exhale slowly.

This feels like another successful step on my road to contact, but now what?

Is this all I can do?

"It was never going to be instant," I tell myself.

Call me crazy, but sometimes *hearing* words like this feels different to just thinking them — even when my voice is the one I hear saying them.

Because I'm right: it *wasn't* ever going to be instant.

I'm a guy in a capsized boat who just let off his first flare. The big ship doesn't show up right away, they have to *see* you first. You have to give them a minute.

Still, I've never felt so tense.

A big part of me feels like if anyone is going to pick up my signal, it will be soon. That's the reality.

I move across to Lily's screen while Harrison's continues to relay the "Transmitting" status of my SOS call.

There's a camera icon that I've had my eye on since I first saw it, and now that I've set off my flare I feel like it's time to take a look.

If this grants me access to security camera footage, it could reveal a lot about our saboteur's final moments and also his previous interactions with others on the station.

And hey, I might as well do *something* while I wait for the SOS status to change…

43

An unwelcome login screen greets me when I tap the camera icon on Lily's touchscreen.

It's different from the ones I saw earlier.

There's no option for biometrics, just a pre-filled username and an empty password field.

The username is Lily's, which would be obvious even if I wasn't using her computer. But the password? I'm stumped.

Quickly enough to prevent myself from lamenting the astronomical odds of success, I reach to type the letter A. I'm not trying to guess the password, just starting at the beginning of the alphabet in the faint hope that the rest might autocomplete once the first letter is entered.

As soon as I hit the key, the password field populates. Not with anything quite as helpful as an autocompleted password, unfortunately, but with something I can work with.

Little underscore-like lines appear in three sets of four, almost like in a game of hangman with spaces indicating the divisions between words. I'm used to seeing this kind of thing for two-factor authorization codes on all kinds of apps and websites, and it tells me that Lily's password has a fixed-length of twelve digits.

This isn't the first time I've needed to guess a password or code, but it is the first time I've felt like there might be a chance.

Let me stress something again: I'm not going to try to guess it. Even a four-digit code has ten thousand possible combinations, and each extra digit multiplies the number of possibilities by ten.

I have an idea, though… one that might — just might — remove the guesswork.

I take Lily's phone from her pocket and gratefully see that it still has a little bit of battery life left. I unlock it as quickly as I can, which necessitates one more biometric approval, then head straight into her browser settings to look for saved passwords.

Most of them are very long, autogenerated and saved by the device. But her email password? You guessed it… twelve digits.

020105290805.

I'll bet those are birthdays.

0201-0529-0805.

Yeah… I'll bet those are the three kids' birthdays.

It's not the best password hygiene but it's also not the worst. What counts now is whether my hunch is right.

I enter the numbers on Lily's touchscreen. I wouldn't say I'm *expecting* to get in, but this is not a blind shot in the dark. She only has one twelve-digit password saved on her phone. If she chose her password for accessing the security system, which I know is twelve digits, there's a reasonable chance she'll have gone for this one.

I hit return.

Score! I'm in.

Straight away, I see thumbnail views of live footage from all over the station. Wow.

There are no cameras in the high-security offshoot labs like mine and Vinner's, but it seems like everywhere else is on here. The Observation Deck's camera is the only one offline, which unfortunately suggests that the power in there wasn't rebootable, after all.

The number of live feeds is cool to see, but I really want to check out the recorded footage. I want to see everything the scumbag did when he enacted his plan, not just the parts I know from his checklist.

I tap into the Canteen's feed.

The system lets me zoom in pretty far without losing any detail, granting another close look at the gloved killer. Once the screen is focused on his position, I click on the time in the top left, hoping I'll be able to change it.

I smile instantly. Things are finally going my way, with one little win after another.

I *can* select a time. I can replay footage of this spot from any time I choose.

First of all I hit the rewind button, which only takes me back ten seconds at a time. Next I jump back by 24 hours, then do the same two more time.

I zoom out to a broader angle and see the busy Canteen just one full day before everything went to shit. I start skipping forward an hour at a time, looking for anything suspicious.

ZolaCore systems are usually state-of-the-art across the board, so I think there might even be an option to hone in on the saboteur and track his movements from camera to camera. That would be hugely helpful, but for now I'm just getting to grips with things and looking for the moment when he set everything off.

After jumping forward a few more hours, I feel my back straighten as though someone has pulled me up by the hair.

But it's not something on Lily's screen that gets me.

No… my head immediately turns back to Commander Harrison's screen, reacting to a very sudden and very noticeable change in the phone-like tone it's been emitting.

There's no more beeping. The tone is now constant.

And when I see the change on the screen itself, it's like the whole world around me stops. The radio is no longer just *transmitting*.

No. It's better than that.

The two words hit me like cool water on a sweltering day, instantly bringing a feeling of relief after far too long in total isolation.

These makeshift glasses I threw together might not be perfect, but I know what the screen says.

STATUS: CONNECTED.

44

"They know," I yell in near disbelief. "Someone knows I'm alive!"

I did it. I actually *did* it.

I survived the shipwreck, I let off the flare, and someone just saw it.

My gut says it's going to be someone at ZolaCore HQ in New Zealand, but right now that feels like mere detail.

STATUS: CONNECTED.

I stare at the words until they change again.

STATUS: ENGAGING.

Wait... is engaging better than connected?

I nod a few times, trying to rid myself of momentary doubts.

It must be engaging the actual radio "call" now, I figure. Opening the channel... whatever the right words are.

This isn't my field of expertise and all I care about right now is that my radio is connected to someone else's and that I'm about to hear their voice.

I might even see them, if any public or private telecommunication satellites are still working.

Radios as people know them on Earth usually live inside

cars and relay audio-only broadcasts, but in telecommunication terms radio waves can do a lot more than that.

While the final "engaging" process goes on, the satellite dish icon in the middle of Harrison's screen disappears.

In its place, a three-dimensional representation of Earth appears. The lines are electric blue, highly contrasted on a black globe like something you might see in a commercial for an international investment bank.

My little station then appears, invisible at this scale but represented by a blinking green dot to the right of the blue-lined globe.

STATUS: INITIATING.

I'm not a big fan of the imprecise words they've chosen to describe the statuses here, but the progressively encouraging images are giving me a good feeling. I'm increasingly confident that we're about to establish a live link.

The graphic is going to show another dot on Earth, too, I realize. It'll show a dot wherever my signal has been picked up.

The bunker in Colorado Springs would be a dream, putting me right in touch with Joe and Eva, but I would settle for the one in Virginia or even New Zealand. Getting back to Earth is what counts.

A pleasant tone chimes from the screen, easing my final doubts even before I see the words:

STATUS: LIVE.

"Hello?" I say. "Hello?! This is Ray Barclay on The Beacon. Do you copy?"

I hear the sound of static, but it quickly gives way to a smooth silence.

"This is Ray Barclay," I repeat. "I'm broadcasting from Zola-Core's Beacon space station and I—"

And I *freeze.*

A second green dot appears on the screen, showing the location of the radio I've connected to.

It's not in Colorado Springs, it's not in Virginia, and it's not in New Zealand.

The signal I've connected to isn't coming from any of those places.

The second green dot doesn't appear on the globe to the left of my station, because that's not where this signal is coming from.

No.

My lungs feel empty. I have no idea what this means.

This signal I've picked up....

It's not coming from Earth.

45

The green dot indicating my location is *just* to the right of Earth. I'm close — low Earth orbit — and the distance is barely noticeable.

But when the visualization zooms out to show the location of the *other* radio I've just connected to, my distance from Earth becomes completely impossible to see. The new green dot appears at the far right of the screen. Earth and my dot are pushed to the far left.

Earth is also a lot smaller now that the scale has changed to show the incoming signal's origin point.

A *whole* lot smaller.

I can't believe what I'm looking at.

It just doesn't make sense.

"Hello?" a female voice booms through the screen's speakers. "Did you say you're Ray Barclay? On The Beacon?"

My mouth falls open.

Until ten seconds ago, *any* reply would have brought only total elation. But the visualization on the screen has knocked my thoughts off that track and now I'm trying to get my head around something that just does not compute.

The Beacon has been the only manned research station,

public or private, for a full seven years. There's not supposed to be anything else out there, let alone so far away.

There haven't been any manned explorations for even longer, either.

These thoughts rattle through my mind almost too quickly to grasp, bouncing off each other like pinballs.

My eyes are stuck on the screen, utterly confounded until a new thought joins the fray. It knocks the others aside in an instant.

Maybe it's an evacuation craft, I suddenly think.

Maybe Zola or the public agencies have been sitting on contingency plans bigger than anything I've imagined? Maybe they didn't just hide underground — maybe the real VIPs took off before things *really* went south?

Yeah, maybe that's it.

They might have fled Earth's sinking ship while they still could, to wait out the storm.

I don't know if that would be good news or bad.

The messages on Lisa Hull's phone said that her family was called to a bunker in Virginia, but Eva's subtle GPS clues told me that my family went to Colorado Springs.

If I had to guess which one of those bunkers might have a secret evacuation craft, it would be the one within easiest reach of the country's political and financial centers. It wouldn't be in Colorado.

"I'm Ray," I confirm after a few uncomfortable seconds. "Who are you? *Where* are you?"

"My name is Mel Lomond," she replies. "I'm trying to get— okay, *there* we go."

All of a sudden, the visualization of our locations shrinks into a small window that floats away to the bottom-left corner of the screen.

The main picture is now a live video link of Mel. There's minimal latency when she speaks, which gives me an idea of the maximum possible distance between us. Everything is relative, but she's not as far away as I feared she might have been.

I reposition myself directly in front of the screen. I have to wheel Commander Harrison's chair out of the way, taking care not to knock off his lifeless body as I do.

"Can you see me, too?" I ask.

My eyes take in as many details as possible as Mel opens her mouth to answer.

She's sitting in what looks like a small room. The wall behind her is very similar to the one behind me. She's also wearing a uniform emblazoned with the ZolaCore logo.

She looks twenty years older than me, mid-fifties or somewhere close, but I could be overshooting. Who knows how many years this stress is putting on both of us right now.

A quick nod from Mel has already confirmed that she can see me, but for some reason she doesn't look like she's as relieved to have made contact as I am.

Maybe she's alone, too, I ponder. Maybe she was hoping to reach Earth and now knows she's just speaking to another helplessly stranded survivor in space?

I try not to read too much into her decidedly unhappy expression. There are all kinds of reasons she could look so unsettled.

But as Mel leans closer to the camera, her whispered words reveal a reason for bleakness that's much worse than I imagined:

"Ray, you need to listen to every word I say. Your life is in immediate danger."

46

I gulp.

I've known my life is in danger since the moment I walked out of the lab and found everyone else dead all around me. But after fixing the air pipe and finally making radio contact with someone, I thought the *immediate* danger phase was over.

Mel's words say it's not.

Her expression says it's *definitely* not.

"Ray, I don't know what's gone on there or how much you know about what's happened on Earth," she continues, "but we have reason to believe there is an infiltrator on board The Beacon. He could be hiding in a secure location. You need to alert your colleagues to this news when you can be sure it's safe to do so, but do not attempt to engage with this man on your own. His name is Oliver Grainger, working undercover as Dale Thorpe."

The image on my screen changes, with the live feed of Mel temporarily replaced by the image of a man I know only too well. It's the checklist-and-gloves killer from the Canteen, whose dirty work I was all set to watch on the security footage right before I made contact with Mel.

"Do you see him, Ray?"

I nod. For now, I say nothing.

"Earth has been hit by what looks like the largest series of coordinated terrorist attacks in history," Mel goes on. "I'll tell you what I know. Three members of the organization behind the initial attacks appeared in public to issue an ultimatum. All three were quickly identified, and the intelligence agents who identified them also discovered complex financial links between two of those individuals and Oliver Grainger. Your station has been offline and unreachable since before this discovery was made. We thought it was too late. Ray... what *happened* up there?"

I blow air from my lips. Where do I start?

"Grainger is dead," I tell her.

Her eyebrows raise halfway up her forehead.

"Mel, *everyone* is dead. It's just me and a parrot, plus some other animals in induced comas inside one of the labs. There's no one else left. It *is* too late. Grainger did something to the air supply while I was in my sealed lab. I think he thought he would survive, but he didn't. I can show you when I figure out how to share footage from the cameras."

"*Everyone* else?" she asks, bringing a hand to her mouth in shock.

I turn the screen slightly so the camera brings Commander Harrison into the shot.

Mel closes her eyes and swallows hard. "Okay," she says, exhaling slowly. "Well, until a minute ago we thought absolutely everyone was dead — you, too — so at least one survivor is better than none. How much do you know?"

I turn my palms upwards in a tired kind of shrug. "Less than you, it seems like. When you say '*we* thought you were dead'... who's we?"

"At the time, everyone thought that," Mel sighs. "The Beacon went dark before anything happened on Earth. No one knew what happened there, but *something* had obviously gone wrong. Then when everything started going crazy on the surface and these maniacs claimed responsibility, it wasn't long before they were linked to Grainger. That's when it started to become clear you had been hit as a precursor to the main attacks on Earth. And when I say 'you'... I know who you are, Ray. I know what you were working on."

I don't know where to start with that.

"I'm asking about *now*," I say, trying to drill down. "Who are you with now? Who are you in contact with? And where the hell are you?"

"Ray, my name is Mel Lomond and I'm the Commander of ZolaCore's publicly undisclosed PetraVista observation station. My three fellow crew members are all in good health and we are on our way back to Earth in the hope of finding survivors. The last broadcasts we received were not promising."

"There are bunkers," I blurt out, because in my mind that's even more important right now than the startling revelation of another manned station. "There are at least two bunkers in the US. ZolaCore *has* to have one in New Zealand, too, so that's three for starters."

Mel visibly perks up. "How do you know that? Can you be sure? We haven't been able to make contact with anyone. It's *possible* that some survivors have evacuated underground, and maybe even that they can communicate between bunkers, but we have no reason to assume any of that. What have you seen?"

Nothing about inter-bunker communication, I think to myself, but that isn't the main thing right now.

I succinctly recount the phone messages I've seen from my colleagues' families and from Eva. I make sure to be explicit and thorough about how I came to learn of the bunkers in Virginia and Colorado.

One thing leads to another and before I know it I'm telling Mel about my experiment, Justin, Yannick, the air leak, my first sighting of Earth, the successful but costly EVA, the makeshift glasses she's been too polite to comment on, the robot... more or less everything that brought me here.

She's a very willing listener.

I probably talk for two or three minutes straight, maybe

more. Hearing it all laid out like this makes me see that it truly has been one hell of a ride.

"Wow," is all she says for a full ten seconds. "You really wanted to survive."

"I promised my family I'd be home at the end of my placement," I reply. "That was supposed to be a day and a half away so I might be a little bit late, but there *is* no quit. I'm going home."

Mel nods firmly. "Us, too. And you said Virginia and Colorado for the confirmed bunkers, correct? Do you know for sure that these are government facilities?"

"Seems like it," I say. "But you don't know anything about a ZolaCore bunker?"

"We haven't been in contact with anyone on the ground for two days," Mel reiterates. "We don't know if the terrorists let off an EMP or what, but all broadcasts from Earth just stopped. The last thing we heard about was the ultimatum on Zola, when those monsters called for him to 'give himself up' and stop all space exploration."

"That's the last I heard, too," I sigh. "I saw some news reports. President Williams was rushed away onto Marine One just before the terrorists' video aired. He was talking about emergency measures to make sure our democracy survived. He said freedom will strike back. He knew something was coming. I only saw all of this a few hours ago. It was like… I don't know how to explain it. It was like hearing the echo of the world being destroyed, when it's too late to do anything about it."

Mel says nothing for a few seconds, wiping her eyes in turn with one hand.

"I can't imagine what it's been like for you, Ray," she eventually says. "We were far enough away to escape their clutches, even if the infiltration at ZolaCore might be deep enough for them to know about our station. We've also had each other to help process it all. You've been all alone in there, fighting to survive and surrounded by death."

"I'm the lucky one," I reply. My voice is low as I try to hold off tears that have been building for untold hours. "I was in the lab when my friends and colleagues on the other side of my door were slaughtered in cold blood. And I was up here when untold millions… billions… who knows how many innocent people breathed their last breaths on Earth. This hasn't been easy but I'm not sitting here feeling sorry for myself. I'm sitting here feeling angry at the bastards who did this. I'm sitting here determined to get home and protect my family while freedom *does* strike back to make those animals pay for what they've done."

Mel replies with a nod, but it's a lot weaker than the one she gave earlier, almost like she wants to agree with me more than she actually does.

"If you're right about these bunkers and about President Williams being taken to safety, there could be a prospect of rebuilding and holding the culprits to account," she says. "But from what we heard about the group responsible, it doesn't seem like they wanted to survive. Ray, this doesn't look like an attack in any traditional sense we're familiar with. This looks more like an ideologically motivated attempt at absolute destruction."

Well, we reached the same conclusion on that one, I think to myself.

When I first ran all of this through my mind, I settled on the feeling that vengeance isn't my main motivator or even a good one.

The rage I feel is just *so* strong, though — it's like nothing I've known. I'm not proud of it but I don't think anyone could criticize it, either.

Getting off this godforsaken station alive and getting home to my family is my number one priority. Rising from the bunker and rebuilding what we can comes next. Those motivations will drive me further than anger ever could.

And then there's making sure my fallen brothers and sisters can have the most dignified send-offs we can give them.

There's making sure Barnet's animals aren't left to die in their tanks. There's Laika, of course, and there's also a lot of data here on scientific breakthroughs that could maybe help us build certain things back better than they ever were.

Okay, I'm really stretching for a silver lining with that last one.

But at the very least, there *is* my theocite research.

I'm in space and I've been working with ZolaCore, so my focus has been on the applications for propulsion. Really, though, the potency and efficiency of the reactions I've catalyzed with tiny amounts of ultra-heated theocite and easily synthesized BioZol is a huge deal. It could bring about a genuine revolution in terrestrial energy generation.

That's without even getting into everything Vinner was working on, with the habitable exoplanet and insanely valuable asteroids that my fuel breakthrough can bring within reach.

I get that I'm also counting on there being some kind of surviving infrastructure for any of this to matter, which the "absolute destruction" and EMP blast Mel speculated about don't make me feel too confident about.

An electromagnetic pulse would kill *all* electronics within range, whether they were plugged into the grid or not. All that would be sure to survive is whatever was very deliberately and very expensively shielded to protect against that specific kind of attack.

But between ZolaCore and the government, I have to believe the bunkers could be shielded against all threats. Surely that would be the whole point?

Call me an optimist, but the super-rich have been buying bunker space in New Zealand for decades. What we know about publicly is probably the tip of the iceberg, too. There has to be more going on under the surface — quite literally — than I can even imagine.

The same goes for government facilities.

So many huge projects have been dismissed as conspiracies,

sometimes for fifty and sixty years, until it turns out they were real after all. Granted, huge bunker complexes don't come cheap. But compared to the logistics of space exploration and even some of the stuff Zola has been trying to do on the seabed? It's a drop in the ocean.

"How much can you see from your location?" I ask. As soon as the question is out, it's like I've broken a seal. "And you said you're on an *observation* station and it's on the way back to Earth, right? So you're on a spacecraft, not an orbital station? What are you observing? The stuff Vinner was working on?"

"You knew Michael Vinner and his work?" Mel replies, clearly surprised.

I shake my head. "I just saw it in his lab before I found the robot. But anyway…"

"Of course," she says. "I'm sorry. There's no rush to dig too deeply into everything right now, Ray. Not when we have action steps to take care of. But I do understand your questions. The PetraVista is an observation station focused on tracking the movements of distant asteroids and other celestial bodies of interest. The instrumentation available to us doesn't allow clear visuals of Earth's surface — we're looking at objects that are much smaller and much further away. *You* are actually in a much better position to access images from any satellites that remain operational, and we can certainly talk you through that soon."

"And you're on the way back to Earth," I say. "Which means you've already altered your course once…"

For the first time, a smile spreads on Mel's lips. "We're not going to leave you there, Ray. We're coming."

I wouldn't quite call it serenity, but a rush of something pretty damn strong floods over me. "When?" I ask. "How far away are you?"

The scale of the radio visualization I saw earlier didn't make it easy to estimate the distance at all. I'm only a few hundred miles from Earth's atmosphere, and my green dot was literally indistinguishable from the edge of the planet when Mel's dot appeared at the far right of the screen. I don't have any idea where they are.

"We'll be there in four days," she answers. There's emotion in the words and she delivers them so flatly that I think she's uncertain how I'll react.

I take a slow breath. Four days.

Four days and I'll be out of here.

That's three days longer than I was hoping for when I prayed someone on Earth might notice me, but the "absolute destruction" Mel referred to makes me doubt there are going to be too many functioning spacecraft laying around down there.

With that in mind, the existence of her secret station is a blessing I should be grateful for.

Yeah. All things considered, it could have been a hell of a lot worse than four days.

"That'll work," I say.

"You have plenty of supplies?" she asks.

I shrug. "Sure. There are supplies here for a lot more people than me. Airflow is good, water reclamation is working. Everything is running. Every extra hour and every extra day brings a risk of something going offline that I don't know how to fix, but at least now I've got you guys to help. Where are your crewmates, anyway?"

Mel glances over her shoulder before turning back to the camera. "Two of them don't know the full extent of what's happened. I haven't informed them of the terrorists' video or their ultimatum against Zola. My Deputy Commander knows everything. Well, not about *you*. He knows everything except what I've just learned. But the other two don't know much."

I can't hide my surprise at this. "You've kept them in the dark?"

"I wouldn't put it like that," she contends. "For all I knew, we were the last four humans alive. You've given me hope with everything you've told me about the bunkers. But even then, if my crewmates know Earth has been hit like it has, they're going to fear for their families even more than they already do. You have a direct and tangible reason to think your family has been successfully evacuated to a bunker. They don't. And this is a dangerous environment for hysteria, Ray — as dangerous as it gets. Controlling the flow of delicate information during a situation like this is one of my responsibilities."

Okay, I see her point.

"So four days," I reflect. "Can you dock here properly, or will I be evacuated through one of the emergency airlocks? I've trained for that."

Mel's eyes narrow. "Oh."

"Oh?" I echo, instinctively leaning forward. I don't like that tone, or the look on her face.

She rubs the back of her neck awkwardly, visibly uncomfortable. "Ray, the PetraVista can't dock at all. You *are* trained to launch your Escape Pod for emergency interception, aren't you?"

My shoulders slump.

I'm infinitely further along in my battle to get home than I was twenty minutes ago, but there just *had* to be a catch.

47

Launching the Escape Pod for an emergency interception?

Yeah... I'm most definitely not trained for that.

"So just to be clear," I say. "You want me get into that tin can and launch it into space, hoping you catch me?"

Mel shakes her head slightly. "There's very little human involvement in the interception process. Pierre, my Deputy Commander, has a great deal of experience in training pilots, too. He can talk you through every aspect of the launch if you don't find everything you need in the emergency guides. You can take remote cameras and radios to the Pod and he can walk you through the process as many times as you want. The four-day journey time might count in our favor there."

She's trying to make me feel better, and in an intellectual sense her words make sense. In my mind I know it's not like I'll be throwing a tiny ball into the air and hoping they catch it with their bare hands, but try telling that to my heartbeat.

Forget launching. Forget being intercepted. Just thinking about getting inside that claustrophobic Escape Pod is enough to send my memories spiraling back to the terrible accident on the day I lost my brother.

Any kind of stressful situation can bring it back to me. Since everything went to hell up here, it's been happening a thousand times more frequently. So many things have brought it back, each flashback playing like an ultra high definition movie on a screen that fills my whole mind.

First it was the sight of Justin… the first dead body I'd seen since all those years ago. Then it was trying to free Yannick from under the vending machine as the spilled water soaked my knees. It was the claustrophobia of the EVA suit, it was the helpless blindness before I made these glasses, it was the feeling of cold skin each time I had to touch someone.

But the idea of *this*? The idea of getting behind the controls of a vehicle I've never used in a desperate attempt to get back to my family, just like I had to do that day? It's almost literally too much. It's too close.

I feel my breathing quicken, and not in the usual sense.

"Are you okay?" Mel asks.

She can sense it, too.

I put a hand on the floor to steady myself, even though I'm already kneeling in front of the screen with both of the Control Center's seats occupied.

My eyes are open but I can't see anything besides that moment… I can't see anything besides the imminent and unavoidable impact that sent me through the windshield.

The coroner's report said the crash didn't kill Jack. He drowned. He would have been dead before I even made it down from the cliff to try and pull him away from the rocks, the report said. But try telling that to my stepfather, Steve.

I killed his son and that was it. He never liked me but after that he *hated* me. I wasn't the only one he took it out on, either, and he always let me know it was my fault he was the way he was.

He never wanted me to forget it was my fault Jack died.

"Ray!" Mel calls, much louder now. "Talk to me! Are you okay?"

Her voice is loud enough to pull me back, or maybe there's just nowhere else for the haunting memories to go. They've managed to run right to the end this time, which doesn't usually happen.

"I'm okay," I say. "Thank you."

She looks beyond relieved to hear me speak and see me looking at the screen.

"You need to sleep," she says.

I can't argue with that, but there are also a lot of other things I need to do. Something Mel said earlier makes it sound like I might be able to access satellite images taken *after* the attacks, which could be priceless for helping us know where to land.

"Nothing else you think you need to do right now is more important than getting some rest," she insists.

Wow, I guess I'm *that* easy to read.

"I'd wager you haven't been eating or drinking much, either," she goes on, "with all the crises you've been jumping between. But your brain needs to rest just as much as your body does. Pierre and I will talk you through as much or as little as you want to hear when you wake up, okay? You've already done harder things than launching that Pod, Ray. Don't forget that."

She's right on all fronts.

Man, it really is good to have someone to talk to.

"You win," I say. "I'll sleep."

"We all win," Mel smiles.

I nod. "Okay. But now that I'm in here and can control all of the station's systems, there is one time-sensitive thing I *really* have to take care of…"

48

"Do you know this computer system?" I ask Mel. "Is mine running the same operating system as yours?"

"Uh, I'd imagine a lot of the core infrastructure will be the same, but we're on two very different stations," she replies. "What do you need to know?"

My eyes flit around the screen to my right, which belonged to Lily, our Deputy Commander. I don't want to do anything on Commander Harrison's screen that might kill the connection to Mel.

"I'm sure I could figure it out," I say. "I'm looking for the atmospheric controls. I need to lower the temperature in certain areas, maybe even with an override to take it below what the system expects me to want. Do you know if there's a shortcut to a full system guide somewhere? Or even a way to share my screen so you can take a look, in case this is the system you're used to?"

Mel can't hide her confusion. "Why do you want to make it so cold?"

"There are a lot of corpses," I say, seeing no need to get into any of the finer — or coarser — details.

The nature of the station's air supply has slowed their

decay enough to spare me from the situation being even more uncomfortable than it is, but that's not a magic bullet.

Mel tips her head back slowly in a silent half-nod of understanding.

"Most of them are in the Canteen and the dorms," I tell her. "If I can turn those areas into cool boxes, most of the work is done. I'll have to move the others from the hallways, and from in here and the Maintenance Bay. Those are the places I need access to, but the temperature in the Canteen and the dorms really has to drop. Can you help me with that?"

Step by step, Mel talks me through how to share my screen so she can see exactly what I'm looking at.

We hit a few snags along the way, and at one point we toy with the idea of a less direct solution involving a small portable camera. It's Mel who spots the small body-cam on Harrison's lapel. As Commander, I guess he had to always share his actions with the top brass at ZolaCore's New Zealand HQ.

Mel's idea is for me to link that to Harrison's computer and point it at Lily's, so she gets a live feed of what I'm seeing on the other screen.

Ultimately, though, we get a screen-share working and Mel is able to look at everything on Lily's system.

"Were those her kids?" she asks, taking in the background image. I hate the sound of that past tense *were*, but we are where we are.

"Her niece and nephews," I say.

Mel sighs sadly. "I'll bet there aren't a lot of young parents up there. Yearly contracts on The Beacon, isn't it? Except for visiting researchers like you. I'm sure it's still been hard for these few months, though. How old is your son?"

I tell her that Joe is seven. There's no need to add that he's not technically my son, or even my *stepson* quite yet, because I'm all he's ever known.

I don't shy away from those labels and being a better father figure to Joe than my stepfather was to me is the most important goal in my life, but I'm also not going out of my way to underline them.

"Seven is a good age," Mel muses. "Mine are grown, closer to your age than you are to mine. I couldn't have left them when they were so young. But back to these temperature controls…"

Before long, we find the zone-by-zone temperature controls. We figure it out via the System Guide, which looks like it's going to be a priceless find for helping me do all kinds of analysis in the next few days.

Better yet, because I'm logged in as Lily I can override the regular minimum temperature and take it as low as the system will physically permit. I make a mental note to grab some food from the Canteen while I'm there, because it's going to get *very* chilly very soon.

"I won't actually lower the temperature until I've cleared the other areas and have everyone in there," I say. "Now that I have the robot, I think I'll secure some trolleys together and have her pull them through the hallway. It would be exhausting moving one person at a time when there are literally dozens to take care of."

"Did you say *her*?" Mel asks with a slight chuckle. "It's a female robot you've found, is it?"

I can't help but laugh, too. "The model name is Robex-2," I explain. "I figured Bex for short. And the parrot felt like a *he*, so a little balance won't hurt."

Mel's eyes widen. "A Robex 2? Wow, I didn't know Vinner was playing with a Model 2. Did it look like he was focusing on the dexterity or the power?"

"I don't know," I admit. "There are all different attachments."

"They're being constantly refined for potential mining applications," Mel explains. "Think of diamond mines, cobalt mines, gold mines… then think of miners who don't get tired, don't need tools, don't even need light or oxygen. That's where Robex-1 came from — ZolaCore's terrestrial research division.

Zola bought out a smaller prototype from one of the legacy mining firms and dialed everything up to eleven for the model 1. You know better than anyone about his fascination with the seabed, especially since theocite was discovered, and Robex-1 is just as good underwater as it is on land. But scaling everything up, we're now looking beyond water or land. We're looking at the *asteroid* mining potential. That's where the Model 2 comes in."

Well *there's* a history lesson I didn't expect, but it's definitely illuminating. Mel knows her stuff and is very forthcoming, which is great for me.

She goes on to tell me a few more things about the Robex-2, including that they're compatible with ZolaCore's so-called "autonomy chips," which essentially function as brains that allow the company's robots to think and act for themselves.

A lot more testing is needed before the cutting-edge brains are paired up with the strong new bodies of the Robex-2 models, Mel says, and I can understand why.

It's interesting stuff, for sure, but we have a lot to deal with.

"Do you want me to leave anything else on Lily's screen while I'm handling this?" I ask. "Anything you want to look over?"

Mel shakes her head. "I can't control the screen so there's not a lot I could do. I'd be looking at the same thing for however long you're gone. Unless you want to take Commander Harrison's body-cam? It should stay linked to his system from anywhere on the station, besides maybe the sealed labs. You could take his headset, too. That way we'll be able to stay in touch."

"Great idea," I say, removing Harrison's wireless headset as delicately as I can.

Now that we've found the System Guide, it's extremely easy to get the body-cam and headset linked up so Mel can see and hear everything I'm doing.

"This will be perfect for your Escape Pod training," she says.

I feel my breathing quicken again as soon as she says it.

"No no no, I'm sorry," she jumps in, evidently seeing my expression change. "That's not something to think about yet. Take some breaths. One thing at a time."

I heed her words and try to stay in the moment.

"You need to sleep," she reiterates. "I understand why you want to do this right now, Ray. You're a good, good man. But please: handle this as quickly as you can and then promise me you'll shut down for at least a few hours."

"When I finally shut down after all of this, I'm going to be out for a lot more than a few hours," I retort, staying as upbeat as I can.

Mel grins. "I can imagine. And speaking of rest... if you found the Robex-2 plugged into a wall outlet or some other kind of charger, make sure to plug it back in as soon as you're finished. It makes sense to keep it ready for anything you might need help with. If you don't know where the charging point is, I'd advise preserving as much of the charge as you can. I know it will be harder moving the bodies that way, but you might later find a task that's impossible without the Robex."

"Like smashing into the last sealed lab?" I ask.

Mel blows air from her lips. "Ray, you've done what you've had to do, but in some ways you've been a very lucky man so far. There's no telling what's in any of the sealed labs. The contents could be extremely dangerous."

"Or extremely helpful," I say. "I didn't get much from the first lab, just my little parrot friend, but the second gave me Bex and she got me in here. If I'd been worried about what I might—"

"We'll analyze Grainger's movements and those of everyone else on the station once you've slept," Mel interrupts. "You're not alone anymore, Ray, and you're not scrambling in the dark. We can look at the footage to see who has entered that lab, and once we find a station manifest on Commander Harrison's computer you'll know what kind of work they've been doing. Just don't do anything reckless in the meantime, okay? Not when you're so close to making it out of there."

Wow.

Did I already say how good it is to have someone to talk to? Because, damn, it is *good* to have someone to talk to.

I would have settled for anyone, but someone as smart as Mel who can relate to life in space is really the best I could have hoped for. I can already tell that she's a great person to bounce ideas off of, and she's also throwing out helpful observations of her own.

By putting our heads together to make the most of the four days until her crew gets close enough to intercept me, I think we can discover a lot more about Grainger. We can also work together to make sure we don't lose any of the important data that's stored here.

Tomorrow holds a lot of promise, what with all the security footage and maybe even some satellite imagery we can pore over as a team. It's also going to involve the start of uncomfortable but necessary Escape Pod training, but I'm trying not to dwell on that part.

The final task I have to do before I can give my body and mind a much-needed break isn't going to be a pleasant one, either. But although I'm not looking forward to doing it, I'm definitely looking forward to getting it done.

"I won't do anything stupid," I promise. "I'll just take care of my colleagues and then shut down for a while. We'll take the next steps when I wake up. Together. I just have to do this first, now that I finally can."

Mel nods slowly. "You'll be recognized as a hero when we get to Earth and reach the survivors," she says.

"I just want to get back to my family," I reply, speaking the whole truth.

She holds my eyes. "Trust me, Ray: we'll bring you home. You just have to hang on until we get there."

49

Making contact with Mel is a real lifesaver — *literally* — but having access to the systems inside the Control Center has a lot of other benefits, too.

For one thing, I'm able to look at security camera footage from all over the station. This allows me to make sure I'm not missing any bodies in the handful of places I haven't set foot.

The main area I haven't checked is the Docking Bay that houses my Escape Pod.

A quick glance on the cameras tells me it's empty. That means I won't need to go there until tomorrow, when I'm hoping Mel's Deputy, Pierre, can ease my mind about my upcoming launch. Right now, I'm glad to put off my first in-person sighting of the Pod.

The cameras also show me inside each of the station's few dozen regular labs. Most of them are locked so it's very good news to find that only two of them are occupied.

Yannick didn't have access to them all and I don't know who worked in which one, so I haven't been able to go search them for information on what the researchers were doing or for items that could be physically useful.

This camera access is a great opportunity for a quick visual overview, and it's an opportunity I don't want to gloss over.

"I can look more closely at the labs," Mel offers. "We can share the load, Ray. You might be better served doing the things that can only be done in person. I don't envy some of those tasks, but you're the only one who can do them."

She's right.

"Thanks," I say. For now, I'll focus only on the two labs that are occupied.

Both of the dead researchers look like they were on the way to their doors, seemingly trying to flee like the others were. Everyone else who was working at the time of Grainger's sabotage attack spilled into the hallways in a desperate bid to escape. These two might have had some physical limitations that slowed them down, or maybe just a higher susceptibility to the toxin.

I zoom in for a better look around their labs and see nothing to raise any eyebrows. I'll be going in to get the guys out, anyway, but the feeling of power from being able to see what's going on in every corner of the station is hard to describe.

For so long I've been scrambling around trying to figure out *anything* about what happened here, and now the whole place is at my fingertips.

Tomorrow we can start looking more closely at what kinds of things were being studied in the regular labs. I've already pieced together a lot from Vinner's exoplanet and asteroid mining research, combined with Barnet's suspended animation trials. Who's to say *what* will show up when we check everything else?

That's without even thinking about the main focus of tracing Grainger's movements to identify any possible allies. It's also without thinking about my unshakeable urge to look inside the last real den of mystery this station has to offer: the fourth offshoot lab.

Seeing the lay of the land on a computer screen also lets me plan the most efficient route for bringing each of my colleagues into one of the newly designated cold zones.

These poor researchers deserve to have some dignity in death. I'm going to do all I can to give it to them.

I head out of the Control Center with my body-cam and headset in place, along with the makeshift glasses I haven't taken off since I engineered them.

I don't even want to think about what I look like right now. These plastic goggles only add to the dark bags under my eyes, along with the unkempt beard that's been growing ever since I isolated myself in my lab for the final BioZol enrichment experiment.

Before I move anyone, I gather as many trolleys as I can quickly find. That amounts to six, each with space for a body on the lower shelf and one on top. By rigging the trolleys together I can have Bex do the pulling, saving a lot of exertion and a lot of time.

At a push I could have moved two people on my own, but even then the weight would be a challenge. It wouldn't be too hard in normal times, but after my lack of food, sleep, water, respite, stronger painkillers... yeah, the last thing I need is to keel over.

Every time I've had to get close to my fallen colleagues, I've felt a horrible mix of guilt and rage. The rage remains, stronger than ever at the scumbag who did this and his cohorts who did even worse on Earth.

The guilt is a tougher feeling to describe. I've been taking my colleagues' phones, moving their hands and heads to use their biometric security data, and effectively using these real people with real families as a means to the end of contacting Earth so I can reunite with my own.

I've always tried to be respectful, and I don't think I could have done *any* of it if I didn't know that reaching Earth is the only way I can try to make sure these people make it home, too.

Now that I have a fuller idea of just how bad things are on Earth, with Mel's term "absolute destruction" still rattling in my mind, I'm finding it harder and harder to assume there's going to be any spacecraft capable of taking off anytime soon.

And even if there are, will whatever government we have left really think it's worth sending a mission to recover the corpses?

"Are you okay?" Mel asks as I stop walking.

I can't control what other people do, I tell myself. The best I can do is bring all of my colleagues together in two cold zones and leave them in peace.

I'll bet every single one of them grew up dreaming of going to space, just like I did. I suppose The Beacon isn't the worst final resting place.

"I'm fine," I reply, setting off again. "This is just… hard."

Mel can see what I'm looking at but she can't see me, just like I can't see her. We can hear each other in crystal clear audio, though, which is a lot better than nothing.

"It says a lot about you that you're doing this, Ray," she says. "It says a lot about what kind of man you are."

"Thanks," I sigh. The words don't make it any easier, but I appreciate them.

I take my six-trolley convoy to one of the emergency airlocks and start positioning my colleagues for the short journey to the Canteen.

"Jesus," Mel mutters. "I… I can't believe what you've had to do to get this far. I really can't. I can't even *look*."

The worst thing is, I *am* kind of getting used to this. The anger that fuels me is like nothing I've ever known, and if any of Grainger's cronies are alive on Earth there's going to be hell to pay like nothing they could ever see coming.

With Bex at my side, I put the glove on and position her to grasp the frontmost trolley.

Mel chimes in with a very helpful tip that I can lock Bex's desired hand position by holding a pressure point on the side of my glove for a few seconds.

That lets me remove the glove and release my empty-handed grip, without affecting Bex's solid grip on the trolley. This makes it much easier to control her feet with the remote.

Once again, Mel's advice is making me very grateful for all the secondary benefits contact is already delivering.

What would have taken hours on my own takes around forty minutes with the help from Bex and the tip from Mel.

In the dorms, I take a few minutes to make sure I've covered every face with the nearby blankets and pillowcases. Relative to the others I still think these people were the lucky ones, passing in their sleep. Their bodies already look restful and I can only hope their souls are, too.

One of the hardest moments comes when I start moving Barnet to the Canteen. Laika, his surviving pet parrot, shows up right on cue.

It tears me up when the little guy lands on the trolley and nuzzles against Barnet.

I don't know how smart parrots normally are and I don't know if there's anything special about Laika, but he one hundred percent knows that Barnet is dead and he is one hundred percent sad about it.

One thing that's common knowledge is that parrots often bond to one person. Laika's person is dead, and I guess I'm pretty fortunate that he's taken a liking to me.

I'm not sure the bird can help me in any real way, but I'm sure he *could* be an obstructive pain in the ass if he wanted to. Hell, the contact lenses incident proves that — and he wasn't even trying to get in the way with that.

A big part of me thinks Laika knows I'm doing what's right for Barnet here, too. As soon as I've wheel the trolley all the way to the Canteen, he flies down and stands outside the door.

He doesn't want to go in.

I can't blame him for that since *I* don't want to, either, but what has to be done has to be done.

Once Barnet is inside, I turn back to see Laika staring straight up at me.

"Leeroy… okay?" he squawks. The intonation sounds like a question.

Leeroy.

So *that's* what the "L" in "L. Barnet" has stood for all this time, I realize.

"Ray Ray," Laika says, shifting his feet from side to side. "Leeroy okay? Squawk. Leeroy no?"

"Leeroy no," I tell him, figuring this is his way of confirming his old buddy is gone for good."

I've never heard Laika say "okay" before, and now I'm thinking he understands a lot more words than I've assumed. Maybe he'll speak more as he grows more comfortable with me.

What he's feeling is only too evident right now, though, and I feel for him in turn.

I crouch down and pat him gently.

A parrot's face might not be as expressive as a person's, but believe me: he's upset.

Minute by minute, I'm growing even more determined to get this little guy safely off the station when I leave.

I'll admit that I didn't have the best first impression of Leeroy Barnet when I saw the rows of animal tanks that fill the walls of his lab, but the way Laika seems to be sad around him makes me think he was probably a pretty caring guy.

"I'll be back soon," I tell him.

I step into the Canteen, which poses a much greater challenge than the dorms in terms of leaving the victims with as much dignity as I can. There are a lot of people and very little to cover them with, for one thing, and it's also down to me to lay them all out in more peaceful postures than I found them.

Emotionally, this is tough. Once I have my colleagues all lined up together, everything feels like it's hitting me harder than ever.

But this is my cross to bear and I can't feel sorry for myself. I'm the only person in this Canteen who can make it home alive, by the stroke of sheer luck that I was in a sealed lab when all of this happened. *I'm* the lucky one.

I end up using a bundle of spare pillowcases I took from the dorms to cover everyone up. When this is done I grab some shelf-stable food from the breakfast buffet, since I never plan to come back in here again after I close the door and turn the temperature down.

I've covered Grainger's face, too. Disrespecting a corpse would only bring me down to his level, and I'm not stooping.

I did put him in the kitchen area away from the others, so that any retrieval crew who might come here will know right away which one he is. I also wouldn't want the surviving families of my dead colleagues to have to think about the killer lying right next to their loved ones.

With a difficult job finally done, I step back to the main doorway. Laika is still there as I pause briefly to take it all in.

"I feel like I should say something," I tell Mel.

She doesn't reply.

"Mel?"

"I'm here," she eventually says. "Sorry. I really couldn't watch. You've done more than anyone could ever expect, Ray. But if you want to say something, I'm here with you. I'll hear it."

I gaze upon the terrible scene before me.

I've been to three funerals in my whole life: Pops', my brother's, and my mother's. I was too young when my other grandparents died and I wouldn't have gone to Steve's if my own life depended on it. Not after how he treated the two of us.

What I'm saying is that I don't really know how these things are supposed to go.

All I can do is give it my best shot.

"Each of these men and women lived their lives in pursuit of scientific progress for the benefit of all mankind," I say. "They gave up comfortable lives on Earth to live and work on this station. These people, who represent the very best of humanity, died senselessly at the hands of an ideologically possessed cabal that sees only the worst in it. Their lives and their deaths will not be forgotten. May they rest in peace."

"May they rest in peace," Mel echoes. "Very touching, Ray. And you're right: these deaths *won't* be forgotten. This will not be forgiven."

50

When I'm finally set to head off to bed, Mel wisely reminds me to recharge Bex.

"See you tomorrow, buddy," I tell the robot. I securely connect her large battery pack to the wall outlet in Vinner's lab so she'll be ready to go again tomorrow. It's been a hell of a first day for our unlikely duo, that's for sure.

Laika has been following me since I left Barnet in the Canteen. His presence reminds me that at least some of Barnet's other animals aren't dead, either.

I can't do anything for them in the short term but I'll keep holding out hope that they might make it back to Earth at the same time as my dead colleagues.

The level of destruction down there has surely wiped out countless animals as well as people. I joked about his lab reminding me of Noah's ark, but Barnet's collection really might end up being an important genetic backup for what nature has lost.

I really have no idea how big the bunkers are and what they contain. In all honesty, I'm still just praying that they offered sufficient protection for the lucky few who made it down.

Mel's mention of an EMP attack, which would likely cripple whatever electrical infrastructure survived the earlier disasters, was just about the last thing I wanted to hear. I try not to think too much about this, telling myself again that an emergency government bunker should be resilient against all threats.

I can only hope.

But in a much bigger sense, my *main* hopes feel far more justified than they did before Bex smashed me into the Control Center and Mel answered my SOS call.

I'm not alone.

I have a ride back to Earth.

Things aren't going to be *easy*, but at least they're moving.

At least *I'll* soon be moving off this godforsaken station, right back down to Earth. Right back into Eva and Joe's arms to fulfill my promise that I'd be back at the end of my placement. Okay, I'll be a few days later than planned. I'm sure they'll forgive me.

Whenever things get overwhelming, I like to remember that I can't control the world but I can do my best to take care of my small part of it. That's harder than usual to bear in mind right now, but maybe it's truer than ever.

In a world of chaos, my family needs me and I most definitely need them. In four days we'll be back together and that's what counts most of all.

Believe me, I know how lucky we are that my family got a bunker invite. There is no way in any world I'm going to let that luck go to waste.

With a busy day ahead and hopefully a bunch of satellite and security camera-related breakthroughs to come, I know I'll want to get right to work as soon as I wake up. With that in mind I decide to grab a quick shower, my first in way too long, and even take a few minutes to shave my face.

It's only when I take my makeshift glasses off in the bathroom that I'm reminded how much of a difference they've been making. They're not perfect and I still sometimes find myself squinting to read small text, but let's just say that shaving with unaided vision is something of a challenge. More to the point, it's a challenge that reminds of how tough everything *else* would be if I hadn't thrown these ugly-looking things together.

When I'm done, I gather the rest of my stuff from my rapidly cooling room in the dorms. I'm taking it with me to where I'll be sleeping.

I put my glasses back on right away, along with the headset. The body-cam isn't so important now that I'm just walking to bed, but I reattach it anyway.

My "bed" for the night — and the next few — is actually going to be Commander Harrison's chair in the Control Center.

There are two reasons for this. The first is that I can't sleep in my dorm. Not when I'm turning that whole zone into a cool box.

The second, pulling me towards the Control Center over anywhere else, is that I want to stay instantly reachable.

Sure, the headset works fine, but I want to be able to see Mel if she calls and I want to be right beside the computer system if she needs me to do something.

I walk briskly back to the empty Control Center and position its chairs as comfortably as I can.

"I'm going to take the headset off while I sleep," I tell Mel. "I'll still hear you through the screen's speakers if you need to wake me up."

She nods. "Okay. But we won't wake you unless we *really* need to. You've done remarkably well to stay on top of things and get this far, Ray. But after so much sustained exertion, you really do need all the sleep you can get."

She's not wrong.

Last time I fell asleep I was inside my lab, stealing a few hours while my last sample of theocite was heating towards its enrichment point. I remember closing my eyes to dream of the difference my results could make to humanity, on Earth and even further afield.

This time, I'm only dreaming of one thing. All I want is to get back to Earth and reunite with the two people I live for.

As I sense myself drifting off and my thoughts start to

bypass the usual filters of doubt and hesitation, that reunion actually feels like a matter of time.

Thanks to Mel and her team, I have a real way home.

All I have to do is stay alive and do what they tell me.

And I've stayed alive all this time without them, I think to myself, drifting away at last.

How hard can a few more days be?

51

I guess if you divide it by the number of nights I should have slept but didn't, sixteen hours doesn't seem like *that* much.

Right?

It doesn't matter. I'm not on the clock like I was when the air supply was dwindling with every breath, and if anything I now have some time to kill.

Not too much, though, since there's still a lot I want to do in the three full days I have left until Mel's PetraVista station-cum-spacecraft arrives.

I feel like a new man when I open my eyes. It's like being genuinely thirsty — you don't know what tiredness is until you really get there, and even then it only comes into the sharpest focus when you finally manage to quench it.

The first thing I see is a new face on the screen.

I grab my makeshift glasses from the desk for a better look.

There we go: detail.

He's younger than Mel and probably not much older than me. Early 40s, if I had to guess.

"Pierre?" I ask, pushing myself up in the chair.

He grins widely and looks at the camera. "Ahhh, he really *is* alive! I was starting to question Commander Lomond's faculties."

Okay, sixteen hours is a long time. I get it.

I'm awake enough to remember that Commander Lomond is Mel, even though she only told me her surname once. I'm pretty good with names.

"Has Mel told you much?" I ask.

Pierre clicks an unseen mouse or trackpad to close whatever else he's been looking at, then shifts in his chair to focus squarely on me. "You've had quite the ordeal, Mr. Barclay," he says. "And from what I've heard, you've handled yourself quite remarkably."

"I've had some help," I say. It's not false modesty, I'm just not used to dealing with praise.

And I *have* had some help, even if it's come mainly from dead people and a robot.

I might be the last man standing, but without Yannick or Bex I'd be down and out by now.

"There's no "*I*" in team, Mr. Barclay, but there's been no team on The Beacon. You've done this alone."

"You can just call me Ray," I tell him. I can handle the back-slapping, at least for a few more minutes, but I don't like that kind of formality. If I was being an asshole I'd tell him that it's *Doctor* Barclay, but that's not my style, either. "And Mel said there's one thing that you in particular *can* help me with. You used to train pilots, right?"

A smile crosses his face. "Happiest days of my life,! And you'll be glad to hear that your Escape Pod practically flies itself. That doesn't mean we can't have some fun, though. You'll have to take off those fetching specs for the ride, I'm afraid, because a pressure suit is an absolute necessity and those things won't fit inside your helmet."

Good news and bad news, I think with a sigh, and the bad is a lot *badder* than the good is good.

Already, the very thought of flying blind is calling back the memories of the accident all over again.

"You good, my man?" Pierre asks.

263

I shake my thoughts away and force a nod. "Yeah. I'm, uh — yeah. I'm good. So you'll talk me through everything?"

"Whenever you want," he says. "Commander Lomond said you have a nice little camera and headset going so I can see exactly what you're looking at."

I nod. "Sure do. And I can show you the security camera footage of the Docking Bay now if you want to take a look at the Pod. I'm guessing it's never been used, so we might need to run some checks."

"No doubt," Pierre agrees. "But the best views I'll get will come when you're up close. If we're going to look at any images on your screen before that, I have a few better ideas than camera footage."

I'm all ears, naturally, and I listen intently as Pierre talks me through how to call up all of the satellite imagery The Beacon has access to.

There are a lot of political complications around access to meteorological and GPS satellites. To my mind the problems lie at the feet of stubborn leaders who resent Zola for spending money on space programs that their myopic worldview see as wasteful. Because of all that, we can't access any publicly funded satellites.

But despite the vast number of satellites we *can't* call upon, Pierre fills me in on how to access images from the TerraVista satellite fleet that ZolaCore launched a few years ago. Its main purpose was to scan Earth's surface — and oceans — for commercial mining opportunities.

Even though very little of this is public knowledge, I know for a fact that the site in the South Pacific where the first theocite deposits were discovered was identified by a TerraVista satellite. At first they didn't know what they'd found, just that it was a highly anomalous mineral deposit. The rest is history.

What I don't know until Pierre tells me is that *he* was the very analyst who spotted the anomaly in that location.

"Do you get the feeling it's not random chance that all this shit happened when it did?" he asks, sighing slowly. "Like that maybe the terrorists knew what you were working on and what Zola thought we could do with it?"

I purse my dry lips and blink away the last of my tiredness. "Pierre, I've been wrestling with that since I heard the terrorists' goal of stopping humanity from leaving Earth. I feel like if I hadn't published my thesis and hyped up the potential applications of the enriched fuel, maybe—"

"Try being the guy who found theocite in the first place," he interrupts. "It's not a competition, brother, but trust me: I know how you feel."

I've never understood the idea that misery loves company, or even that a problem shared is a problem halved. There's an undeniable feeling of a load being lifted from my shoulders right now, though — not because I think there's someone else to blame, but because there's someone else who can understand the guilt I'm feeling.

"You can tell me I shouldn't feel bad and I can tell you the same thing," he goes on, "but we're not going to believe each other. Turns out the road to hell really *is* paved with good intentions, huh?"

I thought the exact same thing yesterday and it's still hard to disagree.

"But what's the best thing to do when you're going through hell?" I ask.

Pierre nods, almost defiantly. "Keep going."

"Bingo. So what are these better ideas of what you want to see from the images?" I ask. "I can share anything you can help me get on this screen."

"Let's see Culpeper, Virginia and the area around the Colorado Springs airport for starters," Pierre says. "That's where you've heard there might be bunkers, correct?"

"There's no *might*," I reply. "And I could zoom in on Colorado Springs from a satellite image, but I don't even know where Culpeper is."

Pierre shakes his head. "That makes two of us. We'll start

with Colorado. We'll look at images from as many time inter-vals as we can. TerraVista is a big fleet so we'll have a lot to work with and we might even be able to see vehicle move-ments that point the way to the bunker. If we see confirmed signs of post-attack life in one location but not the other, we'll know where to land. If we see life in both places — or neither — we'll go where the nearby terrain looks most favorable and where the surrounding infrastructure looks most intact. Sound good?"

"My family is in Colorado," I say, point-blank.

"Okay," Pierre says, holding my eyes. "Then we know where we want to see the best signs…"

52

Pierre shows a lot of patience as he talks me through the mechanics of accessing the satellite imagery. Thanks to him, it doesn't take too long for me to get the hang of it.

Some of the icons and menu options we follow are less than intuitive, though, so I don't know how long it would have taken me to do this on my own. To be honest, I don't know if I could have done it at all.

Another benefit of finally having some human allies, I ponder with a smile.

Starting with a view of Colorado Springs, we cycle through various time intervals and are delighted to see that we have access to images from every few hours.

When I zoom in on the most recent, though, delight is the furthest thing from what I feel.

The streets of the city are utterly lifeless. Dust covers the ground, laying thick on the cars that sit abandoned at all kinds of angles.

Buildings are still standing and the only way I can describe the scene is that it looks like a powerful bomb just went off in the sky overhead.

"Wow," is all Pierre can say. "This happened *days* ago and it still looks like this. Ray, there's no one around. There's no one left."

"There are people alive in the bunkers!" I boom. I'm angry at the sight and those responsible rather than at Pierre, but I still take exception to his fatalistic comments.

"But where?" he asks. "Neither of us know and it's not like we can go online and search for rumors about this stuff. Huge projects like that usually leak out, it's just hard to separate the truth from the bullshit. Doesn't do us any good from here when we can't see the rumors, though."

Before those last words are even out of his mouth, I'm rooting through my bag and looking for my text-reader.

I pull it out and start tapping without wasting a second. "These things are supposed to let us read *any* book registered with the Library of Congress," I explain excitedly. "They're all stored locally on our servers. There have to be books about secret bunkers, right? Even just conspiracy stuff? Like you said, there can be nuggets of truth in those theories!"

When I glance up, Pierre is grinning like a Cheshire Cat. "We make a pretty good team, huh?"

My title search for "*secret bunkers*" brings up way more books than I know what to do with, so I filter these to include only entries which have the words "Colorado Springs" somewhere inside.

There are still more than twenty, so I pick the first one for starters:

Digging For Survival: The Secret History of American Fallout Bunkers.

"Cheyenne Mountain Nuclear Bunker," I read aloud as soon as the book opens to the appropriate page. "Woah... Pierre, I recognize the entrance of this place from movies. Look!"

I grab the body-cam and point it at the page so Pierre can see. The text goes on to say that the bunker, which once served as NORAD's headquarters, is no longer considered viable.

"That's what they *would* say," Pierre contends. "And the best place to build a new modern bunker is where you already have a defunct one from the 60s. Plausible deniability, you know?"

I like the way he thinks and I can see some sense in it. I find a few more names of Colorado-based bunkers, some rumored and some real. All are described as having a considerably smaller footprint than Cheyenne Mountain.

Pierre tells me how to send all my full-resolution satellite images his way via the radio. This will let him look closely for the all important differences across time — the differences that might indicate signs of life and maybe even some movement around the bunkers we're looking for.

I repeat my research process with Culpeper, Virginia in place of Colorado Springs.

This time Pierre sees the results as soon as I do, thanks to the way I've positioned the body-cam.

"No way," he chuckles. "*Again?*"

I'm smiling, too. Because just like in Colorado Springs, the first result for Culpeper is about a government complex that *definitely* exists and is rumored to have been greatly expanded since being officially decommissioned.

This time we're looking at Mount Pony. A shielded facility was apparently constructed here in the 1960s as a place for the Federal Reserve to store emergency cash reserves in case a Soviet nuclear attack decimated the national economy.

It was also a designated "continuity of government" site, which really has my hopes climbing. After all, I've been assuming President Williams was evacuated to the Virginia bunker ever since I saw him being bundled into Marine One. This fits perfectly with that.

"I'm even more sure *this* one is right," I say. "Neither of us have even heard of Culpeper, and now it turns out there's a Cold War bunker that was fit to house the government in the event of an attack? And it's, what, 50 miles from DC? That's too neat and tidy not to be our answer. It has to be."

Pierre is still smiling. "Get me some images with this bunker in the middle and I'll do the rest."

As I call up the Culpeper images, following every instruction Pierre gives, the scene on the ground looks similar to how it did in Colorado. The streets are empty and dusty — so, *so* dusty — but all of the buildings I can see are intact.

We're looking inland here, well away from tsunami danger and well away from any of the main fault-lines. Pierre hasn't asked to see the coasts and I think I know why. We both know the score and we both know where we have to aim.

I'm hoping beyond hope that his expert analysis will reveal undeniable signs of life around both of the locations we've identified.

"That's the images all safely received," he confirms. "I could have Commander Lomond take a look at these now while we do a walkthrough of the Pod, if you like? Or she can be here for that, too, and we could all look at these images later."

I nod. "I'd rather Mel was here, too. I have a… well… I can have certain reactions to certain kinds of stress, in very specific circumstances. It happened last night. I'm not saying *you* couldn't help me with —"

"Say no more, my brother," Pierre says. "She does have a calming way about her. It's almost time for her to wake up for her Command shift, anyway, and she'll be delighted to see you looking so fresh — let alone to hear what we've found already."

"Thanks," I say.

"Sure. So yeah… you could head over to the Pod now if you like, just as long as you bring the camera and headset. Or you can grab a quick bite to eat. You know, whatever you're feeling. We'll be ready for a walkthrough in five minutes."

"Sounds good," I say, standing up to stretch my legs. I'll eat some seeds as I walk, I figure. That might even tempt Laika out of his sleeping place in Barnet's lab.

Something hits my mind just after I stand. I quickly sit back down.

"Hold on, Pierre," I blurt out.

"Uh, yeah?" he asks, either confused or concerned by my sudden return. It's hard to read his face.

"When I launch in the Escape Pod, can I bring my macaw? He won't be any trouble for you guys."

Pierre chuckles loudly. "Brother, if you can get a parrot into a pressure suit, we've got space for one more."

53

As I approach the Docking Bay, Mel does a very attentive and admirable job of trying to keep me calm.

I almost feel embarrassed by how hard she's trying with her gentle, borderline hypnotic comments. I don't say anything to interrupt, though, because I know she's going out of her way in an effort to make me feel comfortable.

She was there last night when I had the closest thing to a panic attack I've had for over a decade, so I guess from her perspective she could be thinking I have them all the time.

There's also the point that I lost control of my breathing when we were only *talking* about the Escape Pod, while right now she knows I'm about to *climb inside* it.

The truth is, after what Pierre and I just learned about the bunkers, I already feel a pretty steady level of calm.

He hasn't analyzed the differences across time between satellite images yet, but we both feel ninety-nine percent certain that we've nailed down the location of the Culpeper bunker. I also have faith in him to find out whether my family is at Cheyenne Mountain or somewhere else near Colorado Springs.

We've even spoken for a few seconds about the different

logistics of landing near some of the possible locations, which makes it all feel so much more tangible than it did yesterday.

That's where my relative serenity is coming from, I think, even as the Docking Bay's door comes into sight.

Launching myself into space inside a tiny Escape Pod now feels like more than a way off the station. It feels like the first step on a mapped-out road back to Eva and Joe. There might not be a big difference there in operational terms, but the psychological difference is huge.

I don't have to worry about fingertips or codes or even robot wrecking balls to pass the Docking Bay's door. That's the magic of the Control Center and Commander-level access to a computer system that lets me disable security locks wherever I want.

Almost wherever I want, at least.

The offshoot labs, because they were staffed by visiting researchers like me instead of ZolaCore employees, are different from everywhere else in *that* way as well as all the others.

Just like there are no security cameras inside and just like they'll automatically detach from the station if any explosions or other dangerous atmospheric changes are detected, the offshoot labs' entry systems are out of the station Commanders' hands.

As I enter the Docking Bay, the surroundings aren't as awe-inspiring as they might sound.

It's a closed room, for one thing, with a large airlock that will open only once a launch procedure is initiated. There are no views of Earth here like there are in the Control Center and Observation Deck, but in the current circumstances I suppose that's more of a selling point than a drawback.

I feel almost like I'm in the Maintenance Bay again, and maybe the clue should have been in that word: Bay. The walls are all light and clean, as slick as anyone would expect, but there's not a lot of character in here.

This entire area feels like an afterthought in relation to the rest of the station's grandeur. When I get my first glance of the Escape Pod, I start to feel like afterthought really is the word.

Seriously… it's like looking at the "before" picture from a renovation-based reality show, when someone buys a rickety old car to turn it into something worth driving.

And forget its worth… right now, I'd settle for this thing being capable of traveling.

"It doesn't even look as good as it did in the pictures," I say.

"No," Mel replies candidly. "The pictures you'll have seen in early footage from the station were probably from the original configuration. The upper section used to house a parafoil landing system but that was removed around eighteen months ago. That's when the Pod was written off as a descent-worthy craft capable of splashing down in the ocean. It was an insurance-related decision. As you know, it can now only be intercepted and docked onto a larger craft or station, like ours."

I walk up to the Pod and tap the side, half expecting it to fall apart. "Why would they take out such a basic safety feature? Surely it had more of a chance with the parafoil than without it?"

"Updated simulations show that it had no chance either way," Mel replies. "Anyone who splashed down in that thing would have been killed, Ray. I think the insurers' logic was that without the illusion of a chance, no one would try and thus no one would die."

There's no point in arguing about this with Mel. I can sense in her voice that she probably agrees with my view, anyway.

"So, Pierre…" I go on. "Talk to me. What do I have to do?"

"Well, you'll be wearing a suit and helmet," he says, "but for now you can go ahead and climb in to see what you'll be dealing with."

I follow his instruction and step into the Escape Pod.

My first reaction, surprising myself, is that it's not as tight as I imagined.

Don't get me wrong: my knees are practically touching my

chin. But this thing is *very* efficiently designed. It almost worries me how thin the walls must be to allow this much interior space within such a small Pod, and I guess that's why there's no chance of it surviving any kind of landing or splashdown.

"You also won't be able to wear your glasses during the flight, but you can leave those on for now, too," Mel chimes in.

I was planning to, since I'm already struggling to make out some of the small writing on the controls and the screen.

Without my adapted goggles, I'd be lost. We'll figure something out though, even if it's a color-coded sticker system so I can press the buttons I need to at the times Pierre tells me to.

"You'll only need to touch any of the lower control section in case of an emergency," he continues. "All being well, you'll set your course before leaving and then initiate the launch. You shouldn't have to touch a single thing after that."

Wow... I like the sound of this plan more than I expected.

"And what actually happens?" I ask. "Does the Pod actively propel itself to a calculated interception point, or do I just have to launch it and let the PetraVista do the intercepting?"

"Somewhere in between," Pierre explains. "You set a course, but The Pod and the PetraVista will both adapt their positions if necessary. The two guidance systems will recognize each other and do all the calculations for us. You and Commander Lomond can step in with minor adjustments if anything unexpected occurs or if something doesn't go as planned, but there is actually very little danger in this procedure. You can't miss us and we can't miss you, Ray. Not in any way that won't be easily rectified."

I nod slowly. True confidence in the plan is still a long way away, but so is crippling anxiety. Mel and Pierre are winning in their efforts to ease my mind.

"We're going to be extremely close by the time you launch," Pierre goes on, "and you're going to be moving pretty slowly. It will only take a matter of minutes from start to finish and I think you'll be surprised to find how comfortably those minutes pass. The sensations you endured during some of your training sessions are far more intense than anything you'll face in that Pod, brother. Believe me on that."

"Thanks, guys," I say, exhaling slowly. "I really do feel better. Pierre, do you want me to show you anything up close like you mentioned earlier? Are there any parts you want to check over more than the rest?"

"We'll do a full dummy run with the suit and without your glasses soon," he replies. "I'll make a checklist in the meantime. It'll be easier if you have the camera beyond arm's length for some of the views I'll need, so it would be good if you could engineer some kind of tripod. Until then... I think we're good. We'll keep running over these satellite images and you can relax, brother. Maybe start gathering the data in your lab, and anything else you want to bring that's small enough for the Pod."

Wow. Thinking about what I'll be able to pack for the journey *really* does make it all feel tangible and imminent.

"Sounds good," I tell them. "I know what I'm going to do today, though. I feel like there's a missing piece of the puzzle that could tie everything together. Now that I have the robot to smash my way in, I'm going to check out the last offshoot lab and—"

"No," Mel interrupts.

And she doesn't just *say* no — she positively yells it.

I don't say anything. I don't know *what* to say.

"Ray..." she goes on, seemingly choosing her words carefully, "there's something we have to tell you. It'll be easier to discuss this when you can see us, too. Come back to the Control Center and we'll talk. Okay?"

I'm on the way before she even finishes asking.

54

I walk back to the Control Center with an uncomfortable feeling of confusion flowing through me.

As soon as I raised the idea of going into the final locked lab, Mel shot it down like I'd suggested setting myself on fire.

These guys are on my side and they're coming to save me, but for the first time I start to think there might be more going on here than I thought.

After all, they work directly for ZolaCore on a publicly undisclosed station. They know a lot more about my work than I do about theirs.

They knew what I was doing in my lab without me having to tell them, and I'm really starting to think they might know what was going on in the other one.

There could be something in there I'm not supposed to see — something *no one* outside of Zola's narrower circle of trust is supposed to see. That prospect only makes me more curious to find out what the something might be.

I sit in front of the screen, ready for some answers.

"You need to be very careful here, Ray," Mel says. "High-clearance ZolaCore offices on Earth have security systems that have *killed* people. You must know that, don't you?"

I gulp. I do know.

A cleaner was once killed by a security system she didn't know about. Rumor has it that the legal fallout was one of the reasons Zola moved all of his operations outside North America — too much scrutiny.

We're not just talking about lock-in alarm systems, either. We're talking honest-to-God booby traps.

The poor woman I remember reading about tripped a laser-based detection system and suffered a laser-based death. I don't want to remind myself of much more detail than that.

"The headline here is that ZolaCore's permanent employees stick rigidly to their permitted areas for a reason," Mel goes on. "I'm amazed you've made it this long, Ray, what with all that sneaking through doors with biometrics and wrecking balls. That almost makes me think Grainger was able to disable the most stringent security measures, but we can't take that for granted."

This is the first time I'm seeing Mel and Pierre next to each other at the same time.

The other screen shows the visualization of our radio link.

It's not immediately obvious that they've gotten closer since last night, because the radio latency was already minimal and their visualization dot is still on the far right while mine is still touching Earth on the far left.

All I have to go on is the visual scale. That *does* show me that they've gotten considerably closer, because Earth takes up a lot more real estate than it did.

Eventually they're going to come close enough that a small gap will appear again between my dot and Earth.

I don't know how close they'll actually get before they instruct me to launch for the interception, but Pierre said it was pretty damn close.

I look at their faces and see concern. I'm almost certain these are expressions of concern *for* me, rather than *about* me, but I don't want to rely on any assumptions.

"Do you know what's in the last lab?" I ask, spitting it out in the plainest terms I can.

"No," Mel says. "We *don't*, Ray, and that's the point. We knew what you were working on — only the details were any kind of secret — and we knew about Vinner, too. We didn't know about the animals you mentioned, or who might be in the fourth offshoot lab. Sometimes one of the labs is empty for reconfiguration work ahead of the next visitor's arrival. For all we know, someone could have been scheduled to arrive tomorrow on the craft that would have taken you home."

Hmm... I guess there's some logic in that.

"I'm with her on this one, brother," Pierre says.

Mel nods. "Ray, there was either no one in that lab, or there was someone even *Grainger* didn't know about. According to the checklist and the document you mentioned, anyway. This is a guy who infiltrated Zola's flagship station and wiped out the whole crew except for you. His people obviously had access to all kinds of systems and probably had moles in New Zealand. If there was someone in there, there would have to be a reason *no one* knew. It would have to be something so especially dangerous that Zola kept it even closer to his chest than your work. Something so dangerous, you *definitely* don't want to walk into it."

"Like what, though?" I ask. "*My* work was deemed too dangerous for Earth — that's why I'm up here — but some people still knew about it. What kind of thing do you think would be even more dangerous? Research into pathogens? Weaponry? None of those things make sense for ZolaCore. I don't know why you'd assume the danger level is why something would be beyond top-secret. Maybe it's AI research, or next-level bionics? You know, the kinds of things Zola has always been obsessed by."

Pierre scratches his chin, deep in thought.

"What?" I ask him.

He takes a slow breath. "Well, the other possibility is that Grainger did know what was going on in there. He was identified as a traitor because the terrorists who went on TV had financial links to him. When investigators on Earth dug into his background they found the deep alias he's been using, and from there they managed to trace him to The Beacon. But that investigation only had a few hours to run before everything went to hell, brother. We don't know if he was acting alone. There could have been someone else who the investigators didn't ID in time."

I feel my heart thumping faster than ever. He's right. And it might go further than that.

"Pierre…" I say. "What if there still *is* someone else? The offshoot labs are totally sealed. There could—"

"Get onto the heat signatures right now," Pierre interrupts. "Do exactly what we say and we can figure this out before it's too late. And if we see something we don't want to see, under *no* circumstances do you storm into that lab like an action hero, okay? We've lost everyone else… we're not losing you, too."

I nod dumbly.

If the heat signatures we're looking for tell us there's someone alive in the fourth lab, there's no way I can go in.

Sure, it could be an innocent researcher who happened to survive, just like I did. But surely Grainger would have known about them, just like he knew about me.

To stick with Pierre's action hero terminology, there's way more chance that a secret survivor is going to be another bad guy lying in wait than there is that they'll be a damsel in distress.

Mel is leaning back and covering her mouth with her hands, clearly running through the same feelings as me.

Pierre, for his part, is keeping it practical and focusing on a next move that makes sense.

He talks me through accessing a new menu option, which he says should bring up a top-down diagram of the whole station with heat signatures showing everyone who's alive.

"He mentioned a parrot," Mel says to Pierre, finally taking her hands from her mouth. "Will that show up? Just so we don't panic if we see two signs of life."

"I think so," he replies, before getting right back to the step-by-step instructions. He's able to see everything on my screen, which makes it a lot easier than if I had to relay what I'm seeing at each step.

I pause with my finger over the option that will bring the heat signatures into view. Everything could change in the next few seconds.

I never wanted to be the last man standing… until now.

All things considered, I *really* don't want to find out that someone else is alive on this station.

The rational part of my brain can't figure out a reason that there would be someone else. I mean, what would they be waiting for? What would they be hiding from? Needless to say, that doesn't stop me from holding my breath and praying for the best as I tap the button.

I close my eyes and wait for Mel or Pierre to react.

"What the *hell*?" Pierre booms.

My eyes open in an instant, reacting to the least welcome tone I could have imagined.

But as my eyes scan the screen, I breathe a huge sigh of relief. There's nothing to worry about.

"Those are Barnet's animals," I explain, staring at the admittedly weird-looking concentration of small yellow circles in one of the offshoot labs.

The only other two circles are in here and in the Greenhouse — one for me, one for Laika.

I hear deep sighs of relief from Mel and Pierre as soon as I explain.

"And this shows us that life signatures *are* detectable in the offshoot labs," Mel says with an assured nod. "So we can at least rest easy on that."

I exhale slowly.

Okay, so there's no one in there. But the curious part of my mind feels like the fact there *might* have been strengthens the reasons for finding out what *is* in there.

I hear what Pierre and Mel are saying about security

systems and traps, because those really are major considerations when we're talking about ZolaCore.

I wasn't even thinking about any of that stuff when I was desperately looking for a way to contact Earth — or other survivors on a faraway station, as it turned out — and no security systems have bitten me on the ass yet.

Granted, the consideration has changed now that I'm safe and will have a ride home in just a few days. But that's not the only consideration here.

An offshoot lab on The Beacon isn't the same as a high-security office in a ZolaCore building on Earth.

By their very nature, these labs house visiting researchers for time-limited stays. How could any crazy security systems be in place without all of the researchers knowing? And even if those systems are only used to guard certain kinds of research, how could they be put in place and maintained without word getting out among the station's tight-knit staff?

Besides all that, though, why would anything so intense *need* to be in place? Each of the offshoot labs has two sealed doors, one at either end of a long closed walkway. There's no way through either door without biometric access.

Okay… I've kind of disproven that point, since Bex can now take me wherever I please.

But the station has a huge inherent security advantage over an Earth-based office, in that no one can get up here without being thoroughly vetted. Admittedly Grainger beat the system by spending *years* living under a very well developed alias, but that doesn't change the core point.

Ninety-nine percent of the work to keep a space station safe happens on the ground, in terms of whoever is and isn't granted access. There aren't going to be any lasers or toxic fumes ready to halt an unauthorized lab entrant in their tracks. It just doesn't make sense.

"Don't tell me you still want to go in?" Pierre asks, reading my face.

I say nothing.

Pierre chuckles. "You've got some balls on you, brother. I'll give you that."

"Let's just trace Grainger's movements," Mel suggests, not seeing the funny side of anything. "Pierre, why don't you go back to your work station and focus on the satellite images around the bunkers?"

She writes something down on a piece of paper and slides it to him.

"This is the clearance we'll need to land," she goes on, tapping the paper. "Find a landing site this size, as close as possible to wherever you find the clearest signs of life. It's smaller than the official guidelines allow — a lot smaller — but the guidelines weren't written for this. If we have to land in an urban area, this is the minimum amount of clearance I'm willing to give you. This is what I think we need, with emphasis on the *need*. I know you'll *want* more."

Pierre, who I know by now is an expert pilot who spent many years as an elite instructor, looks very uneasy as he stares at the paper.

"Can you do it?" Mel asks.

"I *can*…" he replies, sounding sure of his ability but uncertain about the wisdom of the order.

Mel nods then turns back to the camera. "All I needed to hear. Okay then, Ray, let's see exactly what Grainger was up to, shall we?"

Great.

Just when we confirm there's no one hiding in the fourth offshoot lab to ease my fears on that, and just after I start to feel almost okay with the Escape Pod procedures, Mel introduces a concern about our ultimate landing point on Earth.

She glosses over it, but I saw Pierre's unease.

"This will show us if Grainger really was acting alone," Mel goes on, now totally focused on the footage. "I certainly hope he was, but I wouldn't count any chickens just yet."

I think about the other people on the station who knew what kind of work I was doing. Other than the two Commanders I found dead in this Control Center, I can only really think of Yannick and Justin.

Those guys were my friends. The idea of either of them being in cahoots with Grainger makes me shiver, adding another horrible layer to all of this.

It doesn't make sense, though... does it?

Yannick died under a vending machine, so I think I can safely rule out the possibility that he knew anything about what was going to happen.

But Justin?

Justin was right outside my lab.

He was actually in the walkway — past the first door and almost all the way to the second.

I try to stop my runaway thoughts. What if he was in on the attack and thought some pills would make him immune, like Grainger did? What if he was desperately trying to reach my lab for breathable air because the pills didn't work?

Or even worse... what if he wanted to expose *me* to the air, so there would be no loose ends?

I hate these thoughts and I'm glad that Mel is going to help me run through the security camera footage so I can put them to bed, one way or the other.

Before I get home to Earth, I *have* to find out exactly what was going on here.

And on that front, our next few minutes are going to be the most telling so far.

55

The Beacon's security camera system is good. Almost *scarily* good.

Mel doesn't have any direct experience with it, but she's able to guide me through some of the controls thanks to her familiarity with the general infrastructure of ZolaCore's computer systems.

Even while I've been on the station, I've always worked within the university's software infrastructure. There are a lot of differences between the core GUIs. So although I might have been able to figure out most of it by myself, Mel's help saves me a huge amount of time.

What saves us both a whole lot *more* time is a particular feature of the security system: its tracking technology.

I guess I shouldn't be surprised to learn that state-of-the-art facial recognition software has been tracking everyone on The Beacon since long before I arrived. I at least had some privacy in the lab, which is the only thing stopping me from feeling totally violated right now.

By identifying individuals in real-time, the system is able to produce heat-maps of their most visited locations and to provide "associative information" on which other station-dwellers they've spent the most time with.

Straight away, an all-time heat map shows us that Grainger spent the vast majority of his time in three places: the dorms, the Canteen, and the Maintenance Bay.

He was deep undercover as a maintenance worker for several years, Mel explains. The financial links between Grainger and the terrorists who appeared on TV led to analysis of his own accounts, too, with recent savings deposits strengthening the suspicion that he thought he was going to survive. He must have thought he was going to make it.

"Make it to what?" is the question I can't square off, since Earth is in ruins and it doesn't seem like there was any real chance of someone ever coming to bring him home.

Unless Grainger had no idea of the extent of what was to come, I muse.

He didn't know he was going to die, so I guess it makes sense to think he may have thought the station was the only target of the group's long-planned attack.

In any event, it quickly emerges that his most frequent associates were his immediate colleagues in the Maintenance Bay. He spent a broadly equal amount of time in close contact with each of them, indicating no suspicious activity or close relationships.

We can and will dive a *lot* deeper, of course, but the speed at which the system is giving us this useful overview is pretty damn incredible.

As I look at Grainger's full associates list, I'm slightly concerned to see Yannick quite near the top.

I select both of them, which brings up literally dozens of thumbnails showing the times they've been together in the past month.

We could jump even further back in time if we wanted to, but this is more than enough. I change the time frame to a week, which makes the thumbnails larger. What I see eases my mind. In all of the most recent instances when the two of them were together, it was around the chess board in the Canteen.

"What an absolute sociopath that guy was," I mutter.

How could Grainger hang around with Yannick and the rest of his chess buddies like he was one of them, smiling and joking... all while planning to kill them?

It makes me sick.

I feel bad to have doubted Yannick for even a second. He was the best friend I had here and nothing was ever too much trouble. I'm sure he would understand that stress and confusion make the brain go to crazy places, though, so I can't beat myself up for considering all angles.

Speaking of which...

After Yannick, I switch to Justin. He wasn't a chess man and never had any call to visit the Maintenance Bay, so there are reassuringly few interactions between him and Grainger.

I click into the most recent two clips and play the footage. Each is just a few seconds long, featuring nothing more than a quick exchange of pleasantries as they pass each other.

The first time they're in the hallway outside of the Maintenance Bay, and the second time they're standing at the Canteen's breakfast buffet.

While I'm thinking about Justin, I remove Grainger from the search filter for a moment so that I can see what happened right before Justin died at my walkway's inner door.

It doesn't take long to find the precise piece of footage I need. The labs have no cameras and it turns out that the walkways are equally dead zones, but I still see enough to tell me what was going on.

The footage begins with the entire hallway as a scene of desperate panic while people try to cover their mouths and some of them fight a losing and ill-considered battle against the airlocks.

Justin was walking to the nearby dorms when the attack hit, but this footage shows him changing course for my walkway as soon as he realizes something's wrong.

I sit up dead straight, covering my mouth in uncomfortable thought.

There's no alarm blaring in the footage, but I wish there

was. At least that would cover the piercing screams of my dying colleagues.

I watch Justin press his finger against the reader and open the door, making use of his full authorization as my assigned supervisor.

His every move is frantic, covering his mouth with his left hand while he unlocks the door with his right.

He moves out of sight before long, even once the system automatically switches camera feeds to show us a few seconds of him sprinting along my walkway.

In those few seconds that I hear him, Justin's pained voice was close enough to the camera to rise over the others.

"Ray!" he bellows.

He knew better than anyone that I couldn't hear a thing with my door closed, but I know from personal experience that the mind loses sight of things in moments of chaos.

"We've been attacked," he roars, coughing and gasping as his lungs fight the toxin. "You have to detach the lab! Burn something to set it off. You have emergency supplies. Save yourself, Ray! Save the research!"

Just as most of the other screams begin to fade, Justin's does, too. And believe me: the deathly silence is even worse than the hellish panic.

It probably goes without saying that I now feel even worse for doubting Justin than I did for doubting Yannick.

Justin spent his last moments trying to warn me of what was happening. He was trying to tell me to engage my lab's emergency detachment procedure.

"You choose your friends well," Mel says as the silence settles.

I say nothing. I don't know what to say.

"All of this footage is in the black box," she goes on. "You should be able to take that in the Pod and then we can look over every minute of footage from every inch of that station. The box is actually orange, like all flight recorders, but the old names stick. For now I think we should just get to Grainger's final movements, then maybe think about getting all your research findings onto this system so you don't have to fit your computer onto the Pod. It's already going to be a tight squeeze."

I nod at this. It makes sense, so long as I can be absolutely sure everything is transferred. I can transfer most of it to my phone, too, apart from the stuff that's only saved in the specialized software, and I can take backup photos of anything I *can't* port between the systems.

We switch back to Grainger and navigate to just before he sets off the attack in the Canteen. I want to see what he did right before that, though, so I keep skipping back until something stands out.

And when it does... oh boy, it *really* does.

"Hmmmm," Mel utters, biting her lip in concern.

I'm too shocked and intrigued to even make that much sound.

Because in a recording from just two minutes before he entered the Canteen for the last time, we see Grainger emerging shiftily from the fourth lab's walkway.

His hands are empty. Crucially to my mind, he's wearing no protective equipment. Not even the gloves.

"What the hell was he doing in there?" Mel asks. "And how the hell did he get in?"

I skip back and see that Grainger only spent two minutes in the lab. His hands are equally empty when he arrives... at least until he lifts his phone from his pocket, performs some touch gestures on the screen and finally holds it against the fingerprint scanner.

To my disbelief — and Mel's too, judging by her gasp — his phone somehow unlocks the door.

"It can't be a print of someone's finger," Mel muses. "It doesn't work like that, does it? It's touch-based."

I shrug, utterly confounded. "He must have had some kind

of software or maybe a signal that interfered with the lock. Maybe he gained access to some of the security infrastructure from the Maintenance Bay?"

Neither of us have the answers.

There were no other app shortcuts on Grainger's phone and frustratingly his body is blocking the camera angle that could have shown us exactly what he did.

Still, I'll hold his phone against that scanner soon to try to get into the lab, even if it's more in hope than expectation. Any chance is better than none.

A quick "person plus location" search of the system brings up no other instances of Grainger ever entering the fourth lab. Apart from on the one occasion we've just witnessed, he has never been within the viewing angle of the camera that faces its walkway.

I quickly remove Grainger from the search, leaving only the location filter. Intriguingly, I see that *no one* entered that lab for at least a month before he did.

My intrigue grows as I include a wider time range. No one else has entered in the past *year*.

I don't even know where to start speculating about what that might mean.

"Ray, what was he *doing* in there?" Mel asks again. I think the repetition emphasizes her desperate confusion more than any belief I might actually have the slightest idea.

I don't… but I do know the only way to find out.

"Grainger got in and out without any problems," I say, thinking out loud.

Mel inhales deeply. Pierre appears beside her again, watching on in silent shock.

Surely the kinds of traps they were worried about would have gotten Grainger if they existed, I figure. And as far as I'm concerned, that takes away the only real argument against my desire to get to the bottom of this.

"Just be careful," Mel says, resigned to what I'm going to do.

Pierre visibly gulps then forces a nod. "Godspeed, brother."

I rise to my feet and take a deep breath.

Well, Ray, I think to myself. *I guess it's time to look underneath the last rock this place has left.*

56

It's not long since Mel and Pierre were urgently warning me against entering the fourth lab, but what we've just seen has changed the equation in more ways than one.

Seeing Grainger's last-minute entry to the lab has increased two things: my confidence that it's physically safe to enter, and my burning need to know what's in there.

I'm not taking this lightly. I heard their points earlier and I'm not going to take any reckless risks when I'm so close to getting home.

That's the big difference between now and all the times I charged through doorways as soon as I could. The only reason it wasn't reckless to charge in blind earlier was that I *had* to try to find some way to survive, whatever it took.

Now? I'm no longer blind. I know Grainger went in and came out of that lab without any protective equipment.

I'm the only person who can find out what's in there — not just now, but maybe *ever*. Who knows what's left on Earth and whether a launchable space craft will be able to come anytime soon?

A lack of human caretakers could see the whole station deteriorate and ultimately burn up as it falls back to Earth, taking with it all evidence of what's happened here.

That's what's driving me forward most of all. It's not just curiosity, because no amount of that could push me into any level of risk now that a reunion with my family is on the cards in just a few more days.

No. This isn't about curiosity, it's about *responsibility*.

I'm here and I can find exactly what Grainger was up to. And now the footage has given me a strong reason to think I can do so safely, can equals must.

There's no telling what I might find in there. There's no telling what I might learn. The missing puzzle piece in our understanding of the terrorists' plans and motives could be lying in wait.

There could even be something that helps us identify and catch any potential survivors from the evil group, reducing the chance of them being able to do anything else in the future.

As I think through all the arguments for going into the lab, that one feels like the strongest. Looking at what they've done to Earth makes it hard to imagine that things could ever get worse, but the past few days have taught me that's a dangerous assumption to make.

I've felt uncomfortable about the part my work might have played in everything ever since Pierre put the idea in my mind that the terrorists might have targeted theocite deposits to deliver their grand-scale destruction. Particularly given Vinner's documents that show just how much theocite has been discovered, I know what kind of damage an attack like that could do.

So if the terrorists *are* still around, I'm absolutely determined to do whatever it takes to make sure they go down for this. And whether or not they did target theocite deposits for their so-called coup de grace, I have to make sure no one can ever do that in the future.

At the entrance to the mystery lab's walkway, I hold Grainger's phone to the scanner. Nothing happens.

I swipe and gesture on the screen to no avail, hoping to trigger something.

"I guess that would have been too easy," Pierre sighs.

"Worth a shot," I reply.

I'm not too downhearted, though. Getting in so easily would have been a bonus. All that counts is getting it.

My mind retains hope but my body feels heavy as I walk to Vinner's lab to get Bex. This fourth lab is the only place I still need her to smash our way into. She already did the hard work of opening up the Control Center, from where I've been able to remove security locks from every other door on the station.

"Maybe take that drill," Pierre suggests when I reach Bex. I'm wearing the body-cam and headset so I can stay in touch with them.

"Instead of the wrecking ball?" I ask.

"I'd go with both," Mel chimes in. "You're not going to need the dexterity of a hand. If the sealed doors are too strong for the ball, you might still get through with the drill. We could talk you through how to use it."

I look at the size and sharpness of the drill — it's more of a borer, really — and quickly rule it out.

"I'll try the ball first," I tell them.

No way in hell do I want that drill swinging around under the inexperienced control of a newbie like me.

I've also felt the power of the wrecking ball at the end of Bex's incredibly strong arm, so I don't share their doubts that it'll work.

I grab Bex's remote control and guide her towards the locked lab. It's a long way, first along Vinner's walkway and then across a good portion of the station.

By the time we arrive, little Laika has popped out of the Greenhouse to see what's happening.

"Hey buddy," I say.

"Ray Ray?" he squawks back. I don't *know* that there's a question in there, but his unusual intonation makes it sound like there is.

The bird looks at the robot, as if trying to make sense of it.

Bex *is* a weird-looking thing, to be sure.

It's obvious to me that her creators spent a *lot* more time making her strong and dexterous than human-looking. There's no danger of uncanny valley here, when a robot starts to look human enough that it makes people uneasy. Bex's face is like a low-effort mannequin painted silver, but it's what's on the inside that counts.

As I stare at the doorway to the fourth lab, it really *is* what's on the inside the counts.

"Here goes nothing," I say, positioning Bex and then putting on my glove to control her wrecking ball. "Laika, stay back, okay? Back."

"Good luck, brother," Pierre says.

Mel says nothing. In my mind, I wonder if she wishes she *wasn't* counting on the guy who's talking to a parrot about a robot after giving both of them names.

With the biggest and fastest swing I can muster, I direct Bex's wrecking-ball fist to the edge of the door.

I hear a hiss immediately — good news — but it doesn't open all the way.

I punch again, three more times.

The door eventually buckles under the force, clearing my way.

"That a girl," I grin.

"Tyrannosaurus Bex," Pierre quips.

I hear Mel groan at the pun before breaking into a chuckle.

I switch to controlling Bex's left hand, which *is* a hand, and use it to grip what's left of the heavy door. She pushes it all the way down to let us through.

Once our path is clear, I take off the glove and use the remote control to march her along the walkway.

To my surprise, Laika not only follows us but flies up ahead.

I can see from here that the inner door is definitely closed, so he's not flying towards anything in particular. There could be a scent that's attracting him, or it might just be the novelty of a new place for the poor guy to spread his wings.

I don't even know if Laika has ever seen the sky. Part of me thinks it's probably better if he hasn't, since they say you can't miss what you don't know. All I know is I'm not leaving this station without him and he'll be by my side when we finally touch down on Earth.

"Squawk," he calls. "Ray Ray."

"We're coming," I say, my pace constrained by Bex's. She's not overly slow by any means, especially considering the power she's packing, but she's definitely not going to be winning any robot derbies.

"Ray Ray! No-kay!" Laika calls again. There's no question-like inflection here. His tone sounds a lot less happy than usual.

And "*no-kay*?"

Is that Laika's way of saying that something's not okay?

All of a sudden he starts flapping towards me, back the way we've just come.

"No-kay! No-kay!" the frightened bird squawks as he goes.

The moment I turn around to see why, I set off running just as fast.

Oh, shit.

I was wrong.

I was wrong to think it was safe.

They were right.

They were right in the first place when they warned me about security traps.

Because between my current position and the outer door Bex just smashed down, I see a new metal barrier silently sliding downwards from the ceiling.

I'm around halfway down the walkway. The barrier is lowering from a ceiling recess very near the broken door to the main station.

I sprint like I've never sprinted in my life, yelling as the painkiller-managed EVA injury in my leg comes roaring back at the worst possible time. The exertion brings unbearable pain but I push ahead like my life depends on it.

For all I know, it really does.

This barrier could be even thicker than the door, and without the drill I decided to leave behind Bex might not be able to destroy it. Rely on that isn't a risk I can take.

I don't even know how much battery power she has or how much those four massive swings I threw at the door will have taken out of her reserves.

All I know is that I have to make it out of this walkway before the barrier drops.

It's barely a foot off the ground when I get within diving distance, and still dropping. I slide in desperation, bringing the pain to all new levels as my weight lands on the injured leg.

My body makes it underneath — just — but the sliding motion knocks Bex's remote from my hand. She hasn't made it, either. It's just me and—

No no no no no.

Laika… he's not here.

"Laika!" I yell.

"Ray Ray?" he squawks back… from the wrong side of the barrier.

57

The barrier is just inches from the ground now, with Laika helplessly stranded on the other side. Bex is there, too, leaving me no chance of smashing through it.

I desperately reach back under to grab the fallen remote, praying I'll be able to use it to control Bex and have her smash the barrier from the inside.

That's the only way I'll ever have her power at my disposal again and much more importantly it's the only way I can free Laika.

I reach as far as I can and finally feel the remote.

"Ray Ray?" I hear.

Why didn't he make it underneath? Did the barrier freak him out?

I sweep my hand along the ground and feel an ounce of relief as the remote slides out to my side, *just* making it under before the barrier touches down. There's still a ton of panic running through me, though, as poor Laika remains stuck on the wrong side of the barrier with only Bex for company.

Once the remote slides safely by me, I rush to pull my hand all the way to safety.

The next thing I hear is the loudest noise I've ever made.

Even this scream seems unworthy of the sudden pain I'm experiencing, one that's so intense I see blackness as it hits.

My body made it under the barrier at the first time of asking.

The remote *just* made it out at the second, when I stuck my left hand back under to grab it.

Unfortunately, my left thumb wasn't so lucky.

When I manage to open my eyes, I see that my left hand is on the safe side of the barrier with all five of its digits still attached. That's the best spin I can put on it.

The real story is that my left thumb has been crushed by the barrier. That's all there is to it.

It's bent and it's crushed and feels like it's *still* being crushed. The angle my hand was at when it passed under the barrier meant the thumb was the only part still underneath when it lowered to the critical point.

I figure the thumb's presence must have blocked the barrier from fully pushing down, giving *just* enough scope for me to instinctively yank it free before a word like *severed* would have become more appropriate than *crushed*.

My headset has been knocked off at some point, but as I'm laying next to it I hear the words come through:

"Talk to me," Mel yells. "Ray?!"

I don't know if she's been talking the whole time and I'm just able to hear now. I'd guess she probably has.

"I'm alive," I tell them, panting in agony as I force the words towards the mic. Of all the things I know, that's the surest. I'm alive.

"Come back, brother," Pierre chimes in. "We've got to do something about that thumb."

I gasp through the pain and push myself up to a seated position.

"I'll be back soon," I tell them, gritting my teeth as I grab the remote. "But I'm not leaving Laika."

58

As I pick up the remote, I feel a pulsing in my ears and everywhere else.

The full-body shock of the concentrated pain is like nothing I've ever experienced. It seriously makes my EVA collision feel like a gentle tickle.

I can't use my left thumb for anything and my right hand can't grip well at the best of times. I have to leave the remote on the floor so I can angle my index finger to control the joystick.

It's awkward, but it should work.

"Come on Bex," I croak out, gritting my teeth.

I'm staring at a metal barrier, hoping first that the remote will function through it and also that I can maneuver Bex without seeing where she is.

I was guiding her forward in a straight line when Laika raised the alarm about the door, so she should be standing with her back to me. I focus on very carefully turning the right joystick enough to turn her 180 degrees, then awkwardly use the left to march her forward.

I try to estimate how long it will take and definitely err on the side of guiding her too far. At worst, she'll walk into the door. That doesn't matter. I can still pull my arm back and deliver a strong blow even if she's standing right against the target.

Instinct made me reach for the remote with my left hand. It's been my go-to hand for two decades, ever since the accident messed up my right and I had to learn how to do everything with my left. Even when the cast eventually came off, the nerve damage made it hard to go back.

So here I am, kneeling in the walkway with two bum hands.

I'll be up shit creek without a paddle if I have to do anything dexterous anytime soon. Right now, one saving grace is that the glove to control Bex's wrecking ball goes on my *right* hand.

There's no way my messed-up left thumb would get into a glove. It's not even about the pain — the thing is bent to hell. It wouldn't fit.

I put my right glove on, relying purely on adrenaline to push forward. As soon as my hand is in, I tap the button to engage the glove's link-up.

I'm glad to see the little LED blink green. It's *trying* to activate, at the very least.

But this is just step one. All the green light tells me is that the glove is operational and is sending out a signal. I don't know if it's linked up to Bex. I don't even know if the main remote control was able to guide her into place.

Considering that this tech is being developed with mining purposes in mind, I figure it *has* to work through much thicker walls and over much longer distances than this. I can't count on that, but I can sure as hell hope.

"Stand back, Laika," I plead, but I know he won't hear me from the wrong side of the metal barrier.

The poor little guy must be terrified in there.

I really hope he's not flying against the barrier in helpless confusion, right where Bex is about to swing. Surely he's too smart for that.

I get to my feet, ready to punch. I try to harness the pain

301

and my urgent concerns for Laika as I pull my right hand back and throw it forward as hard as I can, slicing through thin air.

I hear a bang.

Yes! Bex is in the right place and the glove is working.

I swing again, and again and again and again.

The barrier completely buckles somewhere around the fourth or fifth impact. As soon as the way is clear, Laika flies right past what's left of it.

He doesn't fly away, though. He stops next to me and teeters over to my legs, then stands on my feet and huddles in.

All of a sudden he looks more like a baby penguin than a majestic macaw.

"You had me worried there, buddy," I tell him, crouching down to put a hand on his shaking back. For a moment, the pain feels secondary. "And hey, thanks for saving my life. If you hadn't squawked, I wouldn't have made it under in time, either. That thing was *silent* when it came down!"

Behind the fallen barrier I see Bex, standing as stoically as ever.

"And I'm running out of ways to say thanks to *you*," I tell her.

I scrambled around and fought like hell to get into Vinner's lab, and boy was I rewarded for it. Bex has made *so* much possible for me, not least getting into the Control Center where I found the biggest reward of all — a ride home. A ride home for me, and a ride home for Laika.

I reach my right hand to the ground at Laika's side, grabbing my headset.

"Are you there, guys?" I ask.

"Jesus, Ray," Mel replies. "Just get back here, okay? We really need to take a look at that thumb. It *has* to fit in the glove of your pressure suit before you launch and there's no way it's getting in unless you can set it back in place. And in the name of all that's holy, no more crazy moves. We shouldn't have okayed this. I'm not going to say we told you so with the first warnings, but I hope you can see now that the security protections in ZolaCore facilities are no joke. Take a step back and remember that all you have to do is stay alive until we get there. That's it."

She's right.

Of course she's right.

Curiosity killed the cat and it almost just got the human and the parrot, too.

I'm definitely going to heed these words.

"You do have to be more careful," Pierre chimes on. "But that *was* a pretty baller double-move when you slid under the falling door and reached back under to grab the remote, brother. Indiana Barclay for the win."

I feel my expression briefly morph into the closest thing to a smile I can manage through this level of pain. I'm so glad to have them on my side to help me deal with this, because my first aid training definitely didn't cover brutally crushed thumbs.

I guide Bex back with me to the Control Center, more aware of her importance than ever. I hold the remote control upside-down most of the time, so I can use my right thumb to keep her moving. I only switch when I need to change her direction.

An unusually quiet and clearly shaken Laika comes with us. He doesn't want to fly, which I'm hoping is down to shock rather than an injury of his own. As little as I know about fixing human bones, it still beats my parrot-related knowledge.

Although he doesn't quite perch on my shoulder like a pirate's companion, he does choose a spot on Bex's head.

Our unlikely trio cast one hell of an odd shadow when I see it on the hallway's floor.

I leave Bex at the edge of the Control Center, but Laika follows me all the way in.

Mel and Pierre's faces say it all: they're both relieved to see me, with Mel's expression having a little bit of consternation thrown in.

That doesn't seem totally fair. Because although she *did* initially try to talk me out of going into the fourth lab with all of her grim warnings, she was pretty much fully on-board with the idea once we saw Grainger's suspicious movements and lack of protective equipment.

That's all in the past, though, and right now we need to do something about this thumb.

I hold it up to the camera.

"*Oof*," Pierre says, visibly grimacing.

"Wow. You need to set that *urgently*, Ray," Mel says, staying much more focused. "You're probably going to need to drain it again before putting your gloves on for the launch, too, but the same tool can deal with both stages."

Sounds delightful, I think to myself.

"Remember where you got the painkillers for your leg right after your EVA?" she goes on. "You know, the medical supply closet down in the Maintenance Bay? According to this station layout, you should find the main Treatment Room in the same place, through a door to the right. The closet leads into the room. You'll know the right tool when you see it, probably in a metal box. I don't have one here to show you, but it's solely for finger and toe injuries like this and you can't miss it. Just keep the body-cam on and I'll tell you once you find it."

I nod.

All of a sudden, that's all I can do.

All of a sudden, words are totally beyond me.

All of a sudden, even meaningful *thought* feels beyond me.

Mel is staring into the camera with a warm expression on her face, but my eyes have just been opened to something else.

All of a sudden, I'm seeing a gap in this story — a story she just blew *all* the way open.

Because how does she know where I picked up the painkillers? That's not the only place you can find them around here. I had some in my dorm, for one thing, and there are packs in the medication and supplements vending machine in the Gym, too.

I categorically did *not* tell Mel anything about going into the medical supply closet downstairs.

All of a sudden, an uncomfortable question fills my mind:

How in the hell does she know exactly what I did in the Maintenance Bay… *before* we made contact?

59

"Ray?" Mel says. "What's wrong?"

You're a lying piece of shit is what's wrong, I want to scream.

It doesn't add up.

Have they been watching me since before we made contact?

At the very least, the connection has given them remote access to the camera system and they've been watching pre-contact footage without telling me, maybe while I was asleep.

At the very worst?

I don't even want to think about it.

"I'm fine," I say. "I just want to look at a map of the area around the medical room, to make sure I know the best route. I don't want this to take any longer than it needs to."

Doing everything with my un-injured but always limited right hand, I navigate into the security camera's control menu. I *do* bring up footage live from the Maintenance Bay's lower level, but only as a way to give plausible deniability for my next move. My *real* move.

That move comes now, as I "accidentally" disable the camera.

"Shit," I mutter. It's part of the plan. "I think I killed the camera down there. Let me try to bring it back. Let's see... activate all cameras... activate all cameras..."

When I get to the menu that gives me that option, I just as "accidentally" ask the system to *de*activate all cameras.

As quickly and subtly as possible, I then close the video connection window before covering the body-cam with the palm of my hand and putting it face-down on the desk.

I place the headset right beside it, ignoring the loud yells telling me that they can't see or hear me anymore.

I'm thinking on my feet with this temporary disconnection. All it's going to give me is some time to think about what I can do next.

My pulsating thumb isn't giving me any respite and I really need to get that tool from the Treatment Room as soon as possible, so I get to my feet and decide to think on the job.

I don't think it's overreacting to feel like *everything* just changed.

It's like a mask just slipped and Mel gave weight to a suspicion I'd been keeping in check for a while, ever since she threw up such urgent and insistent opposition to the idea of me going into the fourth lab.

Sure, it could have been out of concern for my safety. But even at the time, I wasn't totally sold. Now that I know she's secretly been watching what I did before we made contact, all assumptions of trust are gone. It's all shot to pieces.

They're ZolaCore through and through and I'm a visiting researcher.

What if I know too much? What if they've been poring through old footage to see exactly what I *do* know, to determine whether it's better to come to get me or leave me here to die?

Maybe I *am* overreacting, but I don't think so.

Not anymore.

I reach the lower level of the Maintenance Bay without Bex, who I wouldn't know how to get down the stairway even if I needed her for this. There must be an elevator somewhere that I could find on the station layout, but it's not a priority.

Predictably, I do have Laika for company.

I think I'm going to be seeing a lot of him after what just

happened in the fourth lab's safety walkway. He doesn't want to be alone and I can't blame him.

I'm pretty sure about that, to be honest. I don't want to be alone, either.

Inside the small medical supply closet, there sure enough *is* another doorway on the right. I hadn't noticed this first time around when I grabbed the painkillers, purely because I found what I was looking for in the main part of the closet at a time when I didn't have a moment to waste.

I haven't taken any more painkillers since the thumb incident. That's not because I'm worried about taking too many, it's just because they're not made for anything this intense.

The kind of painkillers that *would* dull what I'm feeling are the kind of opioids that would make me way too drowsy and lethargic to retain the mental clarity I need.

I'm counting on the tool Mel mentioned while she was still succeeding in her pretense of being a truthful ally.

There's a fingerprint reader next to the closet's inner door, but those can't pose any issues since I disabled all of the station's core security restrictions.

I walk into a vast Treatment Room, complete with eight beds and more equipment than you could shake a stick at.

There are so many places to look, I start to think I should have kept the body-cam on and not reacted to Mel's slip-up until after this was taken care of.

Easier said than done, I muse.

At the time, it was all I could do not to scream my suspicions at the top of my lungs. Believe me: it would have been easier to stay quiet after the brutal pain of the thumb-crushing barrier.

I think I handled the revelation pretty well, all things considered. The ball is in my court and the next move will be mine when I get back to the desk. I have no idea what comes next, but at least I got over the first hurdle.

One thing at a time.

If I had a watch on, I'd know how long I spend getting

nowhere in my search for the tool I need. The level of pain I'm experiencing skews everything to make time feel like it's passing more slowly than it is, so I can't even make a reasonable guess.

I eventually find a large metal box inside a highly stacked storage closet, and inside I see something that looks suitably torturous to be the finger-setting device Mel told me about.

Something else in the box catches my eye, too, so much so that I reach for it first. It's a smaller box, around the size of my hand, with an intriguingly handwritten label:

PSYCH EVAL.

I grab it and open the latch.

A tiny hard drive meets my eyes. I immediately put it in my pocket. It could be nothing or it could be something, and it's going to cost me nothing to find out.

What clearly *is* going to cost me something — a hell of a lot of pain — is sticking my thumb into this hellish looking device.

How can I even describe it?

The part where I have to stick my thumb is almost like the kind of desk-mounted pencil sharpener my teachers always had in school.

There are a lot of visible mechanical parts, all as uncovered as most of Bex's workings, and it looks like some kind of laser will be used to analyze my thumb before the corrective procedure starts.

Corrective procedure... there's a euphemism if ever I heard one.

I look down at my badly bent thumb. For a millisecond, I actually consider whether taking the Yannick route might be a better way of making sure I can get my hand into the glove before I launch in a few days.

That's if there even *is* a launch, I suddenly consider. Because if my worst suspicions about Mel and Pierre are right, I don't even know if—

"One thing at a time," I say out loud.

Heeding my own advice, I carry the device to a flat surface and hook it up to the nearest wall outlet.

I turn it upside-down and see a few safety notices. They're pretty straightforward, and one bullet point assured me that I'll be able to unplug it at any point without having my finger stuck in there forever.

The worst that can happen is that my thumb somehow gets worse, I tell myself, and it's already useless. There's no option of sticking with the status quo.

I swallow my doubts and put my thumb into position, biting down on my other sleeve as soon as I press the activation button.

I hear a slow whir. It gets louder and louder until it gives way to a single click.

I'm entranced by the odd visual of so many moving parts, almost dancing like piano keys. They move as a red laser passes under my thumb to assess the damage, presumably deciding exactly what needs to be done to correct it.

To me it feels like this kind of procedure might be better suited to a dislocated shoulder than what I'm guessing is a *broken* thumb, but who am I to second guess a high-tech piece of kit like this?

ZolaCore is at the forefront of so many fields that I shouldn't really be surprised to learn that medical equipment is one more string to the bow.

When the laser stops, the beeps begin.

The intervals get shorter and shorter, leaving me in no doubt that this is a countdown. It doesn't take long for them to get as fast as my ever-rising heartbeat. When they overtake even that, I know the moment is coming.

I expect to fall over. I expect to black out.

"Aaaaaagh!" I bellow.

As the device's countless moving parts twist and double-twist my thumb back into position, the pain is somehow even worse than when it was crushed under the barrier.

It's worse… but then it's over.

Within two or three seconds, it's all over.

I look down at my thumb and see a disconcerting amount of redness, but the thumb itself is straight.

It's… *fixed*.

Don't get me wrong, it still hurts more than just about anything I'd experienced until a few days ago, but the excruciating pain of the procedure lasted only a few seconds and I now feel infinitely more comfortable than I did before it started.

Laika understandably freaked out when I roared like a bear with a blister, but he didn't leave the room.

The poor guy is so shaken up, he'll take the scariest version of me over even a few minutes on his own.

"It's okay, buddy," I tell him. "Sorry if I scared you."

I look down at my thumb again and wonder if maybe it wasn't broken after all. Could such a small piece of equipment really fix *that*, with no human oversight?

I just don't know. And to be honest, right now I don't really *care*, either. The device did its job and I suppose I can be thankful to Mel for suggesting… but that's where my thankfulness ends.

I don't know what I'm going to say when I get back to the Control Center.

Before I start talking again, I'm going to check out what this "*PSYCH EVAL*" labeled hard drive can tell me.

There's no real reason to expect I'll find anything useful, but I haven't stayed alive this long by *not* following every possible lead I can get my hands on…

60

When I get back to the Control Center, I'm greeted by silence.

Mel and Pierre have given up on yelling through the headset. I really hope they've bought the idea that I accidentally killed our comms at the same time I killed the cameras.

I haven't decided what I'm going to do next, even now that my head is a lot clearer with the worst of my pain relegated to the past.

Before I plug the tiny hard drive into the port on the side of Commander Harrison's keyboard, I make triple-sure that I'm not still sharing my screen.

I know I disabled the cameras and closed the video connection, but since it didn't feel important to end the screen share at the time I can't totally remember if I—

Nope. I *didn't* kill it before I left.

Damn... that was close. I'm beyond glad I checked before it was too late.

With that taken care of, I stick the hard drive into the port and wait for something to happen. A folder pop ups within two or three seconds, with dozens of subfolders arranged in alphabetical order.

My eyes immediately and naturally fall on one in the second row:

BARCLAY, RAY.

I open the folder instantly — obviously — and I see several photographs of myself along with a text document.

One of the photos is from my ZolaCore security clearance interview, which makes sense. One of the others is my passport photo, and again there's nothing to be surprised about there. But the third is a photo of me with my family on a normal Sunday afternoon a few weeks before my interview.

We're by the grill in our backyard. And because I know the angles so well, I know this photo must have been shot through the hedge next to the driveway.

They were spying on me.

Already feeling violated, I open the document with no idea of what to expect.

The first thing I notice is that it is *long.*

Like *L.O.N.G.* long.

Nineteen pages. Wow, they don't mess around.

At the top of the first page, I see an understandable designation:

"Security Clearance: Visitor."

I skim the rest of the page then start scrolling through the others, looking for parts that jump out.

The main thing that catches my eye is a half-page excerpt from a different psychological report. It's the one that was put together by my post-trauma therapist, more than twenty years ago.

I recognize her name and this text is all in blue, not black like the rest of it, which makes it easy to see the quoted sections at a glance.

There's nothing new here.

It talks about the accident, when my older brother — *half*-brother in the therapist's needlessly precise terminology — jumped from a cliff edge and got into difficulty around the rocks below.

I was 13. Jack was 16.

He was jumping to show me it was safe, so that I would be able to do it next time my friends wanted to.

I didn't want to look like a chicken anymore and Jack wanted to help. He died for that.

I jumped down after him that day, for the first and last time. I made it down, albeit losing my glasses, and I tried my best to free him from the rocks.

I told myself he wasn't dead when deep down I already knew.

I got behind the wheel of his car and tried to drive home. I was 13. I couldn't see where I was going. I crashed into a tree and messed myself up — bad.

No one found us for almost two hours. I was lucky to live.

The coroners said Jack drowned, but Steve wouldn't hear it. His son was dead and I was the inconvenient step-son left behind, who he had never liked at the best of times.

Jack was big enough to keep Steve at bay and he would always defend me, but I lost that protection when I needed it most. I lost it when Steve became ten times worse than ever.

The old report says I was adamant that I didn't want to go into care because I didn't want to leave my mom alone with Steve, without even me to hold off the worst of his turns.

Steve was a big man around town. He owned a chain of gas stations and made donations to the right kinds of people. My word was nothing against his, and it didn't help that my poor mom always felt stuck in the middle.

The report ends there, and every word was true.

I didn't want to leave my mom with Steve, and I didn't. When she got sick and passed away a few years later, I got the hell out of there as fast as I could.

I stayed on friends' couches until one of their dads gave me a flier for a young men's support group at the local church. It wasn't a religious thing, just a bunch of guys who needed somewhere to turn. None of us had dads, or at least any worth the name, and there were a few much older guys who had been through the same thing and wanted to give us something they'd never had.

That was when I learned that there is always a choice. I learned that you can make all the difference in the world to someone — good or bad — and that a biological connection is the least important part of that.

Right until my placement started, I was still going to those meetings twice a month. Nowadays I've been sitting on the other side of the circle, trying to offer whatever help I can to the kids who need it.

I always do my best for Joe, but he has it easy. The other boys are older and usually in situations like the one I was stuck in — most of them have been *worse* than fatherless, stuck in a violent home that still haunts them even if they've broken out.

After the blue text from my therapist, there are a few comments about my recent attendance at these meetings.

Whoever put this report together for ZolaCore says I'm unlikely to volunteer for any longer missions due to my focus on family and community, but that my work ethic and temperament would make me an excellent candidate if my mind could be changed.

For the avoidance of doubt: it couldn't.

These two months were the toughest of my life even before everything went to hell. Any kind of longer mission is totally out of the question.

I scan the remaining pages with increasing speed and don't find much else that jumps out. I can look more closely later.

I navigate out of my folder and back to the list of names. I scan this, too, looking for any that look interesting.

There are hundreds and hundreds — way more than the population of the station. I think this must be a ZolaCore-wide database, or something like that.

I spot Yannick, I spot Justin... and wow.

At the very bottom, I spot Ignacio Zola.

This I have to see.

61

I click on Zola's name even faster than I did on my own.

Only one picture appears in the folder: his familiar portrait.

Since he's such a reclusive guy who spends almost all of his time at ZolaCore's high-security New Zealand HQ, very few photos even exist that are more recent than this one, which looks to be from four or five years ago.

Zola is a handsome man. He'll be 59 now, with tightly cropped facial hair and skin as smooth as money can buy. His brown eyes penetrate deeply even through a computer screen. Everyone who's spent time with him always talks about that arresting gaze and his broader air of magnetism.

I open the notes document. Surprisingly, it's a lot shorter than mine but still fairly long at 8 pages.

Zola's notes naturally open with a different designation:

"Security Clearance: Maximum."

I also note right away that there's a name at the very top right of the page. I recognize it as belonging to the man who co-wrote Zola's official biography almost a decade ago: Logan Conlan.

The two men appeared together in some high-profile media calls. That got huge attention at the time, given how fully Zola usually shies away from that kind of thing.

Conlan is a clinical psychologist by trade and had written some successful pop-science books before Zola approached him to work on the biography.

I didn't realize he did actual work like this for ZolaCore, much less on Zola himself.

I know most of Zola's story from that biography, just like everyone else. Some of it was so dramatic that it almost sounded fictionalized. But now, with Conlan sticking to the narrative even in this internal document, I realize it's not.

No... it's all true.

Ignacio Zola really *was* one of two quadruplets to survive a difficult birth that also tragically cost his mother her life.

He really *was* unable to walk until a cutting-edge medical procedure at the age of 14.

He really *did* dedicate his life to science because of how much science did for his life.

His early pushes into bionics and stem-cell research were particularly motivated by his own circumstances, with the interest in space coming from another angle.

Conlan notes here, like he did in the book, that Zola sees Earth as "an overpopulated womb that curtails the potential of its strongest and most viable inhabitants." He similarly sees egalitarian philosophy as "an intolerable constraint on human development," with potential-driven science being the only route to progress.

One thing I see here that definitely *wasn't* in the book is a note about Zola's full-on hatred of organized religion and absolutist morality. Conlan states his belief that this stems from Zola's parents' refusal to "take the necessary steps to protect the strong in the face of dangers posed by the weak."

It's a pretty warped way to talk about his own unborn siblings, but I already knew that Zola is very different from your average guy.

Space exploration, in Zola's eyes, is apparently the only way to free humanity from its womb-like constraints and to open a door to new worlds of boundless potential.

I agree with *some* of that — for wildly different reasons, obviously — but it's impossible not to feel uncomfortable now that I'm realizing a guy like *this* has been at the forefront of the field for so long.

I quickly skim the rest of the document, stopping when I see the word *brother*.

I already know that Zola's only surviving brother, named here as Valerio, had a developmental disability that was significantly more limiting than Zola's own inability to walk as a child.

Conlan says he was never able to get many details on this. He also says there was only ever one thing Zola flat-out refused to talk about, even in the strictest of confidence: the near-simultaneous death of Valerio and their father.

It happened when Zola was 16 and Conlan speculates that it might have been a tragic case of murder-suicide, with the father unable to cope with the increasing demands of managing a dependent son who was growing older and stronger. This time frame coincided with Zola's departure from the family home, shortly after an untested procedure granted him the ability to walk and a sought after educational scholarship opened doors he had never dreamed of.

Conlan explicitly states his personal view that Zola remains ridden with guilt for leaving when he did. He thinks Zola believes that Valerio — the only person he ever truly loved — would still be alive if he hadn't abandoned him in pursuit of a better life.

I lean back in my chair.

Wow.

The last thing I expected from this was to feel emotionally affected by something I would learn about *Zola*, of all people.

There's no reason to think Conlan is anything but on the money about all of this, given the unparalleled access Zola granted him for so long. It all really does put a new spin on why Zola ended up holding the views he does.

Or the views he *did* hold, if he hasn't survived the attacks on Earth.

I still have no idea what exactly happened after the terrorists issued an ultimatum for him to give himself up. I really don't know where Mel fits into this, either.

What I know is that Ignacio Zola was a self-made man who overcame a lot of adversity with very little help. The parts of his story I knew as a kid were inspiring to me, because he was already hugely successful by the time I left high school.

He struck me as a rare example of a guy who overcame major physical challenges *and* family issues to succeed at a high level. Understandably, that resonated with me after the accident.

It would take a lot to stop Zola and I'd like to think Eva and Joe have a similar view of me.

I'd like to think they're not crying for me just yet.

Granted, things just took a bad turn when Mel's mask slipped.

Granted, I feel like I'm in a worse spot now than before I made contact.

And granted… I no longer think I just have to survive until they get here.

I can't hide from the fact that at some point, I have to act on this new reality.

But what will that entail? Leaving *before* they get here?

Leaving in what… to where?

The idea of launching the Escape Pod for interception was hard enough to accept, but at least it was possible. As far as my desperate mind can tell, no other journey is.

So if I can't leave, what then?

Do I wait for them to arrive, hope Mel's story about not being able to dock was another lie, and launch some kind of guerrilla counter-attack when they storm in here to kill me?

Yeah, I know. I hear myself going crazy, too.

I'll readily admit that last idea is a sign of how desperately my mind is reaching for an answer.

I just have *so* many questions to work through.

Who even is Mel, really? What's her story?

I come out of Zola's folder and stare at the screen.

It takes only a few seconds for my present reality to sink back in as I start wondering what the hell I'm going to do as an immediate next move. I can't maintain this lack of contact for long without Mel realizing I've figured her out.

How much longer *can* I keep pretending like nothing is going on while I come up with an action plan?

My eyes widen as an idea strikes.

Mel's story.

That's a good starting point.

I'll see what the notes say about Mel. That'll tell me something.

It might not be anything I want to know, but I have to find out who I'm dealing with…

62

I navigate to L for Lomond, but I don't see Mel anywhere.

I tap on the search bar and type in Mel. Neither of the two results are her. I open both folders just in case I've somehow misremembered her surname, but the women I see are completely different people.

I sit in thought for a few seconds before having the idea of filtering the master folder to show all of its contained images, then sifting through them at a manageable size. Even with several hundred, it will only take a few minutes to scroll through and see if I recognize her.

The quick process brings forth countless faces, a lot of which I've seen around the station. Before long I spot the one I'm looking for: Mel's.

Only it's not *Mel's* at all.

No.

When I click the option to open the image's enclosing folder, I see that the face belongs to a Jayne Steele, referred to from then on only as *Steele*.

"Security Clearance: Maximum."

Her report is only two pages long. For all I know that might be a much more typical length than mine or Zola's. Either way, I pay even more attention than I did to those.

I quickly find out that Steele used to work in law enforcement, most recently as a hostage negotiator, and that she's been with ZolaCore for more than ten years. The report is glowing:

"Steele's skills and loyalty to ZolaCore are unmatched, making her an easy choice for any sensitive and high-risk scenarios or unexpected challenges."

She apparently now works in risk assessment and advises the board on media relations. You know, just about the furthest thing from commanding a mobile space station that I can think of.

Steele has been feeding me grade-A bullshit from the very start. I don't know what's true anymore, but I know what's not.

I close the folder and remove the hard drive for now.

I'm a pretty good poker player but there is no way in hell I can hide my feelings on this. I think I have to tell them what I've just found.

My only move is to play it cool and say I'm willing to put it behind us if we can get on the same page from here on out. The trouble is, I don't think they're going to go for that.

Looking back at the words in her report, I think *I'm* an unexpected challenge and I think Mel was the easy choice to deal with me.

My survival on the station, and particularly my urge to see whatever is inside the fourth lab, is a high-risk scenario and sensitive situation.

I gulp.

Getting home feels nowhere near as certain as it did an hour ago, and that's eating me inside. But whatever route I might still have can only go through Steele, so I have to resume contact.

I don't want to, but I *have* to.

I call up the menu to bring the cameras back online, all the while thinking of how I'm going to explain what I did before I read the psych reports.

What I see on the system comes as a huge and unwelcome surprise:

The cameras are *already* back online.

I reinitiate the video link as quickly as I can and immediately see Mel and Pierre.

Sorry: *Steele* and whatever the hell Pierre's real name might be. I didn't even get to him.

"Your family is alive in Colorado Springs," Steele says, with a raspy voice and a deathly stare to match. "If you want it to stay that way, you'll sit the *fuck* down and listen to every word I tell you. Capeesh?"

"Talk," I say, struggling to bite my tongue.

I want to scream that I'll rip her heart out the first chance I get for threatening my family like that, because you better believe that's what I'm thinking.

She grins, snakelike all the way. "Okay, Mr. Action Hero. Listen up, and listen good."

63

I'm ready to disbelieve anything and everything Steele tells me, but I have to hear it.

I don't know what the hell I'll be able to do with any of it now that my only route out of here has just turned out to be the worst kind of dead end. All I know is that I have to hear it.

"You're a survivor, Ray," she begins. "I'll give you that."

I'll give *you* something, you lying sack of shit, I want to reply. But I know better. For now, at least, I bite my tongue.

"Like a cockroach," Pierre chimes in.

I can't believe I liked that guy. I can't believe I bought it all. I'm usually a decent judge of character, but these guys? I couldn't have been more wrong.

I should probably cut myself some slack since I *did* have doubts a while ago, even when they came to me like guardian angels and everything inside of me was desperately looking for some hope to cling on to.

And those psych reports said that Steele was a literal hostage negotiator prized for ability to handle delicate scenarios, so maybe anyone would have fallen for it.

Maybe anyone would have fallen for her web of lies and fallen into her trap.

I sit up straight.

Her trap.

The walkway.

"That was you," I say, finishing out loud a thought that started in my head. "You brought the barrier down to trap me in there! You didn't want me to see what was in there so you tried to talk me out of it, but when I was determined to go in you went along with it and tried to trap me. It wasn't an automated trap. It was you!"

So much for biting my tongue.

With a sarcastic chuckle, Steele gives me a slow round of applause.

Instead of saying anything else, she reaches for a button just out of camera-shot. Within seconds, I can feel cold air coming from the vent at my feet.

And when I say cold air, I mean *cold* air.

"Even cockroaches go when you hit them with the right tools," Steele says with a demented grin. "You didn't *have* to die, Ray. We could have used a man of your skills for the next stage. But you've made your choice. And since we have your research data and you just Won't... Stop... Getting.... In... The... Way."

She tilts her head side to side with each of the last few words, taunting me even as she sets about turning my environment into an ice box like I did with the Canteen and the dorms.

They've had control the whole time, I realize.

The radio connection meant nothing for them. She was watching me long before that.

Knowing this, it's harder than ever to make sense of everything that's happened. Was the initial air leak *really* an accident? Maybe one they couldn't deal with remotely?

Either way, they could surely have silenced the alarm so I wouldn't know about it, and they could just as easily have blocked my path to the EVA hatch. At literally any point in the past few days, Steele could have killed me.

There must be something true in her comment about a man of my skills being potentially useful to them, in whatever

325

demented "next stage" she's talking about. Otherwise I'd be dead by now.

The only other possibility I can think of is that Steele has had *observation* access to the station's systems this whole time, but that she only gained *control* when I rebooted everything. I'm thinking at a mile a minute here, and so far this is the most logical answer I've landed on.

Whether she has had full control all along, Steele definitely has it now. I'm almost certain she had it when everything kicked off, too.

Grainger's sabotage mission wasn't a one-man job and I think I'm looking at someone who played a big part of her own.

"You killed the Commanders, didn't you?" I say. "You poisoned the air in here and in the Observation Deck, all while Grainger took care of the open areas. You're with him. You're with *them*. What the hell is this? A coup? Did you kill Zola?"

She shrugs. "You don't have to worry about *him*, Ray. Soon, you won't have to worry about anything."

It's getting uncomfortably cold already.

My only saving grace at the moment is that by having Bex completely knock down the Control Center door instead of just unlock it, I've prevented Steele from locking me in here. Since Steele has control of the station's temperature, control of the security system feels a given.

So is control of the air supply, I figure. The alarm isn't blaring to tell me we're low on oxygen and I'm not choking on any toxins, but I fear those outcomes might not be far away. If Steele wants to kill me, the air composition is as good a way as any other.

It's almost like she's toying with me by changing the temperature first.

I suppose they could be all-out of toxins. After all, those would need to be physically stored on the station. She can't magic the stuff out of thin air. I don't see why the system would be built with a backdoor to allow anyone to remotely change the atmospheric makeup of the air, either.

With that in mind, it could actually be the case that freezing me is her fastest option.

I can hardly believe what I'm facing.

I survived on my own through so many challenges, wishing all the way that I could reach someone else.

I was the last man standing, searching for an ally wherever I might find one, and here I am bitterly realizing that I was better off alone.

I had no way home back then, just like I have no way home now, but at least I had a guaranteed air supply and was in control of the temperature.

Okay, it's turned out that I only ever had the *illusion* of control, but it really sounds like Steele was willing to let me live and help with their "next stage" — if only I'd stayed in my lane.

It's not over, Ray, I tell myself.

It looked like it was over when the air was running out. It looked like it was over when the EVA suit detached from the station. It looked like it was over when the barrier came down inside that damn corridor. But it wasn't over.

It isn't over.

It's *never* over.

Where there's life there's hope, and these assholes haven't killed me yet.

64

There's no way off this station that I can see — no second step — but there has to be a first step that at least gets me out of this immediate predicament.

I need to break Steele's control. I need to cut whatever connection is giving them a link to the station from wherever the hell they actually are, whether that *is* a spacecraft on the way to get me or whether it's a ZolaCore bunker in New Zealand like I'm starting to suspect.

Spoofing the location of their signal would be trivial when they have full control of the system, and nothing in Steele's psych report makes me think she has any business on a space station.

My last hope is that if I can end her control of *this* space station, I can maybe keep surviving long enough to come up with a plan of where to go from there.

I turn to the second screen, the one that belonged to my friend Lily — the Deputy Commander who Steele's cretinous cohorts inexplicably killed in cold blood.

I've never known a rage like this, so strong that I'm fully aware of it even in these truly life-or-death moments.

I tap through some menus, but I'm not looking for an option to disable the link. That would do nothing. After all, there didn't *seem* to be any connection until they answered my radio call, and I now know that belief was a million miles from accurate.

Their method of control has nothing to do with the Commanders' radio system, and I have to get to the bottom of it.

I have to find the core part of the system that enables any kind of contact from the station and anywhere else. By find, I do mean physically *find*.

That's why I'm doing what I'm doing now. That's why I'm looking as quickly as I can through the troubleshooting section of the computer's radio system, for every possible thing that can go wrong with the link-up.

The suggestions to reboot and recalibrate are all meaningless to me, but when I get to the final suggestion I feel like it at least gives me something to go on.

It's pointing me to an area in the Maintenance Bay's lower level, where the electrical breakers and everything like that are located. I don't know as much as I should about electronics — it's just not my field — but I know more than nothing.

I grab my phone, snap some photos of the screen, and sprint out of the room.

"Hey!" Steele's angry voice calls through the speakers. "What part of sit down if you ever want to see your family again did you not understand?"

I keep going without a backwards glance. I don't zip up the back: she's never going to let me set foot on Earth again if she has any say in it, let alone to see my family again.

For now, all I can do is trust my family's safety to the government and military personnel who are going to be right beside them in the bunker.

I don't think I messed up by working with Pierre to find the exact locations of the bunkers, because I think anyone capable of doing what they did will have been tracking flight and ground movements, anyway.

I have so many questions about why they've been lying,

who they were working with, and why they actually seemed to be helping me in a lot of ways.

Was it all just to keep me in the dark about what really matters?

Were they throwing me a few crumbs of truth and some semi-useful ideas to stop me from getting too close to the important stuff?

Maybe.

One person whose words I'm desperate to trust is President Williams. I pray he wasn't bullshitting when he defiantly vowed that freedom will strike back. The best I can do right now is try to stay alive in the hope that somehow I'll be able to help in that quest with all the knowledge I've gained up here.

I run as fast as I can, glad my leg is long past the worst of its movement-restricting pain. I'm also glad to see Laika flying ahead of me. He's not injured after all, at least not badly, and he probably knows me well enough to know something isn't right.

He's a perceptive little guy and I suppose he'll have felt the cold air, too. The hallway isn't too bad yet, which could be because Steele only turned up the chill in the Control Center or could be because it'll take longer to have an effect in this much bigger space.

The Maintenance Bay is colder when I enter, but I'm too relieved that I left the door open to care much about that. Steele can lock doors with her all-access pass to the station's controls, but she naturally can't close them when they're physically jammed.

I sprint to the spot where the computer told me I'd find the electrics, then waste no time in jimmying off the metal coverings.

They're made to come off like this, so it's not hard.

I pull out my phone and look at the photos again. The overhead lights all die just as I do this.

She's on to me.

Steele knew I was going to do something, but now she's seen me on the cameras and knows exactly what that something is.

I activate my phone's flashlight and aim that at the electrics while I look at the instructional images on the screen.

"Stop right now," Steele's voice booms over the emergency warning speakers.

The sound is about as welcome as the alarm those speakers were blaring before I fixed the pipe outside, but it's not going to stop me.

My photos of the communication troubleshooting notes lead me to one physical connection in particular.

I know what I have to do. I don't know if it'll work, but I know what I have to do.

I grab a robot-control glove from my pocket and put it on. I'm using my weaker right hand since my left thumb is still prohibitively sensitive.

Bex isn't here and I'm only wearing the glove to avoid touching any cables with my bare hands. Even though the cables will be suitably insulated, there's no such thing as being too careful.

I grasp the cable and grip as tightly as my nerve-damaged right hand will let me.

"I know where they are, Ray," Steele reiterates. "If you even think—"

I yank the cable loose, cutting off Steele's voice in an instant.

Just like that, all I hear is my breathing.

"Squawk," Laika says. "Ray Ray? Okay? Squawk. Okay?"

I turn to him. "I don't know, buddy. I might have just killed *everything*."

With the light already off, it's hard to tell whether I've successfully disabled all remote contact and controls or if I've done something much bigger that might bring us all-new problems to contend with.

I reach for the nearest light switch and hold my breath.

"Let there be light," I say, more to myself than to Laika.

And light there is!

"Yes!" I say, pumping the air. "Okay! Come on, buddy."

I immediately run back up to the Control Center, as fast as my legs will take me.

The screens are still on, but Steele and Pierre are gone.

The cold air is still coming out. It's already chilled the room to an uncomfortable level in just the few minutes I've been away.

Fortunately I'm able to put things right with a few taps of the screen.

I'm back in control — of the station's systems, at least, if not yet of my destiny.

That comes next.

I sit back in Commander Harrison's seat and turn to Laika, who's now perched on Lily's like a loyal second-in-command.

"I think we lost them," I say.

He just looks at me. If he could talk like a human, I think I know what he'd say:

Now what?

After what happened last time we tried to enter the fourth lab, I don't think he'd like the answer.

But I've just learned beyond any doubt that Steele and Pierre are my enemy.

And when there's something your enemy desperately doesn't want you to see, like whatever the hell is inside that damn lab, I figure you'd be doing yourself a favor to find out what it is.

Right now, I really am all the way up shit creek without a paddle.

That lab is the only way I can go.

Following the rapids might take me over a proverbial cliff even more deadly than the literal one that killed my brother, but maybe — just maybe — something in there could help me find a way out of here.

My family is alive in the Colorado bunker. So when a risky long-shot is all I've got to have any chance of seeing them again, you're damn right I'm going to go for it.

"You don't have to come," I say to Laika, placing a gentle hand on his upper wing. "But me and Bex are going back in."

65

I have to see what's in the fourth lab. I *have* to.

There are all kinds of arguments for trying again. One of the main ones is that my enemies tried to keep me out. Another is that those same enemies can no longer get in my way.

Most of all, though, the best argument is simply that I have no other next move.

I could keep sending signals to Earth and hoping someone else picks up on them, sure. But that's too passive.

On the other hand, I do feel like there's a possibility Steele was blocking my radio from working properly. I might have more chance of contacting Earth now that she and her cronies have no access to my systems.

I know exactly where to aim now, too, ever since I narrowed the likely bunker locations to Mount Pony in Virginia and Cheyenne Mountain in Colorado.

So yeah… come to think of it, I *will* try again to reach Earth.

I'm not putting all my eggs in one basket, though. While I'm doing that, I'm going to make sure Bex is recharging to full capacity in case I still can't make contact with the bunkers.

I won't wait for long. If no one connects or responds to my broadcasts within an hour, I'll take it as a sign that nothing is being received.

I guide Bex back to Vinner's lab and plug her into the wall outlet once again. More so than ever, I'm careful to jam open every door that isn't destroyed.

Some kind of battery indicator would be really useful about now, because I have a hunch that Bex could run for days and that I'm wasting time with these frequent recharges.

But with how important her strength has already proven, it's infinitely better to be safe than sorry.

While she's charging, I get to work on a message to broadcast via the radio.

"This is Ray Barclay on The Beacon space station," I say, recording my words on Commander Harrison's computer via the headset. "I'm the sole survivor of a sabotage attack by Oliver Grainger, AKA Dale Thorpe. I have extensive evidence implicating other ZolaCore personnel, including Jayne Steele, in these recent events. I currently have no means of getting home to Earth. Please respond as soon as possible, even if the news is bad."

With the aid of the computer's user guide, it only takes a few minutes for me to have this message broadcasting on an open frequency. At the same time, I also instruct the radio system to start looking for any signals emanating from the locations I've given.

I figure I don't have much to lose with this. After all, the bad guys already know where I am and what I know. I can't see any harm in broadcasting this far and wide.

A watched pot never boils.

A watched phone never rings.

And believe me: I quickly realize that a watched radio never picks up *anything*.

It only takes five or six minutes for me to lose patience. That's way too soon to give up, obviously, but it's definitely long enough to start making my contingency preparations.

Bex is charging, which was the first thing I thought of.

The next is that I should do something to guard against any more barriers dropping from the ceiling, just in case Steele didn't *actively* do that. There's a chance she just knew it would happen and encouraged me to go into the walkway, confident that the automated security system would sense my presence and do the rest.

I rack my brain for a few minutes. Eventually I get the idea to gather all of the trolleys I used yesterday, when I carried my dead colleagues into the chill zones.

The walkway's descending barrier crushed my thumb without severing it, so I think a much larger metallic object will provide enough of an obstacle to make sure I can escape again if it comes to that.

It won't come to that, though. I'm almost positive. But again, in a battle of safe versus sorry when the stakes are as high as this, I know which horse I want to be riding.

What else... I muse, starting to think more closely about the potential dangers I might find inside.

Grainger wasn't wearing any protective gear when he entered and exited the walkway. But as I think about it some more, I realize that doesn't necessarily mean he wasn't wearing any while he was inside.

For all I know, there could be an automated security protection involving the lab's air. If someone enters without authorization, a toxin might take them out before they even know what's hit them.

Even after what I've seen with the barrier, I know I'm reaching with some of these more fantastical hypothetical threats. I just want to be as prepared as I can for whatever might come up. And call me crazy, but I'd always prefer a risk assessment to a post mortem.

The idea of wearing an EVA suit crosses my mind, or even one of the slimmer pressure suits I was going to wear when the Escape Pod seemed like my rickety ticket out of here.

Thinking about that now gives me shivers.

Was I going to launch to nowhere?

Was I going to launch into space thinking Steele and her crew were there to get me, when really they were spoofing the signal from Earth and I'd have been suicidally launching myself into the ocean of space?

I shudder at the prospect.

I can't believe how easily and convincingly she lied to me.

I guess that's why they chose her for the job. Decorated hostage-negotiation backgrounds like that aren't exactly a dime a dozen.

Exactly who "they" are and exactly how high this thing might go are questions I can't even begin to wrestle with right now. The optimist in me isn't counting out finding some insights in the increasingly tantalizing fourth lab.

First you have to get in safely, I tell myself. *Then you have to survive.*

Returning to my idea to wear a suit, I see two problems. First of all, I wouldn't be able to wear my goggles. Second, I could only wear either Bex's control gloves or the suit's gloves, which are required to seal it off from the external atmosphere.

Quite simply, it's Bex and the goggles or it's just me and the suit.

Hmm.

I think about this for a few seconds before settling on the idea of hooking a filtered mask up to a small backpack-style oxygen tank. I saw some of those in the Maintenance Bay, down on the lower level.

Sure, it won't protect me from any *serious* atmospheric problems in the lab. But it's a whole lot better than nothing and it won't get in the way of my gloves or my goggles. It's certainly worth wearing, anyway. I have no qualms about that.

Laika comes with me as I set off downstairs once more. I feel like I could make this trip with my eyes closed by now. I wonder if he's lost count, too?

I don't have a mask small enough for Laika, but the idea of him wearing a little oxygen backpack and mask at least makes me smile for a second.

If I don't make radio contact and do end up entering into the lab, I'm not sure if Laika will come with me.

I guess I'll find out which is stronger after the poor guy's near-death experience in the walkway: his aversion to being back there, or his aversion to being left alone. My money is on him staying behind. He really *was* shaken up by what happened.

As soon as we get back upstairs, I check the computer to see if the system has picked up any sign of a radio signal since I left.

It hasn't.

This is a major disappointment, but it also feels like a tipping point. If nothing else, it really focuses my mind on the seemingly inevitable march into the fourth lab.

Even if my heart hasn't given up hope of an imminent change to the radio status, my gut knows what's happening.

It's already settled on the reality:

I'm going in.

66

"The trolleys," I say to Laika, thinking out loud.

Gathering them all would be slightly faster if I link them up and have Bex pull them again. I won't do that, though, because it would defeat the point of conserving her battery for the main job of safely getting us into the lab.

It's also possible for me to move them more quickly today than last time, when each was weighed down by two of my unfortunate colleagues.

I get to work on this, feeling like I'm doing as much as one man possibly could with three things running at once. While I move the trolleys, Bex keeps charging and the radio keeps seeking contact with Earth.

Laika takes it upon himself to ride on the trolleys as I wheel them towards the locked lab's walkway. He's much less talkative than he was before the barrier incident, which to me is the most surefire sign that it really shook him up.

"Do you want some food?" I ask as the last trolley clatters into the rest of them at the edge of the walkway. "Food? Food no?"

He doesn't even reply to this.

I left a lot of sunflower seeds and plenty of water near the open cage in Barnet's lab yesterday. It's not like Laika hasn't had access to sustenance. It's just unlike him not to be excited by the very mention of it.

I guess you could say it was a shared taste for sunflower seeds that brought us together in the first place. That was back in the Greenhouse, when he was still shy around me and I still saw him as the unwanted annoyance who cost me my contact lenses.

Once I've been into the lab — with or without Laika — I'll look at some more stuff in the parrot care book I found on my text-reader. I want to see if there's anything I can do to help him, or at least to learn the signs of what could be wrong. I'm worried that he doesn't seem himself.

With all the trolleys gathered, I start placing them in the walkway. I begin at the outer entrance, where the door is already blown off, and line them up without any gaps for as far as I can.

Laika opts to come with me, albeit with some uneasy squawks. I guess that tells me his fear of being alone is greater than his fear of being back here, after all.

He really seems to trust me now, and I'm not going to take that lightly.

Once I get four or five trolleys deep, I notice something different about the door that lies at the far end of the walkway, beyond the barrier Bex crushed to free Laika.

It looks closer, somehow. And then I realize that it *is* closer, because it's not the inner door at all. It's *another* barrier that must have come down at the same time, to trap us between it and the one we smashed.

At least there aren't any more, I think to myself. Bex has already crushed the outer door and the first barrier, so two more obstacles shouldn't be too much.

My extensive trolley collection makes it a fair way into the walkway without coming close to the second barrier.

Still, it's a hell of a lot better than nothing.

I'm also going to make absolutely sure that I never get too

far away from Bex. I don't think Laika will get too far away from us, either.

We're a lot more prepared than last time and we're a lot more on-guard.

I'm now thinking in *wills* rather than *woulds* regarding our lab entry. Increasingly, it really does seem like the radio isn't going to deliver anything.

The pull of what could be inside the lab is hard to resist, anyway, given the possibility that it might offer a tangible next step for getting off the station.

And I can't just wait around by the radio forever.

There might even be something in the lab that can help the survivors on Earth even if they can't help me — something I could include in my next radio message.

I don't want to stay on this station for another minute, but I have everything I need to survive here for *months* if I have to. That's definitely long enough for someone to pick up my signals once the dust or ash clears, when survivors start coming out of their bunkers to assess the damage and set about rebuilding what they can.

That's what I'm telling myself, and deep down I really do believe it.

This isn't a hopeless endeavor. I might be swimming against the tide, but I'm not circling the drain.

I hold my breath as I walk back to the computer for one last check of the radio status.

Nothing has changed.

By now, this is so expected that I don't even feel overly disappointed.

I'm already thinking about other ways to draw the attention of Earth's survivors.

One far-out option is to blow up my own lab so it detaches from the station — posing no danger to me or Laika — thus creating an unmissable spectacle in Earth's sky

If anyone is watching down there, that would absolutely

bring some attention my way and hopefully lead to them looking closely enough at the station to pick up my signals.

Fortunately, my next step is much clearer and much more rational than that hypothetical act of desperation. So with my mask in place and the trolleys lined up, I fetch Bex from her charging point and march her to the walkway.

"Speak now or forever hold your peace," I say to the robot, trying to amuse myself just enough to take the edge off the chronic stress I can feel building in my gut. "If you don't think we should do this, now's the time to tell me."

Laika looks at me like I'm crazy. He's probably not wrong.

I secure the oxygen mask over my mouth and start walking, one step behind Bex all the way. Laika wisely sticks with us, perched on the robot's head.

My breathing speeds up when we pass the last of the trolleys. Once we reach the new barrier, I get Bex in position and put on one of the control gloves.

I shoo Laika away gently, just enough to get him safely behind me while Bex and I swing away.

It only takes three punches to fully knock the barrier down, and I'm relieved to see that the next barrier is also our last: the fully sealed door.

One more obstacle.

I think Laika has picked up on what we do when we meet a locked door, because he hangs back without any need for me to tell him.

Once I have Bex in place again, I pull my arm back and punch the air in front of me as hard as I can. I punch at an angle so Bex delivers all of her force to the edge of the door. This is what worked for us at the outer door, and after three well-targeted punches it works again.

I hold my breath, half-expecting to hear a hiss of toxic gas or see some other deadly trap spring out at us.

Nothing happens.

I turn around to make sure no barriers are coming down.

All-clear on that front, too.

The trolleys haven't been needed. It's all gone to plan.

"Ready?" I ask, turning to Laika with a slight smile. "Laika okay?"

I don't know if my relieved tone made a difference or if he just can't shake his urge to explore. Either way, the little guy flies right in like he's sure there's nothing to worry about.

I step across the threshold right behind him, taking Bex with me and hoping beyond hope that he's right.

Steele didn't want me to see what's in here, and I'm about to find out why.

67

One step.

One single step inside is all it takes to see that this lab is nothing like any of the others.

It's nothing like anywhere else on the station.

Hell, it's nothing like any room I've ever been in — *anywhere*.

I don't only *see* the differences with this first step, either. I physically feel them.

I feel the plush carpet under my feet, giving a cushiony bounce I haven't felt since I left Earth two months ago.

Looking ahead, I see marble-effect walls covered in exquisitely framed paintings.

A grand piano sits to my left, fitting in well with the gentle piano music I can hear from unseen speakers.

When I look up to see where they're hiding, the ceiling brings another surprise. The elaborate blue and white paint job has clearly been designed to create a three-dimensional effect of Earth's cloudy sky, and it definitely hits the spot.

I look back down to the floor and see a hot tub opposite the piano.

Yup. A *hot tub*. In space.

I walk over and hear the gentle hum of electronics.

This water is still being kept hot, I realize.

What the hell is going on? Why was Grainger in here?

And more than that, why is *any* of this here?

There's no sign of any silver metal, unlike in my functionally designed and essentially undecorated lab where I was always completely surrounded by the stuff.

From the hot tub, I turn towards the wall next to the door. I see an imposing four-post bed, immaculately made and obviously empty.

In an outcome that's the total opposite of the one I hoped for, all I have are new questions.

"Squawk," Laika calls from up ahead.

Just don't touch anything, I silently plead, realizing I've lost sight of him.

I glance in the direction of the parrot's call and see that he's settled on the ground in front of some very heavy-looking burgundy drapes that run the whole way from floor to ceiling.

That's no less than twenty feet high. This place is beyond luxurious, I decide. It's straight up decadent.

The curtains diagonally block off the far-left corner of the lab, which is where I walk next.

"Well," I say when I reach them, "we didn't come this far not to keep going."

With that, I yank the heavy drapes to the right, revealing what lies behind them.

I've seen some things in the past few days that have taken my breath away.

I've seen some things in the past few days that have made me freeze on the spot.

But right now, looking down at what we've just found, I truly feel like time has stopped. I feel like nothing else exists.

It doesn't make sense.

Of all the things that haven't made sense, this is in a league of its own.

The chest-high object in front of us is halfway between a

coffin and a tanning booth, closed tightly with a perfectly clear lid.

It's the clear lid that allows me to see the unbelievable sight inside the capsule.

I lean in close.

Breathing slowly, just like Barnet's animals in the other lab, this man is unquestionably alive.

I don't know if the life-signature tracking screen I saw earlier on the station was spoofed by Steele and her cronies or if the lab's intact seal made him untraceable… but either way, he's alive.

And he's not just alive, he's right here in front of me.

I'm not alone on this station and I never have been.

It's me and him.

Just me and him…

Ignacio Zola.

68

Just like Barnet's animals, there are no wires connected to Zola.

He's wearing a plain white t-shirt and white shorts. No socks.

The only other thing on him is a famous ring that never comes off. It's rumored to be valued in the billions of dollars due to the rare metal content and historic value. The various diamonds he crushed to create the speckled effect around the band were supposedly owned by royal families from around the world.

His expression is calm. Sedate.

The capsule gives off an electrical humming sound about as loud as the hot tub.

I look underneath to see what it's connected to. There are no cables running to any of the walls so I figure it must have a power outlet in the floor. But that's not what catches my eye.

On the front of the base, at around waist height, there's a blue numerical countdown. It's going down one second at a time and will expire in 94 hours.

Just under four days.

Until what?

Four days until *what*?

What the hell is going on?

Why is Zola here?

Of all the people in all of the places, why the hell am I finding Ignacio Zola in a suspended animation capsule in one of The Beacon's offshoot labs?

The only answer I can come up with is very unpalatable. It also requires a leap into a theory I don't want to believe.

I can't be sure — of this, or just about anything else right now — but I think Zola might have isolated himself here to survive what he knew was coming on Earth.

This is the safest possible place.

The whole station is isolated, but each offshoot labs is protected from what happens at the other end of its walkway, too. The fact I'm still breathing is testament to that.

If anything had damaged the station's integrity, this lab would have detached at the first sign of trouble just like mine would have.

Sure, the automated emergency detachment protocol was primarily designed to protect the main body from something going wrong in one of the offshoots, but it works both ways.

None of my old assumptions have a leg to stand on anymore.

Now that I see Zola in front of me and know that some of his senior employees have been working against me, I have new ideas about why certain things might have been designed in certain ways.

I'm even starting to wonder if the Escape Pod's design was purposefully weakened. I'm starting to think they removed the parafoil landing system so no one could evacuate directly to Earth.

It's hard to believe they could have expected someone to survive like I have, with the combination of luck and everything else I've needed to stay here.

I don't think they're the kind of people to take chances, though. And besides, I'm being forced to believe things that are a *lot* more far-fetched than that.

I look more closely at Zola. There's noticeable growth in his ordinarily immaculate facial hair. It's still very neat but clearly hasn't been shaven for at least a few days. Then again, I have no idea what effect the suspended animation technology has on things like that. Who's to say he hasn't been in here for months?

There was no sign of him in any of the security camera footage, but that feels like another thing I can't rely on any more. Steele had access to the whole system, after all. so anything she really didn't want me to find would surely have been redacted.

It seems like her game was to keep me distracted until they could arrive here to deal with me, if they were actually coming at all. If they weren't, maybe they wanted to stall me until Zola woke up.

Is that what the countdown is leading to — Zola's reawakening?

It seems obvious as soon as I think of it.

I turn away from the capsule to look around the room for some context-giving clues. I've already looked under the capsule. When I stand on my tiptoes to look *over* the very back of it, I see an open laptop computer resting on a shelf.

Interesting…

I think this is here for Zola when he wakes up, because I can't see an easy way to get around the capsule without risking contact with any unseen connections.

I crouch to the ground and crawl until I can reach it with a fully extended arm. I take major care not to knock against anything. I'm very glad to see Laika standing still while I do, because there's no telling what could happen if either of us touch the wrong thing.

I disconnect the laptop from its charger and carefully pull it towards me.

Right away, I see that the computer is open in more ways than one. The screen is up instead of being folded closed, for starters. But far more importantly, my first touch of the trackpad brings the screen to life with no sign of any security lockout.

I guess the sealed door felt like enough for him. Well, that and the assumption everyone else was already dead.

The screen displays a spreadsheet. Only three cells contain any data.

The first is a date and the second is a time. I do some quick arithmetic.

Yup… it's the moment a few days ago at the exact time Grainger left this lab to do his dirty work in the Canteen.

The third cell contains the letters OG, which has to stand for Oliver Grainger.

A red warning notice runs under these cells:

DO NOT NAVIGATE AWAY FROM THIS TAB.

Okay. This tells me that Grainger was in here *after* Zola got into the capsule. That's something.

I think Grainger left this minimalist message for Zola. I think he was basically clocking in, typing the time and his initials to confirm that he was enacting his part of the plan.

The plan.

Zola's plan.

It's only too clear now. This son of a bitch was working with the rat bastard who killed everyone else on The Beacon. Zola is responsible.

And I know what that means: he's not just responsible for the deaths up *here*.

I put the laptop on the floor behind me and look down at Zola again.

I have half a mind to smash this capsule open and kill him right now. Screw the consequences of whatever anti-tampering security he might have in place — he deserves nothing else.

I place my palm on the capsule, right above his face. I've never deliberately hurt anyone for any reason except direct self-defense, but I want to rip his throat out right now. I want to—

"Squawk!" Laika calls.

As I turn to him, the piano music stops.

I lift my hand from the capsule, but it's too late.

The speaker system buzzes for a second. The next thing I hear is a throat-clearing cough, sending a chill down my spine as the wall ahead of me parts to reveal a huge TV screen.

Ignacio Zola's face stares out at me.

69

I recognize the background behind Zola in the recording. It's *this* lab.

He must have filmed this right before getting into the capsule!

I feel every hair on my body stand up.

"You should not be here," Zola says, speaking in that famously resonant and highly enunciated way that's so unique to him. "You *certainly* should not be interfering with my capsule."

Yup... just as I feared, I've triggered this — and maybe something worse — by touching it.

I'm kicking myself for that. At the time I felt pretty controlled for having the restraint to only place a palm on it instead of pounding two fists through the glass.

"I might look helplessly exposed," Zola's recording goes on, "but be aware that tampering any further will be the last mistake you ever make. Step back and let progress take its course on the path I have laid out, why don't you? If you have survived your role in the plan, congratulations are in order. Please now retreat and wait patiently for the next stage to commence."

Hmm.

This mention of a "role in the plan" suddenly makes me think this might have been meant for Grainger, if he had indeed survived and made any physical contact with the capsule.

"But if you have survived *in spite* of the plan, even greater congratulations are in order," Zola continues with a wry grin.

Ah, so he's covering all the bases. These comments are for someone who might have survived despite his diabolical plan. Sound familiar?

I was already listening with full attention. But now that I know Zola is explicitly addressing someone like me, I hyper-focus on every syllable he utters.

"Humanity's future starts now and you have evidently proven yourself a born survivor. You now face a choice: you can retreat and await the next stage, where your desire to survive might yet earn you a position in our new world. Alternatively, you can stay where you are and die on the edge of this new frontier. The choice is yours."

The recording ends as abruptly as it began, with the wall re-closing as soon as the screen goes dark.

I turn back to the capsule.

"You dirty son of a bitch," I curse under my breath.

The destruction on Earth wasn't really the work of some linen-wearing eco-terrorists.

I can't be sure yet if they were patsies or if they were actors like Steele, but they definitely weren't at the top of the chain.

It was him. It was all him.

A thousand new questions are floating around in my mind. But as soon as I accept this horrible truth, certain other things suddenly make a very uncomfortable kind of sense.

When I fixed the air leak, I might have inadvertently saved Zola, too. After all, this sealed lab only has 24 hours of its emergency life support — not enough to keep the air in here breathable until Zola's countdown comes to an end.

I wonder now if Steele kept me alive in case any other problems came up.

She definitely didn't want me to get into this lab, but she used a soft touch in her efforts to keep me out. With Pierre at her side she told me it was dangerous, and all along they tried to make me think they were allies by helping me with things like the satellite images.

They were distracting me the whole time, letting me discover things that were never going to help me in any tangible way. They tried to convince me they were my friends so I wouldn't get too close to the truth. And damn them... it almost worked.

Thinking back, I see just how devious they were.

Pierre knew I had the text reader when he said I couldn't look online to research bunker conspiracies. He was encouraging me to have that idea... not just distracting me from the fourth lab, but also giving me more reasons to think my family has survived and thus more incentive to avoid unnecessary risks.

I was never getting off this station. They just wanted to make sure I never saw what was in this lab before the countdown hit zero.

How would Zola have dealt with me then? Would he have killed me? Would he have congratulated me for surviving, spinning a web of lies about his own innocence and offering me a place in the "new world" his maniacal recording talks about?

Or would Steele and the others have arrived before the countdown hit zero? Would they have docked after all, to deal with me and be here to take Zola away for whatever "the next stage" of their plan really entails?

I didn't know anything about the PetraVista station until I made contact with Steele, and now I'm doubting every single thing she told me about it. I don't know if it even exists. I've already considered that the signal's origin point could have been spoofed, but what if it's worse than that? What if Steele really *is* in space after all, but on a much larger station or space-craft that Zola's cronies have all been evacuated to?

With what they've done to Earth, I wouldn't count something like that out.

All I have are questions, but it's the ones about what happens next that have me most worried.

Now that I know too much, it goes without saying that I'm in his evil team's crosshairs. So wherever they might be coming from, I have to think someone is coming for me right now.

And not coming to save me — coming to *get* me.

Once I made contact with the others, my main goal became surviving until they get here.

I moved away from that line of thinking as soon as Mel slipped up and let me know she'd been watching all along, but everything has just come into *much* sharper focus.

There's still no way off this damn station, just like when I first thought about having to leave before they get here.

I suppose I now have a new option of trying to hold Zola hostage, but to what end?

I don't know where I'd go with that. At least an unclear option is better than none at all, though.

Maybe something will come to me. Everything in this crazy lab is proof that I'm still finding new leads, so I'm not giving up hope that—

All of a sudden, a sharp sound breaks my focus and evidently catches Laika by surprise at the same time. His frightened squawk is loud and almost instant, but it's not quite the first thing I hear.

No… that honor goes to the deafening alarm that begins blaring overhead.

A pulsing red light catches my eyes underneath the capsule, where I see that a new countdown has appeared next to the one for ninety-four hours.

It's still there, too, with its blue numbers ticking down one second at a time. But now it's joined by far more ominous countdown.

The new red countdown is ticking down one second at a time, too.

Unfortunately, there are already only fifty-four of them left.

Fifty-three.

Fifty-two.

Oh, shit…

70

I have to get the hell out of here. I'd say *we*, but Laika has wisely already high-tailed to the door.

He hasn't gone any further than that, though. He's standing at the threshold squawking his little heart out. There's no doubt in my mind he's warning me to hurry up. He's begging me to join him on the way back to what we can only hope is the safety of the rest of the station.

I don't know what it means that we've destroyed the sealed buffer between this lab and everywhere else. Is anywhere going to be safe from whatever is about to happen?

I can't afford to think too much. All I know right now is that *this* place is definitely not safe and I have very little time to get as far away as I can.

I grab my phone from my pocket and rapidly snap the clearest close-up photos of Zola I can manage.

I'm still wearing the body-cam. It's connected to the computer and has hopefully sent Zola's speech back to the Control Center and the recording software I set up before I left.

The body-cam is too low to get clear shots of Zola in the capsule, though. It's worth a few seconds to use my phone, because I really do need these photos.

If I somehow make it out of here or make contact with

357

Earth, there's literally no chance anyone will take my word for this without proof.

As soon as I have some clear shots, I put my phone back in my pocket and hurriedly crouch to pick up the laptop. I run to Laika without wasting another second.

The alarm stops as soon as I cross the threshold into the walkway.

Ah… so there's some kind of sensor.

It could be a pressure sensor on the ground, or maybe some movement-detection technology in the ceiling. Either way, the alarm automatically stopped when I left the lab.

I need to know if it's ever going to be safe to go back in there. To find out, I slowly put a single foot back on the plush carpet.

The alarm instantly restarts. I also see the red numbers resume their countdown on the base of the capsule, beyond the open curtain. It doesn't start at the beginning, either — it picks up where it left off.

Everything stops just as quickly when I take my foot out again.

It's majorly frustrating that I can't go back in to look around for more information, or anything else that might help me right now.

I'm glad that I at least have the computer, though. And even more importantly, at least the countdown stopped. That was no given.

"Squawk," Laika cries from the ground by my side. "Ray Ray! See? Ray Ray? See! No-kay!"

I don't know what Laika sees or what he thinks is wrong. But by the time I look down at him, I'm worrying about a problem he's causing rather than a problem he has.

He's flying straight back into the lab!

The alarm blares as soon as he passes the doorway, telling me it's a movement sensor rather than a floor-based sensor after all.

What the hell is he thinking? I have to get him out.

"Ray Ray! See?" he squawks, landing just in front of the capsule.

Only when I reach him do I see that he's landed beside my phone, which must have fallen out of my pocket when I crouched for the laptop.

He's trying to pick it up but can't get a grip of it.

I grab the phone and run straight for the door again, holding it tightly in my hand this time. When I get back out, I see that we're down to nine seconds.

Laika, a fast flyer when he wants to be, is already waiting for me.

The alarm stops, killing the countdown at nine.

Breathlessly, I crouch down again and put a thankful hand on Laika's wing.

There's been so much going on since I found this guy, I've never stopped to give much thought to why he was awake in Barnet's lab.

But after some of the things he's done, and especially what he's *just* done, I'm starting to wonder exactly what kind of work Barnet was doing with him.

I still know next to nothing about parrots but surely they can't all be as smart as Laika. He not only recognizes that a man-made stimulus like the alarm can signal a threat, he also seems to understand abstract things like my need to have my evidence-packed phone.

I don't think I'm putting more on to his action than I should. He knew it was dangerous to be in there, but somehow — and rightly — he decided it was worth going in to alert me that I'd dropped my phone.

"You're a smart guy," I tell him.

I still have to make sure he doesn't go back in for anything else, though, since surely not even *this* parrot can read numbers or know how little time we had to spare.

Going back in would almost certainly trigger something we desperately need to avoid. To keep him out, I think I'll hang some kind of barrier from the ceiling at the walkway's entrance.

For now though, there's something I need to see.

I put the laptop under one arm and guide Bex back down the walkway with us, suddenly *very* glad that I hadn't brought her inside. There's no telling if the security sensors would have been tripped by a large robot. But if they had? Well, her lack of speed would have spelled major trouble.

When we get back to the Control Center, I'm pleased to see that my body-cam footage is still transmitting and being recorded on the computer. This means I have indisputable video proof of Zola's involvement, to go along with my close-up photos.

I put the scumbag's laptop on the desk in front of Commander Harrison's screen.

"DO NOT NAVIGATE AWAY FROM THIS TAB."

"Fuck you," I say out loud, clicking to the second of two tabs within the open spreadsheet.

When I saw Ignacio Zola in the capsule, my blood boiled.

But when I see the content of his spreadsheet's second tab, my heart breaks.

71

It gets worse the longer I look, but I see enough in one glance to get the gist of it.

Zola *was* responsible for everything.

Worst of all, he's not done yet.

This tab has fifteen filled rows, with a list of events in a column to the left and a list of corresponding dates and times on the right.

Words like Evacuation and Detonation jump out right away, like daggers jumping into my heart. But the full ordered rundown of events is what really gets me.

It really does get worse and worse.

The first event, almost tauntingly, is labeled *BARCLAY METHOD VALIDATED*.

I look at the date and time in the right-side column.

It only takes me a second to recognize that this was the moment when my penultimate experiment concluded. This was when I became ninety-nine percent certain I could demonstrate the utility and replicability of my enrichment process. It wasn't my final experiment, but it was clearly enough to convince Zola.

Seeing him refer to the process as the "Barclay method" makes me feel sick to the pit of my stomach.

Even though I had the best intentions with my research, it feels more and more like I really have paved humanity's road to hell.

I commiserated about this with Pierre, who I now know was a bullshit artist trying to gain my trust just like "Mel" was, but it hurts much more now than ever before.

The next event is labeled *ENCASEMENT*, which must be when Zola climbed into the capsule. The time stamp here is only five hours after the last one. This means he was already on the station while I was busily preparing my experiments, evidently waiting to know that my method really would work.

The next is equally self-explanatory: *GRAINGER CHECK-IN*.

It's the same time Grainger entered on the other tab, to signify the moment when he entered this lab before callously proceeding to murder all of my colleagues.

When I carefully click on this cell of the spreadsheet to confirm a suspicion, I see that it is indeed a formula linked to the other sheet. Grainger entered the time *there*, on the only tab he was instructed to look at, and it auto-populated here.

Next up is *FOG OF WAR*, coming exactly one hour after Grainger's check-in.

Since Zola was already in the capsule by then, I'm not surprised to see that this cell didn't have a time entry of its own. Instead, it consists of a simple formula: the previous cell's time plus one hour.

I only know what "fog of war" refers to in the context of what else I've seen. That broader context tells me it relates to the misinformation campaign that painted Zola as a victim targeted by an eco-terrorists cabal, rather than the mastermind behind this whole damn thing.

Each of the remaining time stamps is the result of a formula, always the time of Grainger's check-in plus a specified duration.

I figure the initiation time must have been broadcast to Zola's cronies on Earth, too.

The rest of the spreadsheet is clearly a list of what was planned to happen, rather than a definitive post-facto record of what *has* happened. Some of the noted times are in the future, for one thing, but even the ones that have passed were automatically based on the time Grainger entered.

SURFACE EVACUATION comes at plus three hours, not very long after the station's population was wiped out. This one has to refer to a chosen few being taken to the safety of one or more ZolaCore bunkers.

Next is *COMMUNICATIONS WIPEOUT*, at plus twenty-three hours.

With only a little reading between the lines, I can now conclude that Zola's demented henchmen really did use some kind of EMP to disable communications equipment on Earth's surface. This was no doubt when the internet died and all the phones on the station stopped receiving updates.

I don't yet know what came after the blackout, but I'm about to find out.

PRELIMINARY DETONATION comes next, at plus twenty-four hours. These words are underlined, like a hyperlink. I'll check that out in a second.

The word preliminary sends shivers down my spine.

It's less blindingly obvious what *PRELIMINARY EXCAVATION* refers to in the next cell, but context helps once again.

This comes at plus forty-eight hours. Okay, so that's exactly two days after Grainger did his dirty deed and one day after the preliminary detonation. That means it's already happened, or at least has already begun.

The things I learned in Vinner's lab make me think this could be when Zola's people began excavating theocite, maybe from some of the deep deposits they exposed with a colossal detonation.

I look at my watch. Right now, I'm in the time frame between this "preliminary excavation" and the harrowingly named event that comes next:

PLANETARY EVACUATION.

This is timed at plus six-and-a-half days, which means it's still around *three*-and-a-half days in the future.

The self-explanatory *AWAKENING* comes next, at plus six days and twenty-three hours. That's just under four days away… exactly when the countdown on Zola's capsule already told me he'll be re-awakening.

I try to control my breathing as everything sinks in.

So far, Zola's guys have evacuated from Earth's surface and they've blown everything to hell. They're now all set to evacuate from the whole *planet*, and the next event tells me why.

Scheduled for precisely seven days after Grainger set things rolling, which will be just one hour after Zola wakes up and four days from now, something is coming that sounds much worse than the already-apocalyptic preliminary detonation.

The words cut me like thorns:

MOTHERLODE DETONATION.

I feel numb.

I feel so numb, the next two events barely register.

First comes *RENDEZVOUS*, at plus eight days. That has to be when Zola leaves the station, with help from Steele or whoever else is working with him on this heinous plan.

After that comes *MOTHERLODE EXCAVATION*, when his team will clearly begin work on accessing the unimaginably vast theocite reserves opened up by their second detonation.

This is set for *twelve* days after Grainger's check-in, which tells me the seabed is going to be a no-go zone for four whole days, even for ZolaCore's enormous state-of-the-art mining equipment.

There's one more event. It's set for plus twenty-one days — three weeks from Grainger's sabotage attack — and is described in a single word. The word is a proper noun, so unique that it can only mean one thing.

BAYZEN.

Until now I've only ever seen that word in Vinner's lab.

Bayzen 108b is the name of the supposedly habitable planet he was researching. The chilling context I've seen in here now tells me it's the destination where the certifiably insane Ignacio Zola plans to take his chosen few to start their new world.

He always wanted to leave Earth.

He always wanted to leave behind those he deems weak and worthless so the supposedly strong and worthy can reach their potential.

His whole broken psychology has always been based around his view of Earth as an overpopulated womb.

That explains why he's acted so manically and so diabolically, at least as well as anything ever could, and I think I also know why he's acted so *urgently*.

Now that my enrichment process has given him the final piece of the puzzle, this isn't just the chance to leave Earth he's always waited for. In Zola's mind, it's the *only* chance he'll ever have.

If the powerful governments that despise him had ever found out how much theocite was under the seabed and how it could be harnessed for so many applications, there's no way he could have retained any kind of monopoly.

The public wouldn't have stood for it… not with all the poverty and strife in so many places.

At the very least there would have been a temporary moratorium on private excavation. At most, his mining equipment and platforms might have been requisitioned and nationalized.

Even without these huge new breakthroughs in mining and enrichment, there have already been calls for that kind of thing from some political pressure groups. That would have all gone mainstream, and even governments that have been friendly to Zola would have been pressured to cooperate with the bigger nations he's pissed off so many times.

Zola never really cared about the money. He cared about where the theocite could take him.

But even with all of the unbelievable things I've had to accept as harsh realities, I'm really struggling with the idea that Zola has a ship capable of traveling almost six light years.

I don't care how enriched the BioZol is and how easily his

passengers can travel in capsules like the one he's in... how can a spacecraft that size possibly exist without the world knowing about it?

Another thing that jumps out here is that Zola is scheduled to wake up an hour before the final destruction. It's like he wants to see it happening live. That only adds another layer of sickness.

I know too well how clear the view is from the Observation Deck and Control Center, and all I saw was the aftermath of a *preliminary* detonation.

I also wonder if the people Zola has chosen for his new world will even know that he's involved in all of this. I doubt it. That might be why it all started with supposedly natural disasters and why those so-called eco-terrorists claimed responsibility — the whole "fog of war" idea.

The cover story might go that since Zola was up here, bravely surviving a sabotage attack, he couldn't selflessly give himself up like the terrorists were demanding. I'm making some assumptions there about things of secondary importance, but the general idea makes sense.

While I was working my way down the spreadsheet's time-line, I noticed that it looks like each of the detonation events is a hyperlink to another document or hidden tab.

I click *PRELIMINARY DETONATION*. Sure enough, an image of a map pops up in front of the spreadsheet.

A large black X-mark in the North Pacific shows the location of the first blast. This is where the most easily accessible of Earth's large theocite deposits was blasted open.

The image shows the entirety of Earth's landmass and oceans shaded in one of three colors: yellow, orange, and red.

Everywhere near the epicenter is red.

An annotation in the bottom right corner explains what red means:

UNSURVIVABLE.

Great.

Orange means *SURFACE UNSURVIVABLE*. To my horror,

this descriptor applies to the entire United States as well as most of North East Asia.

The affected area spreads outwards in concentric circles, from red in the center to orange and then yellow. Everywhere on the planet is at least yellow, which means *SURVIVAL UNLIKELY.*

This is harrowing on so many levels. It tells me there's little chance anyone survived outside of a sheltered bunker, and that even a bunker wouldn't have helped in the red-shaded areas that include Alaska among countless other places.

And this was only the *preliminary* blast.

When I close this map and return to the spreadsheet, I'm almost too scared to click the second link.

I know my family isn't in a ZolaCore bunker.

There's no way. Eva has been called to Colorado for the same reason one of my colleague's family was called to Virginia: because she can bring something to the table that our government's emergency planners have decided we'll need in the event of a societal rebuild.

A societal rebuild.

That's what I've been counting on all this time... the idea that humanity can rebuild. The idea that *society* can be rebuilt from the ashes of this chaos.

But now?

I gulp.

I really can hardly bring myself to click this link.

From what I've seen so far, I still think there's a good chance the bunker in Colorado Springs has kept my family alive.

But now that I know a second stronger blast is coming?

I close my eyes and click the link.

When the new map appears, I no longer only *feel* sick.

It takes one glance at what's coming. Just one glance and I *am* sick. The only thing I can be glad about is the well-placed bucket next to my chair.

The image hits me like a freight train.

When Zola's motherlode detonation blows four days from now, just off the Atlantic seaboard, the entire world will turn red.

UNSURVIVABLE.

Surface, bunker, it doesn't matter. Zola's chosen few will have enacted their planetary evacuation by then, because the second blast is going to be categorically unsurvivable.

I've seen the damage caused by the first blast, which only turned a small portion of Earth red. What's on the way is an order of magnitude worse. It's genuinely hard to comprehend.

Fallout isn't a strong enough word for what's coming, even at the other side of the world.

Tectonic, geological… God, I don't even know if there's a word for the scale of the damage that's coming.

This is full-on *apocalyptic*, in the truest undiluted sense of the word. Not just the end of civilization or the end of our human world, but the end of Earth as a habitable planet.

Tears stain my makeshift glasses as I stare at the map.

When Zola's monstrous plan reaches its crescendo in four days, there are going to be no survivors on Earth's surface *or* in any bunkers.

Whoever Zola's gangsters leave behind when they evacuate Earth will be left for dead.

Everyone… including my family.

No one is picking up my radio contact, no doubt thanks to the EMP communications wipeout that came earlier in the plan.

I have no way of contacting Earth and I have no way of getting home.

I have no next move.

My eyes close in defeat.

I tried.

I tried so hard, but it wasn't enough.

I survived everything.

I did so much, and for what?

For nothing, *that's* what.

I turn to my right, where Laika is looking up at me with eyes that tell me he *definitely* understands at least some of what I'm feeling.

"I'm sorry, buddy," I say, trying to hold back any more tears before my goggles fill up. "It's over."

72

I lean back and look at the ceiling, taking my goggles off to shake away the tears.

It really is over.

Seriously… what can I do?

The only thing I can think of is to hide somewhere and try to take Zola hostage when he wakes up an hour before the denotation, then say I'll kill him if they don't call it off.

But what's the point? I can't hold him forever.

And even if I could, everyone left on Earth, underground or not, would always be sitting ducks for whenever they pulled the trigger.

Zola would probably tell his goons to continue the plan without him, anyway. For all his insanity, I've never got the impression that Zola is a selfish guy — he's just a sociopath.

His driving goal of freeing human potential from its earthly constraints is much bigger than himself.

And more to the point, they've already destroyed the world as we know it with the preliminary detonation.

The only way forward for them is to the *new* world of Bayzen 108b, as clinically insane as that sounds. Their only route runs straight through the motherlode of theocite, which they'd require to enrich vast quantities of synthesized BioZol if they'll have even half a chance of getting there.

Enriching their fuel using what Zola himself calls *the Barclay method*, I reflect. Talk about rubbing salt in the wounds.

This really is the ultimate, never-to-be-beaten case of be careful what you wish for.

I was never maniacally driven by a goal like Zola was, but I have to admit I always liked the idea that my work could one day enable humanity to expand our reach beyond Earth.

I could never be a real astronaut with my vision problems, or the nerve damage in my wrist, or the psychological issues I've battled with in certain circumstances. Probably for more reasons, to boot.

I just thought I could maybe at least help with the fuel.

And here I am, getting what I wanted in the worst possible way.

The monkey's paw has done its work and the bad guys are going to flat-out destroy life on Earth just so they can leave it behind.

To round it all off, the one thing I want now is the one thing I'm most helpless to achieve: getting *back* to Earth to stop their demented mission in its tracks.

Zola's chosen few will soon be leaving Earth in their planetary evacuation. Most of them will never return, obviously, but I figure some of them might have to. After all, the theocite motherlode they need for the trip to Bayzen 108b isn't going to excavate itself.

The civilization-killing motherlode detonation that will open up those untapped reserves is going to eliminate *everything* on Earth. With that in mind, I can only assume ZolaCore will also evacuate their mining crews and the massive excavation equipment they'll need after the blast.

That equipment might already be in space, for all I know. All that's certain is that everyone and everything they need to excavate the theocite will have to be safely out of range.

It's sickening.

So much technology, so much planning, so many smart people… all directed towards the most heinous and heartless action imaginable.

I feel more and more duped by the liar formerly known as Mel. She probably is on Earth, like I've been suspecting for a while. All the chaos and damage of the first blast was nothing compared to what's coming, which is why she'll be gone before it hits.

Zola and his cronies really must have had *total* faith that their New Zealand bunker would shield its inhabitants from the first blast. If not, they would have skipped that step and gone right for the planetary evacuation that's coming before the much stronger second blast.

Considering this makes me wonder again why Zola is up here.

It doesn't make sense to think he might have deemed the bunker safe enough for low-ranking personnel but not safe enough for himself. Because if *they* didn't make it there would be no future for him, anyway.

I really don't know.

The best I can figure is that he wants most of his evacuees — besides the real inner circle, like Steele and a small number of others — to think he's dead. This crossed my mind earlier and I'm returning to the thought with more certainty now. That would be a built-in justification for why he didn't step forward to negotiate with the eco-terrorists who were supposedly responsible for the disasters on Earth.

Yeah. I think that's the official line most of his evacuees will be fed.

I know humans have a strong survival instinct, but I just can't buy that thousands of people would willingly follow a mass murderer to a new world if they knew he was responsible for willfully destroying the old one.

Fighting an urge stronger than any I've ever felt, it really is all I can do to hold myself back from running into the lab again and smashing his damn capsule to pieces. I feel like I'm bursting with enough rage to kill him with my bare hands in the nine seconds before the security system might kill me, too.

"Ray Ray?" Laika calls from the doorway, taking my attention. His voice sounds different, like he's not enunciating fully.

I didn't even realize he'd left while I've been helplessly staring at the ceiling in defeat. Thank God he didn't go back into Zola's lab... that would have been all we need.

He flies back to his seat next to mine and proceeds to empty his beak of some sunflower seeds. "Ray Ray, food."

I inhale slowly. *This guy.*

"No food. Ray Ray no-kay," he says, contracting no and okay in his idiosyncratic way. "Food. Ray Ray okay."

This sweet little guy.

He knows I'm not okay, and this is all he can think of to help. I pat him gently.

"Thank you, buddy," I say. I don't feel like eating, but now more than ever it's the thought that counts.

Laika is so kind-hearted. So innocent.

Just like Eva and Joe.

Sitting in front of Commander Harrison's computer, all I can think to do is send them a message.

No one has picked up my radio signals yet and there's no reason to think they will. But if anyone ever *does,* I want them to have a warning of what's coming and I want Eva and Joe to know that my hope of seeing them again is the only thing that's kept me going.

Especially in the first few hours when I had to do what I did to Yannick and had to force myself to step into space for an emergency EVA, the thought of somehow getting home was one I stubbornly clung to for dear life.

This parrot by my side makes it hard to give up, too, but he wasn't always such a welcome sight. It's funny how things change.

I stop the body-cam recording, which I only now realize is still running. With the video capturing software free, I start recording myself from the main camera above Commander Harrison's screen.

"This is Ray Barclay on The Beacon space station," I begin, choking out the words through more emotion than I know what to do with.

I don't get any further.

I stop and take off the goggles to rub my eyes with both hands, telling the tears to stay back and doing all I can to psych myself up.

Take two.

"This is Ray Barclay," I say, my voice a lot stronger, "sole survivor of a sabotage attack on The Beacon space station."

I don't put the goggles back on, because I don't need to see any detail of my own tired face. And this feels like it's going to be the last Eva and Joe will ever see of me, if anyone even picks up the signal in time, so I don't want those clunky things in the way.

I give the shortest rundown of what I've just uncovered as I possibly can.

Once I've relayed the urgency of the main threat, I hold up the laptop to the camera so the spreadsheet and maps are visible. A picture really is worth a thousand words, and showing the list of events and times saves me from trying to get through every detail without choking up.

I explain that Zola is alive in a shielded capsule and that he's ultimately responsible for everything. I also explain that I can't touch the capsule without likely killing myself and possibly setting something even worse in motion.

I show the close-up photos of Zola from my phone, too, with thanks again to Laika for alerting me that it had fallen out of my pocket.

I'm going to send this message out on an open frequency while continuing to look for connections on Earth, but confirmation of an EMP-like "communications wipeout" really has lowered my hopes on that front.

Still, I have to try.

I *have* to.

When I've done the best I can to lay out the salient facts, I get more personal and speak directly to my family.

"Joe, Eva… I've done all I can to get back to you and I want you to know that you've given me the strength to get this far. If this message reaches Earth in time, it's thanks to *you* as much as me. I'm sorry I came here. I thought I was helping the world and I thought the payments would set us up for the life we've always dreamed of. I'll never forgive myself for not being there with you, but if you ever see this… I just want you to hear that I love you both and I'm more sorry than I ever thought a man could be."

I bite the insides of my cheeks in an effort to restrain the tears and keep up *some* charade of emotional control. It's a tough battle.

"I have evidence of everything and I'm broadcasting it at targeted locations where there might be bunkers. This general warning about the second blast is going out on an open frequency. I hope you get both. If there was any way I could get to Earth with this news, I would already be on the way. But they ripped out the whole structure of the Escape Pod's parafoil landing system. There's just no way it can possibly land or even splashdown without killing me on impact. If there was *any* chance I could make it down alive, I would already—"

I stop talking. *So* suddenly, it makes Laika squawk in surprise.

"Ray Ray okay?" he asks.

But nothing cut me off — nothing except a sudden thought that's *so* crazy, I know instantly that I'm never going to shake it.

I know instantly that I'm never going back to the mindset of ten seconds ago.

After all, you can't reason yourself out of something you didn't reason yourself into.

My driving goal is no longer survival. This is bigger than that.

The evidence I have is the only thing that can possibly save the world. But for it to have any chance, I need to get it within reach of someone who can do something about it.

That's why as soon as the crazy idea is in my mind, I know I'm doing it.

Under no illusions that I'll ever walk out of it, I need to get into that Escape Pod and aim for a bunker.

The impact will be like nothing a human being could withstand, but that doesn't matter.

That doesn't matter because my fragile human bones don't *need* to survive the impact.

The Control Center's black box is all that needs to survive the impact.

I don't have to make it down alive. I just have to make it down.

The considerations have changed.

I don't have to survive to make a difference. That idea is gone.

I don't have to see my family again to save them. That one is gone, too.

What counts now is that I've survived long enough to give myself a one-in-a-million shot of saving everyone else...

And that's good enough for me.

73

"I'm coming down," I say, deciding my fate out loud, once and for all. "Don't count on finding me alive inside, but keep your eyes open for an Escape Pod hurtling down to Earth."

It's an insane risk. I get that. But sometimes the stakes are so high, the level of risk doesn't come into it. Doing nothing while your family needs help is harder than doing *anything* — believe me.

On the day of the accident, I jumped off that cliff for the first and only time in my life. I didn't even think about how dangerous it was.

When I looked down and saw Jack floating face-down by the rocks, I didn't think about the chance I would end up the same way. *His* only chance of survival depended on me jumping down after him, so that's what I did. I jumped down.

Okay, I didn't succeed that day. I couldn't save him.

But this is different. I don't even have to survive this landing.

This time, I just have to get down.

Finishing up my radio message, I rapidly vocalize some of the logic I've just run through in my head, to the extent it can be called logic. I skip my thoughts about the accident and sign-off with a vow to do whatever I can to get the evidence down safely.

I don't think anyone will hear my communications from up here.

But an Escape Pod falling from the sky? The naked eye could definitely pick *that* up. Someone might see me. Someone might find the evidence I'll bring to warn of the upcoming motherlode detonation.

My family is in Colorado Springs, but I have to aim for the bunker in Virginia.

I *know* that one is at Mount Pony, whereas I only *think* the Colorado bunker is at Cheyenne Mountain.

Besides, I'm not fooling myself into thinking I'll be seeing anyone once I land.

I'll be climbing into that Escape Pod without expecting to ever climb out of it.

I am counting on something else, though. I'm counting on the belief that if I aim for a bunker packed with government and military personnel, *someone* is going to be looking up closely enough to see a spacecraft plummeting out of the sky.

I can't engineer the Pod to land safely. I'm clear on that.

But if I can just engineer it to land without exploding powerfully enough to destroy an airplane-style black box that's designed to withstand massive forces, the world might still have a chance.

It's not going to be easy, but it's not impossible.

I don't have a minute to spare, either. Four days is almost no time to thwart a plan like this, even if my radio warning *is* picked up.

Sure, it makes sense to exhaust as many ideas as possible to give the black box a fair chance of making it down in one piece. But I really have to be out of here in a matter of hours.

There's one idea rolling around in my mind that might just work.

At last, it's one that finally has an irony falling in my favor.

I owe my one chance to the success I had in enriching

BioZol with ultra-heated theocite, making small quantities of a fuel source *far* more powerful than anything else that's remotely stable and usable.

ZolaCore has looked into all kinds of applications for enriched fuel. Aside from enabling distant exploration, one of the main ones relates to the precision landing of unmanned spacecraft on mineable asteroids.

The idea is that tiny amounts of enriched fuel, engaged in the direction of the target object, can essentially provide a reverse thrust effect for rapid but controlled deceleration.

If I can rig the Escape Pod to feed the engines a little bit of my enriched fuel at the right time…

Well, you never know.

It's untested in real world application, but it just might work. All I have to do is control the landing enough for the evidence I've uncovered to make it down intact.

In a weird way, I feel less stressed than I have for a long time. Jettisoning any idea that I might survive is actually liberating my mind to work on solutions for the more manageable problem of delivering an intact black box to Earth.

I set my latest recorded message to broadcast on an open frequency. With that done, I dive right into the system's user guide. I'm looking for maintenance or troubleshooting information on the Escape Pod.

I find what I'm looking for pretty quickly. As soon as I get deeper into the nitty gritty, I start to think this might really be doable.

There's a backup fuel supply. I don't need that extra fuel, but I can sure use its tank. Once I drain it, I can replace the regular fuel with my own enriched concoction.

The guide also tells me everything I need to know in terms of the Pod, like its unloaded mass.

I already know the established facts about un-enriched BioZol's potency. I also know everything there is to know about the theocite-laced stuff I cooked up in the lab. Combining all of this, I can calculate what I need to do.

I grab a pen and scribble down some quick calculations. It's apparent that the Pod's regular fuel supply of BioZol will be almost totally exhausted when I reach Earth's atmosphere. That's not unexpected, because it really isn't built for long journeys.

Almost totally exhausted is fine, anyway. I'll just have to be mindful not to load in too much extra cargo.

When I reach the atmosphere and stop using the Pod's supply of regular fuel, I'll essentially go into free-fall. That'll last until I counteract the descent with some concentrated bursts of deceleration, courtesy of the enriched fuel I'm about to load into the backup tank.

My last moments aren't going to be pretty and they're not going to be fun. But with the help of the research and calculations I've done here, I'm optimistic that I can get a warning to Earth before the help I've inadvertently given Zola dooms everyone to destruction.

There's nothing in the guide about landing, obviously, and I know I'm going to struggle to see any detailed readings or controls without my goggles.

These few minutes still have me feeling much better, though, and I rush off to my lab with something close to a spring in my step.

This right here is a surefire sign of how desperate this situation is, and of how utterly desolate I was a few minutes ago. Having half a chance of *dying successfully* now seems like something to feel positive about.

It's all relative, as they say.

I close my lab before Laika can follow me in. I'll only be a minute and keeping him out is the only move that makes sense.

Accessing the enriched fuel from inside my reaction chamber is a task I'm used to doing safely, but that doesn't mean it's not an inherently dangerous one. Introducing an inquisitive parrot to the mix would *not* be smart.

It all goes smoothly.

I quickly have the theocite-enriched fuel in its suitable container. It's small — we're talking about a few coffee cups worth of the stuff, no more than that — but it is capital-P *Potent*.

I carefully take it to the Escape Pod.

Laika follows as always, bearing no grudge about not getting in.

When I get back, I follow the instructions from the computer. I snapped a few photos of them on my phone for easy reference, and that comes in very handy.

Within five or ten minutes I manage to replace the full backup supply of BioZol with a much smaller amount of my own special brew.

Everything really *is* relative, because working on this tiny and rickety-looking Escape Pod isn't making me feel as terrified as it probably should be.

That's what the acceptance of death will do to a guy, I guess. Not the warmest of thoughts, but at least it's letting me get on with the task at hand.

My life isn't what counts anymore.

This is bigger than me, and I have no time to waste.

74

I've figured most things out, but I still need to run some calculations on when I should start releasing the enriched fuel.

The main thing for now is that I know I *can* feed in the Pod's backup supply at will. I'm grateful for that.

The Pod's two-tank setup works majorly in my favor, because it conceivably could have taken me *days* to work out how to introduce a manual injection system. Needless to say, *days* isn't a measure of time I can afford to think about, much less a schedule I can work to.

While I'm getting into a good workflow at the Escape Pod, I think it makes sense to keep at it.

I'll get to removing the black box from the Control Center later, along with gathering everything else that might help the survivors on Earth to see what's been going on here.

My next task is somewhat less high-tech than the last one, but it has to be done.

My need to wear a pressure suit rules out wearing my goggles, which poses a natural challenge. And if I'm going to be flying this totally unfamiliar thing while halfway blind, I'm going to need something to let me know which button is which.

Pierre talked about this, too, the convincingly friendly son of a bitch he was.

How could he look me in the eye and call me "brother" so many times, like we were buddies, when all along he was lying through his teeth about being on my side? It's like Grainger playing chess with Yannick and the others so many times, all while knowing what he was going to do to them.

These people are bona fide monsters.

I shake the thought aside. Focusing back on what matters right now, for ease of reference I decide to color code the buttons and dials I'll need. Cutting the colored stickers into different shapes will make it all extra intuitive.

A green arrow for go, a red circle for stop… that kind of thing.

"Go" in this case will launch and propel the craft in the usual manner. What I'm marking as "Stop" will actually be the button to engage the backup fuel source, which I've just replaced with my theocite-enriched concoction.

I think of it as Stop because I'll be rotating the Pod 180 degrees before I feed any fuel in with this button. That way the reverse thrust from my enriched fuel will effectively work as an extremely crude brake of sorts, countering the Pod's descent just before it reaches the ground and thus mitigating the force of the impact.

If my initial calculations are correct, it'll only take truly *tiny* well-timed releases of the enriched fuel to bring meaningfully effective deceleration.

I've run the numbers on the assumption that the enriched fuel's potency will be as great in real-world use as it was in my lab, and I'm growing cautiously optimistic as the results sink in. Everything is pointing in the right direction.

What felt like a one-in-a-million shot of getting the black box down intact now feels more like a one-in-five chance. And if the potency holds up like I expect it to, I now even think there might be a one-in-a-million chance of… whisper it… getting *myself* down intact.

I'm counting on my own breakthrough. I'm betting on myself.

I dearly wish I had more enriched fuel, or another few days to make some. But I am where I am. I have a chance, however remote, and that's a lot more than nothing.

One other thing I still want to do is find the safest way to have my goggles in the Pod with me. That way I can hold them at arm's length and hope they'll still let me see any details that might be necessary to read. I look in and see that I'll be able to stow them under the seat, like hand luggage on a regular plane. I don't want loose glass moving around, so I'll make sure they're packed tight.

I can't count on being able to use them, but it's worth a shot.

I take a photo of the Pod's internal controls before heading back to the computer, where I make a note of all the annotations I'll need.

I'm working faster than ever. Hyper-focus comes more easily now that I have a step-by-step task involving some things I'm actually good at — fuel, engineering, risk assessment — instead of the relentless barrage of outside-my-wheelhouse problems I've had to handle around here lately.

The main bottleneck ends up being the most seemingly straightforward step: finding some damn colored paper for my annotations.

In the end I have to go to my lab and take the two Father's Day cards I got from Eva and Joe, which they wrote ahead of time so I could open them here.

Joe's card had a red rocket on the front and the front of Eva's was mainly a field of green grass, so at least I have something to work with.

I don't like that I have to cut up the cards, but it's for a worthy cause. This reduces the chance of me making a big mistake when I can't see the controls clearly, and *that* increases the chances that my family will live beyond the next four days.

By the time I've finished attaching the annotations, the

inside of the Escape Pod looks like a school project. I can't help but chuckle at how incongruous it is — a cutting edge fuel source and some cut-out colored signposts.

Next up is the black box, which is the main thing I have to get to Earth. It contains *everything*… way more than my phone and the few other pieces of evidence I'm going to pack as carefully and protectively as I can.

When I close the Pod's door for now and turn to head back to the Control Center to access the black box, Laika is looking up at me from the ground.

"Go?" he says, clear as day. "Ray Ray go? Laika go?"

I stare at him and crouch to his level. I'm way past being unsure if he knows what he's saying and well into realizing that this little guy is no ordinary bird.

Another thing Pierre The Liar said to me, seemingly in jest, was that I could bring Laika with me during my evacuation if I could get him into a pressure suit.

But this is no laughing matter.

I don't know what's the kindest thing to do here. We're not going to be intercepted by a welcoming crew. We're going to crash into the unforgiving surface of a planet in ruins.

I could sedate Laika and bring him along for the ride. I have access to the parrot care book, along with everything else ever written, and I have all kinds of medical supplies downstairs.

But I'm making this journey in the knowledge it's almost certainly a suicide mission.

The chance of landing gently enough to survive in a Pod with no landing gear is too low to even factor into my equations.

What I'm now trying to factor that against is the likelihood that Laika will die if I leave him here, anyway.

Could I count on Zola to be merciful to a bird when he wakes up? Not for a second.

"It's your call, buddy," I say, rising to my feet and scratching my head uneasily. "Do you want to stay here? Or do you want to come with me? I've got space for one more. Laika go?"

He looks at me for a few seconds. For the first time, he then flaps his wings and flies up to perch on my shoulder.

"Ray Ray go. Laika go," he says.

Well, it doesn't get much clearer than that.

He'll be sedated, I tell myself. He won't suffer.

It's true on both counts.

And I saw him when I took Bex back down the walkway to Zola's lab. Even though he was terrified of that place after what happened with the barrier, Laika still wanted to go back in rather than be on his own.

"We're in this together," I say, heading back to the Control Center with the unusual but not unpleasant feeling of a macaw on my shoulder. "To the very end."

75

Back in the Control Center, I follow the on-screen guide's instructions to locate the black box.

It's only supposed to be removed for urgent repairs, quite understandably.

Fortunately the actual process isn't too difficult once I gather the right tools.

My trusty toolbox isn't enough on this occasion. The main unit's access panel requires one non-standard screwdriver head, and the black box itself requires an entirely different one.

The fact I get mildly frustrated about something like this is probably a good sign. If there had been any worse surprises during my attempts to get the box, there'd be no room in my thoughts for something like this.

But why *does* the world need so many different screwdriver heads, anyway?

Beats me.

Laika comes with me on each of my back-and-forth trips to the Maintenance Bay. He doesn't always perch on my shoulder but he never strays far from my side.

The station's black box is shaped differently from the standard kind you might find in an aircraft. Its core function is the same, though. *Everything* that's happened here is recorded inside, down to the last keystroke on each keyboard and the last pixel on each screen.

Even if Steele and Pierre cut footage or other data from the computer systems before I could find it, it should all be in here. That's the whole point.

This thing is built to survive as much as *anything* realistically can, and I can only hope the storage drives inside will be suitably shielded. Getting the outer shell home in one piece means nothing if the insides are damaged.

And it really is what's on the inside that counts. Nothing Steele did will have gone unrecorded. There should even be records of her redactions.

The records of all of my messages and general workings on the system will also corroborate everything that might be impossible to believe without it — no ifs and no buts.

When I disconnect the black box from everything else, I find that it's a lot heavier than I expected. The name-defying orange color is less of a surprise. Steele mentioned this when she was pretending to be on my side, and I know the so-called black boxes on planes are orange to make them easier to find after a crash.

It's not unmanageable to pull out from the desk's open access panel. It's just not something I want to carry all the way to the small Docking Bay that houses the Escape Pod.

Fortunately, I have someone who can help with that.

I won't pretend I'm not happy to have Bex assist me one last time, anyway. We've done a lot together in a short time.

A certain reassurance comes with our track record, bearing in mind that each of our previous tasks has ultimately succeeded, even if the things I figured out from those successes sometimes left me feeling worse than when we started.

For the few minutes it takes to bring Bex back to Vinner's lab and switch her wrecking ball attachment out for a second functional hand, I feel oddly zen.

I really think it's the step-by-step nature of this task. I'm much more comfortable with this than the mix-and-match disasters I've been lurching between, like I was just thinking a few minutes ago.

I'm not built for blank space on a schedule and I'm not built for open-ended projects. I like structure.

What I'm about to do is objectively more dangerous and more challenging than anything else so far. It doesn't feel like it, though, because I know the steps I need to take.

The scientist in me likes that, even though I'm not kidding myself that the calm will stick around when I actually climb in to launch the Pod.

I position Bex in place to grasp the box's handles. Just like before, I then use the gloves to make her copy my own movements.

Once she's holding the box with her arms outstretched, I hit the lock button on my gloves. That was one of the best tips Steele gave me, when she was giving me just enough help to avoid suspicion.

This allows me to remove the gloves and assume control of Bex's feet with the remote, without her continuing to copy my hand gestures in a way that would make her drop the black box.

It suddenly strikes me how many more applications there would be for a robot like Bex if I had a helmet as well as gloves. A helmet that could read my brainwaves to issue basic controls like "walk forward" or "turn right" would make things so much easier.

I'm sure tools like that exist for other uses. I'm even more sure that combining one with something like Bex would be a real game-changer.

Even some shoe attachments, more similar to the gloves, could do a solid and intuitive job of controlling her basic walking movements.

I feel like I should be writing this down.

From the helmet and shoes, my mind jumps to daydreaming about a full-on mech suit, like the kind I used to love reading about in comic books. I don't know how far away from reality something like that might be.

Are we there yet? Was anything like that ever in Zola's plans?

As I march Bex towards the Escape Pod, I catch myself thinking all of this and pause.

Is it near-death delirium, I wonder?

Is this just what acceptance feels like?

Why am I thinking about screwdriver heads and mech suits when such a huge ordeal lies ahead?

Has my mind been numbed by so many emotional blows? Did the final revelations in Zola's tell-all tracking spreadsheet push me over the edge?

Whatever it is, I'm just glad I'm not a shuddering wreck. Getting ready for the worst and likely last ride of my life is hard enough like this.

As we near the end of our walk to the Docking Bay, I momentarily catch sight of our trio's reflection.

I can imagine someone on Earth praying for a hero to save the day, then getting a vision of *this*. We're a sight to behold.

A brain-fried guy holding a remote control, a half-finished robot grasping a box, and a friendly parrot hopping along for the ride.

I guess we're out to prove that it's not always looks that count...

76

I reactivate Bex's control gloves as soon as we reach the Escape Pod.

I'm glad the Pod is on the same level as the Control Center, not down a stairway like the Maintenance Bay's utility corridor. If it was, I don't know how I'd have gotten Bex down since I still haven't come across an elevator.

A trolley wouldn't have worked, either, for the same reason.

And with my damaged left thumb and weak right-hand, I certainly wouldn't have fancied carrying the deceptively heavy black box on my own. It's one more thing to be grateful for.

I instruct Bex to lower the black box onto the floor of the Pod, which is the only place I'm sure it can go. It has to go under my seat, where I was previously thinking about stowing my goggles.

There's space behind my seat, but the logistics are tough. Bex's arms can't reach far enough in to put it there, and it's too heavy for me to cleanly lift it over.

If I absolutely *had* to get it back there, I'm sure I could find a way. I don't think I should, though. Putting it out of reach of whoever opens the Pod doesn't seem like a smart move.

Even more to the point, I don't want to hide it out of their sight. That would be the worst irony of all, if I got it down intact but no one found the crucial evidence in time.

The nature of my plan means I have to physically secure everything very diligently. With the Pod rotating upside-down for the final stage, that's a given.

I've already gathered some multi-purpose bungee cords from the Maintenance Bay. I left them in the Control Center with some other supplies, but I'll get them before my final pre-launch walk in this direction.

That walk is coming soon, and my heart-rate knows it.

As soon as the black box is in place, I remove the gloves. And as soon as Bex is fully stationary again, Laika flutters up to perch on her head.

It *is* the high ground, so I guess there's some instinct at play.

I've made a checklist of other things I want to bring. It includes some of the phones that have helped me most in the past few days, plus some handwritten notes explaining the main points I've learned.

My research is coming, too.

I'm going to pack Zola's computer and my own in the back, despite Steele's bullshit lie that mine wouldn't fit. There's enough space and the limited weight I'm adding isn't a threat to the main BioZol fuel supply. I really won't have much left when I reach Earth's atmosphere, but I'll make it.

We'll make it.

Even it it wasn't for the black box, I'd have a hell of a lot of proof of almost everything I've seen here. The key thing is that it's so hardy. It's *hardened*. By design, it should be as durable as anything can be.

Needless to say, durability is a major plus-point in a mission like this.

The black box runs on a proprietary ZolaCore operating system and has no industry connectivity cable ports. I could drive myself crazy worrying that no one will be able to access the data, but I won't. There's no point, for one thing, since I can't do anything about it.

But beyond that, I just don't foresee a bunker full of top government and military officials having too many problems. Tech stuff is so important to the agencies these days, I know they'll have the right people on the evacuation lists to do what has to be done.

If they still have power down there, which is the only way *anything* can possibly play out in our favor, I'm convinced they'll be able to access everything very quickly.

I'll pack the extra evidence at the same time I bring the bungee cords, but there's one more thing I have to do first.

"You have to go to sleep for a while," I tell Laika. "And then we're going to go on a trip. Is that okay? Does Laika want to go to sleep? Laika sleep?"

He flutters down from his perch on Bex's head and lies on his side.

This little guy never ceases to surprise me.

At the mention of sleep, he's suddenly striking the pose of a performing sea lion. He also makes the best attempt at a snoring sound his limited vocal range will allow.

"Laika sleep. Good boy!" he says. It's almost as though he's filling in the part when Barnet would normally have reinforced the learned behavior.

He's also very quickly taken to thinking of himself as Laika, which *I'm* taking as another sign that there's something special going on in that bird brain of his. He's no ordinary macaw, that's for sure.

"Good boy," I say.

Oh — and I guess this means he *is* a male parrot, after all! I've never called him a good boy before, so he clearly did pick it up from Barnet.

Laika gets back onto his feet after a few seconds. Now that he's received the praise he's used to, he seems satisfied in a borderline dependent kind of way.

Hopefully he stays this calm when the syringe comes out.

I *will* have to put him in a pressure suit, probably held down in the same way as the black box. I'll need to secure the suit and I'll need to secure his position inside it, so he doesn't get thrown around when I rotate the Pod and decelerate.

This feels like the hardest part of my preparation, because it's getting away from anything resembling science as I know it and back into the realm of unexpected challenges like nothing I've faced before.

Come on, Ray, I tell myself. *It's not rocket science.*

I mean, I guess *some* of this is… but not the part about putting a parrot in a space suit. I think you'd be more likely to find something like that in a surrealist nursery rhyme than a physics textbook.

Speaking of books… I need to use my text-reader to find out how to sedate and transport a parrot. It might show me how to gently wrap his wings in gauze or brace his delicate neck or whatever else I'm not thinking of on my own.

When we're heading back to the Control Center, I decide to take Bex back to Vinner's lab, where I first found her.

I don't plug her into the wall outlet but I do return the hand attachments to their shelf-like holders. I keep the gloves to take with me.

This is cutting-edge ZolaCore tech and I want our surviving leadership on Earth to see it. I would bring Bex in a heartbeat if I had the space and fuel to carry her, but it is what it is.

She won't miss me like Laika would have, and her job here is done.

While I'm in Vinner's lab I grab his handwritten papers about Bayzen 108b and the asteroids he's been studying. This won't take up any space and I figure there's no harm in bringing some more non-digital evidence to Earth.

It won't survive any impact that leads to a fire, obviously, but it also won't be frazzled by any radiation that could be floating around.

I'll admit to having very little idea of what I'm walking into on that front. It's another one of those things I could worry about, but it doesn't make sense to stress about things I can't control.

Besides, it's not like the task I *do* have control over isn't stressful enough.

"Nice knowing you," I say to Bex.

I know she's a robot, but I'll miss her.

"Bye bye," Laika chimes in. He flies onto her head one last time before following my lead out of the lab.

Our final stop after the Control Center will be the Treatment Room on the lower level, where I'll sedate Laika right before we set off.

I'm fully expecting to wince at the memories of the finger-setting device as soon as I step in. My previous visit wasn't all bad, though, since it did fix my thumb as well as ultimately lead me to the psych evaluations that exposed Steele as a fraud.

She couldn't have possibly known that the smoking-gun hard drive had been left in the same metal box as the device, so I doubt she's kicking herself for that part. Her big slip-up came a few minutes earlier, when she referenced the spot where I found the strong painkillers before we made contact.

Steele definitely can't see any of what I'm doing now, ever since I physically eliminated any possibility of remote system access. Childishly, part of me wishes she could see.

I want her to know I haven't given up. I want her to know I've got one last big swing in me to make sure their awful plan doesn't come to fruition.

They're going to get one hell of a fright when they realize my Pod is on the way to Earth, and I really wouldn't mind seeing her deceitful face when the headline sinks in:

She didn't beat me.

There isn't a room on this cursed station I haven't found my way into, one way or another, despite their best efforts and worst deceits.

I had one goal when this shit-show all kicked off: to get off this death-box of a station.

There's a much more important goal tied to that now, but in

a matter of minutes I'm going to be ticking that original outcome off the list.

They didn't kill me and they didn't break me.

Whatever comes next, they'll never have that.

I might not make it home alive… but I'm *making it*, alright.

I'm making it.

77

At last, I head back to the Control Center with Laika. I put everything else I need into a bag. That's the bungee cords, the extra phones, and a bunch of written and printed notes I've deemed worth taking with us.

Before leaving, I boot up my text-reader and open the parrot care book. Happily, it does have a short section on injuries and another on transporting birds safely.

I put the two together to come up with a simple plan. I'll need gauze, as I expected, and also some protective packaging to cushion his body as much as possible.

It's going to be rough and I feel very conflicted about this, but what's the alternative?

I'm not putting Laika in any position I'm not putting *myself* in, and to be honest I wouldn't mind my own hit of a sedative before we take off.

On that point, I need to search for another book. I need something more focused on veterinary medicine. That's where I'll find information on the type and quantity of sedative I'll need.

I know my options will be limited to whatever is in the Treatment Room and the supply closet, but it doesn't hurt to get some ideas before we go down there.

Laika is very comfortable here and I don't know if the same will be true down there, so I do my rapid research before we leave.

When I've found what I think we need, I use my phone to snap some photos of the main parts. I then take one last look around the Control Center before picking up my bag and walking out for the last time.

It feels surreal to think back to how hard I fought to get in here, only for the elation of making contact to quickly give way to the realization that Steele was playing me for a fool.

From the doorway I can't help but glance back at the two empty chairs that once belonged to Commander Harrison and my good friend Lily.

Lily never stopped talking about her own extended family and how much they meant to her.

Steele, Zola, whoever else they're working with... they took it all.

They took it *all*.

The phrase President Williams used about freedom striking back gives me something to hold on to, hoping desperately that I can deliver the information he and the other survivors are going to need to strike back before it's too late.

They have to block the motherlode detonation that's scheduled to hit in four days. And for them to have any chance of even finding out that Zola's cronies are planning this, I have to get my evidence down to the surface.

Stepping into the main hallway brings back all kinds of memories, too, now that I'm in the reflective mood that comes with an imminent departure.

It wasn't too long ago that bodies littered the floor here — again at Zola's hand. They're in the dorms and the Canteen now, where I've done all I can for them.

The living have to be my focus now. I have no idea how many people are left alive in the bunkers or maybe some isolated areas far from the preliminary detonation site. All I know is that their future is in my hands.

Laika follows as closely as ever as I rush to the Escape Pod to drop off my bag. This is one more trip than I expected, but I've just realized that both of my hands will be carrying precious cargo once I'm finished in the Treatment Room.

We head there next, via the Maintenance Bay and its stairway.

For the first time, I feel absolutely sure that Laika *doesn't* know what's happening.

There's no way he'd be so calm if he did, I figure.

I feel increasingly uneasy about the sedation process as it grows nearer, because it's been a very long time since I gave anyone an injection.

As for a parrot? Contain your surprise, but I've never stuck a needle anywhere near one of those.

I know where to aim, at least, thanks to the veterinary text-book. I hope Laika makes it as easy as he can for both of us.

I think he trusts me by now. Even though he won't understand what I'm doing, I'm hopeful he'll know it's for the best.

When I enter the Treatment Room, I catch sight of myself in the familiar mirror from last time.

It shouldn't be a surprise that I have a few more gray hairs than before, considering all I've been through in between, but I'll be honest and say I'd forgotten about them.

The irony is even stronger now, thinking back to my grandfather's expectation-setting comments that my hair would be as gray as his before humanity set course for other worlds.

I've spent years working on fuel sources as my contribution to chasing the dream of space exploration.

But now?

Now I'm trying to get a warning down to Earth in time to make sure the survivors can stop Zola's apocalyptic mother-lode detonation — the one that his chosen few are set to escape with a timely evacuation to Bayzen 108b.

In any other circumstances, the idea of humanity discovering a viable planet and having a viable means to get there would have been the best news I could have imagined. The idea that my work might have played an important role would have been the icing on the cake.

But in these circumstances I literally couldn't care less about any abstract notions of human expansion, and any role I've played is just salt in the wounds.

Earth is the only place I want to be.

"Ray Ray okay?" Laika asks.

So damn intuitive.

I exhale as I walk towards a treatment bed. "Come on, buddy," I say, tapping it a few times.

Like the trooper he is, and *almost* making me doubt my confidence that he doesn't understand, he flies right up onto the bed and stands perfectly still.

"Good boy," I tell him.

He doesn't move in the few minutes it takes me to find an appropriate sedative and a bunch of syringes. This stage goes as easily as it could have, so we're off to a good start.

"Does Laika want to sleep?" I ask, hoping he'll tip over onto his side. "Laika sleep?"

He does. I reach over and gently lay my right hand on top of him. After a few seconds, I apply slightly more pressure.

He doesn't struggle at all, which I take as an invitation to get the job over with.

I grab the full syringe with my left hand and do exactly what the book told me to.

Just like that, with barely a squawk and no meaningful wriggling at all, the sedative is in.

"I'm going to do everything I can to get you down in one piece," I promise. "Good boy."

"Good boy," he echoes proudly.

Optimistically, I try to tell myself that Laika's padding and restraints might give him a better chance than me.

Either way, we really are in this together until the end.

"Ray Ray?" he says, his voice weakening already. "Laika… no-kay."

I keep my right hand in place but ease off on what little pressure I was applying.

"You *are* okay," I assure him.

He looks up at me, straight into my eyes. "Bye bye… Ray… Ray."

"No," I tell him, more firmly than I intend. "It's not bye bye, buddy. It's just see you later."

Within a few more seconds, he's out.

I use some of the gauze I've already gathered to gently swaddle him. When that's done, I just as gently pick him up and carry him to our Escape Pod.

"Laika okay," I whisper, talking to myself more than the unconscious bird. "Laika okay."

78

I'm going to give Laika the best chance I possibly can.

That means utilizing the padding materials I've gathered from various places and doing my best to secure him in the upper section of the largest pressure suit I can find.

I could be doing something massively wrong here that anyone with a non-frazzled brain would be screaming at me *not* to do if they saw this, but I'm only one man and I really am doing my best.

I've modified the suit with makeshift pillars on the inside, to keep it loose around him. That's the only way I can describe the setup. I swear, it's more elegant than it sounds. And between this and the bungee cords I strategically arrange to secure the whole suit in place, I really don't think there's anything else I can do.

"I've tried, Laika," I tell him. "Believe me, I've tried."

With that, the time is upon me to get into my own pressure suit.

But before I reach to grab it, a sudden thought stops me in my tracks.

Speaking of doing things massively wrong, which anyone else might be screaming about if they could see all this...

Am I doing the right thing to leave Zola where he is?

I can't go in and kill him without risking killing myself. That's not risk I can contemplate in this situation — not when an alternative course of action can possibly help humanity avoid a truly extinction-level planetary cataclysm.

But couldn't I rig a slow-fuse explosive to destroy the station just after I leave?

That's not really the question. I'm a jet fuel specialist — of course I *could* rig a useful explosive.

So… *should* I?

If this was a movie, wouldn't leaving the villain alive when there's an easy chance to kill him be the most irresponsible thing the good guy could do?

In general, yeah. But there are almost infinite unknowns at play here.

Maybe if I kill Zola and he no longer has to be met by the evacuees from his secret compound on Earth, the whole time-line will speed up?

Maybe he's rigged himself up to a dead man's switch that would cause spiteful mass destruction the *instant* he stops breathing?

Maybe maybe maybe.

The point is, there are immediate risks to killing him that could get in the way of the only chance I have of *foiling* him.

My mind is totally settled. I can't afford to risk it.

I wish I could kill the son of a bitch with my bare hands, which is something I never thought I'd say about anyone. I don't particularly like myself for thinking it right now, either, but this is what he's driven me to.

As it stands, he's going to be in that weird capsule for almost four more days. If I can get the evidence to Earth intact, the station could be a sitting duck for any military firepower that's survived.

This risk isn't for me to take. This isn't my dice to roll.

My role right now is to raise the alarm in the only way I can, and that's all there is to it.

Confident in my decision, I'm ready to suit up.

I take off my goggles and place them in the tight spot I've left under my seat. It's incredible how much difference they've made, and yet again I can only really appreciate that once they're off.

Next, I step into my suit. I feel similar to how I did when I had to suit up for the EVA, but this time there's a lot more pressure. Back then I was trying to shore up my own air supply, with abstract hopes of finding out what happened on Earth.

But now? Well, now it's not about me. It's much bigger than me. Now I'm trying to ensure Earth has a future at all, by giving my all to stop the terrible event that's scheduled to happen in only four days.

It's a different vibe.

My left thumb protests when I put my glove on. The pain isn't excruciating, though, which would have seemed like an impossible result before I found the tool in the Treatment Room. All things considered, I can grit my teeth and bear it.

I climb into the Pod and strap myself in tight.I can see shapes and colors of the card I've left on the controls, as intended, but all details beyond that really are hard to make out. I reach down for my goggles, which are just barely accessible.

It takes a firm pull, but I get them.

I hold the goggles in front of my helmet. I'm pleasantly surprised to see that they still make a slight difference. Not as much as when they're closer to my eyes, naturally, but better than nothing.

I considered bringing an uncut panel of the glass from Barnet's lab in here. The idea struck me that I could maybe find a way to position it directly above the readout screen just like I found it directly in front of the insects in the lab.

In my defense, it only took a few seconds for me to realize how foolish the idea was.

I mean, bringing exposed glass in to a Pod that's going to spin like a disco ball and land like a golf ball? Probably not the wisest move.

At least it didn't take a screaming onlooker to save me from *that* potential mistake.

Once the goggles are securely back under my seat, for now at least, I pull the door closed and seal the Pod.

Not unexpectedly, the face of my late brother Jack bursts into my mind.

I'm in an unfamiliar vehicle.

I'm halfway blind without my glasses.

I'm facing a more stressful challenge than any I've ever known.

I'm rushing home to try to save a boy — and this time also a woman — who I care about more than anyone else in the world...

And I know I'm going to crash.

The parallels are too huge and too numerous to ignore. But despite all of these parallels to that awful day, no flashback comes.

Nothing.

It doesn't come.

Unlike on *so* many other occasions since I stepped out of my lab and found Justin's corpse on the floor, no flashback comes.

Maybe the intense anticipation of death leaves no room for an older, previously all-consuming memory of it?

Or maybe, just maybe, even in this most challenging of all situations, my well-practiced mind is edging into scientist mode? Because just like earlier, I know what I have to do. I know the steps.

I've run the numbers for our mass and the potency of our two fuel sources, and after some secondary calculations I've figured out when I need to start engaging.

This plan has a lot of moving parts that mean it's not the *exact* science I'd like it to be, but at the end of the day I'm putting my trust in the numbers and I'm putting my trust in the fuel.

I've mentally rehearsed the sequence of controls I have to

engage and I have my markers in place. There are steps to follow and I'm ready to get started on the first.

Without any hesitation, I press the button with a white square on it. This powers up the Pod and brings a whole bunch of the Docking Bay's overhead lights to life for the first time.

I press the button again, as rehearsed, and watch in awe as the wall ahead of me parts to reveal an airlock.

Automatically, a moving platform under the Pod then carries me forward and into the airlock.

The wall re-closes behind me, leaving the inside of The Beacon out of my reach.

There's no going back now.

The second and final hatch then parts, bringing the vastness of space and the curvature of my tragically darkened home world into view.

As I gaze out in slack-jawed wonder, something stronger than awe hits me:

Purpose.

I have a sudden and singular focus like none I've felt before, driven by an absolute need to save every other innocent survivor and the world we all call home.

Only *I* can stop humanity from becoming extinct on Earth in a matter of days, and the drive to succeed is stronger than any fear could ever be.

I hover my finger over the white circle, knowing one more press will launch me from The Beacon and begin a pre-targeted journey towards Culpeper, Virginia.

Our course is set.

With the sharpest inhalation of my life, I close my eyes and prepare to launch.

"Well," I mutter inside my helmet. "I guess it's trial by fire for the Barclay method."

I press the button.

We're on our way.

79

Pinch me.

We're on our way to Earth.

The Escape Pod's combined navigation and information screen has come fully to life, with the coordinates locked down for the bunker in Culpeper.

The navigation system is linked up to satellites that were safe from the EMP blast on Earth, just like the Escape Pod was, and I'm more than content to let it do the bulk of the work in getting us where we need to be.

I'll take over when it comes time to inject some enriched fuel. The process is going to involve turning the Pod upside-down and firing the minimum amount at first, to test how effectively it will slow our final free-fall towards Earth.

Without the emergency parafoil landing system it was initially designed with, this Pod has no meaningful air resistance to speak of.

That's just not what it's for — the only thing it's signed off for is emergency evacuations in space, to be intercepted by a rescue craft.

There are no lifeboats in the ocean of space today, and there are good reasons I'm not aiming for Earth's ocean, either.

It might seem like a hard splashdown would give the black

box more chance of getting down in one piece, and I can't argue against that fact in isolation.

Logic doesn't exist in isolation, though, and someone has to *find* the black box very quickly. That's the whole point.

If I was trying to give *myself* the best chance of surviving the impact of a crash-landing I can mitigate only with an incredibly volatile fuel source whose properties haven't even been peer reviewed, then yeah. In that case, I'd be aiming for the ocean.

But there are no lifeboats in the oceans of my home planet right now, just like there are none in space.

I'm hitching my hopes on getting the warning of Zola's extinction-level motherlode detonation as close to Earth's survivors as I possibly can. That means inland, no two ways about it.

My descent is going to be one hell of a spectacle and I just can't see any way they'll miss it. We're now a few days past the preliminary detonation, so surely they *have* to be out exploring or at least analyzing the surface by now.

Surely?

I feel surprisingly optimistic about a lot of things now that the Pod is en route.

The ride itself is much smoother than I imagined, which sure helps with my mood.

I kind of expected to be white-knuckle gripping the screen like the safety bar of a roller coaster. But I guess Pierre was telling the truth for once when he said the forces here aren't as strong as those I faced in my training simulations on Earth.

I realize only now that today is the day I was supposed to go home all along. My placement is officially over.

After everything that's happened, I'm not even going to be late.

When I made contact with "Mel" and Pierre and bought the lie that they would come for me in four days, I remember chuckling to myself at the thought that I'd be home a few days later than I promised my family but that they'd hopefully forgive me, given the circumstances.

Now? I'm going to be home on time.

If we're using "home" to mean Earth, anyway.

I'm not going to be back by their side today and I'd have to be the craziest man in the world to assume I'll ever see them again.

This mission is about saving them by raising the alarm while there's time for anyone to do anything about it. For the sake of my own sanity, I keep reminding myself of that sole priority. There's way more chance of achieving *that* than of saving myself and Laika.

He's still out for the count beside me, with enough sedative flowing through his veins to last a few hours longer than he'll need. The best I could do was make sure he's not going to feel anything.

With each passing minute, it really is so far so good.

I'll be able to read the information screen pretty well by holding my goggles in front of my helmet if I need to, and even the helmet isn't as oppressive as I expected despite being smaller than the EVA suit's.

The main negative is that Earth truly is a sorry and dark sight. No lack of surprise on that front can lessen the emotional blow that comes with seeing it at closer and closer range.

The worst of the smoke plumes have subsided, at least, but I know I'm not coming down over the worst-hit zones. I timed my launch to come when the station was over the right general area, without waiting around too long for a perfect moment.

Some of the barren-looking areas I can see were yellow in the fallout map for the preliminary detonation — not even orange, let alone red.

Knowing that those lifeless-looking zones got off relatively lightly is a sobering thought. Other places are already much worse than this, and if my mission doesn't succeed then *everywhere* will soon be totally and utterly desolate.

Aside from the views, though, everything really is going pretty smoothly.

The large screen tells me when I'm nearing the threshold of Earth's atmosphere.

I can tell that much without my goggles because the image is so simple and the screen is so large. I reach for them, though, keen to see more detail.

I always thought I'd use them, I just didn't want to have any glass out in the open until I was sure.

I don't expect too much to change when we reach the atmosphere. The main fuel supply is practically exhausted, but I knew that would be the case. It's at a level that fits almost perfectly with my pre-flight calculations, and there would be no "almost" to qualify my accuracy if I'd had time to weigh everything I loaded in here for the journey instead of carefully estimating.

This ride would be one hell of an experience in better times, I think to myself.

Only the very last of the day's sunlight is shining down on the eastern side of the United States, but the lights of our great cities are nowhere to be seen.

If there's any chance of those lights ever returning, everything has to keep going right.

I don't have a mental list of things that could go wrong. Honestly, I wouldn't know where to start. I'd probably just write "everything" on every line until the page was full.

I take a deep breath, knowing that the intensive part of this shot in the dark is about to kick off.

We're about to pass into Earth's atmosphere.

I'm about to cut the fuel.

We're about to start free-falling.

I pay close attention to the screen, waiting for the atmospheric readings to populate.

It's really not going to be much longer, based on the visual representation of our location. One way of thinking about it is that distance is about to become altitude.

And there it is!

Here we are!

Okay… we're in.

I cut off the main fuel supply, as planned. There's as much of this regular BioZol left as I expected, which is very little, but we have no use for it now. I'm just glad it lasted.

"So far so good," I mumble to myself. "*Still*."

Seriously: pinch me. This is actually working.

My eyes fall on a screenful of atmospheric readings as they begin to populate.

My heart falls right behind them.

"No…" I groan.

So far so good?

So much for that.

We gave it a good shot, but we're done.

The screen tells me a lot of things, but it might as well be an arcade machine flashing two words in giant red text:

Game over.

80

Shattered.

My hopes, my emotions, my chances… with the data on the screen, they're all shattered.

My *calculations* weren't wrong, but the assumptions that fed into them have just been shot to pieces.

The readings aren't what I expected. Earth's atmosphere isn't what I expected.

Some combination of the undersea detonation and the volcanic disasters has affected the atmosphere enough to throw an enormous and insurmountable obstacle in my path.

My theocite-enriched fuel isn't going to behave how I expected.

It's a fuel like no other… hence the depths Zola is plunging to secure a theocite supply for his planetary evacuation before word of my research gets out and the whole world wants a piece. And in these atmospheric conditions, it's going to work *too* well.

The disaster-related changes in air pressure, temperature and even air composition, as relatively small as they might appear in isolation, are going to massively increase my enriched fuel's already formidable potency.

I wanted to rotate the Pod and feed some of it in to slow my descent, but that plan is out of the window.

Now, in this post-disaster atmosphere, even the minimal possible injection would fire me so fast and so far back into the sky that I'd eventually land with almost as much catastrophic force as if I didn't do anything.

I try to run some numbers in my head, but the only one I keep coming up with is zero.

Zero chance of personal survival, obviously, but now effectively zero chance of *anything* staying in one piece.

I don't even see how the black box will make it. Durable and indestructible aren't synonyms.

"I had no way of knowing," I say, this time turning to the tightly secured pressure suit Laika is sedated and restrained inside. "I'm sorry, buddy."

I hear my heartbeat thumping, but it somehow seems unusually *strong* more than unusually fast.

The awful feelings running through me are nothing like the high-octane stress I felt during my EVA or even when I was rushing to the Maintenance Bay to cut off Steele's access to the station's systems.

That's because this isn't fear — it's dejection.

This isn't a fight-or-flight quest for self-preservation — it's a helpless realization that I can't even warn Earth's survivors of what Zola is going to do to them in a few days.

I look at the green and red shapes I stuck onto the Pod's controls, cut out from Eva and Joe's Father's Day cards.

I climbed into this claustrophobic craft in a desperate bid to give them some kind of fighting chance. But with each second that passes without *any* new idea of how to possibly salvage my mission, I'm only getting surer that the fight is over.

My enriched fuel is too potent. In the worst irony of all, my greatest success is my greatest failure.

If I had my time again and could have seen this coming, I would dilute the fuel. That does me no good now, though, and neither does wishing there had been a way to modify the Pod to let me drip-feed truly minuscule amounts at once.

Both of those things would have taken time I didn't have on the station, even if I'd had any reason to think they'd be necessary, and I wish I could stop myself from lamenting variables I can't control.

Wait.

Wait wait wait wait wait.

The variables.

The potency of my enriched fuel — that's variable number one.

The minimum injection I can feed into the engine — that's number two.

But there's one more.

There's variable number *three*: the speed of our descent.

I've been thinking about what I can do to counteract our free-fall... but what if we weren't free-falling?

Now my heart is beating fast.

When passivity all but guarantees total failure, doing nothing isn't an option.

So what if someone was crazy enough to fight every human instinct... and what if he decided to use what's left of his *regular* fuel supply to actively accelerate towards the ground and give his theocite-enriched fuel injection a more formidable force to counteract?

Well... we're about to find out.

81

I don't feel like I have any choice.

There isn't enough lower-potency BioZol left in my regular fuel supply to counteract our free-fall. Meanwhile, even the minimum injection of theocite-enriched fuel now swings the other way into being *way* too much to control our descent.

If that doesn't show how much of a leap forward my research has delivered, I don't know what ever could.

My only hope is to use the remaining supply of regular BioZol to fire us faster *towards* the ground. I'll then get back to the original plan of rotating the Pod at the last second and feeding in a minimal burst of theocite to counteract our fall.

What's changing now is that our fall will become a *powered* descent. And believe me, I wouldn't be doing this if I had any other option.

There's no established formula for this. If I'm working on any logic at all, it's the logic that I'm going to fail if I do nothing.

With that in mind, I might as well risk failing harder by doing something that might — just *might* — give the Pod a chance of landing in a manner that doesn't explosively destroy the whole thing.

That's not the biggest goal, is it? It's not like I'm asking to survive.

I'm close enough to the ground now to recognize the ash-laden landscape. I've seen it before — in the satellite images on Commander Harrison's computer screen.

I'll give ZolaCore's satellite designers their due: the Pod's guidance system has done a stellar job to get me this far.

So far, I haven't had to override anything. I figure that won't last. When a deadly impact is already looming, I'll surely have to confirm my desire to accelerate *towards* the ground.

Bearing in mind this possible extra step, I'll give myself an extra few seconds.

Minutes are long gone. We really are in the realm of seconds now.

I hold my goggles in front of my helmet again to double-check each of the controls I'm about to engage. I have to make sure I'm correctly remembering the basic shape and color-coded system I gave myself. I internalized the layout when I placed the markers, but I can't take any chances. Not with so much riding on this.

Everything is where I expected. I'm ready.

Holding what seems certain to be one of my last breaths, I engage the Pod's regular supply of BioZol.

A warning pops up on the screen. I saw this coming, and I'll be able to override it with one more tap.

The override is easier than I expected, but I'm still glad I foresaw it. There really is no time to spare.

My main concern now is that the small amount of regular BioZol won't speed us up *enough* to give the theocite enough to counteract. Because of that, I really do want to leave it as late as I can before making my next move.

Rotating the Pod should take nine seconds, according to the system guide. I've factored that into my decision of when to act. But without any way to run the calculations in real-time I'm going more on feel than anything else.

When I can see the shape of a winding highway, I know it's

time. I can't afford to get any closer.

With a gulp and a prayer, I tap again to engage the regular BioZol fuel supply again. This time, thanks to my override of the warning notice, it fires.

My right hand grips the screen as I feel the Pod start to shake like crazy. The fuel injection only lasts for a few seconds but the screen and it's huge red warnings make it clear just how significantly I've hastened our impact.

Still gripping for dear life, as though that's going to make any difference, I then use my more reliable left hand to rotate the Pod.

I'm suddenly praying that I haven't left this too late.

I try not to look out of the window again as I count the seconds. It's impossible not to.

The disorienting feeling that comes with a sudden rotation like this makes it hard to tell how far we are from the ground, though, which is probably a good thing.

I count ten seconds — not bad given the estimate of nine — and we're now facing upwards like rocketeers ready to launch.

The enriched fuel I've worked so hard for so long to make as potent as possible is now the only hope humanity has.

Now that it's ironically *too* potent, I'm praying that I've increased our speed enough so that the upcoming injection will only boost us back to an altitude that makes a free-fall potentially survivable — for the Pod and the black box, at least.

"Here we go," I say, hovering a finger over the control that will feed in a shot of my recently brewed superfuel.

I press the button.

The force is incredible.

I glance outside as it kicks in and immediately see just how close to the ground I allowed us to get.

I'm not exaggerating when I say we could barely have been any closer.

Truly, I've done all I possibly can.

I grip the screen for dear life as the tiny injection pushes against the fall and boosts us towards the sky.

I'm not hoping I've done enough to save myself. The all-consuming desperation I have to get the black box down in one piece leaves no room for any secondary considerations, even my own survival.

I try to count how many seconds we're sent soaring by the tiny fuel injection, but my brain is a mess.

When the Pod reaches its highest point, the briefest of moments before we start plummeting seems to run and run.

It feels like my stomach keeps going upwards even as we start falling the other way, and looking outside brings a hellish anticipation of the impact to follow.

My last thought isn't the worst, though, because we're actually not nearly as high as I'd feared.

Accelerating towards the ground for as long as I possibly could has made a major difference.

I really think the black box is going to make it!

I think I accelerated hard enough, late enough and for long enough to ultimately deliver a landing roughly comparable to the one we would have experienced if the atmospheric surprise hadn't thrown everything into chaos.

I'll never forget the report card that motivated me to prove my physics teacher wrong and make a solid research career for myself, back when Mr. Lindell pulled no punches:

"Ray Barclay tends to falter under pressure."

All I can say now is that I hope the old guy is alive in a bunker somewhere and keeps on living because of the last-ditch maneuver I've just pulled off.

But infinitely more importantly, I *know* Joe and Eva are alive in a bunker in Colorado.

Increasingly and maybe even *proudly* confident that The Beacon's black box will survive the intense but mitigated impact that's almost upon us, I spend my last few seconds before the crash praying that someone here in Virginia notices me falling from the sky.

"See me," I whisper under one of my last full breaths. "Please… *see me*."

82

They always say your whole life flashes before your eyes.

For me, this time, it's a single image.

It's Joe, smiling next to the Welcome Home banner he made for me just a few days ago.

"I made it, Joe," I hear myself saying as we hurtle towards the ground. "If this is home, I made it."

The next thing in my mind's eye is no image at all.

I see nothing.

All I know is darkness.

83

We crumple.

That's the only word for it.

The impact is blunt, not sharp.

It isn't instant, either. It *lingers*.

I feel the crumple zone give way to the force and I feel the jackhammer vibration through my spine like nothing I've ever known or could possibly describe.

But even as my eyes fill with darkness and my lungs fight for breath, I don't care how bad the pain is. I don't care how bad these injuries are.

Because even in a shell-shocked stupor, I know that pain means one thing: life.

If I'm alive, with all my bones and organs and every other breakable part still within me, even if they don't all feel intact, the black box *must* have made it. It's a thousand times more durable than I am.

I really can hardly breathe, and right now I can't even tell if my eyes are closed or just unable to see.

A jarring alarm from somewhere in the Pod's inner workings is the only sound I can hear, but it's music to my grateful ears.

My vision returns as I force my eyes open, as though the sudden burst of sound has brought all of my senses back under my conscious control.

I try to turn to the side but feel a gnawing pain in my ribs. This is different from the shin, different from the thumb, different from everything else. Those were sharp pains... this is deeper.

Something is definitely not right in there and that's probably what's making it difficult for me to breathe.

But I'm here.

I'm here! Not just in Earth's atmosphere but *on* Earth.

I made it. I actually *made* it.

Maybe the atmospheric readouts throwing me for a loop was a blessing in disguise, my giddy mind considers.

The odds of me surviving the original plan were almost zero, and I would never have thought of something as reckless as the late acceleration idea unless I had been forced to think so far outside the box.

The *black* box I've just safely delivered from the station contains every single thing that was on the Control Center's computers, but my *mind* is full, too.

The final stage of my plan isn't even dependent on the government or military cracking the black box anymore, even though I'm confident they will.

I'm alive. I can *tell* them what happened. I can even show them what happened on my phone, if it's also made it down intact.

The Pod's physical integrity is shot to shit, hence the alarm, but there are no fires. I can hardly believe it... even the paperwork I brought down is going to be okay.

Against all of the odds it seems like everything I—

"Laika!" I blurt out.

I use what little strength I have to unseal and remove my helmet. There's no need for it here — the post-disaster oxygen concentration is fine, at least. That wasn't the issue.

I turn to my right, wincing with every inch of neck rotation, and I see that the little guy's pressure suit is still in place, held securely by the bungee cords.

We weren't thrown around, though, so that's not what I was worried about. I'm worried if the crumpling impact has been too much for him.

I cushioned and braced him as much as I could.

When I manage to get close enough to peer in at Laika, the sedative makes it hard to tell if he's okay. I can't hold still enough to see any breaths, especially since I haven't been able to reach down for my goggles yet, and he's obviously not moving.

My body is in one piece, which is a much better result than I was counting on, but right now I feel like a metal table leg with some loose screws inside. Rattle me around, or even just tip me to one side, and I'm sure you'll hear some ominous sounds.

I'm not sure if we've landed on concrete, grass, or whatever else — the thickness of the ash made it hard to tell before the impact. I'd wager grass.

If I owe my life to only two things, they're the level of desperation that drove me to fire myself towards the ground and the team who designed this Escape Pod's crumple zone.

Let me tell you, race cars have nothing on this.

Like Bex and the thumb-setting device I found in the medical lab, this thing is a marvel of human creation. It's too bad they're all property of a corporation whose dictatorial leader is all set to destroy the world in a few days.

We'll see about that, Zola.

I know he wasn't counting on this. I know he wasn't counting on me.

I force myself to lean forward, feeling my breathing slow. The all-over pain might be growing or it might just be becoming more apparent as an unprecedented flood of adrenaline slowly recedes. Either way, I feel it.

I'm able to grab my goggles again and put them on, and

wow — as always, what a difference they make. The ground outside is *remarkably* thick with ash. It's an upsetting sight.

I quickly find a way to silence the alarm via the screen, and in its place comes nothing but total silence.

Eerie silence.

Not a bird, not a plane, not a distant hum of a highway.

I knew I wouldn't hear any of those things, but you really can't be ready for genuine silence until you're in the middle of it.

Sitting up, I shift towards Laika and reach for the helmet that's sealing his suit. I pull it away then carefully lift him from the brace I constructed. I'm delighted that I *have* to do this, because I'm delighted the brace held up.

I stare and stare at my loyal feathered friend, aching to see just one single breath.

"Come on, little buddy," I beg him. "It's Ray Ray. We're here. Don't quit on me now. Laika okay. *Laika okay.*"

And then I see it. It's slight, but it's there. A breath!

He's alive. Laika is alive.

My head falls forward under the weight of a relief that's almost too much to handle.

It's not just about Laika, as much as his survival is the catalyst for pushing me over the edge — it's everything.

We're here. The evidence is here. *Hope* is here.

The success of this longest of all long shots is only going to lead me into what could be an even *longer* one. I know that. But at least the lucky few of us who survived Zola's preliminary detonation now have any shot at all of preventing his extinction-level motherlode detonation.

Everything hurts, but I force myself to unclip my safety belt and slowly move towards the door. Its structure has buckled, meaning the handle doesn't open it all the way and I have to muster some more strength to force it.

"*Aaaagh,*" I groan. It's these damn ribs again.

Of all the things that could have been badly injured, I guess it could have been worse than my ribs. The welcome fact that my neck and spine and skull have avoided major damage doesn't stop the pain, but the pain doesn't stop *me*.

I'm hurt, but I'm here.

I'm finally back on solid ground.

Now let's see what's left out there…

84

I step out slowly and look around at what's left of Culpeper, Virginia.

In keeping with what I saw in the satellite images, it's not a pretty sight.

From outside, the Escape Pod looks kind of like a hard boiled egg that's been dropped to the ground from head height. It hasn't splattered, as such, it's just cracked at the end that made contact.

A slight bounce under my feet tells me that we are on grass, after all. Kicking aside the top layer of ash confirms my hunch.

"Hello?" I yell into the silent evening. "Can anybody—"

Before I even know what's happening, my face is in the grass.

My ribs are on fire.

My goggles are knocked off and land out of sight.

A powerful body is pressing me to the ground, telling me to shut my mouth and not move a muscle.

I've been tackled.

As soon as I called out, someone sprung from behind and rushed me.

They've got me.

When I manage to turn my face to the side and look up, I see two men dressed all in black.

The first is holding me to the ground. The second is holding a gun to my head.

"Get up and *shut* up," the second guy barks, gesturing with the weapon in a way that tells me he's not messing around. "You're coming with us."

85

It's easier said than done, but I tell myself not to panic.

I just fell from the sky in a ZolaCore emblazoned Pod and I'm still wearing most of my ZolaCore branded pressure suit.

If government and military intelligence suspects any Zola-Core involvement in all of this, and if they haven't picked up my broadcasts, I'm going to look like a bad guy.

These guys can't be ZolaCore.

If they are, everything is *definitely* over and nothing I could do from here would make any difference. But they're not. They can't be.

The guys are chiseled looking — secret service or special forces is my guess — and their voices tell me they're both American.

They have to be from the bunker and I'll gladly go with them. Every shred of evidence in that Pod will prove I'm innocent, even if I have a few uncomfortable minutes in the meantime.

"I'll come," I say, slowly raising my hands. "My name is Ray Barclay and I was the sole survivor of a—"

"What part of *shut up* wasn't clear?" the gun-wielding guy asks.

I nod.

His empty-handed companion holds my hands behind my back and binds them with a zip-tie.

"Please just empty the Pod and bring the evidence with us," I whisper. I know they want me to be silent rather than quiet, but I have to get this message across and I figure that showing some effort to follow their orders won't hurt. "There's a live parrot, too. Sedated. He's important."

"Evidence of what?" my restrainer asks, loudly enough to bring his companion in closer.

I gulp. There's no sense in whispering anymore. "Evidence that Zola did all of this and he's about to do something even worse if we don't stop him," I blurt out. "I was the sole survivor of a sabotage attack on The Beacon space station. I know you're not going to tell me anything but please at least listen. We only have a few days to prevent another detonation that will kill *everyone*. Whoever is in charge in the bunker has to see this. Bring my glasses, too, and please… be gentle with the bird."

The men look at each other, giving very little away. The guy with the gun turns towards the Pod and walks to the door, but the other guy covers my face with a fabric hood before I can see what comes next.

He leads me to a vehicle. It has a high enough step to feel like an armored 4x4.

Since the car works, there either wasn't an EMP-like attack or it must have been shielded in the bunker. Either one is good news, although the first is obviously better.

For now, the good news ends there.

I'm in pain, I'm restrained, and I'm blinded by a hood.

"Take him in and come back," the armed guy yells from the Pod. "I'll get this stuff out. It'll take a minute."

I hear the driver's door close. I don't have Laika or my glasses. I effectively don't have hands or eyes, either, but I'm doing all I can to stay calm.

The one positive I can cling on to is that the other guy said he'll be a minute but still wanted his buddy to take me in.

"In" has to mean into the bunker, and "a minute" has to mean I'm just as close as I thought.

It really is Mount Pony, a historic government facility.

I'm not in a good position at this present moment, but I am in the right place.

To my surprise, I hear the driver's door reopen and then the sound of the guy getting out.

The next thing I know, he's opening my door and a needle is shooting into my arm.

"What the hell are you do—"

I can't even get the whole question out.

I'm fading fast.

Fading....

Fading...

Out.

86

When I come to, I'm in what looks like a holding cell.

My hood is gone but the room is dark. Too dark to see anything beyond the bars.

Bars?

Seriously... *this* is what I get? I've heard of no good deed going unpunished, but this is ridiculous.

The first thing I do is reach for my ribs. They feel different somehow.

My midriff is wrapped in bandages. Ah. No *wonder* they feel different.

So they're not monsters, I reflect. The whole surprise sedation thing had me worried for a second, but that might have been security protocol.

Sure, I tried to explain myself... but wouldn't a bad guy from ZolaCore have done the same?

I guess those guys were just doing their jobs. Their jobs for the Secret Service, maybe. Or special forces... or whatever else is the best I can hope for.

I'm still wearing the clothes I had on under the pressure suit. My phone was in my pocket, so I optimistically reach for it.

Nope. The engagement ring I've had in there since before I started the placement on The Beacon is gone, too.

"Ray Barclay," a voice booms in the darkness. And I would know this voice anywhere.

The next thing I know, a light comes on and brings him into view.

Ruffled, pale, and clearly flat-out exhausted, he looks like he hasn't slept in a year and has just stepped out of a hurricane.

Flanked by the two men who brought me in, it's President Noah Williams.

A week ago this man was almost universally recognized as the leader of the free world. Now, it looks like he's in charge of whoever and whatever is left down here.

"I'm sorry for how you've been treated," Williams says, quickly flicking his eyes between the men at either side of him.

"They were pretty reasonable," I say. They *were*, I suppose, compared to how they *could* have acted. Besides, it's not going to do anyone any good to dwell on a minor mis-introduction when we all have the same common enemy to contend with. "But how long have I been out? And where's my ring."

Williams looks at his watch. "Six hours," he says. "Give or take. Your things are safe, too. And those glasses are the closest match we could find to the lenses you put together for yourself."

I'm glad to hear the ring is safe and, sure enough, I see a pair of glasses sitting to my left.

I breathe a huge sigh of relief at the more important part of his reply, though. It's six hours longer than I would have liked, but that answer is so much better than it could have been.

"What about my parrot?" I ask.

Williams holds my eyes. "Alive. A little banged up, but alive. Much like yourself."

With that, Williams reaches forward and unlocks the cell, then signals for his muscle men to leave.

"I'm sorry," the guy who held the gun mumbles.

"Me, too," his colleague adds.

I tell them not to worry about it then watch as they walk off.

Williams steps inside the unlocked door and sits down beside me.

"We've seen a lot of the evidence you brought down with you," he says. "There's a lot more to get through but the only thing that seems to matter for starters is stopping that second detonation. Do you agree?"

"That's the most urgent thing," I say. "But my family is in a bunker in Colorado Springs. What can you tell me about it? How many people are there? How many people are *here*? What kind of chance do we have of stopping this thing before it's too late?"

"We have a little over eight thousand people here," he replies. "We're well stocked. Are we well enough stocked to react to what you've discovered is coming our way? I hope so. We have a functioning chain of command and some of the best minds from all walks of life. We have a chance, is what I'm telling you. Thanks to you, we at least have that."

"And Colorado?" I push.

Williams pauses to think, then rises to his feet. "Come with me, Mr. Barclay," he says.

I don't budge. "*Colorado.*"

"Although the fallout there is worse than here, we have received some communications," he replies, albeit a lot more uncomfortably and noncommittally than I'd like. "You'll learn a lot more upstairs."

I feel my face turn pale under the strain of this uncertainty.

"Ignacio Zola will pay for what he's done," Williams promises, spitting out the words. "With God as my witness, I will see to that. But please... come with me."

87

President Williams leads me towards several flights of stairs, explaining that we started twelve stories down.

"*Twelve*?" I echo.

Damn, this is a serious facility.

Williams concisely explains that this is what he calls a "new-within-old" bunker that has been quietly undergoing a massive extension project for decades.

The bunker is effectively hidden in plain sight, he says, with a well-known Cold War-era site chosen because it really is easier to play something down than keep something quiet.

That makes sense and is pretty much what I was thinking when I first read about Mount Pony on my text-reader.

It must be all but impossible to construct a massive bunker complex in this day and age without word of it leaking out, so relying on secrecy really isn't a viable option. Renovations and extensions are much easier to keep under the radar.

Despite my repeated questions, Williams continually refuses to give me many specifics about Colorado, telling me he's not the best man to discuss it.

He only reiterates that contact has been established, which apparently can't be said for some of the bunkers whose anti-EMP shielding apparently didn't work as well as intended.

So there *was* an EMP.

Williams isn't desolate about that but it's clearly weighing on his mind. It feels like he's trying to convince himself more than me at some points, like when he says that the radio technology on the surface at other locations could have been fried without any electronics *within* the bunkers being hit.

"The evacuees in our other bunkers could be surviving just fine," he says, "but with no way of contacting anyone else. We've been working on plans for physical reconnaissance and some drones will be ready to go in a few hours. We're very well stocked, Mr. Barclay. *Very* well stocked."

His repeated emphasis of *very* gives me a little bit of hope, since there's nothing to be gained at this point from over-promising.

We walk up several flights of stairs.

There *have* to be elevators, for heavy items if nothing else, but my body isn't complaining about the exertion as much as I would have expected. I've probably been injected full of painkillers. Someone has patched up my ribs, after all, and the guys outside certainly weren't shy with a different kind of needle.

I take my opportunity to ask Williams what he was thinking about everything before I brought news of Zola's involvement.

His reply begins with a slow sigh. "Well, we had our suspicions. The blasts in the North Pacific were concentrated around a ZolaCore undersea mining facility. The X-mark on the map you found... that's the spot. We didn't know at that point whether this really was an external terrorist attack or if that was just a ZolaCore cover story to throw everyone off the scent."

"But why would you even *suspect* it was a ZolaCore inside job?" I ask. "I was working on the guy's station, working with the very material this is all about, and I didn't see all this coming until I found the proof."

"Understandably so," Williams shrugs. "But you have to

understand that we see things you don't, Mr. Barclay. Former senior figures at ZolaCore have spoken about Zola becoming increasingly reclusive and erratic. Our intelligence reports have been getting stronger on that for more than a year. It's almost like when military generals grow concerned about their leader, right before he overstretches. I'd like to believe that the number of people who knew exactly what he was setting in motion is tiny. The people in his bunker, the people he's planning to evacuate before the second detonation, according to what you found... I don't think they're going to know he was responsible for the chaos they're fleeing, let alone *deliberately* responsible."

Wow. There's a lot to take in here.

I agree with the last part, which I've already thought about. Long-term concerns about Zola's erraticism and reclusiveness definitely fit with the reality that he's been hiding in a suspension capsule in space while his minions set about destroying the world on his orders.

"So what's our plan going to be?" I ask, point-blank.

Williams thinks for a few seconds. "We're going to stop the second detonation by any means necessary. I've been briefed on steps that are being taken to get some people off Earth in case the blast *can't* be stopped, but my undying focus is to make sure it can. I'm going nowhere. Plan A is all I see."

I like the sound of undying focus and I like the sound of any means necessary. I understand why a backup plan could be necessary, too, and I'm definitely curious what that entails. For right now, though, *my* undying focus is the same as President Williams'.

Other people can work on contingencies, but we can't afford to start thinking about what ifs. The blast has to be stopped, no ifs and no buts.

"So when you say *any means necessary*..." I probe.

"We're already planning an underwater reconnaissance mission to the key site," Williams replies. "The epicenter on the second map you discovered is another well-documented Zola-

Core mining zone, just like the site of the first blast. If we spot ongoing activity by ZolaCore personnel, we will seek to decisively eliminate them. If we run into a dead-end, we may need to engage the would-be evacuees in ZolaCore's New Zealand bunker."

"And when you say *engage*..."

Williams turns to face me directly, with the hard gaze of a man who has the weight of the world on his shoulders. "Nothing is off the table," he says, and that's all.

I force a nod of understanding.

There's no telling what kind of people are in Zola's bunker, how much they really know, or what kind of *engagement* Williams will seek with them if it comes to that.

The one and only thing I can be sure of is that I hate Ignacio Zola like I've never hated anyone.

I hate him like I've never even thought it was *possible* I could hate anyone.

This must be showing on my face, because Williams calls it out.

"Zola will pay for this," he promises for the second time. "But I have to ask one thing. Why didn't you kill him?"

"There was a *very* ominous security system and I was worried about a dead man's switch," I reply with no hesitation. It's a reasonable question for someone to ask and it's not like it didn't rattle around my brain for a few hours up there, but I don't like the way Williams' tone makes it sound like I did something wrong.

"Do you think there's a mechanism to destroy the station if Zola stops breathing?" he pushes.

"Quite likely," I nod. "If I had done something to his capsule, who knows what could have happened? Sure, if I had literally no way of getting this warning down to Earth then I would have done it. But when I had a chance to bring the evidence down here, I couldn't kill him out of spite and risk dying with him. I didn't ask for any of this, but I was our only chance."

It's Williams who nods now. "Eliminating Zola might have been futile, in any case," he replies flatly. "His plan is in place, with or without him being alive to see it come to fruition. There's no rewind button on any of this, either, so his boots on the ground would still have had no choice but to keep going. There may have been a hit to their morale, sure. But it could just as likely have strengthened his deputies' resolve. In the position you were in, I think you did the right thing."

I'm glad to hear this. Not because I was in any moral doubt and not because I need this dose of presidential absolution, but because it means Williams is more likely to keep me in the fold when it comes to planning our urgent response.

If he saw me as someone who had squeamishly skipped an opportunity to deal with our problem once and for all, rather than someone who withheld a primal urge to kill a mass murderer for the greater good, a seat at the table would have been out of the question.

After a few more flights of stairs and a short walk down a tight concrete corridor, during which we talk some more about Zola and what I read in his psychological analysis file, Williams pauses at a fairly nondescript doorway.

"I understand you found a macaw and a robot on The Beacon," he says.

My eyes narrow. "Yeah…"

"Our robotics experts have some things I think you're going to be very interested in. They've actually already asked for some of your time. They want your help with something important that relates directly to our next steps."

"What is it?" I ask.

I *am* interested in seeing whatever the robot team has, especially when it's something I can help with. Maybe they were impressed by some black box footage of what I did with Bex?

"I don't know all the details yet," Williams replies. He tilts his head towards the door beside us. "But your bird is in here."

Without trying to be rude and without even thinking about it, I reach past him and push the door open.

Sure enough, I see Laika in a large cage. It's *very* large, probably more of a cell, and two people are sitting by a table in front of it. A man and a woman... veterinarians, I suppose.

"Ray Ray!" my little buddy squawks. "Ray Ray okay!"

I feel my smile widen and widen. "Laika okay," I beam, exhaling slowly. "You made it! Boy, is it good to see you."

"Laika okay. Ray Ray okay!" he replies, happily throwing his head back each time. He isn't flying, which fits in with what Williams told me about him being a little "banged up" from the landing.

"Mr. Barclay," the woman at the table says. She rises to her feet and extends a hand, which I gladly shake. "We're greatly in your debt for all you've done. But about this macaw... Laika, as you call him."

"Yeah?" I inquire.

"How much do you know about him? Because I can tell you, speaking from decades of experience, this is no ordinary bird. Not just behaviorally... *neurologically*."

Neurologically?

This is news to me, even if it's not all that surprising. With every hour we spent together on the station, I grew more and more aware of how smart the little guy was.

"I don't know where my phone is, but I took a lot of photos of the lab where I found him," I reply. "I didn't find any notes about Laika, and he was in a cage in the main part of the lab like he was a pet. But you should be able to look into the researcher's psychological evaluation. I brought that hard drive and the data will be in the black box, too, because I looked at it on the Control Center's computers. His name was Leeroy Barnet. You might find clues of what he was studying, besides suspended animation."

The woman nods. "Excellent, thank you. I know we have more urgent priorities to deal with, but Laika could be an incredibly significant creature. I need to stress that this bird is far more special than I think you're grasping at the moment."

I look at him through the bars. "And he's definitely okay after the crash?"

"By and large, considering what he's been through. When the sedative fully wears off he might be able almost straight away. It won't be long until he's right as rain."

Now *there's* some good news. "I'll be back soon, Laika," I tell him. "See you later, okay?"

"Later, later," he caws.

I'm beyond relieved to see that Laika is safe and well.

But above everything else, I just hope this isn't my *last* happy reunion.

88

Once I've extended another *see you later* to Laika's enthusiastic minder, I return to Williams in the doorway.

"I didn't know any of that," he says.

I shrug. "Like she said, there *are* some more urgent things to deal with."

"There are," Williams sighs. "And on that, Mr. Barclay…"

"Just Ray. Please," I say.

He looks down at his watch, as though reading a message, then smiles warmly. "Well, I *was* going to take you to Core Command to introduce you to some of our leadership committee, but I've just heard that direct contact has been re-established with Colorado. We're actively trying to locate your family, Ray. If they're there, it shouldn't be long."

"*If* they're there?" I push. He presented that like good news, then ended it like *that*?

"Look, Ray… if *you're* sure, I'm sure. I just mean that if they can be located quickly, we *will* locate them quickly. I wasn't trying to insinuate anything else."

"How many people are in their bunker?" I ask, for what feels like the tenth time. "If you're not taking me to the others, at least tell me that."

He sighs, more uneasily than impatiently, but I also sense

an element of frustration. "I think Colorado is somewhere around four thousand. We successfully populated fourteen major bunkers, Ray, and our dependable international allies have at least three times that number between them. I don't know the exact population count of each. They didn't all reach capacity. Not everyone made it to the pickup points."

Wow.

The numbers are heartbreakingly small relative to the population before this all happened, but fourteen large bunkers in this country alone is significantly more than I was expecting.

"As soon as it's possible to connect you to your family, we'll do it," Williams reiterates. "It really shouldn't be much longer. But at the moment there are thousands of people in *this* bunker who have spent the past few hours marveling at what you've fought through and grieving over what you've discovered. Would you mind saying a few words to them?"

"*All* of them?" I ask.

He shakes his head. "The Assembly Hall is packed, but not everyone is in there. I spoke to the crowd earlier. As soon as our personnel started poring through your evidence and realizing what you'd found, I knew I had to get on top of the narrative before the mood fell too much. Our people will get a much bigger morale boost from seeing you in the flesh than from anything else I can deliver. Ray, you are the embodiment of the triumph of the human spirit against almost impossible odds. In the bind we're in, that's exactly what we need to focus on."

I'm no public speaker, but more to the point I just want to hear something about my family as soon as I possibly can.

"I need to know my family is safe," I tell him.

I watch as Williams emphasizes the urgency of this point into a small earpiece microphone.

"Our team is on it as a matter of urgency," he assures me a few seconds later, "and we know who we're looking for. But *these* people, Ray… they're obviously grateful you got here to deliver the news you did, but that news has just hit them like a truck. Anything you can say is going to be better than nothing. And it really will mean more than anything I can say. At least step out with me, will you? Please."

A please from the President of the United States — or at least what's left of it — is not something I ever expected to come my way. But Williams is sincere and his request is fair, so I agree to follow him through the door up ahead.

I expect to come out on a stage of some kind, but we actually emerge on a high platform that reminds me more of a diving board than anything else.

I look out at the crowd below and see all kinds of people.

A lot of them applaud when they first see me. The reception quickly spreads as the others realize who I am.

The applause is warm but understandably subdued. I'm not going to call myself a hero, but I understand that some people will. That's why they seem so warm.

But I'm also a messenger bringing awful, awful news… and that's why they're subdued.

The room Williams called the Assembly Hall brings to mind something between an aircraft hangar and the inside of a large stadium when it's being used as a hurricane evacuation center.

I focus more closely on some of the faces in the crowd.

There are all types: young, old, together, alone.

The one thing they all have in common is a shellshocked look I can totally understand. Until I got here, they probably felt very lucky to have survived the most destructive event in human history.

Thanks to me, they now know that was nothing more than a prelude for what Zola still has in store. They now know that we have a little over three days to stop him, or our chance of survival is zero.

I know how they're going to feel after the gut-punch of hearing the news.

I've been there more than enough times myself lately to know *exactly* how bad news feels.

Over and over again I've been the guy who survives and pushes forward to a new discovery, only to be rewarded with even worse news than anything that's come before. I really am the furthest thing from a public speaker, but I can try.

I can say *something*.

When Williams tells me the communications team is working overtime to connect with Colorado — and with Joe and Eva in particular — I believe him.

I also believe him when he tells me my words can make a difference here in Virginia, so I'll give it my best shot.

He hands me a small clip-on microphone and ushers me to step in front of him.

As soon as I take that single step forward, everyone realizes I'm going to speak. Their quiet murmurs give way to total silence. Every ear and every eye is on me.

"Zola and his gangsters don't care how many people they have to kill to get what they want," I begin.

President Williams turns to me with an uneasy expression, barely containing his sudden doubts over whether encouraging me to address the crowd was a good idea after all.

"But let me tell you this," I go on. "Our will to survive is stronger than their will to destroy."

In the middle of the crowd, I see a familiar face.

It's Mr. Lindell, the old physics teacher who said I couldn't handle pressure! What are the odds?

Not *too* remarkable, I tell myself. I knew he had some publications under his belt and wanted to go back to "real" academia, so I guess he made it happen and did something important enough to get himself on the local evacuation list.

He nods when our eyes meet, then smiles widely. He remembers me, too.

Lindell's smile looks pure, not forced or embarrassed or anything like that. For the first time, I start to wonder if his harsh words were just his way of trying to get the best out of a promising student who maybe didn't always apply himself to the fullest.

I smile back at him then look around some more.

I see stoic nods from some of the people near the front. A few people applaud, but it doesn't catch on. The rest know I'm not finished.

"Yesterday I was in a much worse spot than this," I tell them. "And today? Today we know their next move. Can they say the same about us?"

I pause and shake my head for effect.

"No," I continue. "They have no idea what we're going to do and they have no idea what we're capable of. Because we are many and we are adaptable. Together, we are strong."

I turn to Williams and see him nodding approvingly.

"Together, we will prevail," I boom, the tone making it clear that I am finished now.

Short and strong, I hope, if not quite sweet.

A loud and enthusiastic round of applause greets my closing words.

"Ray Barclay, ladies and gentleman," Williams says, holding a hand towards me. "This man has done more than anyone could ever be expected to do, and we all owe him a tremendous debt of gratitude. Aided by the information he has brought our way, we *will* prevail. Our enemies will fall, *not* us, and freedom will strike back."

Sustained cheers and hollers follow. Some people look more upbeat than I personally think the situation calls for, but I'd rather see that than dejection.

I'm living proof of how far a stubborn and resilient hope can take one man, so there's no telling how far our collective hope-fueled determination and our combined efforts can take us in the fight to foil Zola's demented plan.

From the back of the crowd, a waving hand suddenly catches my eye.

"You're sure?" Williams asks at my side, quietly but suddenly talking into his earpiece again. "Okay. Yes, I'll send him."

I feel my heartbeat quicken in hope as Williams turns to me. It's been a long time since it quickened in *hope*.

"Follow him," he tells me, gesturing to the waving man.

My feet carry me quickly across the expansive floor, all the way to the guy and the doorway he's pointed me towards.

When I cross the threshold to step inside, my knees literally weaken. I grab the edge of a huge desk to prop myself up.

The emotion is flat-out overcoming me.

Because up ahead, on a huge screen like the kind I've only ever seen in Hollywood movie war rooms, I see the two faces I've longed to see more than any others: those of Joe and Eva.

"You made it," Eva sobs.

Joe stands beside her, smiling the widest smile I've ever seen.

They're in front of a plain concrete wall, probably as deep underground as I am, but the only thing in the world that matters right now is that they're alive.

Fighting a losing battle against tears of my own, I force a smile with renewed determination to tackle the real battle that lies ahead.

"Shelter where you are," I tell them. "I've made it this far, and I'm not done yet."

AUTHOR'S NOTES

Thank you for reading *Last Man Standing*.

I'm excited to announce that Ray's adventure continues in *Into The Fire*, a direct sequel with higher drama and higher stakes than ever! You can read on to the next page for the story blurb.

~

This book was a long time in the making and I had a lot of fun bringing it to life. I hope you've enjoyed reading it just as much as I enjoyed writing it.

If you did enjoy this book and could spare a few moments to leave a review on Amazon, that would be very helpful.

Reviews are a great way for readers to find books that might interest them and every kind word really does help. Thanks!

~

To stay up to date with news on my future books, as well as promotions and other news, please visit my website:

www.craigafalconer.com

— *Craig A. Falconer,*
Scotland, October 2022

~

INTO THE FIRE
(THE EARTHBURST SAGA, BOOK 2)

Surviving in space was the easy part…

I'm not alone anymore.

I've made it down from the solitude of the station, all the way to an incredible underground bunker complex.

Thousands of humanity's best minds are by my side.

I'm surrounded by secret cutting-edge technologies that almost defy belief.

Too bad none of that is a match for what I'm up against now.

Because in just three days, the final stage of Ignacio Zola's demented plan to reach a new world will eliminate all life on Earth — unless I can pull off a miracle.

The stakes couldn't be any higher. The odds couldn't be any longer.

I'm the man who uncovered Zola's plan. And now, I'm the only man who can stop him.

This fight started in space and brought me deep below Earth's surface.

But that's nothing compared to what comes next…

For purchasing information:
www.craigafalconer.com

BOOKS BY CRAIG A. FALCONER

The Earthburst Saga

Last Man Standing

Into The Fire

Operation Starshot

Not Alone

Not Alone

Not Alone: Second Contact

Not Alone: The Final Call

Not Alone: Fractured Union

Not Alone: Leap of Destiny

Not Alone: Revelations

Not Alone: The Awakening

Not Alone: Hidden Wonder

Not Alone: Endgame

Not Alone: Origins

Terradox

Terradox

The Fall of Terradox

Terradox Reborn

Terradox Beyond

~

Cyber Seed

Sycamore

Sycamore 2

Sycamore X

Sycamore XL

The Complete Cyber Seed Compendium (2023)

~

Sci-Fi Sizzlers

Wanderlust

Pamela 2.0

Sunset Stays

Pumpkin Splice

Happy, Inc.

When Santa Slays

Arise With Us

Replica

Whence They Came

A Scent Of Man

Megaton Murphy

Yester Year

Too Good To Be True

Bound For Glory

Funscreen

For more, visit **www.craigafalconer.com**

Made in the USA
Columbia, SC
23 April 2024

34808925R00271